For Every End,
A New Beginning

Molly McDermott

Printed in the United States of America
For more information or to book an event, contact:
Sullivan Publishing
Email: Sullivanpublishing406@gmail.com

Cover design by Suzanne Hetzel
ISBN – Paperback: 979-8-218-06053-4

To my parents, Helen and Joe McDermott,
who taught me to love reading and writing.
Thank you, Mom, for teaching me the art
of storytelling.

Table of Contents

A Week at the Beach

Stone Harbor, New Jersey, Third Week in August

Tori waded into the water and lowered first the red plastic bucket with the green handle, then the navy-blue plastic bucket with the yellow handle into the unfurling waves. When she lifted them, the weight of the water strained the handles and caused the sides of both pails to bend. Water sloshed over the edges as she walked, forming a parallel path of wet sand droplets from the Atlantic Ocean to that spot on the beach where her two best friends sat. Those two women, Pat Murphy Malone—Murphy to everyone who knew her—and Mary Louisa Roberts, whom everyone called Lulu, were entertaining Lulu's eleven-month-old son, Jackson, by filling colorful plastic molds with damp sand. Jackson delighted in smashing each sandy brick as soon as it was released from its plastic form.

As Tori joined her friends, she handed one of the buckets to Lulu, who slowly poured the salty ocean water into the shallow hole in the sand where her son sat. Tori did the same with water from the second bucket. The toddler's attention was immediately drawn to the small sandy pool, and he giggled and slapped the puddle's surface.

A shout of "Wahoo!" drew the women's attention twenty feet up the beach where their three husbands were playing bocce ball. The apparent winner, Lulu's husband, Tom, was jumping in place, his hands above his head in a Rocky-style gesture. Nico, Tori's husband, was bent at the waist, his hands on his knees. Dylan picked up and organized the blue, green, and red balls.

"Looks like Tom won," Tori said, "and I bet Nico's demanding a rematch. Deep down, he believes the bocce balls should just know they're being thrown by an Italian and do whatever he wants them to do. He isn't going to accept this defeat well."

"According to Dylan, Nico's always been a 'leave it all on the field' kind of player," Murphy said. "Even as a kid. But the last couple of weeks, when we've gotten together for pizza and cards, it's been more 'winning at all costs.' Is everything okay with him, Tori?"

"Last night, Nico told Tom he was in line for a major promotion and salary increase at the end of the year," Lulu said. "He should be celebrating."

Tori winced. "I wish he hadn't said anything. Nothing's definite, but he's got his hopes up. I just worry in case it doesn't happen. I think he brought it up because he's particularly sensitive right now. Sal and his partners were just named one of the best ob/gyn practices in New York Magazine's 'best of' series. Nico's proud of his brother, happy for him. But you know my mother-in-law – Jenny's expecting a call from Stockholm any minute announcing Sal won the Nobel Prize for Medicine."

"How is Jenny?" Lulu asked. "Still mispronouncing your name, Veek Toria?

Tori nodded. "Still sounds like nails on a blackboard every time she says it."

"Dylan says Sal is first in their mother's eyes—first born, first at everything," Murphy said. "When does the magazine come out?"

"The end of October. There's a reception at the Ritz Carlton in Battery Park just before the issue hits the stands. Jenny has already made appointments to have her hair and nails done that morning, and she and her favorite daughter-in-law are scouring the stores for new dresses."

"Speaking of Princess Eena," Lulu asked. "What's she up to?"

"Shopping and packing for Stockholm," Tori quipped.

Tori stood and brushed off the sand before reaching into her beach bag for a tube of sunscreen. As she applied it to her arms and legs, she asked, "Do you remember when we came here the September before junior year, and I got that horrific sunburn?"

Lulu nodded. "I think you were still peeling in December."

"You both tan beautifully. So not fair."

"The three of us have had a lot of good times on this beach," Murphy said. "Do you remember how cold it was the first time we came here together? It was mid-May after our first year at Dickinson, and the water was freezing. No one could go in. Except Lulu."

"We Mainer's are a hearty stock," Lulu said.

"Your parents, Murphy, are so generous to give us the use of their beach house, this week in paradise," Tori said. "I look forward to it all year. It's true what they say – the sun, sand, and surf weave a special magic. Maybe it's all that extra oxygen when the waves roll to shore?"

A loud "Noooo!" came from the bocce ball game. Nico was shaking his head back and forth in denial. One of the other men had landed a perfect pitch, smashing into Nico's ball and sending it spinning out of competition.

"Ouch! That's gotta hurt," Murphy said. "Looks like Nico was close to winning that one."

Tori watched as her husband turned away from his friends and kicked the sand in frustration. She could see his clenched fists from where she was standing. To her friends, she said, "All part of the game." Keep it together, she silently warned her husband.

"Anyone else ready to go in?" Lulu asked. "Jackson's ready for lunch and a nap."

As they gathered toys and folded towels, Tori said, "Please don't say anything to Tom and Dylan about Sal and the magazine or what I said about the promotion until after we've all left."

"Of course, we won't say anything," Lulu said. "We have three more days in paradise for him to soak up the ocean's healing powers."

"I hope so," Tori said.

"Looks like the guys are going for a swim," Murphy said. She put her thumb and middle finger in her mouth and whistled. When she had Dylan's attention, she signaled they were returning to the house.

When the men returned from the beach for lunch, Jackson was napping, and the women were enjoying lemonade on the screened porch. As soon as they'd eaten, Tom announced they were returning to the beach for yet another bocce ball game.

"We have reservations tonight at the Sea Breeze. Then we're going to the Boardwalk," Murphy reminded them as they left. "My parents will be here at seven-thirty to babysit. So, no water pistol fight after the beach."

Hours later, as she was getting dressed, Tori heard aluminum chair frames clanking together and the thud of the bocce ball bag hitting the cement carport floor below her bedroom window. Seconds later, she heard, "Now you're gonna get it."

"The guys are back from the beach," she called to Lulu and Murphy, "and it sounds like the evening's water pistol battle has begun."

"They have to come in and get ready," Murphy called from the master bedroom.

"I'll get 'em," Lulu said.

Tori heard Lulu call through the screen door, "Guys, the two bathrooms and the outside shower are all yours. Come in and start …."

Then, she heard Lulu scream.

Tori and Murphy raced toward the kitchen. Both women were slipping and sliding—trying not to fall. They clutched the backs of chairs, the door frame, anything to remain standing. The kitchen floor was soaking wet.

Lulu stood at the screen door. Water streamed from her just-straightened hair and down her face. It combined with her eyeshadow, mascara, and foundation, leaving clownish streaks on her cheeks before dripping on and staining her emerald and white striped silk blouse. The wet fabric was transparent and clung to her skin and bra. Her once perfectly creased navy linen pants were plastered to her thighs and calves.

"Oh. My. God." Tori said. "What did you three do?"

All three men began to speak at once.

"Quiet," Murph said. "Only Tom gets to speak."

Careful to avoid puddles, Tori led Lulu back to the bedroom. Once she was sure her friend was all right, she returned to the kitchen to hear Tom's explanation. For that night's water pistol fight, he and Dylan planned to alternate standing guard at the spigot, one of them always there, ready to prevent Nico from re-filling his water pistol. The strategy was working. Tom had trapped Nico near the steps at the back door when Dylan, armed with a bucket of water, had snuck around the side of the house—to lob the final shot in tonight's water war.

Nico had been running up the back stairs when Lulu opened the door. But it was too late! The water from the bucket was a torpedo heading for its target. But the intended target ducked—just in time!

When Lulu emerged from the bedroom—in dry clothes, her make-up re-applied, and her auburn curls bouncing, she said to her husband, "We're leaving now. The three of you can take care of Jackson, clean the floor, and wait for Murphy's parents to arrive. We're heading to the Sea Breeze to get a head start on the cocktails."

Murphy picked up her car keys and led her friends out the front door.

When their husbands arrived at the restaurant, the three women had finished their first round of Midori Coladas. After the men apologized, their wives forgave them, and more cocktails were ordered and served, Tori raised her glass and said, "To friendship, forgiveness, and another amazing week together. Next year when we're all here, together again, we'll remember this evening's escapades and laugh."

Six glasses were raised and met in the center of the table to a chorus of "here, here." At that moment, none of them could imagine they would not all be there, at that beach, one year later.

Chapter 1
The Best of Everything

Saturday evening, Late October

Tori turned her back to Nico and lifted her hair. "Zip me?" she asked.

"My pleasure."

She felt his right hand move up her back, and he kissed the nape of her neck to signal he was finished. "This sapphire suits you, makes your eyes look bluer, but I thought you were wearing your black dress."

"Thank you." She turned toward the mirror and fastened the dress's thin jeweled belt. "Your mother was horrified I was wearing, and I quote, 'that old thing.' Besides, Eena's new dress is black. That makes the color off-limits for everyone else because, as your mom has often reminded us these past months, 'tonight belongs to Sal and Eena.'"

King Sal and Princess Eena, she silently edited. Her secret nicknames for her brother and sister-in-law. Nico's mother, grandmother, aunts, and uncles looked up to and admired them. It was always Sal's advice they followed. His opinion they sought. Eena had been born in a suburb of Rome, and her family had emigrated to America when she was ten years old. In the eyes of the Italian-American Morgano family, that made her the "real deal." Together, they were the perfect couple, the model against which everyone else was compared.

"But that dress isn't new," Nico said.

"It is to your mother."

He held up the traditional black bow tie in his left hand and a two-toned blue striped one in his right for her consideration. "The blue," she said, "with the matching pocket square. More festive. And I prefer the thinner cummerbund."

She walked to the window and looked out. The weatherman had been right last evening when he'd forecast an all-day steady rain. It was the perfect evening to stay home—curl up on the couch with a bowl of warm, buttery popcorn and watch a movie. But she and Nico were preparing to drive into Lower Manhattan to attend a reception hosted by *New York Magazine* to honor the nominees for their "Best of New York" issue, which included Sal and his partners. It was all the family had discussed since the nominations were announced three months ago. *At least tomorrow, it will finally be over, she thought.*

Nico slid his arms into his tuxedo jacket and adjusted the cuffs. "Very handsome," she said, smiling in approval.

"You look pretty. Ready?" he asked.

"As I'll ever be," she said and picked up her small evening bag.

As their car approached the New Jersey side of the Holland Tunnel, Nico said, "I'm not looking forward to tonight. I'm happy for my brother, but I'm ready for all this hype to be over, aren't you? I wish we weren't going."

"I'm glad we are," Tori said. "It's what we do for family and friends—we show up. And we're going to be eyewitnesses to this evening."

"What do you mean?"

"Do you remember a couple of years ago Murph and I attended the wedding of a former classmate from Dickinson? We'd been surprised we were invited because we hadn't been close with Joan in college."

"Maybe. Was that the wedding Dylan and I weren't invited to?"

"Yup, that's the one."

"The invitation made the wedding sound like a big deal. But you two came home making jokes about it if I recall correctly."

"Yup. Everything was so elegant—on paper. Wedding at St. Patrick's Cathedral, reception at the Plaza. Even though it was difficult to hear over the crowds of tourists coming and going in the church, enough of us heard the priest get their names wrong during the ceremony. The elegant reception was nothing more than a slice of dry cake and a glass of warm champagne. If we hadn't gone, hadn't experienced it ourselves, we'd have believed the pictures Joan posted on social media. I think tonight might be very similar. Your mother will embellish every aspect of the reception, and we know Eena lives in an Instagram world—perfect pictures of a not-so-perfect life. But we'll 'be in the room where it happens.'" We'll know the truth.

Nico turned his car over to the garage valet and handed the parking ticket to Tori to keep in her purse. They took the elevator up to the hotel's mezzanine, where the ballroom was located. They could see and hear the crowd from the hallway leading to the large room.

At the entrance to the ballroom, Tori pulled out her phone. "I'm texting Sal. Asking where he and your family are."

"It's too loud in there. Sal won't hear a text coming in," Nico said. "Let's go home and tell everyone we came, looked for them but didn't find them."

"Oh no," Tori said. "It's important your mother and brother know we came. Sal should have his phone on vibrate. He may not be on call tonight, but I'm sure he's prepared if a patient needs him."

Minutes later, her phone buzzed. "From Eena," she said, reading the text aloud. "Delayed. Arriving now. Meet at coat check."

When Nonna Morgano, Jenny, Eena, and Sal walked off the elevator, Tori could feel the tension. She looked over at Nico, raised her eyebrows, and whispered, "What do you think's going on?"

"What do you mean?" he asked as the foursome walked toward them.

"Just look at them," Tori said. Nonna's cheeks were flushed, and she was strangling the gloves she held in her hands. Jenny's lips were set in a tight-lipped smile, her brow furrowed. Eena's eyes bore a hole in the side of Sal's head. His jaw and fists were clenched.

When Tori stepped in to kiss Nico's grandmother, the woman was rigid, her body unyielding. "Is everything okay, Nonna?" she asked. The older woman just nodded. Tori thought she heard Eena, who was standing behind Nonna, hiss the word "unforgivable" in Sal's direction. *That can't be good.* Tori thought and fought the urge to roll her eyes.

Sal and Nico helped their grandmother and mother off with their coats before Sal helped Eena with hers. Jenny's gasp was audible, and Nonna grabbed Tori's forearm tightly. Eena's new black dress was a sheath, with a plunging neckline and sheer bodice. Tori swallowed a laugh. *Definitely a showstopper!* The dress was so predictable.

In the minutes it took Nico to drop off the coats and return with the claim check he handed to Sal, Tori asked about the drive in and received a curt, "Fine" from Jenny. Sal took his grandmother's arm. Eena wrapped her arm in Nico's, so Tori was left to walk with her mother-in-law. In the ballroom, they found an unoccupied high-top, but neither Nonna nor Jenny was comfortable on the high stools, so everyone remained standing. The noise of hundreds of people talking at once and the background music made conversation nearly impossible.

Servers balancing trays of champagne passed by frequently, and Eena helped herself to a new glass every time one passed. Nico whispered in Tori's ear he was going to the bar to get his mother and grandmother glasses of white wine, and Tori said she'd go with him. "You can't manage their drinks and something for yourself," she said. "And I'd like a glass of sparkling water."

When they returned to the table, Nonna and Jenny were standing alone. "Where did Sal and Eena go?" Nico asked.

"Mingling," Nonna said. "Tori, would you walk me to the ladies' room? There are so many people here. I'm not sure I could find my way back."

As Tori led the older woman across the floor to the exit, she spotted Sal laughing and talking with a young woman who looked up at him adoringly. A few minutes later, she spied an inebriated Eena leaning into the man standing next to her. *I wish Jenny could see the perfect couple now,* Tori thought.

The line for the ladies' room was long, and Tori waited for Nonna just outside the door. A woman she recognized as Lauren, one of Sal's two partners, joined the back of the line. "I cannot believe he brought his wife and invited his girlfriend. It's bad enough she works for the practice, but to invite her here? Beyond tacky. And his drunken wife, who's practically falling out of her dress, is draped all over my husband. After this, we're heading home. What about you and Max?" Tori overheard Lauren say to the woman standing next to her.

Max, Tori realized, was the third partner in the practice. *So the 'he' who brought his wife and 'luvah' to the same event must be Sal,* she deduced.

Ninety minutes later, Tori almost cheered when Nico's car was the first to arrive at the front of the garage.

"Hmph!" Jenny said. "The attendant should have brought Sal's car out first. After all, he's the honoree."

Tori turned and smiled. "Good night, everyone. Congratulations again, Sal." Then, she got in the car, slammed the door shut, and fastened her seat belt. As soon as Nico secured his, she said, "Drive."

He chuckled. "I will never doubt you again. Glad we went, glad it's over. Want to grab a sandwich on the way home? I'm starved."

"Let's stop at that coffee shop on Anderson Avenue. The one that makes those wonderful maple-glazed Virginia ham and gruyere cheese sandwiches."

"If I can find a spot to park, I'll go in and order. If I can't, you go in, and I'll drive around the block," he said.

She nodded. "Yeah, okay. Nico, your grandmother told me tonight how thrilled she was about your upcoming promotion. When I tried to downplay it, say we expected it to be announced in December, but nothing was guaranteed, she told me you'd assured your mother it was a sure thing. I thought we'd decided we wouldn't say anything to anyone until it was final, announced."

Nico and Tori were assistant vice presidents of First Dominion, a sizeable bank with headquarters in midtown Manhattan. Nico worked in the international division while Tori ran a department within compli-ance. One evening almost three months ago, as they were walking to Port Authority to catch the express bus home, Nico announced he would be promoted in late December. "It makes sense. On January second, I'll have been with the bank four years," he'd said. "After today's staff meeting, the new boss mentioned he wanted me to take on more responsibility next year."

At the time, Tori had been excited for her husband but cautioned him not to say anything. She reminded him her first promotion at the bank had been delayed. "When he hired you, Jeff may have made certain commitments. But he's gone, and Wayne's the guy in charge now," she'd said when Nico argued his former boss had told him he was on the "senior management track."

At First Dominion, like the other large banks, two promotions were considered the "big ones." Being promoted to assistant manager, the first rung of the junior management ladder, came with annual merit bonuses and an additional two weeks' vacation. The leap from junior to senior management, the jump Nico expected to make in December, brought more responsibility and perks. Managing directors enjoyed stock options and bonuses tied to the bank's profitability. For a new managing director, that could mean a payout in the low six figures.

But for Nico, Tori knew, it wasn't just the prestige, money, or his boss acknowledging and rewarding his hard work. He believed along with the promotion would come his family's pride and respect—the same pride and respect Sal had enjoyed all his life.

"I know. I didn't intend to say anything," he said. "But Mom was going on about Sal and the practice. How she always knew he was des-tined to do great things. I tried to shake it off."

"It's just you mentioned it to Murphy and Dylan when we played cards at their house two weeks ago, and it came up again last weekend when we visited Lulu and Tom in Boston, and now...."

He nodded. "You're right. Just let it go, okay?" She heard the annoyance in his tone.

"So, what do you think was going on when they arrived? And what did you think about Eena's dress?" he asked, changing the subject. "I thought Nonna was going to have a stroke. That dress was…." He grimaced.

"Provocative is the word you're looking for. Sal's partner, Lauren, didn't think too much of it. Or the way Eena was fawning all over her husband," Tori said. "Who was the woman Sal spent most of the evening talking to? I overheard Lauren tell Max's wife she works for the practice."

"Bobbi. She's his new nurse and latest conquest," Nico said.

"He's living on the edge. I suspect Eena knew Bobbi was coming to the reception tonight because I heard her tell Sal something was 'unforgivable.' Their attraction was apparent, and Eena was drunk and angry enough to make a scene. Your mother and grandmother may have just been reacting to the tension between them.

"And please talk to your mother about Thanksgiving. She cornered me again this evening to complain we're spending it with my family in Pennsylvania. That's the third time in two weeks. I get she wants you to spend all holidays with her, but that's just not how it works."

"Okay." He sighed. "I'll try. But you know my mother. There's a parking space. Two ham and gruyere on onion rolls with lettuce, tomato, and mayo coming up."

Chapter 2
A Weapon of Mass Destruction

Christmas Evening

"That was an incredible dinner, Sweetheart. You outdid yourself." Nico smiled at Tori across their dining room table. "I propose a toast to our extraordinary hostess, my wonderful wife."

"Thank you," Tori replied.

Sal sat to her right. He raised his wine glass and toasted, "To Tori, an elegant and gracious hostess. Your standing rib roast rivals any I've had, was an inspired choice for this year's Christmas dinner and a pleasant change from the usual capon."

Tori's mother, Anna, who sat to her daughter's left, added, "Dinner was delicious, darling."

"As my husband said, dinner was a most interesting choice," Eena added. "So very American. No pasta, salad before the meal."

Tori repressed her urge to snicker. Eena hated sharing the spotlight! Her sister-in-law preferred to be and usually was the recipient of Morgano family compliments.

One more compliment and she'll dredge up the fake Italian accent, Tori thought.

"Mother, do you need more wine," Nico asked, "or do you want to join in the toast with water?"

Jenny moved her empty wine glass toward her younger son, who filled it. Then she raised her glass to join the others in the toast. Now

Tori wanted to laugh out loud. Jenny looked like she was about to drink a gallon of white vinegar.

Best present of the day, she thought.

"My husband deserves the credit for the menu," Tori said.

In response to his quizzical look, she said, "When we had dinner with Murphy and Dylan at the Reef a couple of weeks ago, you debated between the flounder stuffed with crab and the prime rib. When you chose the flounder, I decided prime rib would be an excellent choice for today. I'm so glad everyone enjoyed it."

"And I'm glad you picked the flounder. How are Dylan and Murphy? I haven't seen them in months." Turning to Tori, Sal asked, "Is Murphy still enjoying teaching at Northern Valley High?"

Before Tori could respond, Jenny rolled her eyes. "Argh! I hate that you girls have these horrible nicknames. You, Veek Toria, and your friends calling yourselves Tori, Murphy, Loco."

"Lulu," Tori, Nico, and Sal corrected in unison.

"Whatever! You were named for a queen, Veek Toria. Such a shame."

Nicknames are acceptable for your sons and favorite daughter-in-law, but not me or my friends? How typically Jenny, Tori thought.

"My daughter was named Victoria Helene after her two grandmothers, an Irish tradition," Anna said. "I think their nicknames are delightful and suit them. Those three are—what do you three call yourselves?"

"Friends with history." Tori smiled at her mother as she reached under the table to take Anna's hand and squeeze it three times—her silent signal for I. Love. You.

Jenny continued, unfazed by the interruption. "And Valentina, the most beautiful name in the world, has that dreadful nickname, Eena. Outrageous!"

"But what a toddler who loved his baby sister could pronounce, Mom. It's sweet."

"No," Jenny contradicted her older son, "it is not, and you should call your *Bellissima* Italian wife by her beautiful Italian name."

Tori looked around the table. Anna was wringing the linen napkin in her lap. A frown creased her forehead, a sign she was annoyed. Tori guessed it was because Jenny had deftly redirected the conversation away from the compliments she and the dinner had received. Eena smiled at her husband, but he was looking not at her but at the Tag Heuer stainless steel watch his mother had given him for Christmas, a watch Tori knew retailed for over a thousand dollars. She glanced at her husband, ready to suggest he help her clear the table while the others moved to the living room, but she caught him watching his brother, eyeing that same watch, and saw the look of longing in his eyes—not for the watch or even another expensive gift, but for everything the watch symbolized. Tori clenched her fists and dug her nails into the fleshy part of her palm, forming dents she could imagine having the next day.

My husband is your son, too! We all saw you gave him yet another sweater.

"We're going to leave soon," Sal said. "It's getting late, and I'll need to swing by the hospital later to check on a few patients."

"*Sono pronta,*" Eena said,

Tori struggled not to roll her eyes. *Right on cue!*

Surreptitiously, Nico glanced at his watch, winked at his wife across the table, and smiled triumphantly. She responded with a slight pout. Their private joke. Sal used his patients as the pretext for arriving late to every family get-together and the excuse for leaving early. Before each family gathering, Nico and Tori placed bets on Sal's arrival and departure times, and today Nico had nailed it

"But that was an excellent meal, Tori," Sal said, ignoring his wife's announcement she was ready to leave. "We never had a rib roast at home growing up, and Eena doesn't make it. Eena, you should get the recipe from Tori."

"Valentina is a superb cook. She does not need Veek Toria's recipes,"

Jenny said. "Everything she makes is exceptional. You couldn't get better in a restaurant, here or in Roma. Her pasta is *deliziosa*!" She cupped the tips of the fingers and thumb of her right hand, brought them to her lips, and sent a kiss and a smile across the table to Eena.

"*Grazie*, Mama Jenny," Eena said.

I wouldn't know since I've never eaten anything she's made, Tori thought as she looked down at her lap, stifling her urge to laugh at Jenny's and Eena's predictability.

"Mother, we're discussing **this** dinner which was exceptionally good," Nico said, exasperation clear in his voice, "and praising Tori's cooking, and this dinner has nothing to do with Eena or her cooking."

"Not to mention the prime rib was an unexpected and very pleasant change from our usual holiday meals," Sal said.

"What's wrong with capon? Why do we need a change?" Jenny asked both her sons. Turning to Tori, she said, "You have been married to Nico for four years, engaged a year before that. You know our family always has capon on Christmas. And where was the lasagna or spaghetti Bolognese? Traditions are important to this family."

"Mother, Tori and I are family. We're starting traditions that work for our family, hers and mine. Maybe a standing rib roast will be part of that, or maybe our traditional Christmas dinner will be that we don't have a traditional Christmas dinner, but together, we'll figure that out. I, for one, enjoyed not having an Italian meal before the main course."

Jenny's criticism continued. "This meal is so expensive. And look, no leftovers. So wasteful."

"It's once a year and a holiday, Mother," Nico said.

"A standing rib roast was my father's favorite meal and the meal my mother traditionally made at Christmas," Tori said, trying to defuse the growing tensions.

Her mother smiled and added, "And when we had company, a dinner party, or sometimes just because."

"Such a rich meal," Jenny said. "All that red meat isn't good for you."

Then, turning to face Anna, she said, "Your husband died of a heart attack at a very young age, didn't he? Don't you think all the rich food you made him might have caused his death?"

Anna's smile disappeared; her eyes filled with unshed tears. Her sharp intake of breath and single, soft whimper—the only sounds in the dining room. And just like that, a weapon of mass destruction had shattered the Christmas peace.

Tori felt as if she were in a theatre, hearing and watching a scene play out in front of her, one in which she seemed unable to participate. Nico's and Sal's angry voices erupted around her. She heard a muffled thud, but there was a several-second delay before her mind identified it as her husband's chair that had fallen back onto the carpet and hardwood floor when he'd abruptly stood. Tori felt, rather than saw, Sal's fury directed toward his mother. Rising from her chair, she placed her hand gently on his upper arm to quiet him. Then, she instructed her husband to get their guests' coats and help them carry their gifts to the car. Dinner was over. It was time for them to leave.

Only after Sal had activated the remote start on his Mercedes SUV. and Nico had retrieved everyone's coats and collected the Christmas gifts did Jenny say 'thank you' or wish Anna a safe flight home the next day. She excused their abrupt departure by reminding everyone Sal had patients he needed to check on. *And* Tori silently added, *enjoy a Christmas quickie with his mistress.* She and Nico had recently discovered Sal was having an affair with his nurse, Bobbi. Only when she heard Nico close and lock the front door, did Tori breathe a sigh of relief. Christmas was over. Joy to the World.

"I'll clear the table and finish up in the kitchen," her husband said, taking Anna's and Tori's coats from the hall closet. "You and your mother take Baron for a walk. The evening air is pleasant, and I think the three of you need a walk along the water's edge."

Anna, Tori, and Baron basked in the view of the Manhattan skyline reflected in the Hudson River's shimmering waters. When they returned from their walk, the dishwasher had been started, stemware was drying upside down on the counter, and Tori had tucked her anger away until the next Morgano family command performance.

Chapter 3
Boxing Day

Monday, December 26th

The next morning, Tori knew, without consulting the charging cell phone turned upside down on her nightstand, that it was approximately five a.m. Her internal clock woke her every morning at the same time. In fifteen minutes, the slumbering house would begin to awaken. The smart thermostats on the first and second floors would raise the temperature. In approximately thirty minutes, Nico's internal clock and the external alarm they set each evening would wake him. But these thirty minutes were hers alone. Every morning she burrowed under the duvet's warmth and reviewed all she had planned for the day.

This morning—*Boxing Day, what an appropriate name!*—she was angrier than when she'd gone to bed. Like the yeast dough her mother had made to create the warm, crusty bread for yesterday's Christmas dinner, Tori's anger had been kneaded and poked by Jenny's insults and Eena's back-handed compliments, then tucked into bed under the warmth of the covers until her anger had doubled in size. On their walk along the riverfront the prior evening, Anna had advised her daughter to overlook Jenny's nasty comments and Eena's insensitive remarks. Fat chance!

Growing up, Tori had thought holidays, particularly Christmas, were magical. Now, she admitted to the darkness, she saw them only in terms of obligations, a series of tasks to be completed, get-togethers to be dreaded. Tori had debated over Jenny's gift before deciding on a scarf and gloves to match her mother-in-law's new camel dress coat. When Jenny opened the scarf, a delicate blend of cashmere and silk, the color of homemade peach ice cream, and then the box containing the buttery leather matching gloves, she'd smiled at Nico before turning to Tori with her verdict. "This scarf won't keep my neck warm, Veek Tori, and these gloves are too impractical."

"*Yeah, I'm done.*" Tori decided.

Three years ago, she'd suggested she, Nico, Sal, and Eena begin a tradition of going to dinner and a Broadway show in January instead of exchanging gifts. Tori'd thought it would be the beginning of an enjoyable holiday ritual—two brothers and their wives trying out different restaurants, enjoying a night at the theatre. But the tradition had disintegrated into a contest Sal and Eena were determined to win. Every year Tori and Nico backed down. It wasn't worth an argument.

Tori was lying on her side, her back to her husband when she felt him awaken beside her. He rolled over, put his arm around her waist, and instructed Alexa to cancel the alarm.

"Morning," he yawned, his voice still hoarse from sleep.

"I hate Christmas. All holidays, actually, but Christmas especially," she said.

"No, you don't."

She hesitated, then said. "Okay, maybe I don't hate them, but I don't particularly like them."

"By 'them,' do you mean my mother, Sal, and Eena, or holidays?"

She paused before answering. "That's a tough one—your mother's reaction to her gifts, Eena's shock I cooked the meal all by myself. Seriously! A little Jenny and Eena go a long way, ya know? It didn't help you announced Lulu, Tom, and Jackson are flying in from Boston for the New Year's weekend, and we aren't going to your Aunt Checchi and Uncle Frank's. The mood of the day changed with that reveal."

"Yeah, but I also said Aunt Checchi was fine with it," he said.

"Really? That's all you've got? I'm in the doghouse, Nico, not you. Your mother won't forgive and forget anytime soon. My friends, my fault you're not going to be where she thinks you're supposed to be."

"Do you know this will only be the third time since you and I've been together that my brother attends a family dinner, and I don't? Which will make it harder for him to back out, which we know he had to be already thinking about."

"Eena bragged they were going to a New Year's Eve party the hospital administrator was throwing, so I bet Sal is planning an emergency c-section or the birth of quadruplets as the excuse to skip the next day at your aunt's. I'm sure Bobbi won't make it easy for him to change plans," Tori said.

"He still may use work as an excuse. My family thinks Sal and Eena have 'real' jobs. A doctor is a career they understand, and how many times have you heard someone in my family explain that Eena's degree is the equivalent of a doctorate in pharmacy? We, however, work in a bank. They don't get what we do because we aren't tellers or customer service reps. Maybe, when I'm promoted tomorrow, mom will finally appreciate my job. At one point yesterday, I almost said something. I was so frustrated," Nico said.

"I'm glad you didn't. We expect it to be tomorrow, but you never know. Besides," she said, "it deserves its own day and celebration!"

"Nothing *should* delay it. This is my anniversary month. I'm due. Tomorrow it will be a done deal."

Tori kissed him, "Now we need to get up. My mom has a plane to catch."

Later that morning, as they drove home from the airport, Tori turned to face her husband and said, "I can't believe Lulu, Tom, and Jackson are coming in just a few days. That was an incredible gift you, Dylan, and Tom came up with. Thank you. I miss Lulu so much, and you couldn't have gotten me anything I'd want more. What made you think of it?"

Nico reached over and put his gloved hand over hers. "Remember a few weeks ago when you told Murphy you'd seen a woman on the street who reminded you of Lulu?"

"Yes," she said, "I saw her only in profile. She was looking at her phone, and I couldn't see her face. But there was something about her that reminded me of Lulu. I missed her so much at that moment. It took my breath."

"You, Murphy, and Lulu saw each other every day for four years. During grad school, you got together at least once a month. Now, between family and work, the three of you haven't been together since early October. I called Dylan. We hooked in Tom and worked it out."

"Thank you. It's the perfect gift."

The horn text tone rang from Tori's purse. "Oh no," she said, "That's work!" She grabbed her phone. The screen showed a text from Carlos, the most senior of the four section heads who reported to her, that began "911."

"I have to call him back," she apologized as she dialed Carlos's number. Then, she said, "It's Tori. What's up, Carlos?"

She listened for a few seconds, then said. "No, you were right to call. I have the emergency contact list at home, and I'll get started on my calls in about ten minutes. Tell the others how sorry I am. I'll check back later in the day." She was quiet for a few seconds, then said, "What?! Okay, thanks for the heads up. I'll be ready." She hung up and looked at her husband.

"What a mess!" she said.

"What happened?"

"A couple of products were set up incorrectly. The error wasn't discovered until the income posted last night, which triggered several compliance issues. All the problems and issues must be corrected before the bank's books close at the end of the week and customer statements are run. Carlos warned me senior and executive management are monitoring this closely, and Don's going to call," her phone rang, "and that's him now."

Don Howard, the Executive Director of Finance, and Tori's boss's boss, began speaking as soon as she said, "Hello."

"Tori? It's Don Howard. How was your Christmas?"

"Fine. My Christmas was lovely, Don. Yours?"

"Good," he said. "You've heard about the mess we have here?"

When she confirmed she'd heard the news, Don asked, "So what's the plan?"

Tori updated him on the contingency plans she and her team had developed to manage situations like these.

"Good. It sounds like you have everything under control, Tori. Let's meet tomorrow in my office at eight to go over where we are. Keep me posted throughout the day, and let your staff know if they face any resistance, they have only to ask for my help."

"Okay, see you tomorrow, Don, and thanks," Tori ended the conversation.

"I'm very impressed at how prepared you were for something like this," Nico said.

She unbuckled her seatbelt and turned to face her husband as he pulled into their driveway.

"You sound surprised. Which is a bit insulting if you want to know the truth."

"I meant it as a compliment. You don't just know your job but have an amazing grasp of the bank's systems. The plan to correct this, the one you described to Don, is well-thought out and through."

She shrugged. "I consider that all part of my job. I've got at least an hour of calls to make and emails to send. Sorry."

Once inside the house, Tori handed Nico a hanger and hung up her jacket. "I'll use our office to make my calls," she called over her shoulder and began to climb the stairs. She stopped on the third step and turned to face him. "You could amuse yourself by calling your mother. She's left you enough voicemails."

"You certainly know how to kill a mood. I'm still angry with Mom, but I know from her voicemails Sal told her she was out of line several times on the drive back home. He also said her comments about the gloves and scarf were 'ungracious,' and he reminded her of the lectures she gave us growing up about accepting gifts with a smile and a thank-you, even when we weren't thrilled."

"My intentions were good," Tori said. "I'd been thinking about the first time my parents and I went to Italy. Dad went for business, and Mom and I tagged along. One afternoon, she and I discovered the Madova Glove Factory as we walked back to the hotel from the Pitti Palace. Mom bought gloves in the most stunning colors for my aunts, her nieces, and me, but for herself, she selected black. That night, she fanned the gloves in a rainbow of vibrant colors, like a peacock's tail, across the hotel's white bedspread. I can still picture it. Dad asked her why she'd selected such exciting colors for everyone but herself. She'd said something about black being more practical. The next day, when he returned to the hotel after work, he had a shopping bag from Madova with the hydrangea blue gloves Mom wore when we went out to dinner the other night and to midnight mass. She was wearing black gloves when we dropped her off just now because she'll be stuffing them in her pockets, pulling her suitcase behind her. But when she gets dressed up, is going someplace special, she wears those lovely blue gloves. I thought your mother might like special gloves like that."

"Oh, sweetheart, I'm sorry she didn't appreciate the gift or that she didn't put any thought into the gift she gave you, or me for that matter. But then, I've had many more years to get used to her than you have."

"Your mother's never going to change, and I learned long ago she doesn't always put her claws away at night. She knows her words at dinner hit their mark, but she would never apologize. If you and Sal can't get through to her, nothing I could say or do will make a difference. I know it bothers you. Maybe, in a couple of weeks, I'll invite her to the

City for lunch—you know, extend an olive branch."

"I love you," he called after her as she began to climb the stairs again.

Chapter 4
Everything Changes

Tuesday, December 27th

The following day Nico and Tori caught the first express bus from Fort Lee to Port Authority. Nico had promised to help her move into her new office, and Tori wanted to set everything up before her meeting. Before the Christmas holiday weekend, Tori had moved her laptop and personal items into the office and neatly packed the contents of her desk and overhead cabinets into two large moving boxes. As she unlocked the office door, Nico balanced one of the two boxes on a desk chair and rolled it through the door.

"Great view into that office across the street!" he teased.

After he helped her unpack the boxes and set up her desk and credenza, Nico looked at his watch. "Time for me to go and you to get ready for your meeting," he said.

They walked to the elevators, and she kissed him before he pressed the button.

"Call me the minute you hear about the promotion," she whispered.

Then, she walked to Don Howard's large corner office and the meeting she'd been dreading since yesterday's phone call.

By the time she and Don had checked and double-checked the list of things to be done, it was after nine o'clock.

"Thanks. I think we've got everything covered," Tori said as she stood to leave.

"Before you go," Don said, "there is one more item of business we need to discuss."

She sat back down. Don opened the desk's center drawer and removed a small white envelope. An envelope that wasn't sealed. An envelope Tori could see was the same high-quality stationery as those that contained…. *Wait, it couldn't be, could it?* She felt her face flush.

"Congratulations!" Don said. "Your promotion to managing director is effective today."

He continued speaking, but Tori's ears were catching every third or fourth word – she was struggling to concentrate. "happy," "glad…," "our team," "well-deserved."

It was only when Don said, "Tori, did you hear me? You have to go to the twenty-sixth floor to meet with Amber Reynolds in HR. She's going to go over benefit changes that come with this promotion," that she realized the meeting was over.

"Okay," she said as she stood on shaky legs. "Before I go. Just a couple of things. First, thank you so much. Second, I think I'm in shock. You said something about a raise, but I'm sure I misunderstood. Could you repeat the amount?"

Don did. Then he chuckled when she sat back down on the chair.

It was past eleven when Tori finally returned to her office. She couldn't believe Nico hadn't heard her news yet. And why wasn't there a voicemail telling her about his promotion? She smiled. Of course! They'd probably been in human resources, at the same time, hearing the same things about the benefit changes that came with their new status.

"Nico, honey," she said when he answered the phone with his signature, "Morgano," "you'll never guess what happened this morning!"

"I take it the meeting went well, and from the sound of it, maybe very well."

"Oh, the meeting," she laughed, "With everything else, I forgot about the meeting. Nico, I got promoted today, too. To managing director. Don told me after the meeting. He just opened his center drawer and took out the envelope. And that's not even the best part."

There was silence on the other end of the line. Tori looked at the phone console on her desk. The light was still lit. They hadn't gotten disconnected.

"Nico? Nico, are you there? Did you hear me? Can you believe it? I got promoted today, too."

"Did you know. This. Was happening. Today. Tori?" His icy tone chilled her.

"No, of course not. Are you okay? You sound angry. Why are you angry?"

At that moment, several colleagues walked past her office door and called, "Congratulations, Tori." She waved back and mouthed, "Thank you."

"Nico, you didn't answer me. What's going on?"

"I didn't get promoted."

"What? Maybe Wayne hasn't had a chance to announce promotions and raises yet. Maybe he's waiting until the afternoon, and Don just told me because I was already in his office. Maybe...."

"No, Wayne's handed out the promotion envelopes. We have several new junior officers but no promotions to senior management this month."

"Oh," she said. "Well, I know you're disappointed, but you know it's coming, right? I mean, you and Wayne have had this conversation. We're going to the Pool Bar to celebrate. Let's meet in the lobby and go over together."

"No. I'll go home. To walk and feed your dog."

"Come on. Help me celebrate. We'll only stay for one drink, I promise. The boys next door can walk and feed Baron."

"No," Nico said and hung up.

It was nearly eight-thirty when Tori sank into the comfort of the town car's leather and fabric seats and kicked off her heels. She opened one of the complimentary bottles of water that sat in the cup holder on the armrest beside her. The icy water soothed her throat made scratchy from several more-than-one cocktail and hours of louder-than-normal conversation. It had been a long, exciting day, and she was exhausted. For hours she had smiled, made excuses for her husband's absence, and lied to her colleagues and staff.

She'd repeated the story so often during the evening that it had begun to sound like the truth even to her. "No, Nico couldn't join them. He had gone home to walk and feed the dog. Wanted her to stay out, enjoy herself, and celebrate without worry. This was her night. The young men who walked and fed Baron when she worked late couldn't do it this evening—one was sick, and the other had a basketball game. Yes, it was a shame, but she and Nico would celebrate this weekend."

Tori opened and raised the second bottle of water to her lips before leaning her head back and closing her eyes. She listened to the sounds the tires made as they traveled over asphalt, then metal, and finally asphalt again. The signal the lattice-steel tower on the New Jersey side of the bridge was dead ahead. She was less than fifteen minutes from home.

When she opened the front door, she was startled to find Baron, who was not allowed beyond the boundary of the family room, bouncing on all fours in the foyer. Around his neck was a bowtie of three-inch wide red silk wired ribbon left over from Christmas. An envelope was attached to the large bow with the crinkly green ribbon used to make curly ques. Every time the dog leaped off the ground, the sharp points of the envelope's corners poked him in a different place—his jowls, neck, and ears. She dropped her briefcase and gave him her full attention. She didn't want him to get hurt, and she wanted to see what was in the envelope. As she calmed the dog, she removed the bowtie and read the apology note in her husband's handwriting.

"Congratulations.

I am so proud of you.

Love, Nico"

What a pathetic apology note!

Tori walked into the family room. Lit candles and a roaring fire cast shadows around the room. She noticed the tall Waterford crystal vase from the hall credenza now held red roses, eleven, she assumed, and baby's breath and had been set in the center of the coffee table. Nico stood beside it, holding a single rose.

"Am I forgiven?" he asked.

"When was Baron walked last?"

"You're still angry?"

"No. I was angry when you hung up on me. I was furious when you didn't call back to apologize or come up to congratulate me. Right now, I'm livid. I understand how disappointing this is for you. I'm heartsick you weren't promoted today, too. But being angry with me, as if I'm somehow to blame? Do you know how much that hurts me? How embarrassed I felt that you didn't even call—to apologize or congratulate me?"

She snapped Baron's leash on his collar and walked to the back door.

"I hate that we aren't celebrating together, and I'm sad and angry that you wouldn't join in my celebration. Baron and I are going for a walk. We won't be gone long. Either move the clothes you'll need for tomorrow out of our room and into the guest room or come up with a sincere, from YOUR heart apology." She turned on her heel and led Baron to the boardwalk.

Fifteen minutes later, she found Nico sitting at the kitchen table.

"Honey, I'm sorry. I was jealous. I love you, and I'm very proud of you. But that promotion is my dream, my ambition."

Tori sighed. She knew this story by heart. "Nico, that's an excuse, but it's not a reason for mistreating me. I know you were disappointed today. I get it! You were counting on this promotion. You'd planned on it being today."

She shook her head. "This morning, you were angry with me, like I'd done something terrible to you. All day, you've acted as if I'd done something illegal, immoral, and scandalous. Something you should be ashamed of, not proud of."

"But I am proud of you."

"Really? Who'd you tell?"

"What?"

"Did you tell anyone? Brag about my accomplishments? Maybe even as a way to ask Wayne when you'd be promoted?"

When he didn't answer, she continued, "Yeah, I can tell from the look on your face that the answer is no. Ask yourself how you would feel if, when you're promoted, I told no one—not my mother, our friends, or my colleagues. What if my behavior then mirrors your behavior now?"

She called Baron to follow her upstairs. "You're sleeping with me tonight, Buddy."

The following morning, Tori awakened to rain pelting against the window. Great! Weather to match my mood, she thought. Last night, she'd cried herself to sleep. During the night, she'd gone downstairs for a glass of cold water and an ice pack to reduce the swelling around her eyes.

I'm angry and hurt, but he has apologized. At the end of the day, I'm not going to leave him over this or end my marriage. We'll get past this. We have to, she decided.

Chapter 5
The Accident

New Year's Day

"Here, sweetheart." Nico extended his right hand, and Tori pinched the two ibuprofen tablets in his palm between her thumb and middle finger and placed them on her tongue.

"Now this," he said, holding out the glass of water. She took it with both hands before raising it to her lips. She swallowed once, then several more times, closing her eyes, imagining the pain medication dissolving and flowing through her body. Nico pushed a strand of hair behind her ear, caressing the shell of that ear with the thumb of his left hand while tugging the empty glass free from her hands with his right and placing it on the vanity's counter.

"Your bath, Mrs. Morgano, is nearly ready," he whispered in her ear, his breath and words tickling that sensitive shell. And then his touch was gone. She opened her eyes. He was bent over the wicker basket she kept by the whirlpool tub for body lotions, department store perfume samples, and small bottles of scented bath oils. He selected one of the small cobalt blue bottles and allowed several drops of lavender oil to scent the water. She smiled. From the just-shy-of-overpowering smell, she knew he had put in an extra drop or two.

This was her husband's 'tell.' Nico believed if one of something was good, two of something was better. The first time he'd made her dinner in his small New York apartment on the Upper East Side, he'd applied that theory to the garlic. After dinner, the two of them had raced each other to the tinier-than-should-be-allowed sink in his very small bath-room to brush their teeth. He'd squeezed too much toothpaste onto each of their toothbrushes, and when she'd slid hers under the faucet to wet it before putting it in her mouth, most of the white paste had fallen off the brush and down the drain. The day she was offered and accepted a job at First Dominion and then had called him to share the news she'd be moving from Washington, DC to New York City, where he lived and worked, he had sent her flowers. The bouquets, not one but two, were so large they were practically funereal.

And then there were the "I love you's." There had been a time when Nico thought one was never enough. She remembered all those early days of their courtship when they'd walked to work together from his East 82nd Street apartment to Park Avenue and 53rd Street. He'd kiss her goodbye, tell her he loved her, and as she'd walked toward the build-ing, he'd call her name, walk up to her to kiss her again, say he loved her one more time. When he'd left his job at a competitor months later and joined her bank's international staff, the routine hadn't changed—it was just moved inside, to the lobby of the building, before they parted for their respective elevator banks. She couldn't remember when that rou-tine had changed to the "call me when you're ready to leave" peck on the check they now shared.

Sadly, this idiosyncrasy had a dark side. One biting remark, one nasty comment, wasn't enough. There always seemed to be a backup. Ready. Aim. Fire. She willed those thoughts away before taking his hand and allowing him to help her into the soothing hot water.

"This is divine. Join me?"

"I cannot resist such a tempting invitation, Mrs. Morgano."

She closed her eyes, leaned against the rubber and terry cloth pillow he had secured behind her head, and allowed the soothing waters to do their job.

"Skootch forward, honey, just a little bit." When she opened her eyes, she saw her husband had replaced the harsher lights over the vanity with a more romantic option—the cool glow from the light in the walk-in shower and flickering candles. She moved forward, and he sat behind her, straddling her with his legs, pulling her back against his chest before he turned on the whirlpool jets.

"I was so scared when I saw how much damage there was on the car's passenger side. You were so stiff and sore getting out. Then, when the EMT suggested you go to the hospital to get x-rayed…."

"I'm fine, Nico. The ER doctor, the MRI, and I say so. The bruises won't be attractive, and I admit parts of me are tender," she winced when Nico moved the washcloth over the places where the seatbelt and airbag had done the most damage, "okay, really tender."

"Sorry," he whispered in her ear, then kissed the nape of her neck.

"I'm glad you called Sal and Murphy and Dylan. Your brother can be a pain in the ass, but he is a good doctor with many connections. I'm very grateful he knew the ER doc, and we could get in and out as quickly as we did. Murphy and Dylan were wonderful—waiting for the tow truck, meeting us at the hospital, and driving us home."

"I'm so sorry, Tori, for the accident, for wrecking your car, for causing you pain."

"You have nothing to apologize for, Nico. I'm sure your quick reflexes saved us from a more serious accident. Nothing that happened was your fault. We were going downhill on a slick road. You couldn't have been going more than two miles an hour. I'm grateful we hit a tree, not another car, person, or animal. The only reason my car is totaled is because of its age. I did love her, though. She was the first brand new car I ever owned."

"Maybe you should take my SUV. It's heavier, and we could use the insurance money to upgrade what is our family car. What do you think?"

"My nose is wrinkling at the suggestion," she said, "I say this because you can't see it from your vantage point. No, I'm more a sedan person. I find the SUV too big. I'm not comfortable driving it. Besides, Baron doesn't like the SUV."

"Your dog doesn't like that *I'm* in the SUV. He tolerates me because I'm the chauffeur and for no other reason. Although he was very cooperative tonight when I told him there would be no long walk, just a quick trip out back because you'd been hurt. He negotiated a tough compromise, and I agreed to let him sleep upstairs on your side of the bed."

She smiled. Nico preferred her dog to sleep downstairs and not in their bedroom. That had been *her* compromise when they'd moved to the townhouse, and she'd adopted Baron. The two men in her life only tolerated each other.

"This weekend was such fun," Tori said. "Having Lulu, Tom, and Jackson here was wonderful. I hate they live in Boston, and we don't see them much. Thank you. I couldn't have handled dinner at your aunt's with your mother. It's too soon after Christmas."

"You'll have to face or talk to her at some point. Thank God the number of times she calls every day has decreased significantly. I think she is sorry for what she said."

"You do? I don't know. I'm enjoying the radio silence. She's sorry you and Sal are angry with her, but I don't think she's sorry for what she said to my mother or me or that she even thinks she said anything wrong. Not going to your aunt's house today gave Jenny a chance to play the martyr and retell the story her way without contradiction. She didn't miss us, or at least me, at all. Besides, she had the golden couple, which has always been enough for her.

"Mom most likely blamed you because we aren't there."

"Your mother blames me for global warming and every downturn in the stock market. I don't care, but I am sorry it bothers you. I'd be devastated if you and my mother weren't speaking. So I'll try, Nico. And I accept that I'll have to be the one to take the high road, be the bigger person. It's just—I don't anticipate a growing spurt anytime soon, okay?"

Nico kissed the top of her head. "I can give you more time to reconcile with my mother, but not more time here. I think we should get out of the bathtub. I'm waterlogged, and you've been in the tub longer than I have. It's time for you to go to bed."

"Okay, I think that's a plan."

He got out of the tub first, wrapped a towel around his waist, and then helped Tori get out of the tub and dry off.

"I'm fine, Nico. Don't worry," she said, raising her eyebrows up and down in the move she called 'her Groucho Marx,' "and I was hoping to get lucky tonight. Start the New Year off on the right foot."

He kissed her. "I don't want to hurt you. I think you'll have some serious bruises in the morning."

"But it isn't morning—yet."

Chapter 6
Dinner and the Theatre

Friday, January 6th

"You have got to be kidding me twice!" Tori exploded. "Let me get this straight. We are heading to a restaurant I don't particularly like. Would never have chosen. That isn't even convenient to the theatre. To see a show we've already seen and didn't particularly want to see again! All because your brother and his wife insisted. Now, he has some emergency that may not be over in time for the curtain, and we'll be subjected to Eena's endless prattle without Sal as a buffer all through dinner. Is that about the gist of it?"

Nico nodded.

The first Friday evening of the New Year was the night the two brothers and their wives traditionally met for dinner and the theatre. Nico and Tori had been walking west on Fifty-second Street to Sal's favorite New York steakhouse when Nico had dropped the bomb—his brother would not be meeting them for dinner and might not be joining them at the theatre.

"Yeah, I'm not buying that crap," Tori said. "His so-called 'emergencies' are too frequent, too well-timed. What did you say when he called?"

"Eena called, not Sal. She sounded upset. Sal probably forgot about the theatre, made plans with Bobbi, and then when Eena reminded him, had to come up with an emergency. Eena's not stupid. She has to know about Bobbi. But there's something different about this affair. It's as if he sees them as a couple. Last week, he suggested we meet for dinner one evening—the two of us, he and Bobbi."

"What? No! I am *not* Eena's champion, and I'll admit I enjoyed Bobbi's company the night we met her. But meeting for dinner? That would betray Eena and your mother, not to mention our principles. I have enough guilt now just knowing about Bobbi."

"He used to be very discreet about his affairs, but he's almost reckless with this one. Like he wants to get caught. My brother has short arms and long pockets but is very generous where Bobbi's concerned."

"That's because she makes him pay for what he wants. Eena makes him pay for what he doesn't want," Tori said.

As they approached the restaurant, Nico spotted Eena exiting a taxi. He called her name. She turned in the direction of his voice and waited for them at the restaurant's entrance. Although she only nodded in Tori's direction, she leaned in and kissed Nico on both cheeks. Just as he reached out to open the door, a couple approached the restaurant's front window, a glass-encased meat locker.

"Could you take our picture?" the man asked.

After Nico had taken several photos of the couple, the man asked if he could reciprocate.

"Yes," Eena said, just as Tori wrinkled her nose and said, "No."

"Come on, Nico," Eena said.

He stood beside her and placed his arm around her waist. Just as the man completed the one, two, and three count, Eena turned to kiss her brother-in-law on the cheek.

When the tourist handed her back her phone, Eena said, "Grazie," and then checked the photo. "Perfetto," she said, "I'm going to send it to Sal before I post it. Let him know we're enjoying ourselves without him."

Inside the restaurant, the hostess instructed them to follow her to their table. Eena linked her arm in Nico's, and Tori walked behind them. She lowered her eyes as she passed refrigerated shelves of marbled steaks, ribs, and roasts. This restaurant had, in her opinion, the ambiance of the meat counter at her local Whole Foods. As she passed the bar, an inebriated customer staggered off his bar stool and slammed into her bruised right shoulder. She winced. Nico turned at her groan. He disentangled his arm from Eena's and went to his wife's side.

"It's fine," she told him. "Just tender." She cupped her hand protectively on her shoulder. "I should have been more aware of my surroundings."

"Are you still experiencing pain from the accident?" Eena asked after they had been seated. "Didn't the ER doc prescribe pain meds?"

"I was offered some at the hospital," Tori said, "but I've been managing with over-the-counter drugs and ice. Pain meds make me so foggy."

She rubbed her shoulder gently, then reached into her purse and extracted a small bottle of ibuprofen. "That jerk at the bar gave me a good knock, though."

"The seat belt and the airbag caused some serious bruising," Nico said.

"It's not that bad," his wife said as she swallowed two pills.

After the waiter had taken their drink and dinner orders, Eena asked, "Tori, have you ever thought about alternative pain treatments, like acupuncture? I go to a wonderful acupuncturist for my headaches. I'll text you his information." She took her phone from her purse and shuffled through her contacts.

"Thanks, Eena, but no. I'm fine. Just bruised and a little stiff. If I need anything, I'll contact my doctor."

"Stiff? Have you considered a chiropractor? Mine does wonders for my back. Maybe you just need an adjustment. I'll send you his information, too." Eena swiped her index finger across her cell phone.

"Thanks, but I'm good. I just need time for the bruising to settle."

"No worries. Already done," Eena said, then placed her phone face down on the table.

The waiter brought their meals, and conversation at the table slowed for a brief time. Eena's phone buzzed, and she turned it over to read the message.

"Sal can't meet us at the theatre," she said, as her thumbs flew across the keypad, composing a response. "That's the third time this week he's supposedly had an emergency that derailed our plans." She returned the phone to the table. "So, what are you doing about a new car, Nico? Sal said yours was *fatto per, kaputt.*"

"Not mine," Nico corrected, "Tori's. We're expecting the money from the insurance company soon. We'd planned to shop tomorrow until Mom reminded me Sal and I had promised to take her to the cemetery so she could put flowers on Dad's grave for his birthday. Sal missed the pre-holiday pilgrimage in mid-November. I hope he's planning to make this one."

"What do you mean?" Eena asked. "He went. He told me you picked up your mother, and he met you at the cemetery. Then you all went to Talk of the Town for brunch. I remember because we were supposed to…."

She frowned. "Never mind. I must be mistaken," she said, her voice barely above a whisper as she put the last piece of the jigsaw puzzle in its place and concentrated on buttering her bread roll.

Nico and Tori glanced at each other. To cover the awkward silence, Nico said, "About the car. We'll replace Tori's car, of course, but we've decided to trade in our SUV, our family car, and upgrade that as well."

Eena raised her eyebrows. "Nice. That expenditure should run you serious cash, especially after the holidays. Good news your promotion's coming this month, right, Nico?"

"Yes, a raise will certainly help," he said.

"It's a shame you can't blame someone for the accident, recoup some of your medical expenses, and be compensated for your pain and suffering," Eena said.

"You mean like suing Mother Nature for black ice?" Tori chuckled. "She'd counter-sue for damages to the tree we collided with."

"I know what you mean, though," Nico said. "It would have been much better if someone had just taken the car to a chop shop. Tori wouldn't be hurt, and we'd still get some money from the insurance company."

"And you could have reported expensive presents in the trunk," Eena said in a stage whisper. "You could've made up all kinds of things—presents for your friends, Tori, and their husbands, expensive toys for your friend's little boy...."

"Ah, no, no, we couldn't, Eena," Tori said. "That's not legal. That's stealing."

"From the insurance company," Eena said. "Don't be a fool, Tori. You won't be defending them next week when you get the reimbursement check. It won't be as much as you expect it to be."

"You're probably right," Tori said, "but what you propose is...." She shook her head and then took the last bite of her meal.

But Eena wasn't letting go of this. "You should receive compensation for your pain and suffering and the inconvenience."

"Like what?" Nico asked as he signaled the waiter for their check. Tori frowned when she saw Eena's cunning smile.

"Well," Eena whispered in a conspiratorial whisper, "what if I were to tell you that I know people, several people—doctors, physical therapists—who could help you inflate your claims for medical expenses? Maximize your injuries. Be willing to treat more—let's call it, difficult to diagnose chronic pain."

The waiter delivered the check. Nico scanned the bill and placed his American Express card in the black plastic portfolio.

"There are medical professionals who help patients, financially, I mean. Help them handle expensive medical treatments," Eena continued after the waiter had left the table. "These men and women understand how challenging serious injury and illness can be. They charge the insurance company and share overcharges with patients. For example, say you visit the doctor once every other week. He could bill the insurance company for weekly treatments. The doctor gets paid, and the patient gets a cut. Everyone benefits."

"Eena," Tori said, shaking her head, "that's unethical, immoral, not to mention illegal."

"You're naïve, Tori," Eena hissed through clenched teeth, "Everybody does it."

"Sal? Does your husband do it? Do the doctors in his practice do it?"

"Keep your voice down," Eena warned. "Sal's practice doesn't lend itself to…."

"Really?" Tori said, "because I can think of many ways, without working up much of a sweat, his practice could participate in your proposed scam. I'm fairly certain had Sal been able to join us, you wouldn't have introduced this topic. If you thought everybody was doing it, you wouldn't want me to lower my voice so I couldn't be overheard." She shook her head in disgust. "I'm going to the ladies' room before we leave. Please, could we change the subject? This talk of filing false insurance claims is making me uncomfortable."

Later, as Tori was walking back to their table, she saw Eena stop talking as soon as she saw Tori, place her hand on Nico's arm, and give an almost imperceptible nod in Tori's direction. *What am I interrupting?* Tori wondered and made a mental note to ask Nico about it later.

On the sidewalk outside the restaurant, Eena turned to Nico. "*Grazie*, Nico. Dinner was *molto buono*," and turning to Tori, she said, "I'm sorry if I slapped the panda."

"What? Oh, poked the bear? I'm fine. As long as we don't talk about it again, I'm fine."

"I see you're wearing flats," Eena said as she slid her arm into Nico's and leaned against him. Balancing on one royal blue Louboutin stiletto, she held her other leg up in a provocative pose. "You chose practical, Tori, and I chose style. I'll need the support of your strong arm, Nico, for the hike to the theatre. You don't mind, right, Tori?"

"And if I did?"

"Ladies, ladies, don't fight over me," Nico joked. "No, Eena, Tori doesn't mind, do you?"

Tori shrugged, turned, and walked down the Avenue, soon lost in the frenzy of New York's theatre district just before show time. She skirted around tourists ogling flashing neon lights, garish window displays, and now-tired-looking holiday decorations. She hummed along to familiar songs played by street musicians and inhaled the rich, sweet smell of freshly roasted chestnuts rising from pushcarts. Her steady pace put her under the theatre's marquee well ahead of Nico and Eena. The initial crowd of audience members had already gone through the theatre's open brass and glass doors, and she was surprised to see her brother-in-law waiting alone by the entrance. The shells of his ears and cheeks were red from the cold night air, while his balled fists were outlined in the pockets of his navy-blue cashmere overcoat. The steam he exhaled wasn't just from the warmth of his breath as it hit the frigid air—he wasn't happy to be there.

"This *is* a surprise," she greeted him. "Eena said you had an emergency."

Sal kissed her on the cheek. "Yeah, well, per my wife's text, this was a *command* performance. How are you feeling, by the way? Still stiff and sore from the accident?"

"I'm fine, Doc. Your wife gave me contact information for her chiropractor and acupuncturist, but as I told her, I'm just bruised."

"Those quacks?" He rolled his eyes. "My wife's a hypochondriac, and those guys are taking advantage if you ask me. Which she doesn't. Where are Nico and Eena anyway? They didn't abandon you at the restaurant, did they?"

"No. Eena asked Nico to escort her. Her heels, while stylish, are not made for the mean streets and grates of New York CIty, and she said she would feel more comfortable taking his arm. They should be arriving momentarily. If they don't, I have Nico's and my tickets. I'm assuming Eena has yours. They might miss the curtain, but we won't.

"Before they get here, Sal, I want to say something. Nico mentioned you wanted to arrange an evening out—you and Bobbi, the two of us.

I want to be very upfront. I like Bobbi, but I'm not comfortable doing that."

"I get it. I do. I just thought it would be great for you to get to know Bobbi, and I like spending time with you and Nico." He blew on his hands. "How was dinner tonight? What did you have?"

"Well, our dinner conversation was," she paused, "interesting, to say the least. I had the usual—crab cakes."

Sal chuckled. "You go to one of the finest steakhouses in the City, and you don't order a steak—ever."

"I have a thing about ordering a steak there, with all the raw meat on display. I always feel the other steaks are judging me—like I'm enjoying one of their friends. The restaurant's ambiance creeps me out. I can't help it."

"If you dislike the restaurant, why do we go back year after year? There are plenty of other restaurants to choose from."

"Because it's your favorite, the one you prefer to go to. Eena insists, and Nico and I don't mind. Anyway, why don't we go in? The theatre won't seat you until about twenty minutes into the first act if you're late. The opening number is my favorite, although the number that closes act one will probably be chosen for the Tony's."

"You and Nico have already seen this show? You should have said something."

"We did, Sal. First, I said something to Eena, then Nico spoke to her. She told us this was your first, second, and third choice for a show this year. Since you only want to see a musical…."

"What?" His question was so loud several audience members turned to look at him as he followed her to their seats.

Once he helped her with her coat and they were seated, he turned to her. "Tori, I like spending time with you and my brother. I don't care where we have dinner or what show we see. What else has Eena been telling you?

As Tori turned to answer him, she saw Eena and Nico following the usher down the aisle. "They're here."

Just as Nico and Eena were seated, the house lights dimmed. Sal leaned over to whisper in Tori's ear, "This isn't finished. Tell me at intermission."

But she didn't tell him. Sal stepped outside to listen to voicemails, Eena hurried off to use the ladies' room before the start of the second act, and Nico slid over to sit next to his wife. Not until she was in the car heading home did Tori remember her unfinished conversation with Sal, a conversation that would remain unfinished for several months.

After the curtain calls, the two couples began to inch toward the aisle. Cold air from the now-open doors overpowered the warmth in the theatre. The outside temperature must have dropped at least ten degrees since they'd arrived nearly three hours earlier. As they left the theatre, Tori scanned the parked town cars and drivers, looking for the one she had booked. When she saw George, the driver she'd requested, she raised her hand and waved to let him know she'd seen him, then pointed his location out to Nico.

"Our car is at the end of the block," she said. "Good night, Sal, Eena. Hope you enjoyed the show. See you soon. Safe home." She leaned in to kiss her brother-in-law on the cheek.

"See you tomorrow morning," Nico said to Sal.

"Tomorrow?" Sal asked.

Fearing this might be a more extended discussion than she was willing to stand on the sidewalk and listen to—the cold from the pavement already seeping through the soles of her shoes—Tori said, "I'll wait in the car. Good night."

"Yeah, tomorrow, Dad's birthday. Tori ordered the flowers," she heard Nico say as she walked toward the car.

"Thanks, George," Tori said as she got into the town car. Before leaning her head against the back headrest, she turned on her seat warmer and Nico's. "My husband is just saying good night to his brother. He'll be here in a minute."

Several minutes later, she heard the vehicle's front door open, and then her husband's voice called, "Stay in the car, George. I'm good." Tori sat up and saw Nico walking briskly toward the car. Then the passenger door on the other side of the vehicle opened, and he slid in beside her.

"Hi, George," Nico said. "How have you been? Good Christmas? It sure feels great in here. I think we might be in for some snow tonight."

"Yes, sir, Mr. Morgano. My wife and I had a terrific Christmas. Hope you and the missus enjoyed yours. And I think you're right about the snow."

As George slowly moved into the traffic, heading west then north toward the George Washington Bridge, Tori asked, "Sal forgot he was meeting you and your mother tomorrow?"

"Yeah. But he's going. And Eena said she wanted to join us. Do you want to come?"

Tori shook her head. "For so many reasons, the answer is no. Your mother would prefer to have you and Sal all to herself tomorrow. In some ways, visiting your dad's grave for his birthday is like her family's back together for a little while. She won't mind that Eena has joined you, but I'd be—well, let's just call me an unwelcome interloper." She covered his hand that rested on the leather seat beside him with her own. "Who's getting the coffee tomorrow?"

Nico and Sal's father had loved McDonald's coffee, and many Morgano family stories began with or included a stop at the golden arches so he could get his favorite cup of joe. The first January Tori and Nico had been dating, Nico had forgotten to order flowers to bring to the grave. She suggested he stop at a McDonald's and pick up four cups of coffee —for his mother, brother, and himself, and one for his father. Nico had loved the idea, as had his mother and brother. It had become an annual tradition. No one but she and Nico knew where the idea had originated.

"Sal said they would stop tomorrow after they pick up Mom. When I asked him if he could make the McDonald's run, Eena didn't know what we were talking about." He laughed. "She suggested they stop at the Starbucks at Continental Avenue." He shook his head. "I'm beginning to wonder if those two talk at all. Anyway, I'm glad Eena's going—she'll remind him, at least."

"Was this evening weird or what?" Tori asked. "That conversation at dinner with Eena about the doctors and insurance was just—I don't know—creepy is the word that comes to mind. Do you think that was just talk? You don't think she's doing what she suggested we do, do you?"

"Yeah, I don't know what that was all about," Nico said. "What did you and Sal talk about before we got there?"

"I told him I wasn't comfortable getting together with Bobbi. He said he understood. He just enjoyed being in our company."

"Not enough to remember family obligations," Nico said.

"Your family can be overwhelming. Eena mentioned your promotion tonight as if it were a done deal."

He shrugged. "I guess Mom told her it would finally be official at the end of the month."

We hope, Tori thought as she crossed the fingers of her left hand and wished with all her heart Nico's boss had submitted the paperwork.

Chapter 7
The Lunch

Friday, January 13th

Whenever Tori walked into the Pool Restaurant's cocktail lounge, she wished she was an artist. If she were, she would paint this bar. Each backlit glass shelf was a palette of jewel tones. Together the bottles' glistening contents created an enticing and intoxicating ambiance. From aperitif to liqueurs, the sparkling liquids dazzled—the Chartreuses' lemon citrine, the Amaretto's garnet topaz, the rich ambers of an array of whiskeys, scotches, and bourbons interspersed with shocks of crème de menthe emerald, Curacao sapphire, Grenadine ruby, and Midori peridot. And then there were the shapes of the bottles—the Massenez pear-shaped decanter, the Finlandia textured glacier. Each bottle begged to be taken from its perch, its contents savored.

Today, Tori could not be hypnotized by the bar's beauty, even though she would have loved to slide onto one of the smooth leather counter stools and run her hand along the polished cherry wood of the bar. The Pool's bartender, Skylar, was one of the few in the City who made her favorite drink, a Jack Rose, to perfection. Today, for this lunch, she would have enjoyed the courage from the fuchsia-colored cocktail—the one she had fallen in love with that long-ago summer she'd 'met' Lady Brett Ashley and Jake Barnes in the pages of *The Sun Also Rises*. But today, she needed her wits to be razor sharp. She was having lunch with Jenny. Today was the first time the two women would be in the same room since Christmas dinner.

Tori walked through the bar to the maître d's station. She wanted Duane, the maître d' on duty, to know she was here and would be waiting for the other half of her party by the restaurant's door, and instructed him to give her guest one of the menus without prices, as she would be taking care of today's check. Then, she returned to stand watch by the restaurant's entrance.

She glanced at the clock above the coat check—she was early. Tori had been taught keeping someone waiting was rude. Her mother-in-law would be late. Jenny felt conspicuous waiting for her dining companion to arrive or being left alone in a restaurant. She always said this was one of her pet peeves, and because Jenny had so many, Tori had assigned this complaint number one hundred twenty-three for identification purposes.

Jenny knows I have a job and can't take all afternoon for this lunch. Where is she? Tori thought and realized she was impatiently tapping her right foot.

For several days after Christmas dinner, Tori had imagined confronting her mother-in-law, demanding an apology. In those early morning dialogues with her reflection in the bathroom mirror, she had delivered persuasive arguments and parried each of Jenny's retorts with a spot-on response. Then, after several days of wrapping herself in self-righteous anger and basking in her prowess as avenger, Tori had let go of her anger. After all, Jenny's sons had spoken to their mother about her behavior on Christmas Day, and no apology had come.

Jenny was more than fifteen minutes late. Tori looked at her watch, then confirmed the time on the clock. *Come on, Jenny. I have a job I have to get back to.*

Tori had finally accepted she couldn't change Jenny's behavior. She could only change how she reacted to it. She'd be polite and respectful, but she wouldn't take Jenny's rudeness anymore. Nico needed his wife and his mother to be civil to each other. And Tori had known she would have to be the one to make the first move.

She'd carefully choreographed everything she could for today's lunch. She'd chosen the Pool because it was close to her office and the first stop in Manhattan for the express train running from Jenny's Forest Hills co-op. The restaurant's ambiance was elegant and sure to impress her mother-in-law. In the center of the dining room, flowering trees stood at each corner of a reflecting pool. Highly polished brass chains formed drapes that shimmered and swayed on the restaurant's two walls of windows and allowed ambient light to fill the dining room.

When Tori had invited her to lunch, her mother-in-law had been gracious. Tori had had high hopes this lunch would go well. When Jenny entered the restaurant, however, she was scowling. Hopes dashed!

"You said this restaurant was in the Seagram's Building," Jenny said. "I was expecting to enter on Park Avenue, and then, I saw the sign on East Fifty-third. It's tiny, easily missed. And it's very chilly in here. I do hope the dining room is warmer."

"It is. Duane is waiting to seat us," Tori said.

As the maître' d led them to the table in a discreet location by the window as Tori had requested, Jenny questioned why they couldn't be seated at a table around the aqua waters of the reflecting pool. When she was handed her menu, she complained there were no prices.

"Jenny, I requested this table because it affords us more privacy, and lunch is my treat," Tori said. "Please don't concern yourself with price."

Their waitress appeared moments later to get their drink orders. Jenny ordered a glass of Pinot Grigio. Tori said she was fine with water.

"I'm so pleased you were able to join me for lunch. We should look at the menu and order soon because I'll need to return to the office. I have meetings this afternoon," Tori said.

"What do you recommend' Jenny asked.

"The crab cake here is outstanding, and your son swears by the red snapper. But I think I'll have the lobster salad today, which is also fantastic."

"It's freezing outside, Veek Toria. Too cold for salad. What soups do they have?"

"The lobster bisque is wonderful, and while I've never had the she-crab, I've heard good things."

"So rich. It will just sit. Here," Jenny put her hand in the center of her chest between her breasts. "Just like your Christmas dinner. *Agita* all night and the next day." She shook her head.

"I'm sorry you had heartburn Christmas evening. Then perhaps something light today. The grilled chicken or Dover sole," Tori said. She was growing increasingly annoyed. "Are you about ready to order?"

Jenny shrugged and rolled her eyes. "I'll find something."

Tori signaled the waitress to their table. Jenny ordered sautéed red snapper, chose French Fries as her side dish, and selected one of each type of the three bread choices they were offered. Tori ordered the lobster salad.

"Veek Toria," Jenny began when the waitress had left, "this is an expensive restaurant. You should not be spending my Nico's money so frivolously."

"Lunch is my treat, Jenny. I have a good job, too, which I'll need to get back to in about an hour."

"My Nico is about to be promoted to Managing director. I am so proud of him."

"As am I. Although we don't know exactly when Nico will be promoted, we hope that...."

"No, Nico said it would be this month. Later this month," Jenny said.

"Promotions and raises are not official until the Bank's board meets," Tori said. "It's pro forma, but until that hap...."

"Everyone missed Nico on New Years' Day," Jenny interrupted, "and of course, he didn't get a chance to see his father's side of the family at my sister-in-law's Christmas Eve. Our family has celebrated the Feast of the Seven Fishes with the Morgano family since I was engaged to Nico's father. First at my mother-in-law's and now at my sister-in-law Angela's. Two years in a row, he wasn't there. Keeping my son from his family isn't right, Veek Toria."

Tori tried to interject, but Jenny spoke over her in a voice loud enough for the woman at the next table to turn and look at them. "The holidays are about family, Veek Toria. Those girls are only friends. They are not family. You and Nico should have been with family on New Year's Day, not with your friends."

The two women paused their conversation as one waitress refilled their water glasses, and another served Jenny's glass of wine.

"Jenny," Tori said when they were alone again, "I have a family too. It's important we spend some holidays with my family, follow some of my family's traditions. We came home early from Pennsylvania to be with the family at Nonna Morgano's the Sunday after Thanksgiving. And you, Sal, and Eena were with us Christmas Day."

"I told you before you and Nico were engaged, family is the most important thing. The first time I met you, I knew you weren't a good match for my son. You still can't even make a decent gravy."

When Tori tried to respond, Jenny raised her hand to stop her. "I'm not finished. Valentina understands this. Even when Sal and Valentina spend a holiday with her family, they can drop by and celebrate the holiday with us. Your family lives too far away."

"Yet, they never have. Sal and Eena have never just dropped by—at any holiday gatherings I've attended." Tori said. "Sal has patients, or Eena has a headache. They spend the holiday with her family and then call to explain why they can't drop by."

"I know you were upset about my reaction to the gloves and scarf, but they were very impractical. Although the quality of the Italian leather is remarkable, that *color*!" Jenny shook her head. My mother-in-law told me the story of your mother's gloves. I *do not* appreciate you talking behind my back, Veek Toria, or complaining to other family members about me."

The waitress arrived with their lunch, and the two women didn't speak until the server had left.

"I didn't say anything to Nonna Morgano about the gloves. If she knows the story, it didn't come from me," Tori said.

For a brief time, their conversation ended while they ate.

"What are you planning to celebrate Nico's promotion?" Jenny asked.

"Nothing yet. As I told you, we don't know when Nico will be promoted. We hope this month, but we don't know for certain," Tori said.

Jenny tsked. "I'll organize something for my son's big day. His family will want to do something special, even if you don't."

"Of course, I want to celebrate Nico's promotion. His boss, colleagues, and subordinates will take him out for drinks after...."

Jenny interrupted her. "I said I'll take care of it, Veek Toria."

"Jenny, Nico and I both have vacation days we need to take before the end of March. I'm planning a surprise getaway, just the two of us, to celebrate Valentine's Day. Please check with me on dates before you schedule something, okay?"

"Where are you going?" Jenny asked.

"Right now, I want to keep it a secret. I'm sure Nico will tell you about it when he finds out. I'm hoping to finalize the details this week," Tori said.

"Tell me as soon as you've arranged everything for this little surprise trip. I need time to plan, Veek Toria," Jenny said. "There are a lot of people who will want to come and celebrate my son's success. I have arrangements to make."

"And you'll need a guest of honor at the party," Tori said, "and not one at a beach resort."

Jenny glared at her.

What could possibly go wrong? Tori wondered.

The waitress refilled their glasses and handed each of them dessert menus. Tori asked her to box her lobster salad, which she'd hardly touched.

"Nothing for me," she said as she glanced at her watch and returned the menu to the server. "I really need to get back to the office."

Jenny ordered coffee and a crème brulé.

"I'm going to use the ladies' room before I leave." Tori stood. "When I return, I'm going to have to go back to the office. My time for lunch is nearly up."

On her way to the ladies' room, she stopped at the servers' station and handed their waitress her American Express card. "I'll stop by to sign the receipt and pick up my card on the way back."

After retrieving her credit card and signing the receipt, Tori returned to the table. The waitress followed her, carrying a tray with Jenny's dessert, a small French press of coffee, a silver creamer, a sugar bowl, and the boxed lobster salad. Tori didn't sit down.

After the waitress had served the dessert, pressed and poured the coffee, and left, Jenny said, "Sit down. Why are you just standing there?"

"I need to return to the office. Thank you for joining me for lunch, Jenny. I've taken care of the check. Enjoy your dessert and coffee. We'll talk soon."

"Where are you going, Veek Toria? This is very impolite to leave me here in the restaurant to eat alone."

"I'm sorry, Jenny. I need to return to work. Perhaps, if you hadn't been nearly fifteen minutes late…. Good-bye."

Unlike Eena, who works Monday, Wednesday, and half of Saturday, she thought, *I work for a living.*

Then, she turned and walked out of the restaurant, through the bar —admiring the dazzling jewel-tone display reminiscent of stained-glass windows and wishing one more time for that icy cold Jack Rose.

January was a busy month for Tori's department, and she was soon caught up in the maelstrom of that day's issues. She didn't have time to review her frustrating lunch with Jenny. Only when the day transitioned to twilight and the glaring fluorescents in the ceiling were her sole source of light, did she realize it was late afternoon.

She noted the time on her phone before texting Nico.

On for the 6:45 express? Meet in lobby at 6:15?

At six o'clock, she realized she hadn't heard back from her husband, and after packing up her messenger bag, she headed for the elevator. She'd just go and pick him up.

As she rounded the corner and headed for Nico's cubicle, she heard her name and turned toward the sound.

Nico was standing at the entrance to the workstation of one of his staff members, Siobhan, with their boss, Wayne Wright. Tori realized it had been Wayne who had called out to her.

"Congratulations, Tori!" he said. "I haven't seen you since your promotion. Well done. Well deserved."

Siobhan, seated at her desk, rose and waved to Tori over the cubicle's divider. "Belated Congrats! I hadn't heard the news until just now, or I would have said something sooner."

Tori smiled and called back. "Thank you," before continuing to her husband's desk.

A few minutes later, Nico joined her. His only greeting was to drop papers and files on his desk and announce, "Let's get out of here."

"Do you want to make sense of this chaos before we go? We have time before we have to leave."

"We're leaving now," he said through gritted teeth.

He retrieved his overcoat from the hanger near the cubicle's entrance, threw some papers and his laptop into his briefcase, and looked back at her expectantly.

"Well, are you ready? Let's go."

She followed him to the elevator, and since they were the only two waiting, she lowered her voice and asked, "What's wrong?"

"You left my mother in a restaurant and stuck her with the check," he hissed.

"No, I paid the bill. You know I'd never do that, don't you?"

"Don't you?" she repeated when he didn't respond.

"My mother said you did. She said you took her to the Pool and then left her. You know she hates sitting alone in a restaurant."

"I had to get back to work, Nico. I'd been there for over an hour and a half. I explained that, and I apologized. What else did she say?"

"She said you ordered an expensive salad and encouraged her to have wine and the snapper. Twenty-two dollars for a glass of Pinot Grigio, she said. And then, you left when her dessert and coffee were served."

"Yeah, that all happened. We met at the Pool, I ordered a lobster salad, and she had the snapper, and yes, I left to go back to work before she'd finished dessert. I had to get back to the office. I explained that. To her. Several times. But I paid for the lunch. If she was charged for any portion of that meal, ask her to text you a copy of the bill. I'll have them reimburse her. I did *not* invite her to lunch to stiff her with the bill. No way!"

"Then why would she say you did?"

"Who knows why your mother says what she says? By the way, do you know she thinks you and I should never have gotten married? She's also decreed I will never learn to make a decent spaghetti sauce because I'm not Italian. I guess, she'll never make a decent corned beef and cabbage or Irish whiskey cake because she's not Irish," Tori tossed over her shoulder as she boarded the empty elevator cab ahead of her husband.

"But you left her. She said she got a menu with no prices and was horrified that the bill was over $100 with the tip. How would she know that if she didn't get the bill?"

"I don't know, Nico. Maybe she asked the server the cost of the lunch —it wasn't a state secret. Maybe she asked for a menu with prices and figured it out. I've been completely honest with you about the lunch, what happened, and I own my part. What I don't understand and need you to help me understand is what I've said or done to make you doubt me and my honesty. A few weeks ago, you wouldn't have immediately concluded that your mother's version of the story was the correct version."

The elevator stopped on the second floor, and several home-ward-bound employees got on. Tori smiled and said, "Hello," but Nico didn't acknowledge the new passengers. They resumed the conversation when they'd left the elevator and were walking through the lobby toward East Fifty-Third Street.

Tori said, "Your mother thinks I abandoned her in a restaurant. I say I had to leave. You know me, and you know her. You know, or should know, I would have more respect for your mother than to invite her to lunch and leave her with the check. There was a time, just a few weeks ago, when you would have believed me. But now I'm being questioned. I'm the one you don't believe. And she's convinced you're getting promoted at the end of this month. Have you talked to Wayne? Did he say something? What if it isn't this month but later in the year? What will you say if it doesn't happen in a couple of weeks?"

"It's going to be this month, Tori. Stop being so negative. No, I haven't talked to Wayne, and stop nagging me about it. Just because you're senior management now doesn't mean you know everything there is to know about how promotions work. And I'm still angry you left my mother at lunch."

"Well, you'll have to build a bridge and get over it. It didn't happen the way your mother said it did. By the way," she said, "did you tell your grandmother the story about the gloves? Because your mother accused me of being a tattletale. I so didn't see that one coming."

Since the noisy subway station made conversation in a normal voice no longer possible, Tori and Nico didn't speak again until they settled on the express bus waiting to pull out of Port Authority. She was tired of talking about Jenny and lunch. She ignored the work in her messenger bag and lost herself in music and the City's lights as the bus headed for the George Washington Bridge. When she saw Nico pull out his phone, she removed her right earbud and said, "Please text your mother and ask about the lunch check. If she could text you a copy of the receipt, I'll take care of it tomorrow. I promise. The last thing I intended, the last thing I wanted, was for her to get stuck with the bill."

Nico nodded and sent the text.

After they had gotten off the bus and were in the SUV driving home, a notification that Nico had a text message from Jenny flashed across the navigation screen. Tori tapped the "read" button. The text appeared on the screen, and the vehicle's computer voice read, "I don't have a bill. I didn't get charged. You misunderstood what I said."

"She's accusing me of misinterpreting what she'd said about the check? She's a piece of work, my mom."

"And she's not going to change," Tori said.

They rode the rest of the way home in silence. Only later did Tori realize Nico had neither apologized nor explained why he hadn't trusted her.

Chapter 8
A Not-So-Friendly Game of Bridge

Friday, January 27th

"Damn it!" Nico threw his remaining card on the table.

"Last trick is ours, and you're down two," Dylan said.

"Maybe if we'd had a better trump split or the club finesse had worked," Tori said.

"Maybe if you'd bid your hand correctly," Nico said.

"I would have bid the hand exactly the way she did, so what would you have done?" Murphy asked.

"Let's take a break," Dylan said. "Nico, what the hell is with you tonight? Ever since you walked in the door— you want to pick a fight with someone."

Both Dylan and Murphy looked from Nico to Tori and back at Nico.

"Nothing. Nothing's wrong. Okay? Drop it."

Maybe, if he's alone with Dylan, Tori thought, and she willed her husband to open up to his best friend.

"I'm hungry. When I ordered the pizza, Ray's said it would be about forty minutes, and that was a half hour ago," Tori said. "How 'bout we get everything ready, Murph? Nico, Dylan, do you each want another beer?"

"That'd be great. Thanks," Dylan said.

In the kitchen, Murph took plates from the cupboard while Tori took two bottles of Corona from the refrigerator, opened them, sprinkled sea salt on the rims, and inserted slices of lime into each bottle. When she delivered them to the card table, the two men were talking basketball!

Damn it, Nico. Tell him. Maybe you'll listen to his advice because you sure won't listen to mine, she thought.

Just then, the doorbell rang. Dylan went to answer it. He returned seconds later, holding a large pizza box, and headed for the kitchen.

"Follow me," he said as he lifted the lid of the box, and Tori followed the enticing aromas of melting cheese, oregano, and garlic into the kitchen.

"I didn't realize how hungry I was," Tori said. "Ray's Pizza is sooo good, isn't it? It tastes as good as it smells." She held out her plate to Dylan. "Two, please."

Dylan placed two slices on her plate, served his wife two slices, and placed two more on the plate he held out to Nico. "Nico, pizza."

Murphy, Tori, and Dylan took their plates and drinks to the kitchen table and sat down. Nico remained seated at the counter, picking the label on the beer bottle with the thumbnail of his right hand.

"Everything set for your long weekend in Saint Martin?" Murphy asked Tori.

"We're not going," Nico said.

"What?" Murphy asked, looking at Tori. "What happened?"

"Nothing," Tori said. "This is the first I'm hearing about it. I'm going, and if he doesn't want to go, do you want to? If you can take Friday off, it's the Presidents' weekend. We can sit on the beach, enjoy some fun and sun."

Nico stared at her. "You'd still go? Just leave me here?"

"Yes."

"Does this mood have anything to do with your promotion?" Dylan asked.

The silence that followed seemed endless to Tori. Finally, she said, "You might as well tell them. They're two of our best friends, and it's not going to be a secret for long."

Nico glared at her. "Since you're so eager to spread the bad news, why don't you do it?"

She sighed. "Nico's boss told him today he isn't getting promoted."

"You mean next week," Murph said.

Tori shook her head. "No. Wayne said his job isn't a senior management position, so no promotion."

"You might as well tell them the rest."

"He's maxed out the salary scale for his job," Tori said,

"What does that mean?" Murph asked.

"What do you think it means?" Nico said. His tone was biting and sarcastic.

Dylan glared at Nico, then turned to his wife. "It means Nico won't be eligible for merit raises in the future, Honey."

"So, what's next?" Dylan asked. "What are your options?"

Nico said nothing.

"He could ask to have his job description reviewed, see if there are responsibilities that aren't listed. He could put in for a transfer within the bank, or he could look for a job outside the bank," Tori said. "He has options."

"All of those sound good. Dare I ask how Jenny took the news about having to cancel the party?" Dylan asked.

"She doesn't know yet," Tori said. "He'll have to tell her when he talks to her this weekend."

"I'll tell her when I'm ready to tell her."

"Okay," Tori said, holding her hands up in surrender.

Later, when she was helping Murphy clean up in the kitchen and Nico and Dylan were putting the card table and chairs away, Murphy asked, "Isn't the party only four weeks away? Yeah. It's the 27th of next month. I wrote it on the calendar when Jenny called Dylan."

"Yup. But that's not my problem. I didn't run around telling people about the promotion. He did. His mother, his problem. Next weekend he, Sal, and Eena are taking Jenny to brunch for her birthday. Thank God I'm flying to DC for a two-day conference and will, unfortunately, miss those festivities. The weekend after next, we were supposed to be in Saint Martin. I was serious. Do you want to go?"

"You gave him that trip for Valentine's Day. He's going to change his mind," Murphy said.

"Maybe. We'll see. I'd rather go with you if he's going to pout the entire time."

On the drive home, Nico told her he'd go to Saint Martin—not that he wanted to.

"I planned this trip as a romantic getaway for us. I want you to go because you want to, not because you feel you have to. Think about it and let me know your decision by the end of the weekend. I'm sure Murphy can arrange a sub for her classes. You cannot continue to treat me as your punching bag, Nico. Where's the man I married? Since Sal's practice was honored by *New York Magazine*, you've been obsessed with this promotion. A few days apart might do us both some good. Then, maybe you and I should see someone, like a counselor, to talk about this."

"A counselor? Like a marriage counselor? No." He shook his head. "No."

"Well, I'm going," Tori said. "With or without you."

Chapter 9
Has the Tide Turned?

Friday night, Mid-March

February seemed to last forever. The weather was cold and miserable almost every day. Soot-covered snow stood in mounds, knee-high, on every corner. Sanitation crews drove garbage trucks, converted to snow-plows, past the ever-growing piles of black, plastic trash bags along the streets. But the plows were no match for the snowstorms that blew in from the west every week.

Tori's workshop in DC had been a pleasant respite from the dreariness of New York and Nico's career drama. When she'd called from the Hay-Adams Hotel that Sunday to let him know she'd arrived, he'd complained about the brunch with his mother, brother, and sister-in-law.

"Sal and Eena were late. Sal had to leave early—of course. So I got stuck with the check and had to take Mom and Eena home. And Eena wanted to talk about Sal without Mom being there, so I had to drop Mom off, then double back and take Eena home—a good fifty miles I didn't need to be on the road."

If Tori had to pinpoint when Nico began to change, be less disagreeable and argumentative, she would have said it was after she and Murphy returned from Saint Martin. For days after that January evening at the Malones, Nico would announce he wanted to go to Saint Martin. Hours later, he would change his mind. Finally, she called his bluff.

He hadn't believed she'd go without him—until she went. When she'd returned from the trip rested and relaxed, he was more thoughtful, less combative. She'd also made an appointment with a psychologist, Dr. Jessica Avery. Although he refused to join her, she'd gone anyway. Her weekly sessions with Jessie, as the psychologist had encouraged Tori to call her, gave her strategies, things to say and do when the situation at home got too tense.

At the end of February, Nico announced he was going to look for a new job. One afternoon, as they were waiting for the E train to take them to Port Authority, he told her he'd hired a career counselor, a suggestion she'd made in early January, and he'd rejected. "I'm meeting him tomorrow evening after work to punch up my resumé," he'd said.

A few nights later, as they got off the express bus, Nico told her he'd joined a committee at the American Institute of Certified Public Accountants. "The career counselor thought it would be a great place to begin networking," he said. "There's a dinner tomorrow evening, and I signed up to go."

Even Dylan and Murphy commented on his change of mood. "The counselor, the networking, and whatever else you're doing seems to be working," Dylan said.

But the most significant change came one Friday in mid-March.

Tori was waiting for him in the bank's lower lobby when she spotted him walking toward the escalator. Her heart danced when she saw him —just as it had nearly six years ago when they'd met at Murphy and Dylan's engagement party.

He looks so handsome. And he's smiling. Haven't seen that grin in a while.

That morning, she remembered, he had chosen to wear his navy-blue wool suit—one of two she'd given him last week as a birthday present—five months early. As she had promised last January, she'd offered job search and career suggestions only when asked, and she'd supported everything he'd wanted to try, including buying a couple of new "interview" suits.

Maybe he wore one of the power suits and new ties today because he had a job interview. Maybe he's smiling because it went well.

Last Saturday, when they'd picked up the suits after the final tailoring, she and the salesman had selected two Ferragamo ties and matching pocket squares that perfectly complemented both suits. Early birthday presents from her mother, she'd explained when he'd balked at the additional expense.

"Power suits need power accessories," she'd said. "Think Superman —great suit, but It's the cape and boots that make the outfit!"

As soon as they were home, he'd taken the garment bag upstairs while she went to the kitchen to make the grilled cheese sandwiches they'd decided on for lunch. Ten minutes later, the sandwiches were made, but he wasn't downstairs yet.

Going to the foot of the stairs, Tori called, "Nico, lunch is ready. Come eat while it's still hot from the grill, and the cheese is gooey."

No answer. She waited a few minutes before calling his name again. No answer. She climbed the stairs and walked into their bedroom. He was sitting on their bed and seemed—sad. She sat beside him, took his right hand in her left, and leaned her head on his shoulder.

"Hey, what's wrong?"

"I was just thinking how much money we spent. Your mom, too"

"Those suits are an investment in our future. And you look amazing in them," she said as she stood. "Just to be clear, in five months, I plan to put a bow on both hangers, wrap up the ties and pocket squares and give them to you again! Now, let's eat. I'm starved."

He stood and took her in his arms. "I haven't been the husband you deserve," he said. "I've made so many dumb, some might even say reckless, mistakes. I don't deserve you."

Reckless? Odd choice of words, she thought but didn't press him further.

The rest of that weekend had been wonderful—and just theirs. That night, they went to dinner at one of her favorite restaurants. After a leisurely brunch Sunday, they went to the movies, shared a tub of buttered popcorn, and held hands. Reminiscent of the early days of their relationship when he would fly to DC, or she would fly to New York so they could be together. Yes, last weekend was fantastic! His smile this afternoon suggested this one might be too!

Maybe the worst is behind us, she thought.

When he joined her in the lower lobby, he kissed her on the lips—instead of his usual peck on the cheek. He hadn't greeted her that way in a while, and she realized how much she'd missed it.

"Wow! That's nice," she said. "I like that much better than the pecks on the cheek my husband gives me. Let's get out of here before he comes."

He laughed. "Yeah, let's get out of here and start the weekend. I talked to Dylan this afternoon. Rather than our usual Friday pizza night, we thought we'd go to the Patrick Henry for burgers and then back to our place for cards. Sound good?"

"I will never turn down a Patrick Henry cheesy, messy burger. We have to go home first and get our bibs, though!"

He laughed—again. "Yeah, we need to change. We aren't meeting them until seven, so we have time," he said.

"You're practically buoyant," she said. "Good day?"

"No, not good. Great!" he said, his smile getting wider. "Next month I'm going to London for two weeks!"

"Okaaay," she said. "You go to the London office once or twice a year for meetings, and I've never seen you this excited." She crossed the index and middle finger of her right hand and shoved her hand in the pocket of her coat.

Was the job interview in London? Is he thinking of taking a job outside the United States? Please, God, no. Not when my career is taking off!

"Well," he said, "I've never been accepted to take the Bourse Course before. I'm going for two weeks—the first will be the course, and the second will be meetings in the London office. Maybe I'll even get to spend some time on the trading floor, put my new skills to the test."

Tori grinned—a mixture of pride that Nico had been chosen to take this prestigious workshop few Americans attended and relief they weren't talking about an overseas relocation! He had wanted to participate in this workshop on the European stock exchanges for a couple of years.

"Wow," she said. "That's fantastic, Nico. I'm so proud of you for being nominated and getting accepted."

"I'd suggest you go with me," he said.

"No, no. From everything I've heard about the course, you won't have a free minute. The only time we'd have together would be the weekend, and even then—doesn't the course go from Monday to Saturday morning?"

He nodded.

"I'd rather we plan a trip together, just the two of us."

"Yeah, I'd like that," he said.

"When are you going?" she asked.

He laughed. "Last two weeks of April. So yes, I'll be here for Easter and my brother's birthday party."

The Patrick Henry was busy. Everyone, it seemed, was hungry for a Huzzah burger—the house specialty. Dylan and Murphy arrived at the restaurant minutes after Tori and Nico, and the two couples were seated immediately. After they'd ordered their usual, Nico shared the news of his upcoming business trip.

"I've wanted to take this course for a couple of years. It's hard as hell, but you learn a lot."

"Preference is given to the employees in Europe," Tori said. "It's a fantastic opportunity and, from what I hear, an amazing workshop. Every day is a simulation of different European exchanges. The participants are put in groups that compete against each other to see who makes the most money."

"Congratulations. The course sounds amazing," Dylan said.

"Sounds like something that would look good on a resumé," Murphy said. "Do you think you could leave what you're doing now at the bank, maybe do something more related to this course?"

"No, but it will give me a better understanding of what goes on at the different exchanges," Nico said. "Another great thing about the trip, after I take the course, I'm going to the London office for a week. I'll be able to sit at the trading desk, see the action. Maybe they'll even let me execute a few trades."

"When do you go again?" Murphy asked.

"The last two weeks of April."

Chapter 10
Where's Nico?

Friday, April 21st

Although Tori held her phone away from her ear, she could still hear everything her mother-in-law said—loud and clear. She opened the storm door and stepped onto the front porch of her townhouse just as Murphy's white Highlander turned off the road. Tori's heart was breaking. Her two best friends were here. Help had arrived.

Tori quickly pulled the phone away from her ear and rang her doorbell twice. "Jenny, there's someone at my door. I've gotta go. I know. I'll tell Nico to call you." She paused. "Yes. As soon as I hear from him. Gotta go." She disconnected the call.

"Was that Jenny you just gave the bum's rush?" Lulu asked as she walked toward the house. "I can't believe you're still using that old trick. And that she falls for it."

"I see you found Murphy circling the airport. Thanks for doing the airport shuttle this time, Murph," Tori said. "And yes, that was Jenny, and she still buys it. But then, I have several strategies. I'm not a one-note show—I alternate. In addition to the doorbell, there's the oven timer signaling the nonexistent meal or cake is ready. Needing to walk Baron is another good excuse, and then there are the sounds of a knock at the back door and a tea kettle whistling that I've recorded. I also set reminders on Alexa. When she starts talking, I pretend I have company. Whatever works."

"Group hug," Murphy said, and she and Lulu dropped their overnight bags and pulled their friend into a hug. Tori was suddenly overcome with emotion, the news she needed to share with them overwhelming her. "You guys," she said, a lump forming in her throat. "I'm so glad you're here. Let's go inside and get this weekend started!"

Murphy and Lulu propped their purses and suitcases against the banister before joining Tori in the kitchen. She was unpacking take-out containers from brown shopping bags. The aromas were intoxicating.

"Oh. My. God!" Lulu said, "Is that Caprese chicken from Café Scalinatella?"

"With fettucine alfredo?" Murphy asked.

"Yup," Tori confirmed. "And their amazing garlic bread. There are several bottles of Santa Margherita chilling in the fridge." She handed Murphy the corkscrew. "Do the honors?"

"This reminds me of senior year in our little house on High Street," Lulu said, "Us, together for the weekend, except with gourmet food and much better wine."

The cork gave a satisfying pop, and Murphy poured three glasses of cold Pinot Grigio.

They sat at the dining room table when each had helped herself to chicken, pasta, and bread.

"Tori, you didn't take much," Murphy said, looking at her friend's plate. "Everything okay? You feeling all right?"

"Yeah, just a big lunch." She didn't want to spoil the mood just yet.

"How are King Sal and Princess Eena?" Lulu asked. "Any good gossip?"

Tori shrugged. "Eena hosted a birthday dinner for Sal a couple of weeks ago, and it was evident from the tension between them the guests had interrupted a Battle Royale! It was as if we'd all arrived at a prize fight in the middle of round three, and each fighter had gotten in a few good punches."

Lulu laughed. "Not too awkward! Wonder what they were arguing about now?"

"I'm sure he would have rather spent the evening with Bobbi than a room full of relatives and friends," Murphy said. "I bet she had an extra special present for him too."

Tori chuckled. "But wait! Eena had the dinner catered! Jenny raved about the food and complimented Eena on how delicious everything was."

"Plus ça change!" Lulu said.

"Yup," Tori said, "In the bad mother-in-law department, I caught the brass ring on the merry-go-round!"

Murphy said, "Sorry to break this to you, but it's too late to demand a do-over."

"Anyway," Tori said, "Eena was so exhausted from planning the party, she told the family she needed a rest. She's *supposedly* gone to a spa in the Poconos for a week. No phone, no internet—just rest, yoga, massages, and facials."

"You sound like you don't believe her," Lulu said. "Where do you think she is? Do you think she's following Sal's lead and taken a *luvah?*"

"Yes. Yes, I do." Tori took a deep breath and exhaled slowly. "I know exactly where Eena is. She's in Paris. In a hotel room. With my husband."

Two forks clattered on porcelain.

Murphy swallowed her pasta without chewing and nearly choked as she asked, "What?" between coughs. Lulu reached over and grabbed Tori's hand. "What the hell?" She looked from Tori to Murphy, "What the hell?"

Tears rolled down Tori's cheeks. "I guess I ruined dinner."

"No, no, you didn't," Murphy said. "Lulu, help me take the plates to the kitchen. We can nuke everything later. Then pour us more wine. While you're at it, get the second bottle and open that too. Let's get comfortable in the family room. Light some candles and turn on the fireplace. Make it cozy."

Turning to Baron, she said, "You know what? I think you should join us. Go sit by Tori," and the Boxer sprang to his feet and followed his mistress into the family room.

When the three friends had settled on the couch and loveseat in front of the fire, their wine glasses full, Lulu asked, "Are you up to telling us the whole story?"

"I thought Nico was in London," Murphy said. "At that workshop. He was so excited about it." Turning to Lulu, she said, "The last two Fridays when we got together, that's all he could talk about—how he'd wanted to go for years, what an honor it was—like he'd been nominated for an Academy Award or something. Then he planned on being in the London office for a week."

"Yes," Tori said. She reached down to pet Baron. He laid his head in her lap. "That's what he said. Being nominated to attend that workshop in London is prestigious, especially for an American. The worst part? I encouraged him to go. I was excited for him, excited his boss had nominated him, and he'd been accepted."

"Of course, you were excited for him," Lulu said. "What wife wouldn't be?"

Tori shrugged. "I keep thinking of that song in *My Fair Lady*, 'What a fool I was, what an addlepated fool!'

"Anyway, I know the workshop is intense—lots of late-night sessions and competitions among groups, so I told him to call me when he could. I offered to drive him to Liberty Airport last Saturday, but he'd arranged a town car to pick him up. Of course, I know now he didn't want me to see what airline he was flying. Or, God forbid, see Eena getting out of a town car. So I just kissed him goodbye."

"So far, everything sounds believable," Lulu said. "What changed?"

Tori sighed. "About a month ago, an acquaintance of mine, a senior partner at a Wall Street law firm, invited me to lunch. We've worked together a lot over the past two years. When we met, Esta, that's the lawyer, confided in me that in October, she'd be leaving the law firm and going to run the compliance, legal and regulatory divisions at a major investment firm. She negotiated, as part of her package, being able to pick the heads of each division. She's asked me to head the compliance division."

"What?" Murphy asked. "Like you'd have the job your current boss has?"

Tori nodded. "Even a bit more responsibility than he has."

"I can't wait to hear what Nico said when you told him," Lulu said.

"I didn't. I didn't tell anyone for lots of reasons. First, at the time, I didn't have a job offer," Tori said. "I still had to interview with several people in the investment bank."

"Didn't? or Don't?" Lulu asked.

"Didn't," Tori said. "The investment bank, Loftus & Hunt, is putting together a formal offer, but Esta has told me what it is, and I'll accept it when it's officially made. Anyway, there were other reasons. Esta's appointment wasn't even scheduled to be announced until the beginning of August. I thought I had months to soften the blow, prepare Nico a little bit."

"Tori, do you hear yourself? Soften the blow? Prepare Nico?" Murphy said. "What is he? Two?"

"I soften the blow for Jackson—and he *is* two—when he goes to another kid's birthday party and doesn't get to keep the presents," Lulu said. "Nico should be, and frankly, you should expect him to be—proud of you, thrilled for you. This is a great opportunity!"

"You're right. I thought Nico was getting used to my promotion, and he was—or pretended to be—more interested in doing something about his job situation. He said he was networking with colleagues at other banks. They'd meet for drinks and dinner. I wasn't suspicious because I have a similar relationship with my counterparts. He even told me he had gone to a career counselor, like I'd suggested, to punch up his resume and post it on the best online sites. But these were lies." She took a deep breath and exhaled. "All lies. And I believed them, all of them. So, I repeat, 'What a fool I was!'"

"No, you weren't," Lulu said. "His story sounds believable—even now that I know it's all lies."

"Lu's right. I'd have believed him too. Go on," Murphy said.

"Wednesday morning, I got a call from Esta. She told me the news of her appointment had been picked up by Barrons' digital magazine. L&H agreed to give them an exclusive on Esta's appointment, an interview with the retiring director she's replacing in exchange for a twenty-four-hour publication delay. Her appointment was announced yesterday, and that sped up the entire timeline. Esta's taking over in July, not October, and she wants me and the two men she's hired to run legal and regulatory to start right after that. Suddenly, I had days—not months—to tell Nico."

"You thought you'd run out of time," Murphy said.

Tori nodded.

"Was the announcement of your new job in the article?" Lulu asked.

"No," Tori said. "I don't have the written offer and haven't accepted the job."

"Then what happened?" Murphy asked.

"Wednesday afternoon, I left Nico a voicemail. When he didn't call me back, I texted him—asking him to call me. When I still hadn't heard from him by Thursday morning, I called the Savoy, where he'd told me he'd be staying. The Savoy confirmed his reservation—starting *this coming* Sunday night, for late check-in. I called the Mayfair, where the workshop is usually held, thinking he probably stayed there for the first week, and then planned to move over to the Savoy on Sunday. He wasn't staying at the Mayfair, and the seminar wasn't even going on."

"No way!" Murphy said.

"Then what did you do?" Lulu asked. "How did you find out where he was?"

"I asked a friend, who coordinates travel for the bank's top executives, for help. I told him I had to get in touch with Nico. Said it was a serious family matter, which it was. Nico had made the reservations through the First Dominion's travel office—just as I knew he would. He's lazy, and he'd want all the perks an employee enjoys when traveling on bank business, like the use of the first-class lounge and corporate hotel rates. Jim pulled up the reservations—two business class tickets to Paris, a week at the Hotel Splendide Etoile. One of my favorite hotels in Paris! Eena flies home Sunday. Nico flies to London."

"Geez," Murphy said. "Now what?"

"I had just gotten the news about Eena and Nico when Esta called. I was upset and blurted out I was getting a divorce. I asked if she knew a good lawyer. She gave me the name of a former law school classmate of hers. Last night, I had a good cry on the phone with my mom. This morning, the lawyer and I had a teleconference. I like her. She gave me a list of things to do—including files to copy. But right now, we're going to heat dinner and finish the wine."

The friends stood in a group hug for a few minutes. Tori thanked her lucky stars for Lulu and Murphy. They'd been with her through triumphs and losses.

"And tomorrow, we're going to help Nico move out," Lulu said.

Their teamwork in the kitchen was the result of years of being roommates. They worked in comfortable silence, never getting in each other's way, the choreographed dance of best friends who had shared similar moments many times over the years. They were soon sitting in the dining room enjoying the feast from Café Scallinatella.

"Did you ever think he might be having an affair?" Lulu asked

"And where do you think they did it?" Murphy asked. "They couldn't have afforded a hotel. Eeew! You don't think they did it at her house, do you?"

Tori shook her head. "No, Murphy. Eena's godmother, Mehta, is financially comfortable and owns a brownstone on West Seventy-First

Street. She lives in West Palm Beach and doesn't come to New York that much anymore, and Eena looks after the house for her. She and Sal used to stay there overnight when they had plans in the City and didn't want to head back to Long Island. I often wondered if Sal takes Bobbi there. I'm sure he has a set of keys or knows where Eena keeps them, and unless Eena changed the security code, he knows that too."

"Wouldn't it have been a hoot if Eena and Nico were in their love nest, hear a key in the lock, and in walk Sal and Bobbi!" Lulu said.

"You're evil," Murphy said.

"But to your earlier point, Lulu, now that I know, I keep thinking of little things—lies he told so easily. I swatted gnats and swallowed camels, as my mother would say."

"Like?" Lulu prompted.

"Like one night Nico came home smelling of Bottega Veneta perfume—the perfume Eena always wears. I was already in bed. When he leaned down to kiss me, I said something like, 'Eew, you smell like Eena,'" The next morning, he said he'd been in meetings all day with a group from the Rome office, and one of the women must have been wearing the perfume. I didn't question it. Especially when it didn't happen a second time—he never came home again smelling of her perfume. Part of me believes he told her about that night, and she deliberately decided not to wear the perfume when they planned to meet."

Lulu rolled her eyes. "Seriously? You honestly believe that?"

"No, I can see that," Murphy said. "The target of Eena's revenge sex was Sal, not Tori. And who better understands the pain of smelling another woman's perfume on your husband's clothes than someone who's experienced that pain repeatedly?"

Tori looked at Murphy and smiled. "There were other things that should have made me suspicious, made me question what he told me. As I review the past few months, Nico weaponized his non-promotion. He became argumentative and defensive if I asked too many questions and dropped the subject. Or worse, I apologized. I censored everything

I said, reviewed everything I did—for fear of setting him off. I behaved like an abused wife—but the abuse was emotional."

"Yeah," Murphy said. "I've heard him do it. And I've watched you back down."

"The first time Nico said he'd gone out to dinner with colleagues from the other banks, I asked where they'd had dinner. As I think back, he was distracted when he told me they'd gone to Café Luxembourg. I even questioned him about it at the time. Asked why they hadn't gone to Fraunces Tavern, which is right across the street from where they were meeting. I didn't put two and two together then—Café Luxembourg is a block away from Mehta's townhouse. He got annoyed and accused me of not trusting him. He said several members of the group lived in that area and wanted to eat near their homes. Since he was new, he hadn't wanted to be disagreeable—so he went along. He'd even used it as the excuse for why he was later than he'd said he'd be."

"He covered all his bases, didn't he?" Lulu said.

"I trusted him. Even when things were tough after my promotion, I always thought of him as my husband, lover, best friend, and someday the father of our children. Never did I cast him in the role of a liar and cheat."

"So, what's the game plan? How can we help?" Murphy asked.

"At lunch, I picked up a couple of new flash drives, and the lawyer gave me a list of items from our computers, like tax returns for the past few years, brokerage and bank statements, to transfer to the drives. One for the lawyer and one for me. Then, we'll need to visit Kinko's to make copies of all our receipts and backup information for those tax returns. Nico prepared them, including the ones we just filed. Everything seemed okay, but I want to protect myself, just in case.

"We've got this," Murph said."

Chapter 11
Fraud!

Monday, April 24th

Why am I here? This question ran in an endless loop in Tori's mind.

Here was a small interior conference room on the thirty-third floor, just two floors below her own office. Here was a charmless room with four listless gray walls. Three, the color of dense morning fog, while the fourth, perhaps intended to be an accent wall, was painted a dark charcoal, the color of threatening storm clouds.

She looked around the room, more for something to do than for any other reason. There was no artwork on the walls, nothing of interest in the room. The conference table looked inexpensive, of poor quality—its surface scratched and unpolished. Surrounding it were four uncomfortable chairs. An overflowing trash can, ignored by the cleaning staff, stood sentry by the door.

Even the cleaning crew doesn't want to come in here.

She sat on her hands to keep them still and wished she had something to do. Pretending to be occupied, even doodling, or making irrelevant comments in the margins of a memo, might have made her feel better. Whoever had summoned her here wanted her concerned, wanted her nervous.

Why am I here?

The Internal Audit Department occupied the thirty-third floor. Tori and her staff, who oversaw the Bank's compliance with government regulations, often worked hand-in-hand with the internal auditors who ensured departments were following bank policies. In the five years she had worked for the bank, despite the number of times she had been to this floor, she had only been here in this conference room, sometimes referred to as the 'interrogation room,' once.

When a young woman, Connie, who had worked in Tori's department, had been suspected of stealing from two of her colleagues, Tori had received a call from an investigator of the Employee Investigation Unit, the EIU, a small group within the larger Audit Department tasked with investigating employee wrongdoing. She had been instructed to send Connie to this conference room.

Why am I here? Am I like Connie? Am I being accused of something?

This morning her boss had stood at the entrance to her office and knocked awkwardly on the metal doorframe. When she'd looked up, he'd walked into her office and closed the door. He stared first at a point over her left shoulder and then down at the floor, before telling her she had been summoned to Conference Room 33 A. That was the same message Tori had delivered to Connie nearly five months earlier. Just after Connie had left Tori's office that morning, two security guards appeared, packed up Connie's personal belongings, and left with them. An hour later, Tori was asked to come to this conference room to pick up the former employee's desk key and bank-issued cell phone.

"Why?" she'd asked him. "Do you know what this is about?"

He continued to stare at his black tassel loafers and shook his head before adding, "I'm sure it's nothing to worry about."

But one didn't get summoned to the interrogation room to meet with investigators for something that was nothing to worry about.

Absentmindedly, Tori touched the onyx and marquisate brooch of a peacock in profile pinned to her left shoulder. It had belonged to her maternal grandmother, who gave it to Tori when she'd gotten her first job after college. She thought of the pin as her talisman and wore it on those days when she needed a little extra luck. Now, unconsciously, her left hand reached up to her shoulder to stroke the bird's smooth onyx body, as if it were Aladdin's lamp, and a genie would appear in a puff of smoke to grant her three wishes—that she was back in her office safe and sound, that she was just about to start her new, dream job, and that her husband wasn't having an affair.

How long had she been in this room? Tori avoided looking at her watch, even clasping her right hand around the left sleeve of her suit jacket so she wasn't tempted to peek. She estimated she had been here a good twenty minutes. Just as the door to the conference room opened a small fraction, and Tori could hear a fragment of a conversation between a man and woman, did she dare look at her watch. She was startled to see only seven minutes had passed since she exited the elevator. Four hundred twenty seconds that seemed like four hundred twenty hours! When the conference room door finally opened wide, a woman and a man walked in.

"Good morning, Mrs. Morgano," the man began as he pulled out a chair opposite her, dropped a yellow legal pad on the table, and sat down. "I'm Douglas Carroll. This is my colleague, Dorothy Stager. Together, we oversee the fraud section of the EIU. We have questions about medical insurance claims filed on your behalf."

"I'm sorry, but I don't... I mean, I must have misunderstood you. Could you please say that again?" Tori asked.

"Over the past several months, many health care providers have filed claims with our insurance company on your behalf," Mr. Carroll began.

"Quite a few claims from doctors, physical therapists, and an acupuncturist have been filed," Ms. Stager said. "As well as many claims for prescription drug reimbursements."

She opened the green file folder she had been carrying when she entered the room and began to spread papers—some single sheets, others several sheets stapled together—in front of Tori.

"I'm sorry," Tori said, "but I'm very confused. I've never been to an acupuncturist or a physical therapist. I haven't seen my primary care physician since the beginning of this year, and I take only one prescription drug, which I have filled through our insurer's pharmacy plan. The only claim I've filed this year was an emergency room visit after a car accident on New Year's Day."

"Not according to these invoices," Mr. Carroll said as he pushed a stack of papers toward her.

Tori reached for a small stack of invoices. That was her name, Victoria Morgano, and her address, Fort Lee, New Jersey.

"Mrs. Morgano, we are investigating this matter as fraud. These insurance claims were filed under your old insurance number. If, as you claim, you did not receive these medical treatments, do you know how someone might have gotten access to that number and filed these claims in your name?" Mr. Carroll asked.

Tori had been so focused on verifying her name and address on each invoice that she'd almost tuned out Mr. Carroll's voice. Something had to be wrong on these papers—although, she had to admit, as she reviewed each one, everything appeared to be in order. The answer was dancing on the edge of her mind, but her mind couldn't grasp it. Then, after a several-second delay, she processed what Mr. Carroll said.

"What do you mean about the claims being filed under my old insurance number? You mean like identity theft? You think someone is using my old medical insurance card?"

"No, Mrs. Morgano, we don't believe this is related to identity theft," Ms. Stager said. "We believe this is a case of a person or persons trying to defraud the insurance company for money. We believe someone is claiming to have an injury, such as whiplash from an accident, and is colluding with at least two physicians, an acupuncturist, a chiropractor, a physical therapist, and a pharmacy to defraud the medical insurance company out of tens of thousands of dollars by filing false claims for medical treatments and prescriptions."

"Ms. Stager, Mr. Carroll, I...I don't, I don't understand," Tori stammered.

"As you know, your medical insurance number changed, effective this January, due to your promotion to senior management last year. Your insurance number is still your employee identification number, but your group number now ends in an 's' and not a 'j,'" Mr. Carroll said.

"Yes, that was all explained to me when I met with human resources. There's something I'm missing, something that's right...."

She picked up a printout of charges submitted directly to the insurance company from the physical therapist—someone she had supposedly seen three times a week for nearly four months. Although she'd never been to any physical therapist, there was something—something she wasn't remembering. What was it?

Next, she picked up the invoices from the acupuncturist. For some reason, she felt something about these invoices was familiar. She looked at the name of the practice—Summerall Acupuncture. *'Like 'All Summer in a Day,'* she thought. She felt the blood drain from her face. She was suddenly cold, and she felt as if she were shivering.

No, no, no! This cannot be happening!'

She grabbed the pile of invoices from the physical therapist. Something was odd about her name. The spacing! There was a double space between the "M" and the first "o" of Morgano. Victoria Morgano—could it be?

The invoices and claim forms that had been like a kaleidoscope, changing patterns and directions each time she'd picked up another piece of paper, were now forming a picture—a picture she didn't want to see but couldn't turn away from.

Hadn't Ms. Stager said several Claims for Patient Reimbursement had been filed? Someone had to have completed and signed those forms, attached invoices, or proof of payment before submitting them to the insurance company. Tori needed to see those forms and invoices.

She began to rifle through the papers on the table. "You said there were a number of claims for reimbursement filed? I don't see them here."

Ms. Stager removed a group of papers held together with a small binder clip from the green folder and placed them in front of Tori. There it was. A "Patient Claim Form for Reimbursement" was on top, and she recognized the printing. It was the same printing that had routinely added items to the weekly shopping list that hung on their refrigerator. It was the same printing on the to-do lists he made and left around the townhouse. Then, she examined the signature—the signature that appeared on birthday, anniversary, and Christmas cards over the years, "Love, Sal and Eena." The neat Catholic school printing belonged to her husband, but the signature? The person who had signed Tori's name was Valentina Marie Morgano!

Suddenly, the milk that had moistened her morning cereal began to curdle in her stomach.

"I need a glass of water," Tori said. "Please, may I have some water? Then, I'll tell you everything I know."

Mr. Carrol left the conference room and returned a few minutes later, carrying three bottles of water. He handed one bottle to Ms. Stager and another to Tori. She tried and failed to turn the bottle cap. The cap was small, the bottle was wet with condensation, and she was nervous. Seeing her struggle, Mr. Carroll offered her his now-open bottle in exchange for hers. She took a long swallow. The cold water was soothing as it slid down her throat.

"I don't know where or even how to begin," she said as she reached for the stack of Patient Claim for Reimbursement Forms. "Here, I guess."

Tori pointed to the printing, "This is my husband's writing. I have samples of his printing at our home in New Jersey, but I'm certain you could find examples of his manuscript and cursive writing on his desk. He works here, on the fifth floor. Oh, but he's not here now—he's on a business trip this week. In the London office."

She paused and took another swallow of water. *Calm down*, she silently reminded herself. She took a deep breath through her nose and exhaled through her mouth.

"The signature is my sister-in-law's handwriting, Mrs.—Doctor," she corrected, "Valentina Marie Morgano. She's married to my husband's older brother, Dr. Salvatore Morgano." Tori turned to the invoice attached to the claim form. "This pharmacy, Green River Pharmacy in Manhasset," she pointed to the logo printed at the top of the invoice, "is owned by a couple, a married couple. The Hoppers. Eena, Dr. Valentina Morgano, works there part-time. She shares a job with the wife. That's why Eena was hired—to job share with her when she got pregnant two years ago."

Mr. Carroll ripped off the top sheet of the legal pad where he had scribbled some notes and then slid the pad and pen over to Tori. "Please print and sign your name, Mrs. Morgano." Tori did as he'd instructed and slid them back across the table. Mr. Carroll ripped off the page where she'd printed and signed her name and handed it to Ms. Stager, who left the conference room with the yellow paper and the packet of stapled pharmacy invoices.

"Please go on, Mrs. Morgano," Mr. Carroll said.

"In January, my husband and I had dinner with Eena—that's her nickname—at Benson's Steakhouse. Can I just refer to her that way and not Dr. Morgano?"

Mr. Carroll nodded.

Tori continued. "Anyway, it was right after our New Year's Day accident. During dinner, Eena recommended I try several of her doctors. She even texted me their contact information. Their surnames were something like Freehold or Friedman."

"Freelander?" Mr. Carroll suggested.

"Okay," Tori said, "that could be it. The other was," she frowned. "When Eena texted me the contact information that night, I associated the practice's name, Summerall Associates, with the title of a short story I've loved since I was a girl, Ray Bradbury's *All Summer in a Day*. When I saw the name on the invoices just now, I immediately thought of that short story. Just like I'd done that night. I probably still have the texts on my phone, which is in my office. Upstairs."

"Anyway," she continued when her interrogator didn't offer to let her retrieve her cell, "at dinner, Eena told Nico and me that she knew people —doctors, therapists, acupuncturists—who deliberately over-charged insurance companies, like billing for weekly treatments when patients were only receiving treatments every other week. She said the doctors gave the patients a cut of the reimbursements. I think the names she texted me were two of those doctors."

Mr. Carroll made more notes. "Go on," he said.

"That's it. I said the conversation made me uncomfortable, and we stopped."

Tori took the last swallow of water from the bottle, stood, and walked to the trash can. "Should I throw this in here," she asked, "or do you recycle?" Just getting up, walking around a little, and being close to the exit door felt good.

"Just leave it on the table," Mr. Carroll said. "We'll take care of it when we're finished."

Tori gave a curt nod before returning to her chair.

"I don't think my husband knows senior management is enrolled in premium medical insurance. I didn't until HR told me when I got pro-moted." She paused. "My husband wanted, was counting on the promo-tion I got, so I don't talk about the additional benefits and perks I have as a result of my promotion." She stared straight ahead and took a deep breath. "So, I don't think he knows about the enhanced medical insur-ance coverage I now receive or the change in the group number.

"My husband has—had," she corrected, "my second health care card, and I have his." She took another deep breath. "Every year, when the new cards arrive, I'm the one who replaces the old insurance cards in each of our wallets with the new ones. This year," she paused again and lowered her eyes, "I only changed out *my* card in *my* wallet. He should still have my old card, the one with the 'j' and not the 's.'"

"I see," Mr. Carroll said. "Is there anything else you think we should know?"

Before she could respond, Ms. Stager came back into the room and sat down. She was holding another green folder.

"Mrs. Morgano," Ms. Stager said, "tell me about the bank accounts you and your husband have and if you remember, the branch or branches where you opened them."

"Well, we have a joint checking account and a money market that were opened in the branch downstairs, and we each have personal checking and savings accounts and IRAs at that branch, too. Our individual and joint brokerage accounts were opened through the investment bank and are monitored downtown."

"No other accounts?" Ms. Stager asked.

"No," Tori said. "Well, I have a Christmas Club account."

"Nothing at another branch?" Ms. Stager asked.

"No," Tori said, "of that, I'm certain." She paused. "At least I'm certain about myself."

"Good," Ms. Stager said. She opened the file folder and turned several sheets of paper—copies of signature cards and W-9 Forms—in Tori's direction. "Can you confirm these are your signatures and social security number?"

"Yes," Tori said. "Each signature is mine, and that's my social security number."

"What about these?" Ms. Stager pushed two more papers—a Form W-9 and a signature card—across the table.

Tori gasped. Her heart thundered in her chest. The name and social security number on the W-9 Form were Tori's, but the signature was Eena's! That bitch!

"What are these?" she whispered.

"Copies of the signature card and Form W-9 for an account opened in the Manhasset branch closest to the Green River Pharmacy," Ms. Stager answered. "The account where the reimbursement checks for the drugs were deposited."

"Can you identify the people in these photos?" Ms. Stager asked.

Tori stared at security camera photos from a cash machine until the tears blurred her vision. She pointed at the first one. "This is Valentina Morgano," she confirmed, "and this," she pointed to the second picture, "is my husband, Nicolino Morgano."

There was a knock, and then the conference room door opened. A young man entered the room, handed Ms. Stager a stack of papers, and left. She pressed her lips in a taut line as she looked through them.

"Another investigator has contacted Dr. Delaney Hopper. The doctor emailed her work schedule and Dr. Morgano's since the beginning of the year. The schedules confirm Dr. Morgano was working every day an invoice from the pharmacy was created. Dr. Hopper and her husband have also confirmed they and Dr. Morgano were the only people who had access to and could add and delete information on the pharmacy's computer. An insurance company representative and a detective from the Manhasset Police Department are on their way to the pharmacy now to take their statements."

Tori felt lightheaded. "Police? Is Eena going to be arrested?" she asked, her voice barely above a whisper. "Could she go to jail?"

"That will be up to the Manhasset DA," Ms. Stager said. "Dr. Morgano's employment will be terminated when she comes to work Wednesday, and her pharmacology license will most likely be revoked. Our insurance company may pursue civil action if Dr. Morgano and your husband don't make restitution. The pharmacy's insurance company has been notified, so I imagine an investigation into her medical claims for the last few years is underway or soon will be. She may be able to trade her knowledge of the doctors and their practices for probation."

"And my husband?" Tori asked.

Mr. Carroll pulled his cell phone from the inside pocket of his jacket and typed in his passcode. Then he dialed a number and put the cell phone on speaker.

"Wayne Wright," came the voice on the other end of the phone.

Tori clasped her hand over her mouth to smother her gasp. Mr. Carroll was calling Nico's boss!

"Wayne, it's Doug Carroll, and I have Dorothy and Victoria Morgano here with me. You're on speaker. About that matter we discussed earlier—we need you to call Mr. Morgano back to New York. He has reservations on the first flight out of Heathrow to Liberty tomorrow. Details should be in an email to you. When you talk to Mr. Morgano, you can NOT say anything," Mr. Carroll looked at Tori, "and that goes for you, too, Mrs. Morgano—that would give him a heads up as to what's going to happen when he comes to the office on Wednesday."

"Got it," Wayne said. "I'm planning on telling him we have a serious legal and accounting issue that's time sensitive and could cause significant embarrassment if the details became public. Due to the sensitive, confidential nature of the situation, I won't be able to discuss the problem with him over the phone."

"That's good," Mr. Carroll said. "Tell him you need him to get to the office early Wednesday morning and bring him up here as soon as he arrives. I've blocked conference room B for the entire day. We'll follow the interrogation with a lie detector test before he's escorted out of the building."

"Is a security team set to box his personal items and take them downstairs to the guard's station?" Wayne asked. "How will they know when we've left to come upstairs?"

"Don't worry, Wayne," Mr. Carroll said, "Security has that covered. Do you have any other questions?"

Wayne said, "No," and then Mr. Carroll looked at Tori, who shook her head. "Okay," Mr. Carroll said, "See you Wednesday morning, Wayne. Thanks, and good luck."

After he had disconnected the call, Mr. Carroll said, "I know this is a bit awkward, and I'm sorry. We don't want to tip off Dr. Morgano or your husband before Wednesday morning."

"Then what will happen? Will Nico be arrested? Does he need a lawyer?"

"His employment will be terminated effective Wednesday morning, but we don't have the authority to arrest him. The bank, the pharmacy, and the insurance company may file civil suits against him. At that point, he would be well advised to seek legal counsel."

"May I ask? How much money are we talking about?" Tori asked.

"Over $250,000."

Chapter 12
The Homecoming

Tuesday, April 25th

Just after two o'clock, Tori heard Nico's town car from the airport pull into their driveway. She had been sitting in the family room listening to Barbra Streisand's *Til I Loved You* album. She turned it off before she heard his key turn in the lock and his off-key whistle of a song she didn't recognize. She stood in the dining room, so she was the first thing he saw when the front door opened.

Yesterday morning, when she finished telling Mr. Carroll everything she knew about the medical insurance fraud her husband and his lover were perpetrating, the scam for which they'd set her up, Tori had been sworn to secrecy. Mr. Carroll was apologetic when he'd told her she couldn't tip Nico off, give him a heads up. But Mr. Carroll hadn't known about Nico's affair. She didn't need an excuse to avoid having sex with her husband that night—she was planning on kicking him out.

When Nico called to let her know he was coming home, that something big was going down in his division, something that would finally lead to the promotion he desperately wanted, she judged her feigned excitement and joy at his news as so realistic, she awarded herself a second glass of Pinot Grigio. Tori spent the morning preparing for Nico's return by preparing to throw him out, rehearsing what she would say, imagining his denials, and checking the time every few minutes—on the oven and microwave clocks, her watch, her cell phone, the cable box. Now time was up. He was here.

"Hey, babe, what are you doing home from work? You didn't mention possibly being home when I called you yesterday. It's nice not walking into an empty house."

He dropped his suitcase and messenger bag by the stairs, flashed her what she always called his "panty-dropping" smile, and strode toward her. She could tell by his confident air he had no clue.

"I wanted to be here when you arrived. I wanted to talk with you about your trip. I want to hear all about how Eena liked the Hotel Splendide Etoile. Did your room overlook Sacre Coeur and Montmartre or the Etoile? Both views are spectacular, but I prefer the view of the Arc de Triomphe. At night, when it's lit, it personifies romantic Paris. Did you take her to that little café I love so much across from Le Comedie Francaise? The one with the profiteroles to die for?"

His smile fell from his face as he processed her words.

"Yes," she continued. "I know. I have proof—screenshots of boarding passes and a copy of the hotel confirmation. So, I know what you did. I know where you did it and with whom. What I don't know is why? What I don't understand is how you could do this—to me, to your brother, to your family, to us?"

He sagged into the navy-blue wing chair and put his face in his hands.

"Who else knows?"

"That's the first thing you want to say to me?" She sighed. "If you're asking if I've told your brother that you've been having an affair with his wife. If you're concerned, he's on the George Washington Bridge right now on his way here to beat the crap out of you? The answer is 'No.' Do you have any other questions I can answer before you pack your bags and get the hell out of my house?"

"How long have you known?"

"Again, can't believe that's your second question, but I haven't known long. All I'd ever known from my parents and friends was love, and with that love, respect, trust, and honesty. So, when your deceit, your lies began, that history of love and trust made it harder for me to recognize your dishonesty for what it was."

"It's not what you think, Tori."

"What I think is you and Eena got laid, and Sal and I got screwed."

"I'm sorry, but I didn't know how to handle everything—you got the promotion I wanted, the one I worked hard for. When you got that huge year-end bonus and moved from a cubicle to an office, I thought, I really thought, your boss was softening the blow, throwing you a bone—you weren't getting promoted. Your job wasn't senior management like mine was. Except, your job was, and mine wasn't. Wayne let me believe my job was, well, that I would be promoted to managing director. And then I wasn't. And then everything I thought was true was not. It was thrown in my face every day, every time we entered that building."

"By whom, Nico? Not by me. My success is not your failure. I get you're disappointed. I'm disappointed for you. But you've dismissed every offer of help, derided every suggestion I've made. Aren't you tired of playing the victim? Everybody else is sick to death of it. You don't want to change your situation—you just want to bitch about it.

"Back to the matter at hand—you moving out. Your suits are in the large garment bag, and your large suitcase is lying on the bed, ready to receive your shoes and the contents of your drawers. I've put the business card of my divorce lawyer on the nightstand. Please hire an attorney as soon as possible."

"Wait! You want me to leave now? I just got here, just got off a plane from London. Eena means nothing to me. You know that. It was just…."

"Just what? Revenge sex? My trust in you was just an acceptable casualty? Our marriage was just collateral damage?"

"I told you yesterday. Something big is going on in the division. Wayne insisted I had to come back to help with the 'crisis,' he called it. Before he even called me, his PA had made the reservations on the first flight back from Heathrow. I mean, he didn't tell me much, or anything really, but he called it a 'top priority.' This could mean great things for me, for us. If this, whatever it is, is so damned critical I had to fly back after only one day, if I'm the only one who can fix it, don't you see? He can't say I don't deserve to be promoted. He can't say my job isn't senior enough. I'll fix whatever it is, no matter what it takes, and I'll get that promotion, and everything will be all right again."

"Yes, the answer to your question is yes, I want you to leave now."

"I know this is bad. I was stupid. I shouldn't have started up with Eena. I don't know what I was thinking. I swear, the whole flight back all I could think of was coming home to you, how to end it with her. I'll end it tomorrow, right now, but don't give up on me, on us—don't kick me out. We could try counseling. You wanted to do that, remember? I'll make the appointment with that psychologist you found. What's her name?"

"Jessie, Dr. Jessica Avery. I remember telling you about her, about wanting to go. I remember you rolling your eyes. I remember making an appointment, and I remember you making an excuse as to why you couldn't go."

"But things are different. I'll make them different; we'll—I'll be different. You'll see. Give me another chance, Tori. Please."

"I've told my lawyer we'll be filing a no-fault, no spousal support divorce unless you'd prefer adultery with Eena as co-respondent. No? Then no fault it is."

Tori looked down at her penny loafers and noticed how dull the pennies were. Suddenly, all she wanted were new shiny copper pennies in her Weejuns, right then, right now. She picked up her purse and rummaged for her wallet. Hadn't she received some new pennies when she'd paid for groceries yesterday?

"Wait. What are you doing? Are you leaving?" Nico asked.

"No. I'm not. You are."

She extracted two sparkly pennies from her coin purse, dropped her purse on the floor, and tucked the coins in the pocket of her jeans before removing her shoes. She replaced first one dull penny and then the other with their newly minted replacements.

"Tori, what *are* you doing?"

"Out with the old, in with the new. That, dear husband, includes you."

"But where will I go?"

"To quote Rhett Butler, 'Frankly, my dear, I don't give a damn.' Let's explore some options, shall we? How about Dylan's couch?"

"He may be my best friend, but he's married to one of your best friends. I'd be afraid to close my eyes. Murphy might murder me in my sleep."

"Actually, I think it was Lulu who suggested castrating you and shipping you off to the Boys' Choir in Vienna, but I take your point. How about your brother's house? Now THAT would be convenient. When Sal is called out on an emergency in the middle of the night, your booty call would only be feet away."

"I've never heard you be so bitchy, Tori. What's brought this on?"

"Seriously? I have endured years of subtle and not-so-subtle abuse and slights from your mother and your mistress and months of put-downs, digs, and criticisms from you. In short, I have been taught by masters."

Chapter 13
The Confrontation

Friday, April 28th

When, at last, she was alone in the elevator, Tori allowed herself the luxury of a full, open-mouth yawn. She had had little sleep the night before. She had had little sleep since she'd learned her husband was an adulterer, a thief, and a fraud. Each night's sleep was interrupted by a nightmare that left her gasping for air, thrashing to free her arms and legs held hostage by the bedsheet and blanket, and her heart pounding in her chest.

In the building's lobby, Tori headed for the wall of cash machines and joined the short queue of customers. She looked up when she heard a familiar voice call, "Hey Tori," and turned to see Dylan leaning against the beige travertine tiled wall. He slid his phone into his suit jacket pocket and came to meet her halfway.

"What brings you to mid-town in the middle of a Friday afternoon, counselor?" she asked and leaned in to give and receive a kiss on the cheek.

"You okay, Tori?" he asked. "You look tired."

"I'm okay. Just not sleeping well these days."

He took her right hand in his larger one and held it. A deep 'v' formed just above the bridge of his nose. "You look like you've lost a little weight, too. Are you eating, Honey? "

Tori glanced at the floor and then looked up. She focused on an advertisement for IRAs on the wall behind him, steeling herself before answering.

"I'm miserable. Every morning I'm shocked the sun has risen, surprised the birds are chirping. I see people on the streets going about their business as if everything is normal and want to shout at them, 'Don't you know the world has blown up?'"

He nodded. "I'm sorry. We're still on for our usual pizza tonight, right? Your house, seven-thirty?"

She nodded and gave him a weak smile. "I couldn't get through this without Murphy and Lulu. You and Tom, too, of course."

Dylan looked over her right shoulder toward the revolving doors at the building's East Fifty-Third Street entrance.

"Uh, Tori, I'm meeting Nico. He should be here any minute. We have a meeting upstairs."

"What? Why?" she asked. "Does he need a lawyer? Mr. Carroll and Ms. Stager told me it was unlikely the bank would press charges. I thought he would just lose his job and have to repay the money."

"What are you talking about? Nico and I have a meeting with a couple of people from human resources about his severance. I think one of them may be a Ms. Stager."

"Ms. Stager's not from HR, Dylan. She's from the Audit Department, specifically the unit that investigates employee fraud. She and Douglas Carroll questioned me on Monday when they thought I was the one filing the fraudulent claims."

"I'm not following. What fraudulent claims?"

"The ones Eena and Nico have been filing since the beginning of the year. Oh. My. God. I can tell by your expression, he told you something else!"

"Eena? What's she got to do with this?"

"Eena is not just Nico's lover," Tori said.

"Lover? No, you're wrong! You have to be. Murph told me Nico had an affair, but not with Eena. She's not his lover. She's married to his brother," Dylan said.

Tori nodded her head several times. "Yes, yes she is, Dylan. She's his lover and his co-conspirator. Actually, this scheme was all her idea. That night we were supposed to go to dinner and the theatre with her and Sal, and only she showed up at the restaurant? At dinner, she suggested we make some money from our New Year's Day accident by filing false medical insurance claims. She even said she knew doctors and therapists who would help us."

"This is nuts, Tori," he said, shaking his head. "Lovers? Co-conspirators? Tori, do you hear how crazy you sound?"

"I need to go *now*. I'll get cash on my way home," she said, more to herself than Dylan. "I don't want to run into him today or any day."

She tugged her hand loose from Dylan's. "Two pieces of advice: first, make him tell you the whole story before you go upstairs," she said. "He owes you the truth, Dylan. He's asked you to sit beside him, be his attorney. And second—be careful."

"Wait!"

"I can't, Dylan!"

"No. Sorry." Dylan whispered, "Too late. He's here."

Nico strode toward them. His expression was menacing.

"You bitch!" he hissed through clenched teeth. "You told my mother I was home from London. I was no longer working at the bank. You told her to check with Eena. That she might know where I was? You are some piece of work, some vindictive piece of work. You know that?"

Tori thought back to Wednesday afternoon. She'd been ready to leave for a meeting when the phone on her desk rang. She was tempted to ignore the call, but what if it had to do with the meeting? So she'd reached across her desk and picked up the receiver, unable to see the caller ID. Jenny had been on the other end of the phone.

Now Tori said, "You could have returned your mother's calls, and then she wouldn't have called me on Wednesday. I only told her the truth—that you were already home from London, and you'd moved out of the townhouse. When she asked me to transfer her to your old work number, I thought the news you no longer worked here might be less embarrassing coming from me than an analyst assigned the job of answering your old number and redirecting calls. You could have told your mother the truth when you returned from London. You could have not gone along with Eena's ridiculous scheme last January. And you could have kept your pecker in your pants."

"I. Am. Furious, Tori. You *will* pay for this. For now, though, I think an apology is in order," Nico said.

She waited expectantly. "Oh," she said when she realized he expected her to apologize to him. "Oh," she said again. "All right."

She raised her head and looked him directly in the eyes.

"Nico," she said, "I'm sorry you're not the man of honor I thought you were. You could have, you should have told Eena to go to hell, and I'm very sorry you didn't. I'm sorry your moral and ethical compass wasn't strong enough to withstand a career disappointment. I'm sorry that you were and continue to be frustrated your ambition did not meet your abilities. And finally, I am so very, very sorry you continue to believe there is an employment situation on this planet where I wouldn't, where I couldn't be your equal in both rank and pay."

She turned to Dylan and said, "Make him tell you the entire truth before the meeting. And it's your turn to order the pizza. I vote for extra cheese, pepperoni, onions, and mushrooms."

"My family despises you, Tori. Everyone thinks you're a bitch."

"What you and your family think of me is no longer any of my business," she said before turning and walking into the building.

Chapter 14
And the Hits Just Keep on Comin'

That Evening

As soon as they returned to the townhouse after their walk, Tori un-fastened Baron's leash and hung it on the hook in the kitchen. The dog walked, with single-minded focus, to the dining room entryway and stared at the front door. His stance was rigid with muscles so taut they appeared to tremble. His favorite after-walk bacon, egg, and cheese dog treat sat forgotten on the kitchen counter.

"What?" she asked as she looked back at the French doors they had just entered to reassure herself the deadbolt lock was engaged and the alarm reset. She had been unsettled since her confrontation with Nico that afternoon.

Baron's ears were pitched forward, and his right ear twitched as if swatting away an unseen fly— just before she saw the glare of head-lights and heard a car pull into the driveway.

"Murphy and Dylan won't be here for at least another hour," she said aloud.

She pulled her phone from the back pocket of her jeans and checked the driveway camera. Sal's black Mercedes SUV was just pulling in.

"And the hits just keep on comin'! Do you think we could pretend we're not home?" she asked the dog, who cocked his head to one side. "Yeah, it was just a suggestion."

She texted Murphy. "911. Sal here. Come now."

Then, she took a deep breath and walked to the foyer. Only after she'd confirmed Sal was alone did she open the front door and lock the storm door.

"What are you doing here, Sal?" she called out in a voice loud enough to be heard through the glass barrier as he walked toward the front porch.

Sal raised his hand in a half-hearted wave and stood at the bottom of the steps.

"Hi, Tori. I'm glad you're home. I took a chance. I was afraid to call, afraid you'd send me to voicemail. In the past forty-eight hours, I've left more voicemails—for my wife, her friends, my brother—than I have my entire life."

"So, you thought ambushing me at home was a better idea? You didn't answer my question. Why are you here, Sal?"

"May I come in and talk? I just want to talk. I just want, need some answers. There's so much I don't know, and I think, maybe…."

"What do you want to know, Sal? What questions do you think I can help you answer? What information do you want from me—that you and your family would believe?" she asked.

"Tori, what's wrong? Are you mad at me? Did I do or say something to hurt you?"

Tori stared at him as she processed his words. Of course, he didn't know all she knew, all that her tight circle of friends and family knew. She made her decision—she turned the lock on the storm door, twisted the handle, and held the door open.

"Of course, come in. I'm sorry—you're right. My problems are with your brother, not you."

In the light of the entranceway, she studied his face—he looked weary, worried and the bluish black circles under his eyes signaled more than one night's lost sleep. He wore black pants and a white dress shirt rumpled around the collar. Since he wasn't wearing a tie, she imagined him tugging at the knot to loosen it, yanking it from his neck and abandoning it, maybe on the seat of his car.

He told her he'd come because he needed her help. "In forty-eight hours, my whole world has spun out of control," he said, "No! Less than forty-eight hours! Every place I turn for answers, I have more questions."

She nodded her head and assured him she understood. "Fasten your seat belt—you're in for a long and difficult evening," she said. "Murphy and Dylan will be here very soon with pizza, and I need to make a salad and feed Baron. You're welcome to stay, join us for dinner. You can open a bottle of Pinot Grigio for Murphy and me. Dylan'll have a Corona and fix yourself whatever you want. Wedges of lime for the beer are in a baggy in the fruit drawer on the right."

Just as she headed for the kitchen, the timer she had set for the brownies she'd put in the oven before she and Baron had taken their walk along the Hudson River went off. She took the pan out of the oven when Sal walked through the family room to the kitchen.

"Smells good," he said as he opened the refrigerator. He found the wine and the two bottles of Corona, but the location of the limes eluded him.

"There," Tori said as she came up behind him and pointed to the drawer in front of him. Then, she put Baron's bowl on the floor.

"What can I do?" he asked after he'd opened the bottle of wine.

"Sit," she said and indicated, with a tilt of her head, one of the counter stools opposite where she was cutting onions and peppers for the salad. She took a sip of wine before she asked, "What's going on, Sal? Tell me what's happening."

He told her his mother had called him, terribly upset, after her conversation with Tori Wednesday afternoon. He had reassured her he hadn't heard from Nico since his brother had left for London.

"I was sorry and surprised to hear Nico moved out," he said.

Tori nodded her head. "Yeah, I'm sorry, too," she said, looking away so he didn't see the tears welling in her eyes.

"This is awkward. I'm not sure how to ask this," Sal said, "but is this it? Are you going to try counseling? I always thought of you two as a great team. I mean, if you guys can't make it…."

"No, Sal," she said. "We won't be reconciling."

Oh. My. God. Could this be any more difficult? He doesn't know.

She shook her head and focused on what Sal was saying.

"Wait! Did you just say Eena's missing?" she asked.

"Yeah. She left, and I don't know where she is, and I'm not sure when she left."

Sal explained he'd had two high-risk pregnancies ready to deliver, and the Wednesday afternoon and evening hours had soon blurred together. It had been early Thursday evening when he'd finally gotten home.

"I was exhausted," he said. "Eena wasn't home. Our bedroom was a mess—clothes still on hangers, lingerie, shoes, and purses strewn on the floor, as if they'd been removed from the closet or drawers and then just dropped."

Most disturbing, the leather accordion folder where they kept important documents such as passports and titles to their cars lay on the floor, the contents scattered.

"Tori, it was crazy! Eena, her passport, the suitcase, and overnight bag she'd used for her trip to the spa, and her SUV and its title were gone," he said. "I tried calling her, but my call went to voicemail. I tried tracking her phone, only to find it was in the house, abandoned on the kitchen table. Mom's frantic—about Eena and Nico. Do you know how to get in touch with my brother? Honestly, I'm more angry than worried about either or both of them."

"Nico's fine. I saw him about three hours ago. He's mean, nasty, but healthy. Not lying in a ditch or physically hurt or sick," Tori said as she walked to the refrigerator to gather bleu cheese, cranberries, and a Macoun apple for the salad.

"You saw him? Where? What did he say? Where's he staying?" Sal asked.

"Yes, I saw him at the bank. He and Dylan had a meeting there. I accidentally ran into them in the lobby. He said I was a vindictive bitch, and everyone in your family hates me." The knife punctuated her words with a satisfying "thunk" as the blade sliced through the apple and hit the wooden cutting board.

"I don't know where he's staying but based on things he's let slip over the past few months, I'd wager he and Eena are holed up in her godmother's townhouse," she said.

"Geez! I never even thought of Aunt Mehta's! Yeah, that makes sense Eena'd go there. But why would Nico be there?"

"To answer your question, I need to tell you a story. One that has several beginnings," Tori said. "Last December, when I got the promotion Nico wanted so desperately, bragged he would be getting. Last January,…"

"Wait! You got promoted?" Sal asked. "Nico never said anything. That's great! Congratulations! So, you're both managing directors now."

"Thanks, and no. Only I was promoted. But I'll get to that," she said. "The second beginning was last January when Eena, Nico, and I met for dinner—the night we met you at the theatre. But for me, it all began a little more than a week ago." She set the knife down on the counter, "when I found out my husband and your wife were having an affair."

"What? No, no, you're wrong. You must be wrong. Nico wouldn't…," Sal said and shook his head. "You're wrong, Tori. Eena may be having an affair, but with Nico? No, no. That's not right."

She reached across the counter to place her hand on his forearm. "I'm sorry, Sal, but it's true."

She had proof, she said—screenshots of their boarding passes from Newark to Paris—when Nico was supposed to fly to London for a workshop and Eena was supposed to be at a spa in the Poconos. She had copies of their hotel confirmation—at the Hotel Splendide Etoile for seven nights with one king-size bed.

Sal sucked in air through his clenched teeth and exhaled—emitting a sound between a groan and a growl deep in his throat. He slammed the beer bottle down on the granite countertop. The sound exploded in the kitchen. They both starred as the first crack appeared, propagating another crack and another, until the bottle shattered into sharp, irregular pieces. A patina of beer floated on the countertop, and streams of lager, the color of pale straw, poured over the sides and splashed onto the hardwood floor. Liquid dripped off the counter and down the right leg of Sal's creased black pants. He didn't seem to notice.

Tori was the first to recover. Opening the drawer to her left, she pulled out a stack of dish towels.

"Here," she said as she held out a towel. "Here, Sal, take this. Blot the beer off your pants."

He shook his head as if he'd been daydreaming. As if the world had intruded and called him back. He took the towel and stared at it as if he'd never seen one before.

"Your pant leg," Tori prompted as she gathered shards of glass from the countertop, placing them carefully on an old dish towel so as not to cut herself before throwing the glass and the towel away. She grabbed a roll of paper towels and began to drop them on the floor to absorb the liquid pooling. Then she returned her attention to the counter, dropping more dish towels on the surface to soak up the remaining puddles of amber liquid.

"You okay?" she asked.

Sal nodded, then shook his head.

"Okay. I know this is earth-shattering, so take a minute. But this is only the beginning," Tori said as she handed him another bottle of beer and a wedge of lime. "Let me know when I can continue."

She gathered the soaked dish towels in her hand, commanded Baron to stay on his bed, and walked to the laundry room. On the way back to the kitchen, she stopped to pick up the broom and dustpan from the utility closet. Carefully, she swept any remaining slivers of glass from the kitchen and family room floors. When she finished, she asked Sal if she should continue the story.

He nodded, then listened in stunned silence as she relayed the story of how she'd discovered, with the help of a colleague, their spouses' overseas assignation.

As she was putting the finishing touches on both the salad and the story of Paris, the doorbell rang.

"That'll be the Malones," she said. "Are you okay answering the door? I'll carry the salad and utensils to the table, and we'll continue the story in the dining room."

But he didn't move. "Sal, you okay to answer the door?" she asked.

"I guess so," he said.

He disappeared into the front of the townhouse, and then Tori heard Murphy's voice.

"You're inside? Did she invite you inside? Tori, did you tell him he could come in?"

"Yes, Murph. I invited him in and invited him for dinner. I'm filling him in—I forget not everyone knows what we know."

"Yeah," Dylan said, "like me, Nico's best friend, who didn't get the deets from my wife."

"I explained all that this afternoon. I told you the essential parts—Tori kicked Nico out because he was having an affair, and he'd been fired," Murphy said.

Turning to Sal, Dylan asked, "How are you holding up?"

Sal took the last swallow of beer. "If I smoked, I imagine I'd be out on the deck lighting up about now. But I think I'll follow you to the kitchen for another one of these," he said as he raised the empty bottle.

"Do you want something stronger?" Dylan asked as they walked through the family room.

"Yes, but no. I need to hear the rest of this story, and I have to drive home," Sal said.

The two men disappeared into the kitchen. Tori could hear their voices but couldn't make out what they were saying. They returned to the dining room a few minutes later, each holding a bottle of beer with a lime wedged in the opening.

Dylan caught Tori's eye and nodded slightly before he said, "Let's eat!"

Tori filled the salad bowls, and Murphy opened the pizza box, allowing the aromas of the warm dough, onion and garlic, oregano, basil, and crushed red pepper flakes to fill the room.

"Smells great, and I'm starved," Dylan said as he lifted a slice from the box and placed it on Murphy's plate. "How about if I serve everyone." He turned to Tori and asked, "Where are we in the story?"

"We're up to the insurance fraud."

Sal rubbed his hands up and down across his face several times and cleared his throat before speaking. "I called the owners of the pharmacy where Eena works. Worked," he corrected. "Thursday morning. At first, all Delaney Hopper, the owner who shares—shared—a job with Eena, would tell me was that my wife didn't work there anymore. Only after I told her Eena was missing did she tell me they'd fired her Wednesday morning. Before I left the office tonight, I had a message from a Detective Kaminski of the Manhasset PD. Are all these things related?"

"Yes," Tori said. She began a detailed account of her Monday morning meeting with the Audit Department's fraud investigators and wove in details from the January pre-theatre dinner conversation.

When she was finished, Sal shut his eyes, put his elbows on the table, and massaged his temples with his index and middle fingers. Eena had insisted on having her own health insurance when she'd accepted the position at Green River Pharmacy, he told them. "I bet she's been doing this since she started working there. But why would Nico go along with her scheme?"

"He was intrigued, Sal. Eena had disclosed a titillating secret," Tori said. "For days after that evening, we'd be on the bus or walking to the subway, and he'd blurt out something like, 'you don't think Eena's doing that, do you?' I think Nico decided to be a part of her scheme after his boss told him he had hit the salary ceiling for his job. He was furious—at the bank, Wayne, me. That devastating news came just days before the first fraudulent invoices were filed."

"This is so unbelievable," Murphy said, "This isn't the first time I've heard the story, and I still can't wrap my brain around it."

"I know," Tori said, "Everybody grab something and head for the kitchen. We can refill our drinks and sit in the other room. We'll be more comfortable."

"Sal, why don't you go sit in the family room? The four of us will only get in each other's way in there," Murphy said.

"Good idea," Tori said, "Sal, do you want a glass of milk, coffee, another beer?"

"Decaf?" he asked.

She shook her head. "No, regular."

"Good," he said, "That's what I'll have with...."

"One sugar and a splash of cream," Tori finished and smiled. "I remember."

She removed cups and plates from the cupboard and poured the coffee she had set to brew while they ate. Dylan loaded the dinner dishes and utensils in the dishwasher while Murphy returned the salad dressings to the refrigerator and took out the creamer. The trio worked in silence, each sneaking glances into the adjacent room to see Sal deep in thought. When they were settled on the sofas in the family room, dessert and coffee served, Dylan said, "I think this is where I pick up the story."

He turned to Tori. "I'm so grateful I ran into you before the meeting this afternoon, and I have to say, 'Brava.' You handled the situation masterfully and gave me enough valuable information so I wasn't blindsided."

Turning to Sal, he said, "Nico and I had a meeting at the bank today. I arrived first and ran into Tori in the lobby. She assumed Nico had been honest with me. That I knew he had had an affair with Eena. I didn't—or at least not all of it. I knew he'd had an affair, but he told me the woman was a colleague. Tori assumed I knew about the fraud, but he'd also lied to me about that. She gave me just enough information for me to proceed with caution."

Tuesday afternoon, when he learned Nico had returned from London and he and Tori had separated, Dylan called his friend but had been sent to voicemail. Wednesday afternoon, he learned Nico had been fired, and he left a second voicemail and sent a text.

"I was working late on a brief for an important case," Dylan said, "and honestly, I didn't think about Nico until he called me Thursday afternoon. When he needed my help."

"At least he called you back," Sal said, "that's more than Mom and I can say."

Nico had been quite distraught on the phone. "That he was upset didn't surprise me," Dylan said. "what he was upset about did." His friend hadn't been distressed about either his separation from Tori or his termination, Dylan clarified. He was unhappy about his severance package!

"He didn't mention anything about the fraud, being frog-marched to an interrogation by the bank's investigators, or being given a lie detector test," Dylan said.

"My brother was given a polygraph?" Sal asked.

Tori and Dylan nodded. Sal rubbed the dark stubble on his chin with his hand but said nothing.

"Nico told me he'd known since the end of January that to get the position and monetary compensation he deserved, he would need to leave the bank," Dylan said, "and he'd been goading—his word, not mine —his boss to ask for his resignation or to fire him."

"Oh my God, he wanted to provoke a buy-out," Tori said. "Nico's entitled to five months' severance pay."

Dylan nodded. "Yeah, that was his plan. When his boss called him back from London, Nico decided to give Wayne an ultimatum—a promotion with a raise retroactive to the beginning of the year in exchange for help with the issue. Nico said Wayne fired on the spot."

The next day Nico called Human Resources to review some outstanding items regarding his termination. When he was told he wasn't getting severance pay, he'd demanded to speak with someone more senior. "He was transferred to Ms. Stager, who invited him to meet with her and another colleague Friday afternoon. He asked me to come along—as a witness, moral support—and it didn't hurt that I'm an attorney," Dylan said. "So, I agreed, thinking the meeting was about supporting him on the severance issue.

"What?" Dylan asked as Murphy rolled her eyes. "He is, was, my best friend, and he needed a favor. Don't tell me you wouldn't do the same for Lulu and Tori. Admit it."

"No, you're right," Murphy said.

"Why did Nico think he'd see a dime of severance? EIU is thorough—they would have had him sign an agreement that the bank would use his severance and any accrued vacation pay to offset the stolen money. Those funds plus whatever's left in the Manhasset account would make a significant dent in what he owes," Tori said.

"You mean what he *and* Eena owe, right?" Murphy asked.

Dylan exchanged a look with Tori before he explained the bank had no leverage over Eena, only Nico. "He'll be holding the bag for the money," Dylan said. "It's Eena who has the greater legal jeopardy."

"How much trouble do you think my wife's in?" Sal asked.

"A lot," Dylan said, and he began to tick off the offenses on his fingers. "She forged documents to open a bank account, including signing one form under penalties of perjury. She submitted fraudulent insurance claims for more than $200,000. Using Tori's name, social security number, and medical insurance. That's identify theft. And she's most likely been submitting fraudulent claims on her *own* medical insurance for years.

"We also know there's a group of—I'm loathe to call them medical professionals, who are conducting this insurance scam. We don't know whether Eena is just another patient submitting false claims or if she is the pharmacist in the scam."

The weight of Dylan's words hung in the air. Sal was the first to break the silence.

"Thanks for being so honest with me, Dylan. Murphy, it was good to see you again. I just wish…." He shook his head and rose from the sofa. "I think I should get going. I have a bit of a drive and a seven-thirty meeting tomorrow morning with Detective Kaminski. Not to mention a lot to process. Walk me out, Tori?"

Tori followed him to the foyer, where they stood and talked for several minutes. She stood on the porch and watched the ember glow of his taillights turn onto the street and disappear. When she returned to the family room, Dylan was seated on the couch, bent forward, his elbows on his knees, his hands covering his face. Murphy was beside him. She was rubbing his back and speaking softly. Tori felt a wave of shame wash over her. *I've thought only of me, then Sal. But Dylan's just found out his friend of twenty years, his friend with history, lied, cheated, and stole.*

"How are you feeling, Dylan?" she asked.

Dylan dropped his hands from his face, and she saw the look of pain and sadness in his eyes. His attempt at a smile failed, and the composure, bravado he'd shown all evening was gone—replaced by weariness and grief.

"I don't know. It's tough," he finally said, shaking his head. "When Murphy told me Nico had had an affair and you two were separating, I was sad for you both, disappointed in Nico, but I said to Murphy, no one knows what happens in a marriage. Then, when she told me he'd been fired, my first thought was that his combative attitude, saying provocative things—as if he always wanted to start an argument, had caught up with him, and he'd pissed off the wrong person.

"At this afternoon's meeting, he introduced me as if my firm and I were representing him. I shot that down right away. Said I was there solely as a friend. Then, I listened as Ms. Stager laid out all the evidence the bank had against Eena and Nico, replayed Wednesday, starting with Nico being brought to the thirty-third floor by two security guards. I was furious. They set you up to take the fall—all the evidence appeared to implicate you. You could have lost your current job, your pending job offer, your reputation. He was ready to put me in a compromising position and involve my firm." Dylan shook his head. "And when the meeting was over, he was angry with me for not playing along with him. I don't know what's happened, but he isn't the guy I grew up with. I don't even know who he is anymore. I told him I didn't want to be around him, that if I wanted to see or talk to him, I'd call. Then, I took the train back to my office. Wondering when I should have stopped trusting the man who was my best friend."

"I'm sorry, Dylan," Tori said. "I just assumed you knew. That Murphy had told you."

"And I wanted Dylan to hear Nico's version first," Murphy said. "But now, how about all of us take Baron for a walk, and then we'll head home."

Chapter 15
A New Beginning

Saturday Morning, Mid-July

As Tori waited for the light to change at the Broad and Water Street intersection, she stared at the building across the street. *Who would design a fifty-story building with an outside that looks like the inside of a waffle iron?* she wondered. Even set against today's picture-postcard backdrop—an azure blue sky, the shimmering Hudson River, a pair of orange and black ferry boats crossing paths on their way to and from Staten Island—the building had no charm, she decided. But this building was to be her new work home starting Monday.

Thinking about Monday made her anxious, and her stomach did a backflip. *It's not the job that's making you nervous, she reminded herself. It's the change—new faces, learning who's who, navigating from department to department.*

She'd worked in mid-town Manhattan for First Dominion Bank since moving to New York just over five years ago. She'd known her job —inside and out, confident she would know where to go, who to see to solve any work-related problems that came her way. Tori had known the neighborhood, too—everything from which deli had the best pastrami on rye to when the Museum of Modern Art held lunchtime docent tours. The financial district in lower Manhattan was an entirely different world. She didn't know where the best of anything was down here. *It will take time to get used to this new world*, she assured herself.

The downtown streets were deserted, she noticed. Even on an early Saturday morning in July, midtown would be bustling with pedestrian and vehicular traffic. Here, in lower Manhattan, she hadn't seen another person or even a passing taxi since leaving the Broad Street garage. She looked right, then left, and finally, she looked behind her. There was no one. *Only my closest family, friends, and former boss at First Dominion know where I work now,*" she reminded herself. *Nico won't think to look for me down here.*

Today was hot—already eighty degrees and not yet eight o'clock in the morning, according to the time and temperature gauge on the side of one of the buildings. The blacktop on the downtown streets was soft and sticky under her sandals. The leaves of the potted plant she cradled in the crook of her left arm slapped her cheek and tickled her nose and chin as she crossed the street. She had no extra hand to swat the leaves away or even scratch her nose. In her right hand, she carried a canvas bag containing recently taken framed photographs of her with Murphy and Lulu at the beach and her mother and Baron at her Fort Lee townhouse. The tote was heavy. And the shoulder strap of her pocketbook was trying its best to slip down her arm.

Four weeks earlier, on her next to last day of work at First Dominion, Tori had packed up most of her personal items and arranged to have the boxes delivered to her new office. Last week, Esta, her new boss, emailed her that Ben Cooper, the managing director of the legal department, had agreed to come into the office today. Tori could set up her office and get the "lay of the land" before her new employee orientation Monday morning. Jack Graham, the new managing director of the regulatory department, was also starting work on Monday and would be joining them this morning. Esta had asked Ben to give his new colleagues a mini tour of the building and acquaint them with the location of essential services, like the ATMs, cafeteria, and executive dining room. At eight o'clock, Tori and Jack were scheduled to meet Ben in the building's lobby. She was right on time.

As she walked across the building's large outdoor plaza to the front doors, she noticed a man, whom she estimated to be in his early thirties, standing by the door, watching her. His auburn hair glistened in the sunlight as if it had been woven with shiny copper wire, and he wore the business-casual uniform—khaki pants, a long-sleeve dress shirt, both fresh from the dry cleaner's plastic bag, and boaters. *Ben or Jack?* she wondered. *I'm going to bet you're Ben.*

"Excuse me," she called out to him. "Would you hold the door for me, please?"

The man smiled and nodded, then stood aside as she walked ahead of him through the open door and into the cool lobby.

"I think you're here to meet me," the man said. "I'm Ben Cooper. Let me help you with that." And he reached for and took the planter she had been clutching like a squirming toddler. "This is heavy."

Tori shifted the canvas bag from her right to her left hand, pushed the sagging strap of her purse back onto her shoulder, and extended her right hand. "Thank you. Hello, I'm Tori Mor…," she began, "Harrigan," she corrected.

Ben smiled. "Pleased to meet you, Tori Mor Harrigan," he said.

"Just Harrigan," she answered.

"Got it," he said, and she knew he did from the way he glanced at the empty third finger of her left hand.

A dark-haired man, dressed in an ensemble almost identical to Ben's and who appeared to be in his early thirties too, entered the door pulling the ubiquitous New York City shopping cart behind him. The cart was filled with bankers' boxes.

Ben called out, "Jack? Jack Graham?"

"Yes," the man pulling the cart said as he approached Tori and Ben, "I'm Jack. Are you Ben?" When Ben nodded, Jack extended his right hand to shake Ben's before saying, "Nice to meet you, and thanks for doing this. We'll lose the morning and part of the afternoon with orientation on Monday."

Jack turned to Tori, who extended her hand to shake his. "Hi. I'm Tori Mor...," she said, shaking her head. "I mean, Harrigan, just Harrigan."

"Nice to meet you, Tori," Jack said.

"Tori here is struggling to remember her name," Ben said, "and I say, since Esta is already calling us the Three Musketeers, we help her. From now on, I'm going to call her Harrigan. How about it, Jack?"

"Okay," Jack said. "And just to show you I'm a team player, call me Graham."

"Good," Ben said. "Almost everyone here calls me Coop. Cooper, Harrigan, and Graham has a ring to it."

"Not as much as Harrigan, Graham, and Cooper," Tori said.

"Or Graham, Harrigan, and Cooper," Graham countered.

"Let's say we go in order of 'seniority,'" Ben said. "I started two weeks ago, Harrigan here, beat you, Graham, by about two minutes."

The three laughed. "Agreed," Tori said.

"Is that tote bag all you brought with you?" Graham asked Tori as they followed Ben past building security to the elevators.

"The planter Ben's carrying is mine," she said, "and I have two boxes waiting for me upstairs. I had my stuff delivered."

"Great idea. Wish I'd thought of that," Graham said as Ben held the elevator door open and then pushed forty-five.

"Our location is terrific," Ben said as he reached into his pocket and took out two office door keys. "We have extraordinary views of the New York skyline and, of course, the Harbor, Liberty, and Ellis Islands. We're next door to the downtown heliport, so we often see dignitaries arriving and departing. We're just too high up to tell who's who."

When they exited the elevator on the forty-fifth floor, Ben led them through the reception area to a row of offices. "This is your office, Graham, and these three smaller offices and these cubicles house the regulatory department," he said while unlocking the office door. "Your desk and credenza keys are on the desk—same in your office, Tori, I mean Harrigan, and the file cabinet key is hanging in the lock. Next to you is the conference room. The corner office is Esta's. Harrigan's office and mine are next to each other on the other side of the floor."

Ben and Tori walked across the floor to the office he indicated would be hers, and he unlocked the door. "Your compliance department is here," he pointed to an area of three smaller offices and cubicles to the left of her office. "My legal staff is here." He nodded to the offices to his right and the area directly in front of them.

"Desk or credenza," he asked, holding out the potted plant.

"Credenza, please," she said.

Ben put the plant on the credenza, left, and returned a minute later. "I have a welcoming present for you," he said, handing her the six-volume set of the Internal Revenue Service Code and Regulations and the Blue-Sky regulations.

"Just what I've always wanted! You shouldn't have, but I'm glad you did," she said and laughed. She pulled a set of book ends from one of the boxes and set up the books between her phone and her laptop.

Tori had her boxes unpacked, broken down, and her office set up for business before nine-thirty. She could see Graham was finishing up, too. Ben took them on a quick tour of the building, and by ten-thirty, she was waiting in the garage on Broad Street for her car to be brought around, feeling more relaxed and ready for Monday morning.

As she drove up the West Side Highway, Tori realized how much she was looking forward to spending a quiet afternoon and evening at home. The last three months had flown by, and she was ready for life to settle down. So much had happened.

Twelve weeks ago, Tori had learned of her husband's affair with their sister-in-law.

The following week, she was accused of fraud, asked her husband to leave their home, met with a divorce attorney, and told her brother-in-law his wife and brother were having an affair.

Nine weeks ago, she'd replaced the furniture in the master bedroom and the home office she and Nico had shared.

Eight weeks ago, she'd selected new paint colors for her bedroom and office.

Seven weeks ago, she took Baron to his favorite dog sitter's and moved into the Park Lane Hotel on Central Park South for three days and two nights while her handyman painted over what remained of Nico in the townhouse. She signed the papers to refinance the mortgage and purchased Nico's share. The townhome was now hers and not theirs.

She pampered herself those three days—eating at her favorite restaurants, going to the theatre and museums, and enjoying a hot stone massage and a passion fruit facial.

Six weeks ago, she'd accepted a new job and resigned from First Dominion Bank. Deciding to leave what had been her 'work home' for five years had been a difficult decision, and she hoped she'd made the right one.

Three weeks ago, she and Baron drove to Sunset Beach, North Carolina, where she'd rented a house on East Main Street. For two months, she had thought of herself as a shark, needing to move continuously for her lungs to receive oxygen, so she would survive. She took two days to drive the nearly nine hours from Fort Lee to Sunset Beach. She and Baron had listened to the latest "beach reads" and a couple of self-help books on Audible.

Those first few days at the beach, Tor forced herself to stop, to let the grief of all that had happened envelop her, shatter her. She allowed herself to cry the 'ugly cry'—the one that had her gasping for air and left her with a throbbing headache. Each night she sobbed into her pillow. Every morning she took a pre-dawn walk on the beach. As she had known it would, the majesty and magic of the sea, the beauty of each morning's sunrise, and each evening's sunset began to heal her.

Two weeks ago, Murphy, Lulu, and Lulu's now two-year-old son Jackson had joined her. They built sandcastles and flew kites. They laughed and cried. With the help of her forever friends, she continued to heal.

Then, a week ago, she and Baron were alone again. But her heart was less heavy, and she found contentment for the first time in three months.

Chapter 16
Let Me Introduce You

That Afternoon

"Do you want your water straight up or on the rocks?" Tori asked. Baron looked up at her and cocked his head to the side.

"On the rocks it is. Excellent choice," she said as she dropped two ice cubes into the cold tap water in his dish. "I'm going to carry my tray out first, and then I'll come back for you and your tray. Let me check I have everything we need."

She inventoried the items on the first tray—an acrylic pitcher containing lemonade, a matching tumbler filled with ice and a circle of freshly cut lemon, and a plate of flatbread crackers topped with spreadable pub-style cheddar cheese. She surveyed the other tray—the water bowl with two floating ice cubes, a glass with additional ice should it be required, and a napkin with two of Baron's favorite after-walk dog treats. Then she pushed the button on the remote control, and the awning over the deck began to unfurl. Within minutes, she and Baron were settled outside under the shade of the awning with drinks and snacks, enjoying the majestic view and the cool breeze coming off the swiftly flowing Hudson River.

"Lulu and Murphy will be wondering where we are," she said to the dog lying beside her lounge chair as she started the FaceTime call.

Murphy's phone rang only once before she answered, but it took a minute for Lulu to jump on.

"Good afternoon, Ladies," she said. "Tori Harrigan here, waiting to be debriefed."

Lulu laughed. "Inquiring minds need to know. What'd you think?" she asked.

"What are Ben and Jack like?" Murphy asked. "What's your office like? What kind of view do you have? Tell us everything. Don't leave out a thing."

Tori told them about the incomparable view of Liberty and Ellis Islands she had from her office and how they could see the downtown heliport from Graham's office across the hall. "Lots of VIPs land there, Cooper said. But the only time anyone can remember being able to identify who was who was the last time the Pope came."

"That's funny," Lulu said. "Of course, his outfit would set him apart from the suits."

"What's up with all this 'Cooper and Graham' stuff?" Murph asked, "What are they like? Do you think you'll like working with them?"

"Yeah," Tori said, "I think I will, very much. They're both really," she paused, thinking of the right word, "kind."

Tori explained how she'd stumbled on her last name when she'd introduced herself first to Ben Cooper and then Jack Graham. "Calling myself 'Tori Morgano' came so automatically this morning," she said. She told them how Cooper had come up with the idea of calling her "Harrigan." "Just like college," Murphy said, "lots of people at Dickinson called you 'Harrigan.'"

Tori nodded before continuing the story of how the three new colleagues had christened themselves the team of Cooper, Harrigan, and Graham.

"They do sound like great guys," Lulu said.

"When they saw the picture of the three of us on the Sunset Beach pier and Mom and Baron's picture at the townhouse, they wanted details," Tori said, "and, of course, they figured out, after I kept stumbling over my name, I'm not married, or soon won't be."

"What kind of details?" Lulu asked.

"Like where we met," Tori said, "what you each did, where you live, the names of your husbands."

"What did you learn about them?" Murphy asked.

"Graham's a Virginian through and through," Tori said. "William and Mary undergrad. He waited tables at the historic taverns, like the King's Arms, to supplement his scholarships and loans. After graduation, he got a two-year analyst job at an investment bank, which he credits for his switch from the 'rainmaking' side to the regulatory accounting side of the business. He went to Darden Business School, where he met his fiancée, Gemma. She works for an engineering firm near Times Square. They're getting married this November. He has a wonderful picture on his desk of Gemma with his two sisters, Shannon and Emily, at the Lincoln Center Christmas tree, after a performance of *The Nutcracker*."

"What about Cooper?" Murphy asked.

"He went to NYU undergrad and Yale law school," Tori said. "He has an older brother, Knox, also a lawyer, who's moving back to New York after a three-plus-year stint in London. Coop's very excited about that. I got the impression they're close. Cooper doesn't have a girlfriend, and he's never been married. And he has nothing personal in his office —no pictures, no plants. Graham teased him a lot about that."

"But you think you'll like working with both of them, working there?" Murphy asked.

"Yeah," Tori said, "it's all good. But, it'll take some getting used to. Until today, I didn't realize how deserted the lower Manhattan streets are on the weekends. Coop said they're just as empty after six o'clock during the week. I'm used to midtown, where there are always people and cars at all times of the day or night. Downtown was kind of eerie. Makes me even more grateful Nico doesn't know where I work."

"Tori, has the security company installed the additional cameras outside the townhouse?" Lulu asked. "I'm still nervous about the—what are the police calling it?—while you were at Sunset Beach."

"' Suspicious activity,'" Murphy said. "They're calling it 'suspicious activity.' What an innocuous way to say, 'your lying, cheating husband tried to break into your house!"

"Yeah, Lu," Tori said, "last Wednesday. I'm glad Dylan and Tom suggested it. I feel better knowing the new cameras are there. But, as the Fort Lee police kept reminding me, the figure in dark pants and a hoodie the cameras caught on my porch while I was at the beach could have been a man or a woman. The cameras didn't catch a face, and the police officer who came to check the house that night didn't find anything."

"It was Nico," Murphy said. "We all know it was Nico."

"And then there's that pesky thing called 'evidence,'" Lulu said. "The police don't have any. This isn't a TV crime show where the intruder leaves a cigarette butt with DNA or a shoe print behind. Although I am surprised Nico didn't make some stupid mistake. I can't believe he, of all people, was smart enough to prowl around your house and not get caught."

"I agree with you, Murph," Tori said, "I'm sure it was Nico, too. I shared a pillow with that man for years, and the movements, the posture of the shrouded figure on the porch were very familiar. But Lulu's right—we have no proof that it was. So, for now, I'll increase the number of cameras as a precaution. And, of course, I have my wonderful watchdog. Baron would alert me if a stranger were on the property."

"But Nico isn't a stranger," Murph said.

"Well, Baron was never a fan of Nico's. When Nico and I would fight, and he raised his voice, sound angry, Baron would stand in front of me and growl at him," Tori said, "as if he were trying to tell Nico, 'Back off, Buddy.'"

"Good boy," Lulu said. "Of all of us, you're the best judge of character, Baron!"

Tori reached over the arm of her lounge chair to pet the resting dog, who acknowledged her attention by opening one eye and wagging his stump of a tail.

"Yes, he is. But now, can we please change the subject?" Tori asked. "I don't want to think about deserted streets and angry estranged husbands. I especially don't want to talk about why I need additional security or the possibility there could be prowlers lurking outside my house. So, tell me what's new with each of you."

Chapter 17
A Too-Close Encounter of the Nico Kind

The First Monday in August

As Cooper walked past the glass wall of her office, Tori called out, "Welcome back! How was your birthday and your trip?"

He stood in the doorway of her office and grinned. "It was an amazing three days! Knox flew in from London and surprised me at the Greenbrier! He, Dad, and I went white water rafting on the Lower New River. We played several rounds of golf. Ate incredible meals. And I have pictures!" he said.

Since that Saturday, when Tori and Graham had unpacked their boxes and set up their offices, they had teased Cooper about his décor, or lack thereof. There was nothing personal in his space. No pictures on his desk or credenza. When they met with the interior decorator from the Maintenance Department to select art for their office walls, he'd found "nothing I want to look at all day, every day." He refused to have a plant in his office—even one under the care of the professional gardening company hired by the firm to water and maintain the office plants and replace any that died.

"As in framed photographs that will adorn your desk and credenza?" she asked. "Should I call Graham? Will you cover them with a dark cloth until they're unveiled for the world to see?"

"Yes, they're framed," he said. "Nothing as fabulous as yours," he pouted. From the first time he'd seen the frame that housed the picture of Tori with Murphy and Lulu on the pier at Sunset Beach, he liked it. Around the border was the inscription, "Partners in Crime, Friends for Life." Lulu had found the frames years earlier and bought one for each. Every year, the trio updated the photo.

"That goes without saying," she said. "When is the unveiling? And you remember we're on for lunch—you, Graham, and I."

"The unveiling is now, and how could I forget a free lunch?" he asked. "Where are you taking me?"

Just then, Graham joined them and said, "Harrigan and I are going to let you decide. The empanada or the taco truck—your choice. Unless you'd prefer a dirty water dog. Did I hear we're having an unveiling? What are we unveiling?"

"Photos," Tori said. "Of his family, I think. Maybe of his vacation. Maybe both."

She lowered her voice to sotto-voce, mimicking a play-by-play announcer at a golf tournament. "Ladies and gentlemen, suspense is building. Ben Cooper has returned from a long birthday weekend celebration with his family. He is about to unveil never-before-seen photographs of the event. Let's watch."

Ben rolled his eyes before opening his messenger bag and removing two pictures. The first contained a photo of an older couple, seated at a restaurant dining table, with Ben and a man who was obviously his older brother, Knox, standing behind them. In the other picture, Ben and Knox were standing in soaking wet T-shirts and board shorts and grinning from ear to ear.

"The title of that picture should be 'Pure Joy,'" Tori said. "I don't think I've ever seen you grin like that!"

"Excellent choices, Mate," Graham said. "We approve. Great start."

"Start?" Coop asked. "The beauty of these photos is they are a start, a middle, and an end. Look at that incredible landscape in the background, for example. Notice the great foliage? This one picture checks the family photo box, the art box, and the plant in the office box. Now get out of here. I have work to catch up on. Come get me when it's time to eat."

By noon the hostess at Fraunces Tavern was leading them to their table. Once their server had taken their orders, Ben described his white-water rafting trip with his father and brother. "We transitioned from patches of calm water to Class III, IV, and a few Class V rapids in a matter of minutes," he said. Steep drops between massive boulders had been both exhilarating and frightening, he admitted, and the three men had been awed by the expanse of the New River Gorge Bridge as they floated under its nearly two-thousand-foot-long arch.

Their server approached the table with a glass of white wine. As he placed it in front of Tori, he said, "Pinot Grigio, compliments of the gentleman at the bar."

Tori smiled. *Probably, Dylan*, she thought. The law firm where he worked was ten blocks away. She swiveled around in her chair as far as she could to see who had sent the wine. It wasn't Dylan—it was Nico, who stared back at her.

She felt the hairs on the back of her neck stand up. Suddenly, she was no longer hungry.

Oh God, she thought, *he's found me! How? What should I do? If I send back the wine, what will he do? Will he notice if I accept it and just leave it on the table?*

"Thank you," she said to the server.

"Are you all right?" Graham asked. "You suddenly went very pale."

"My estranged husband sent over the wine," she said. "I don't know what he would do if I'd refused. So, I'm just going to let it sit here. This is Coop's birthday lunch, and I don't want Nico to spoil it. Although if he's still here when we're ready to leave, and if he tries to talk to me, I would appreciate it if you would both stick to me like glue."

"So your husband's name is Nick Mor?" Cooper asked.

She shook her head. "No, his name is Nico. Nico Morgano," she said.

"Which one is he?" Graham asked. "I think I have the best view of the bar."

Tori described what Nico looked like and his location at the bar.

Graham stared ahead for several seconds. Then he said, "Harrigan, I think your soon-to-be ex has been over-served. From his body language and the expression on the bartender's face, I think your ex has just been told he's cut off."

"I bet he's regretting I didn't send back the wine. He could have drunk it himself," Tori said. "And stop staring."

While he was looking at and listening to Cooper and Tori, Graham positioned his chair, so he could simultaneously and surreptitiously monitor the bar activity. "He seems to be settling his tab. Yup," Graham paused, "he's standing. He's walking. He's heading for the door."

Forty minutes later, when the three colleagues left the restaurant, Nico was outside, leaning against the restaurant's brick façade—waiting. Graham had been right—Nico had had too much to drink.

"Tori, can I have a word?" he asked. He spoke slowly as if he were trying to form the words without slurring them.

"We have nothing to talk about," she said. "If you have a message for me, have your lawyer call mine."

Nico walked toward her, invaded her space, and she stepped back. The sweet smell of the alcohol mixed with sour sweat and the stale odor of laundry left too long in the washer turned her stomach. She took another step back, then raised her right hand to her nose, inhaled the remnants of the jasmine-scented body lotion she'd used that morning, and forced herself not to gag.

"My colleagues and I need to return to work," she said. "Thank you for the wine. You didn't need to do that."

"That was the same wine my mother ordered when you took her to lunch at the Pool. When you stiffed her and didn't pay the bill? Remember?"

He tried to block her way, but she skirted around him.

"You never asked me what I saw in Eena, why I started the affair," he shouted at her back as she walked away, "She's great in the sack, and you're not."

Chapter 18
What Should I Do?

Later that Afternoon

"Health and Social Services. Mary Lou Roberts."

Hearing her friend's voice made Tori feel better.

"Lulu? It's me. Do you have a few minutes?" Tori whispered into the receiver.

"Yeah, sure, but why are you whispering?" Lulu asked.

Tori chuckled. "I'm not sure. No one can hear me. I've got my office door closed."

"What's the matter?" Lulu asked.

"I just had a close encounter of the Nico-kind on my way back from lunch," Tori said.

Then, she described what happened at the restaurant and her altercation with a drunk Nico.

"Coop and Graham were shocked," Tori said. "The two-block walk back to the office seemed endless. We kept slipping into uncomfortable periods of silence that Cooper would try to fill by thanking us again for lunch, or Graham would mumble about some meeting. Except there is no meeting. The two of them are sitting in Graham's office, with the door closed, pretending to have a meeting and watching me."

"You mean like they're staring at you?" Lulu asked.

"No, nothing so obvious," Tori said. "But they each keep glancing over here every few minutes. Do I sound paranoid?"

"Yes. What *are* you doing?" Lulu asked.

"Staring at a page in an open volume of IRS Regulations, hoping I look like I'm talking to a salesperson about a compliance issue," Tori said.

"Okay, you haven't asked for my advice, but here it is anyway," Lulu said. "Remember who you are—a strong professional who is friends with two colleagues. Go over there, interrupt their fake meeting, and acknowledge what happened today. Yes, it was embarrassing. But you didn't do anything wrong. You and a friend took another friend to lunch for his birthday, and you ran into someone you knew who was rude. The awkwardness you feel isn't going away until you clear the air."

"You're right. You're right," Tori said. "Thanks, Lu."

"My bill should arrive via email later today," Lulu said.

Tori waited a few minutes after she and Lulu had said goodbye before standing up, smoothing her skirt, and opening her office door. She squared her shoulders and began to walk toward Graham's office. With each step, Tori gained a bit more confidence. From the way each man had straightened in his chair, by their efforts to pretend the so-called meeting was ending, she knew her intentions to join them had registered with Graham, and he had relayed that information to Cooper. Before she could knock on the door, Coop opened it.

"I'm not disturbing you, am I?" she asked.

Coop mumbled, "No, not at all." Graham shook his head.

"I'm sure you both have questions about today's lunch, what happened afterward," she said. "So, you each get to ask one question, and I reserve the right not to answer."

"I cannot believe you were married to that ass," Graham said. "How did that loser get someone terrific like you to go out with him? Wait! Don't answer that. That was an observation, not my question."

"Who's Eena?" Cooper asked, "As a follow-up, what kind of a name is *Eena*?"

Tori took a deep breath and exhaled. "Her legal name is Valentina. Valentina Marie Morgano." His raised eyebrows, the straight thin line of his mouth, told her he recognized the surname she'd disclosed at lunch. "Eena's married to Nico's older brother, Sal."

"Geez," Graham said, shaking his head. "He slept with his brother's wife? While his brother was living with her, and Nico was living with you?"

Tori nodded.

"That name's familiar. Why do I know that name?" Cooper asked.

"She was arrested at the beginning of June," Tori said. "The tabloids dubbed her the *Fraudster Pharmacist*."

Before Cooper had a chance to ask more questions, she turned to look at Graham. "Next."

"Has he ever harassed you like that before today?" Graham asked.

Tori hesitated. She'd only shared the information she was now considering telling her colleagues with four other people—Murphy and Dylan, Lulu and Tom.

"Yes," she said.

Both men sat straighter in their chairs. Coop pulled out the empty chair next to him, and she sat down.

"I'm embarrassed to admit this, but when Nico moved out in April, I didn't block his number on my phone. All communication was going through our attorneys. It didn't even occur to me. At the end of May, I got a call from him, which I sent directly to voicemail. Later, when I listened to the message, I realized he was drunk. I deleted the message because it was too difficult to understand what he was saying. That's when I finally blocked his number. A week later, when I was deleting voicemails, I noticed I also had a blocked call. The phone log indicated he'd called a couple of days after the first call, in the middle of the night. Since then, according to the blocked call log, he calls about every five to six days."

She looked down at her hands folded in her lap. "The last week I was at the beach, something triggered my home alarm in Fort Lee." She told them about the prowler the security cameras had caught on her front porch. "There's no evidence it was Nico," she said, "but I'm convinced it was."

"Did you call the police?" Coop asked.

"The security company did, and an officer came out but found nothing." She told them about the extra security cameras she'd had installed at Dylan's suggestion.

"Have you told Dylan about what happened after lunch?" Cooper asked. "Was that who you were talking to?"

She smiled. "No, I was talking to Lulu. She'll probably call Murphy in a few minutes—she'll be finished teaching for the day—or Lulu may call Dylan. Telling one of us is a worldwide hook-up. You tell one, it's a sure bet the other four, I mean three, will know within minutes."

"Good," Graham said. "What else can we do?"

"Nothing you aren't already doing," Tori said. "You had my back this afternoon. I admit running into Nico, having him lurk outside the restaurant for as long as he did, has shaken me. Seeing him was the last thing I expected to happen today." She shook her head. "But now I think we all need to get back to work, don't you?"

That evening, Tori did what she often did when she had a problem—talked it over with Baron. He was an extraordinary listener, and while he didn't offer much advice, he was the perfect sounding board. Saying the words aloud, talking through different solutions had always helped her.

After recounting her confrontation with Nico and her phone call with Lulu, Tori said, "Remember I told you downtown is so much more deserted than midtown? Well, now that Nico knows I work in the financial district, it won't take long for him to figure out what building I'm in. To be honest, I'm scared. The gym offers a six-week self-defense training workshop. If I signed up, the boys next door would walk and feed you twice a week after they got home from school. What do you think? Would that be okay?"

Baron gave her a glance she interpreted as skeptical.

"Okay, I know I've never been the most athletic person, which may be all the more reason why I should sign up for the classes. There are probably a lot of good strategies they could teach me. Anyway, nothing's definite, but I'll check it out Saturday."

On Saturday morning, Tori arrived at the gym forty-five minutes before her water aerobics class began. She met with the self-defense coaches, and after getting an overview of what the course included, she signed up. Once she decided, she felt less anxious and more in control.

Chapter 19
Game! Set! Match!

Fourth Thursday in August

I loathe changing clothes in a ladies' room! Tori thought as she wiped the granite around the sink. She removed lemon-yellow jeans with blue and white cornflowers, a pressed long-sleeved white blouse, and her sky-blue V-neck sweater from her overnight bag. She placed them on the now clean and dry counter next to her favorite yellow baseball cap—the one sporting embroidered flip-flops and the words Sunset Beach on the front panel. Finally, she removed her navy boaters and placed them on the floor. *Yep, if we didn't have those amazing seats in Center Court at tonight's match, I wouldn't be doing this,* she assured her reflection.

Two weeks ago, just three days after the infamous birthday lunch, Cooper had returned from a meeting with one of the investment banking teams, entered her office, and plopped himself down in one of the two guest chairs in front of her desk.

"From your Cheshire cat grin," she'd said, "I gather the meeting went well."

"An understatement, Harrigan. Call Graham. Tell him to get in here."

Once Jack Graham joined them, Cooper had removed four tickets to tonight's US Open Tennis match from his inside jacket pocket and spread them like a fan in his right hand—a gift from one of the Executive Directors for Ben's help closing a big deal. The tickets were for seats in the first row of the loge section, Center Court, at Arthur Ashe stadium! Three tickets, Cooper had said, were for the three of them. The fourth would go to his older brother, Knox, who had moved back to New York from London last week.

When they were dating and all through their marriage, Tori and Nico had gone to the US Open every year, and each year, they'd had the opportunity to upgrade their seats. Last year, they'd finally made it to the loge section, but not the front row! She received the ticket renewal form for this year's Open the day after Nico'd moved out. That day, she couldn't imagine ever wanting to return to Flushing Meadow, watch a match—too many memories. But last month, when the annual hype began to grip the City, she was surprised how much she regretted throwing that notice away.

I'm going to the US Open! Tori telepathically told her reflection as she brushed her hair into a ponytail and threaded it through the half-circle opening at the back of her cap. That makes changing in the ladies' room worth it, she thought as she draped the sweater over her shoulders. After she surveyed her appearance one last time in the mirror, and because she was the only person in the restroom, she broke into a happy dance before picking up her overnight bag and returning to her office.

After exchanging her suitcase for her purse, she locked her office door and poked her head into Cooper's office. Graham was there too. They'd just finished a conference call, and neither had changed into casual clothes yet.

"You guys need to hustle. Aren't we supposed to be meeting Knox in the lobby right about now?"

Graham leapt to his feet and ran to his office to grab his change of clothes. Cooper let out an expletive before grabbing his bag and heading for the men's room.

"Meet you downstairs," Tori called after Cooper.

In the lobby, she had no trouble identifying Knox. He was about two inches taller than his brother. His brown hair had golden highlights and undertones and reminded her of cappuccino. It was clear both men had been products of the same gene pool.

She smiled as she approached him and extended her hand. "Hi. You must be Knox. I'm Tori. Your brother was on a conference call that just ended. He'll be down very soon."

"Thank you, Tori. Are you joining us this evening?"

She nodded. "I am, yes."

"I'm looking forward to this evening. I haven't been to a match for more than five years, and I understand my brother's two colleagues, Harrigan and Graham, are coming, too. Ben speaks highly of both men, and I'm looking forward to meeting them."

Men? she thought. *Ben probably only referred to me as Harrigan, and Knox doesn't realize I'm a she and not a he.*

"Yes, Harrigan and Graham are both coming," she said.

"You must work with them too. Ben says they're both brilliant and good at their jobs."

"Yes, yes they are! Graham is the firm's regulatory expert. He's fantastic. And Harrigan's whip-smart. The encyclopedia of compliance. A real pleasure to work with. Everybody says so."

Tori saw Ben and Graham exit the elevator. They walked to the corner of the lobby where she and Knox were waiting.

Ben introduced Graham to his brother and said, "And you've already met Harrigan."

Tori extended her hand again to Knox. "Tori Harrigan, Knox. Nice to meet you."

"You're Harrigan?" Knox asked and shook his head. "You really are something."

In the town car Ben hired to take them to the stadium, he told his brother the story of how he, Tori, and Jack had become the team of Cooper, Harrigan, and Graham.

Less than forty minutes later, they were pushing their way through the turnstiles of the Billie Jean King National Tennis Center, following the signs to Food Village.

"Once we've secured a good table, I'm heading for the Fish Shack,"

Tori said. "If you listen closely, you'll hear the Maine lobster roll calling my name. And, of course, I'm having a Honey Deuce."

"What's a Honey Deuce?" Knox asked.

"The signature drink of the Open. Lemonade, vodka, and Chambord. To be official, the vodka needs to be Grey Goose, and the drink should be garnished with three frozen honeydew melon balls. They are yummy and go down easily on a hot summer night."

"Come here often?" he asked. "You seem to know your way around, Tori."

"Yeah, I've been a regular the last few years. Straight ahead is Food Village. Let's look for a table with an umbrella before we grab the food and drinks."

Tori and Knox had their taste buds set on lobster rolls, while Graham and Cooper had decided on the Texas-style brisket barbeque. Tori remained behind to secure the table while the men went to the various stands to order the food and drinks.

Tori settled back in her chair, watching the couples and families pass by on their way to the different food stalls or one of the stadiums. Behind her, a voice she knew but hadn't heard in months called her name. She turned around.

His clothes were the first thing she noticed. *These past four months have taken their toll*, she thought. Since she'd first met him, Sal had always been well-groomed, fastidious about his appearance. She'd even teased him he could go from the examining room to a GQ photo shoot without missing a beat. But today, Sal looked disheveled. He'd lost at least fifteen pounds. His pants were baggy, his shirt collar was loose, and the shoulder seams drooped onto his upper arm. As he walked closer to where she was sitting, she saw other changes—his hair was grayer, and the laugh lines around his eyes had become deep creases.

"Sal. Hi." Tori said.

As he leaned down to kiss her cheek, she recognized the woman standing behind him. "Bobbi, it's good to see you."

"Can we sit down for a minute?" Sal asked, looking around the table and then toward the rows of food stalls. "You aren't here alone, are you? I know you and Nico used to come every year, but…."

"Please sit. I'm here with friends from work. They've gone to get our sandwiches and drinks. I'm surprised to see you here. I don't remember you ever coming to a match."

"Usually, I was working and Eena," he stopped. "Well, Bobbi likes tennis, and my hours are more flexible right now. What match are you here for? We're going to the women's doubles in Louis Armstrong."

"Our tickets are for the men's match in Arthur Ashe."

"That should be a good one. I've been meaning to call you, see how you're doing. I've left the practice. My partners and I thought it best—with all the publicity. I'm on staff at Mount Sinai now, and I'm, we're," he corrected, "renting a one-bedroom on the Upper East Side until we decide what we're doing."

Tori nodded before asking, "Bobbi, do you work at Mount Sinai too?"

"No, I'm at Lennox Hill."

"You look tan," Sal said. "Just come back from your usual week at Stone Harbor with Murphy and Lulu?"

"You've got a good memory. I'm surprised you remembered our annual mid-August week at the beach. I was there last weekend, but only for three days. I couldn't stay the entire week this year because I changed jobs in July."

Tori turned to Bobbi. "My friend's parents own a house a block from the beach in Stone Harbor, New Jersey. They generously let us use it a week every August."

"How's your mother doing, Sal?" she asked.

His smile faded, and he glanced at Bobbi before answering. "Mom's struggling with everything. Nico and Eena still being together doesn't help. She's called 911 a couple of times, thinking she was having a heart attack. Fortunately, both times were only panic attacks."

"I'm sorry, Sal, but glad it wasn't a more serious health problem."

"How's your mother?" he asked.

"Good. Mom flew in the beginning of July. I'll be going to Pennsylvania for Thanksgiving, and she's coming here for Christmas."

"I don't know if you've been following the case in the news," Sal said.

Tori shook her head. "Not since Eena's arrest."

"She cooperated and pled guilty to reduced felony charges. If or when the cases against doctors and therapists go to trial, she'll have to testify as a condition of her plea agreement. Her sentencing hearing is in mid-October. She may only serve a year behind bars."

"Is a maximum-security prison like Bedford Hills too much to hope for?" Tori asked.

Sal nodded. "Yeah, she'll go to a low-security facility because her crime was non-violent."

"So, my fantasy of Eena being shoved against a gray cinderblock wall by a convicted murderer?"

Sal smiled. "Let it go."

"Damn! It was a good fantasy while it lasted."

Sal sighed. "Yeah. I've had a few of those myself. Eena and I are divorced. I flew to Santo Domingo in early June for the hearing. One of us had to be there. After she was arrested and couldn't travel outside the state…."

"Good for you," Tori said. "Nico and I won't be divorced until the beginning of October. And I can't wait. Sorry, I know he's your brother, but…."

"Are you kidding? I want nothing to do with him. According to Mom, he's having a hard time. Did you know First Dominion and their insurance company filed formal complaints against him with the State Board of Accountancy for acts of fraud and dishonesty and for violating the rules of professional conduct?"

"I didn't. Losing his CPA license will tank what's left of Nico's career. No legitimate business will hire him. But I can't say I'm sorry, Sal. Frankly, I think they're both getting off way too easy. Even now, when I think about…," she shook her head. "Well, let's just say karma better not be finished—with either of them."

He nodded. "I get it. And you've been more than fair where Nico's concerned. I know you bought his share of the townhouse. He was able to pay back the insurance company. Otherwise, they'd have pressed charges, and he might be looking at jail time, too."

Just then, Tori saw Graham looking around for their table. She raised her hand and called his name. He saw her and signaled to Cooper and Knox, who were behind him. Sal and Bobbi stood as the three men approached the table carrying trays of sandwiches and drinks.

"Guys," Tori said, "This is Sal Morgano and his friend, Bobbi De-Bose. Bobbi, Sal, meet Ben and Knox Cooper and Jack Graham."

"Nice to meet all of you. Tori, take care and enjoy the match. It was wonderful seeing you tonight." Sal leaned over and kissed her on the cheek.

Then, he and Bobbi disappeared into the crowds.

Tori reached for one of the baskets with a lobster roll and fries and pried one of the drinks from its slot in the cardboard tray. "I've been thinkin' about you all day," she said to the sandwich before taking a bite.

"You okay?" Coop asked. "I mean, is everything all right?"

Tori saw Graham poke Cooper under the table. She smiled and nodded. When she'd swallowed, she said, "I'm fine. Running into them was unexpected but not unpleasant. Now, tell me, aren't the Honey Deuces wonderful?"

Chapter 20
The Morning After

Tori grinned as she walked down the hall and saw the lights were off in Cooper's and Graham's offices.

"Slackers!" she mumbled, thrilled she had gotten to work ahead of them.

Although she had to admit, she would have loved to stay in bed for at least another hour this morning. By the time she'd gotten home from the U.S. Open match the night before and taken Baron for one last walk, it had been nearly two a.m. before she'd gotten to bed. Then, she'd had too much on her mind, been too wired to sleep. Even Alexa reading the next chapter in the new audible book she'd started hadn't calmed her. It had been a choc-a-bloc night—running into Sal and Bobbi, watching a nail-biting match where the lead had passed back and forth in a five-set battle with two tie-breaks, and of course, meeting Knox.

For so long, Tori had been emotionally numb. Without a doubt, she noticed Coop and Graham were good-looking men—she wasn't dead. But for months, she'd viewed the men she met or knew like an attractive outfit in a department store window display. Yes, it was pretty, and if she were in the market for a new dress, she might consider trying it on. But she wasn't, so she kept on walking.

Last evening, however, had been different. Knox had been great company. He was smart and had a terrific sense of humor. Not to mention he was easy—very easy on the eyes. There was an energy about him—she felt it as soon as she'd seen him in the lobby of One New York Plaza—that electrified the atmosphere, made her aware of everything he did.

They discovered they had many common interests throughout the evening—a love of the beach, baseball, and ballet. Knox had anticipated Coop's teasing comments and had had comebacks warmed up and ready —especially about baseball and the ballet. Then Graham surprised them all by revealing he and his fiancé, Gemma, had season tickets to the New York City Ballet.

"Me too!" Tori had said, "Where do you sit? When do you go?"

She and Graham discovered they had the same subscription, and both had seats in the center section of the first ring. Unlike Tori, who, together with Murph and Dylan, had had the same subscription for five years, Graham and Gemma just changed from the Saturday afternoon to the Saturday evening performances.

"What's the program for the fall season?" Knox asked.

Between them, Tori and Graham came up with the program and performance dates for the five ballets scheduled from mid-September to December, starting with *A Midsummer Night's Dream* and ending with *The Nutcracker*.

"Anytime you want to go, Knox, let Coop know," she said. "My friends and I have an extra seat."

"I'd like that. Thanks."

"Are you going to the gala?" Graham asked her.

"Maybe," Tori answered. She swallowed before adding, "I mean, I have the tickets, so yeah, I could go."

Then, she looked away—needed to change the subject. She loved the New York City Ballet gala. *Who are you kidding?* she scolded herself. *You aren't going to the gala this year, Cinderella. You'd be the third wheel!*

Cooper tried to catch her eye, but she avoided his gaze. Shortly after meeting Tori, both he and Graham had noticed that when the conversation got too personal, when she felt her composure slip and needed the subject to change, she broke eye contact. After they alerted her to her 'tell,' as they called it, she would sometimes add commentary, like "turning away now" or "time for a subject change" when she turned her head.

So, Coop changed the subject. "You should have been with us a few weeks ago, Knox. Each division has to entertain the business school interns, and Graham, Harrigan, and I took them to a Yankee game. Harrigan arranged the whole evening. We had incredible seats, and she even arranged to have a message for us, and the interns flashed on the jumbotron—not once but a couple of times."

Knox looked impressed. "How did you manage that?"

"I have connections," she said.

The man who played the organ and organized the messages on the jumbotron at Yankee Stadium was a neighbor of Jenny's. For nearly ten years, Eddie had been a widower. His children and their families lived in Colorado. From the moment Tori met Eddie, they became instant friends. When she and Nico were in the apartment building, Tori stopped to visit him. She brought him Irish whiskey cakes, brownies, or cookies she'd baked, and they talked about the team and the prospects for the season.

Every year for her birthday and Christmas, Eddie gifted her two tickets—his seats—for a game. After she and Nico separated, although she wasn't going to visit Jenny anymore, Tori continued to call Eddie, send him a funny greeting card, an email, or a text—just to check in and say hello. When Graham suggested they take the interns to a baseball game, she volunteered to get tickets, and Eddie was pleased to help. Their seats were extraordinary, as Tori expected, but a jumbotron sign that began, "The New York Yankees are proud to welcome," and ended with each of their names, at the start of the game and the seventh inning stretch, delighted the interns and stunned Cooper and Graham!

As great as last night was, this morning demands caffeine and lots of it, Tori thought as she removed the lid from her cup. She took a long swallow of coffee before unwrapping her toasted bialy with butter. Graham passed by her office door, carrying a grease-stained bag in one hand and a cardboard tray with two coffees in the other. He appeared to be headed for Cooper's office, but when he saw her at her desk, he took a detour into her office and sat down.

"When did you get here? I'm half asleep," he said. "Talked to Coop. He's on his way and sounds as bad as I feel."

He removed a round object wrapped in parchment paper and aluminum foil from the bag and placed it on her desk. She saw a greasy bacon, egg, and cheese sandwich on a hard roll as he began to peel back the aluminum foil.

"Why is that thing on my desk and not yours?" she asked as she handed him extra napkins from the stack she kept in her desk drawer. "And you're just tired, not hung over. The grease isn't going to do what you might have thought when you ordered that thing."

"Coop said this was just what we needed. There's one in here for him too. He said you probably wouldn't want one, so I didn't order you one. Sorry."

"*I'm* not."

Seconds later, Cooper joined them. He grabbed the bag, removed the other sandwich, unwrapped it, and took a bite. While he chewed, he grabbed several napkins from the pile Tori had just given Graham to wipe his now-greasy fingers.

"Why didn't we take today off?" Graham moaned.

"Because Esta's out, you're in charge, and we all can't take the same day off," Tori said. "It's the Friday before Labor Day—the markets will be closing early, and it should be a slow day. Besides today's TML."

Every Friday, the three colleagues got together for lunch. It was an excellent time to check in on each other's departments, exchange ideas, and tackle problems. They had dubbed the lunch the Three Musketeer Lunch—TML for short. The locale varied. But two Fridays, both sunny summer days when it had been too lovely to be indoors, they'd ordered lunches from the deli next door and rode the ferry from Battery Park around the Statue of Liberty and Ellis Island and back to Battery Park.

If you didn't disembark, the cruise was only twenty dollars and took about fifty minutes. And, no matter what sandwich they ordered from the deli, they unanimously agreed it tasted ten times better cruising on the Liberty ferries than any place on land.

"Wasn't last night amazing?" Graham asked. "I was wired when I got home. Gemma was already asleep, so I couldn't tell her about it until this morning."

"Yup, I think we saw what will be one of the tournament's best matches," Tori said.

Coop laughed. "I was glad to see you're an equal opportunity freak-out, Harrigan. You were jumping up and down, shouting, cheering—just like you did at the baseball game, and you aren't even hoarse this morning. By the way, Knox enjoyed meeting you both last night. He even texted me this morning. Wanted me to be sure to tell you. He's looking forward to seeing you again."

"Meeting him was terrific, too. Sad he got all the good taste genes," Tori said, shaking her head. "Likes baseball, ballet, the beach."

"Yeah, he's great company. What do you want to do about TML?" Graham asked, stifling a yawn. "I, for one, would love a lunchtime on the water."

"Sounds great," Coop said. "Mind if I ask Knox if he wants to join? We don't have anything serious to talk about, right?"

"Only thing on the agenda—scheduling training sessions for the new sales teams," Tori said, "which we could knock out this morning. Please, invite Knox to join us."

She was surprised to find her bialy had come with a side of butterflies!

Just before noon, the trio picked up the four pre-paid brown-bag lunches waiting for them behind the cash register at the deli next door and headed to Battery Park to meet Knox and catch the ferry. Tori felt the static in the air, felt Knox's presence before she turned around to see him walking toward them. Her action caused Cooper to stop talking, follow her gaze, and wave to his brother.

Knox insisted on paying the fares for all four of them, and when they boarded the boat, he took the seat next to her.

The sun was shining in a nearly cloudless sky, and the breeze on the water was refreshing and cool. The breathtaking beauty of the New York skyline, Lady Liberty, and Ellis Island were on full display. They argued about which baseball stadium had the best hot dogs, who they thought should win the Cy Young Award, and which teams would make it to the playoffs and World Series. All too soon, fifty minutes flew by, and the ferry returned to its dock in Battery Park.

"That was wonderful!" Knox said. "Like a mini-vacation in the middle of the day." He pointed to a historic tall ship sailing majestically into its berth. "Look at that beauty!"

"The Union Clipper," Tori said, "My favorite, but I haven't been able to talk these guys into it yet."

"I'll go with you," Knox said. "Today is the last day of the relocation leave my law firm gives. Next week I'm back to work full-time, and my office is next to yours on Old Slip. Let's plan on it."

Her stomach did a front full in, half-out somersault worthy of Simone Biles, and her heart skipped a beat. Knox was looking at her lips as if he wondered how they would feel, how they would taste. *Oh. My. God.*

"Let's," was all Tori managed to say.

Chapter 21
The BIG Bet

Later that Evening

Tori glared at her iPhone. *Ring already!* she ordered. It was Lulu's turn to initiate their evening FaceTime call. With a toddler to put to bed, Lulu often ran late. *Please not tonight,* Tori pleaded with her phone. She hummed the opening bars of From a Distance, Lulu's ringtone, hoping to give the phone an incentive to sing along. Finally, she laid it on the kitchen counter and walked into the family room. *Maybe, if you think I'm ignoring you, you'll ring!*

Her strategy worked. Just as she sat down in the other room, she heard Bette Midler's voice. Tori ran to the kitchen and retrieved the phone before Ms. Midler had finished the opening bars.

"Hi! You're not going to believe who I saw at the Open last night. I have tons to tell you two."

"Don't tell us you ran into Nico!" Lulu said.

"No, but close. I ran into Sal and Bobbi." Then, she told them everything she had learned the night before.

"How do you feel about Nico and Eena still being together?" Lulu asked.

"I'm not surprised. Nico doesn't have a lot of options. And Eena's great in the sack—or so I've heard."

"Did you know about the complaint the bank and insurance company filed?" Murphy asked. "Or that he's going to lose his CPA license?"

"No. Remember how hard Nico studied for that exam? What a waste! He'll never be able to get an accounting or finance job now. But since he can't or won't accept responsibility for anything, I'm sure that's my fault, too. Might explain all his efforts to harass me."

"Do you think Bobbi and Sal will get married?" Lulu asked. "I mean, for one of his mistresses, she's had a pretty good run, and now he doesn't have the 'I'm married' excuse anymore."

"Who knows?" Tori said. "At first, I was surprised when he said he'd gone the Caribbean divorce route, but it makes sense. He needed to separate himself from Eena and her arrest as soon as possible."

"But the stench from her scandal lingers. Sal can say he and his partners made the decision together, but I bet they didn't give him a choice." Murphy said.

"Who do you think posted Eena's bail?" Lulu asked.

"Maybe Nico," Tori said. "She was arrested right after I wrote him a great big check for his half of the townhouse. And you know Nico—no one likes to show off more than he does."

"Are you all right? With running into Sal and everything?" Lulu asked. Tori nodded. "Yeah, I'm okay."

"Now," Murphy said, "tell us about the match. I watched the beginning. But it went past my bedtime. How did you get up this morning?"

"I almost didn't, But last night was totally worth it—from start to finish. One of the best evenings I've had in a while." She told them about meeting Knox in the lobby of One New York Plaza and how he'd assumed Harrigan was a guy! "That's priceless!" Murphy said.

Tori told them she'd learned Graham and Knox both liked the ballet. "Can you believe it? Graham and Gemma have the same ballet subscription we do, Murphy." Knox had asked about the programs for the season and seemed to know a lot about the New York City Ballet Company. "I told him about our extra ticket," Tori said, "in case he'd like to join us sometime."

Coop, she told them, had invited Knox to join them on their lunchtime cruise, and she detailed every moment of their time together—from meeting in Battery Park to seeing the Union Clipper sail into port.

"Knox said he'd go with me on that cruise," Tori said.

"Wait. You just met Knox yesterday, and you were with him again today. And you're planning a third meet-up?" Lulu asked.

Dylan's head appeared on screen behind Murphy's right shoulder just then.

"Happy Labor Day weekend, ladies," he said. "Although I've just caught bits and pieces, Murph will give me the full run-down of your important news and gossip in the car tomorrow. Don't keep her up too late. You know how she gets when she's had too little sleep and is stuck in a car for several hours."

"What time are you guys leaving for Stone Harbor?" Tori asked.

"Dylan wants to be in the Big Apple Bagel parking lot, waiting for their doors to open at six, so we can collect the two dozen bagels we promised my family. Do you know he even made the owner swear he'd be there, have the bagels bagged and ready for him to run in, grab and leave? I've called him the Bagel Bandit for the past two days."

"Would you rather sit in traffic all morning?" Dylan asked. Murph shook her head. "Before I go to bed, Lu, what's your tally? Murph's up to eleven."

"I've counted only ten, but I'm willing to concede I might have missed one."

"What are you talking about?" Tori asked. "What tally?"

"The number of times you've mentioned 'Knox,'" Murph said.

Tori rolled her eyes. "He seems like a great guy. Smart, funny. Do you know how long it's been since a good-looking man showed an interest in me?"

"Wait!" Dylan said. "On behalf of Tom and myself, I object. We're both handsome as hell, have scintillating personalities, and we pay attention to you."

"Damn straight," Tom's voice could be heard in the background.

Tori chuckled. "I mean someone who isn't faux family. Better?"

"No," Dylan said.

"Absolutely not," Tom called to them.

"Well, that's the best I got."

"When Knox joins us for the ballet," Murph said, "I'll get some pictures, Lu."

"And I'll take him aside, like a good older brother would, and find out his intentions toward our girl," Dylan teased.

"You two will do no such thing," Tori said. "I'll bet you cash money he won't take me up on my offer. Who's willing to lose some money on this? Say twenty dollars?"

"Okay," her four friends answered.

"Time limit is the end of ballet season—not including *The Nutcracker*," Tori said. "And the bet is with each of you—no couple discount. Deal?"

"Deal," came the chorus of voices.

"Love me some eeeeasy money," Murph said.

"Seriously, I'm holding you goofballs to this bet," Tori said. "I'm already looking up dates in November for the ninety-minute hot stone massage you all just committed to contribute to."

"Don't count your chickens, sistah," Lulu said. "Tom and I are investing our forty dollars in lobster rolls. And I bet we won't have to wait until the ballet season ends to collect."

"Good idea. Bandit, how 'bout we get Huzzah burgers at Patrick Henry with our free money?" Murph asked.

"Sounds good," Dylan said. "Good night, ladies."

Now, with just Murphy and Lulu on the call, Tori said, "I enjoyed the attentions of a handsome man, the flirty back and forth." She paused. "I felt noticed. For the first time in months. He made me feel attractive, interesting, and I liked feeling that way again."

"Just see how this plays out," Murph said. "Enjoy the attention. Continue to flirt. Get your confidence and dating equilibrium back."

Tori hesitated, then said, "Maybe I'm reading too much into this. I thought there was something—a spark. But maybe I'm wrong. Maybe he was just being nice."

"Sounds to me like he's interested. But you set the pace—baby steps if that's what you're comfortable with," Lulu said.

"We know you're worried about trusting someone again," Murphy said. "All of us get that. But remember, while *your* Spidey-sense was off with Nico, so was all of ours. None of us thought he would ever have an affair. And the scam he tried to pull still blows my mind.

"So we're going to Stone Harbor. Lulu and Tom are entertaining his parents. What did you decide to do, Tori?

"I may go to the craft fair at Lincoln Center tomorrow. I invited my neighbors to come over Monday for a cookout. I thought I'd try that new grilled shrimp recipe I found."

Baron walked to Tori's side, his leash in his mouth. A chorus of "Hi Baron" greeted him. He looked briefly at Tori's iPhone screen before staring at her with soulful brown eyes.

"Someone wants a walk," Lulu said.

"Our new neighbors walk their dog, ZuZu, right about now. Young love is in the air," Tori said, rolling her eyes.

She lowered her voice to a whisper, "I don't think this thing with ZuZu will last. But for now, he's smitten. I better go."

The friends agreed they would check in Monday night to discuss the holiday weekend events before saying, "Good night."

Chapter 22
The Art of Losing Gracefully

Tuesday, September 5th

Whaaat was I thinking? Tori glared at her reflection in the mirror. *Twice in less than three weeks, I'm changing clothes in the ladies' room!*

When she'd gone through her mail after three weeks at Sunset Beach, she'd found the invitation to the Lincoln Center's annual docents' reception. While the food and drink at these events were mediocre, the attendees and programs were exceptional. The principals and soloists of the New York City Ballet, stars of the Metropolitan Opera company, and members of the New York Symphony would stop by to thank the volunteers. Each year they were treated to extraordinary performances—a preview of a not-yet-premiered ballet and Johann Pachelbel's Canon in D Major performed by the strings of the New York Symphony had been the highlights of last year's reception. Her friend and fellow docent, Elaine Meyer, had called her in mid-July to suggest they attend the reception together, have dinner afterward. Tori had been enthusiastic when she'd made those plans with Elaine, but now, as she dried the granite countertop with paper towels, she was having second thoughts. *I just feel like going home, putting my feet up*, she thought.

From her hydrangea blue overnight bag with a lower case "h" embroidered in white on the side—a recent purchase to celebrate her soon-to-be official name change—she removed her black column dress. She brushed her blond hair to add body and fluffed it with her fingers.

Around her neck, she wore a simple filigree chain, and diamond studs twinkled in her ears. Then she slid her feet into a pair of strappy black sandals with heels high enough to flatter her legs but low enough to be comfortable for the entire evening. The nights during this mid-September Indian summer were warm and breezy, so she threw her red cashmere pashmina over one shoulder before leaving the ladies' room.

The doors of an up elevator were opening as she entered the floor's reception area. She heard Coop's voice calling, "Excuse me, getting off," as someone held the door. When he exited the elevator, he wasn't alone —Knox was with him. Tori had to smile—he looked handsome in his dark blue suit.

She stepped forward to press the down button. Coop did a double take when he saw her, and Knox smiled.

"Wow, Harrigan, you clean up nice," Coop said.

"Thanks."

"Tori, you look lovely. Special plans this evening?" Knox asked.

"Thank you. Tonight's the annual docent reception at Lincoln Center."

Cooper frowned. "You're not riding the subway looking like that, are you?"

"No, I ordered a town car. George, the driver I always request, just texted me. He's here."

"Hey, do you mind if I bum a ride with you?" Knox asked. "The apartment I'm subletting is right near Lincoln Center."

"Of course. The number 1 train's loss is my gain," Tori said. She noticed Cooper was frowning, staring at Knox as if he wanted to say something. "If you guys need a minute, I can wait downstairs," she said.

"No, we're good," Knox said, just as a down elevator arrived. "Talk to you later, bro. Tell Graham I'll catch him next time."

When they were seated in the town car, Tori introduced Knox and George. "George and I go way back. He's my go-to driver," she said.

"And Miss Tori's my favorite passenger."

As George navigated the town car onto the West Side Highway, Knox asked Tori about her volunteer work at Lincoln Center.

"Mostly, I work at the souvenir table during intermission. We sell everything from autographed toe shoes to Christmas tree ornaments. Sometimes I lead tours through the three main buildings. Occasionally, I usher at special events, like the American Ballet School graduation. I love it."

He challenged her to give him a fun fact from her docent tour.

"Well," she said. "Oh. I've got one—this is one of my favorites. Wallace Harrison was the lead architect for the entire Lincoln Center Project and the architect for the Metropolitan Opera House. He wanted the Met to be much larger. But he wasn't given the land or money to make that happen. So he was forced to make the Opera House more compact. Executive and administrative offices he'd planned to be hidden from public view had to be put on the upper floor—behind all those lovely arched windows."

"I walk by that building twice every day, but I've never seen anything that would suggest people are in offices working or walking around up there," Knox said.

"That's because the most exquisite and priceless camouflage hides all that—the two Marc Chagall murals, *The Triumph of Music* and *The Sources of Music*."

"Whoa! I'll have to look at those windows and murals more carefully. Tell me something else."

"I would, but we're here."

As George was pulling up to the curb, Tori's phone buzzed. She frowned as she read the text.

"Bad news?" Knox asked.

"I was meeting my friend, Elaine, tonight for the reception, and then we were going to have dinner. Her little girl isn't feeling well, and she's bailing on tonight. I'd invite you to come with me, but unfortunately, it isn't a 'plus one' type of event. George, can you take me home?"

"No. You look too beautiful to just go home. Have dinner with me tonight. You can tell me more behind-the-scenes stuff about Lincoln Center."

Tori thought a minute. *Is this a bad idea?*

"Okay," she said, "that sounds like fun. Where shall we go?"

"Where were you and Elaine supposed to have dinner?"

"The Leopard at des Artiste."

"Perfect. George, Central Park West and West Sixty-Seventh Street, please."

"Right away, Mr. Knox," the driver answered.

Over drinks and dinner, they shared favorite books, movies, and plays. They talked about places around the world they wanted to visit or return to. Seconds later, two and half hours had passed. Tori's phone buzzed—George was texting her he was on his way. Knox signaled the waiter and asked for the check.

"Knox, thank you for saving this evening." She reached into her purse for her wallet.

"Tori, this was wonderful, and I had a terrific time. Please, dinner's on me."

"I don't know what or how much Coop—Ben," she corrected, "has told you, but technically, for several more weeks, I'm married. Attractive unmarried men buying me dinner isn't in my wheelhouse—yet."

"Tell you what. Let's call it an exchange. If the offer you made at Flushing Meadow is still open, I'd like to join you for this Saturday's performance of *A Midsummer Night's Dream.*"

"That would be terrific!" You'll meet my friends, Murphy and Dylan. Graham and Gemma will be there too."

And I can't believe I've lost the bet already! she thought and grinned.

Knox escorted her outside, motioned for George to remain behind the wheel, and opened the door for her.

"Thank you again for a terrific evening," Tori said. "Looking forward to seeing you Saturday—say seven by the fountain?"

"I'll be there."

Chapter 23
Moon Magic

Tori settled into the town car's comfortable seat, closed her eyes, and sighed. *This evening was just what I needed, she thought.* She snuggled into her pashmina, imagining it was Knox's fingertips caressing her arm, not the cashmere's softness. The hum of the sedan's sunshade retracting startled her. She opened her eyes and sat straighter in the seat.

Through the glass of the panoramic view rooftop window, a waxing gibbous moon, the color of soft candlelight, shone warm and wondrous above her. By Saturday, the moon would keep the promise it was making tonight. It would be full.

"Thank you, George."

"You're welcome."

I should call Knox, she thought. *This is too beautiful. How could we have missed this when we left the restaurant?*

Tori reached for her purse. *I should at least text him*—grateful Knox had suggested, over snifters of Amaretto, they exchange contact information. She was startled when, just as she opened her purse, the theme of *Downton Abbey*, her default ringtone, began to play. The caller ID read Knox.

"Hi," Tori answered. "I was just going to text you."

"Have you seen the incredible moon? Can you see it from the car?"

"George opened the panoramic window for me, and I have a ringside seat. It looks close enough to touch, doesn't it? I'm embarrassed to admit this, considering the glorious meal we just finished, but it reminds me of a buttery shortbread cookie."

He laughed. "Sounds delicious. What were you going to text me about?"

"The moon. Which will be full Saturday night, so we'll have a great view from the theatre's balcony."

"Okay, sounds like a plan. As I was walking home, I realized there were a couple of things I meant to ask you."

"Oh?"

He cleared his throat. "When we took the lunchtime cruise on the Liberty II, we saw that incredible tall ship coming into harbor. We said we'd go. The weather's supposed to be great Thursday. If our schedules are good, do you want to go? Thursday?"

"Yes. Unlike the Liberty II, where you can just pay and hop on, we'll need reservations for the Union Clipper. Since you took care of the ferry, I'll order our tickets for Thursday. Should I mention it to Coop and Graham, or do you want to say something?"

"Yeah, okay. Why don't you mention it to them tomorrow?" He didn't sound enthusiastic—or was that just her imagination?

"Okay. You said there were a couple of things."

"Yes. Dinner Saturday night. May I take you to dinner, or do you already have plans?"

"Murphy, Dylan, and I go to dinner at Shun Lee West on Sixty-Fifth Street," she said. "It's a pre-ballet tradition. We've done it for years. I'd love for you to join us."

"Are you sure that would be all right?"

"Absolutely. Our reservations are for five o'clock, under Malone. I'll ask Murphy to add another person. And I'd like to apologize, in advance, in case my best friend and her husband give you the third degree."

He laughed. "I'd expect nothing less from a best friend and her husband."

Suddenly, Tori gasped. "Oh. My. God. I wish you could see this, Knox. We're on Riverside Drive in Washington Heights. Almost at the entrance to the George Washington Bridge. I can see the lights of The Met Cloisters, and the moon is like a halo behind the monastery's turret. It's spiritual! I'll take a picture and send it to you, but I doubt it will come close to the reality."

"The Met Cloisters? Geez, I haven't been there since," he paused. "A high school field trip, I think, was the last time I was there."

"You should go," Tori said. "I haven't been for about a year, but just like the Cloisters of the Middle Ages, it's a place to reflect and recharge. To paraphrase J.D. Rockefeller, those who come under the influence of the Cloisters leave with 'new courage and restored faith.'"

"I just got the picture, and you're right. It's beautiful. I see what you mean," he paused, "spiritual. Is the museum open Sundays?"

"Yeah," Tori said. "It's open every day."

"Then, are you free Sunday to take me on a tour of the Cloisters?"

"Yes, I'm free. But don't you think you'll be a little sick of seeing me by Sunday? Tonight, the cruise Thursday, followed by dinner and the ballet Saturday?"

"I can't imagine that."

"Okay. Let's do it. Usually, the museum closes at five o'clock, but it's open late for the next couple of weeks for the Vatican vestments exhibit. If we go in the afternoon, say three-thirty, we'll have a few hours in the museum before it closes, and if the moon cooperates...."

"Perfect."

"I'll text you tomorrow about Thursday," she said. "Knox, thank you again for a wonderful evening."

That night, as she took Baron for the day's final walk, she took a picture of the moon's shimmering reflection in the inky black waters of the Hudson River. Later, just before she turned out the light on her nightstand, she texted Knox the new picture and added the caption, "On an evening stroll with the guy I live with, enjoying the view from our boardwalk."

She knew she should let Murphy and Lulu know she had lost the bet and transfer the money she'd lost, but she wasn't ready to share her evening and all that had happened—just yet. Morning would be soon enough.

Chapter 24
Grand Pas de Deux – Entrée

Saturday, September 9th

"Tori!" Murph said. "Earth to Tori. Come in, Tori."

"Wha? What?" Tori asked.

Murphy turned her head to look at her friend seated in the back of the SUV. "You're a million miles away, girl."

"I think it's only about twenty miles between the New Jersey side of the George Washington Bridge and the waters off the tip of Manhattan. But you're right. I was daydreaming about last Thursday. So, what were you saying?"

Tori had been lost in the memories of her cruise with Knox on the Union Clipper. Although on Wednesday morning, as promised, she asked Graham and Cooper if they'd like to join them on the lunchtime cruise, both men had had prior commitments. Graham was meeting Gemma in Times Square to check off several wedding-related errands, and Coop had a lunch meeting in mid-town. She wasn't disappointed neither colleague could come, and Knox hadn't seemed upset either.

On Thursday, everything had been perfect—as if the gods had aligned the stars and the planets to create one perfect day. Even her job cooperated—there were no mid-morning crises or last-minute phone calls. Knox had been waiting when she arrived in the lobby of One New York Plaza. Together, they walked to Slip 2 in Battery Park and joined the queue of tourists lining up to board the Union Clipper. Up close, the sailing ship was breathtaking and big, with masts that seemed to reach up to and touch wispy clouds dotting the cerulean sky.

Once the captain navigated the ship out of its berth, deck hands invited any passenger wishing to haul on the sails to join them at the ropes. Tori held Knox's suit jacket, tie and cuff links while he undid the top button of his dress shirt and rolled up his sleeves before joining the crew and fellow passengers pulling the sails' thick ropes to make them taut. She took several pictures documenting his hard work and texted them to his phone as souvenirs of the experience.

When all five thousand square feet of white canvas had been hoisted, the winds off the peninsula filled the schooner's sails until they became vertical wings, lifting the ship high in the water. It was as if they were gliding on the surface of the Hudson River. Deck hands encouraged passengers to take a turn at the wheel, and soon Knox was steering a course for Liberty Island. Later, Tori and Knox stood against the ship's waist-high railing to capture the perfect tourist photo of Lady Liberty. A fellow passenger offered to take their picture. As they stood, side-by-side, against the ship's railing, Knox put his hand on the small of her back. Startled, she turned to face him. He must have felt her body shift and turned to look at her, too. Behind their smiles was a heat, an intimacy that her camera captured. Each time she'd looked at that picture in the past day and a half, which was often, she felt her cheeks flush. They looked like a couple.

When the captain and crew secured the ship in its berth and the passengers were preparing to disembark, Knox said, "Thank you for arranging this. I can't remember when I've had such a terrific time! But then, every time we've been together has been amazing."

Now, Tori forced herself to concentrate on Murphy's question.

"I asked if you thought we'd get there first or if Knox would," Murph said, "and if he's there when we arrive, will he be inside or outside?"

"He'll be waiting for us outside the restaurant."

Dylan parked the car in the garage on Broadway they always used when they came to Lincoln Center. As they waited at the light to cross Columbus Avenue, Tori saw Knox waiting outside Shun Lee West. He smiled when he saw her. After she made the introductions and the maître'd showed them to their table, Knox helped her off with her cape and told her in a soft voice meant for her alone that she looked stunning.

Last Wednesday morning, when Dylan learned Tori had lost the bet and Knox was joining them for dinner and the ballet, he'd teased her by emailing Lulu and Tom with a copy to her, promising he would grill Knox Saturday evening and inviting them to submit questions. Although he later promised he wouldn't follow through on his threat to interrogate Knox over dinner, Dylan did confess to checking his credentials in Martindale-Hubbell, the directory of attorneys. Knox had graduated from NYU and Harvard law school. He was four years older than Tori.

Armed with this information, Dylan skillfully wove questions into their dinner conversation. Over sesame cold noodles and scallion pancakes, they learned Knox played bridge, enjoyed an occasional pick-up game of basketball, and sometimes played golf at the Long Island Country Club Knox and Ben's parents had belonged to since they were boys. Over chicken with three different nuts and firecracker scallops and prawns, Knox told them he married his high school sweetheart right after NYU. "Our parents had been close friends for years," he explained, "and they wanted us to get married. It was just assumed we would." *Wow! So that's why he didn't think my divorce was a big deal, Tori thought.*

Over the pistachio ice cream they all needed to douse the heat from the spicy seafood, he told them the job opportunity in London had presented itself shortly after the divorce. "It was easier to deal with what I perceived to be my parents' disappointment by putting an ocean between us," he said. A decision, he admitted, that had been good for his career but had made him realize how much he needed and missed his family's support during that time.

After dinner, the four of them walked to Lincoln Center. As Tori walked up the stairs to the Promenade of the David H. Koch Theatre, she spotted Graham and Gemma standing near the bar and waved to them before leading Knox, Murphy, and Dylan over to join them. After all the introductions had been made, Graham said, "I hear I missed an amazing cruise on Thursday. Coop said you couldn't stop talking about it."

"It was incredible! You saw the ship in the harbor—it's beautiful, right? But being part of the experience, hoisting the sails, taking the wheel? I want to go again, soon." Knox took out his phone, opened the pictures, and passed the phone to Graham. Gemma leaned against her fiancé's arm so she could see them too.

"Dylan and I have taken the sunset cruise a couple of times," Murph said to Gemma. "It's very romantic."

"Maybe we should go," Gemma said to Graham, "Knox looks like he's having the time of his life."

"I think you both would enjoy it," Dylan said. "Murph's right—the sunset cruise is romantic. But I'm with Knox. Helping with the sails, taking the wheel—a one-of-a-kind experience."

As Graham scrolled through the pictures, he and Gemma looked at each other and then at Tori. They both gave her a big grin. Her cheeks flushed. She knew they were looking at the photo of her with Knox at the tall ship's railing. She was grateful the ushers chose that moment to open the auditorium doors, and she suggested they make their way to their seats.

As they walked through the theatre doors, Gemma said she and Graham would look for them at intermission. Then, they headed for their seats near the back of the first ring. Dylan led Murphy, Tori, and Knox down the steps to their seats in the first row.

"These seats are wonderful," Knox said.

"Five years ago, when we started coming to the ballet, we were two rows behind where Gemma and Graham are. Each season our seats improved, and finally, we were assigned these seats last April," Tori said.

"Have you ever seen the Balanchine choreography of *A Midsummer Night's Dream*, Knox?" asked Murphy.

"No. I've only seen this ballet performed once about five years ago, but it wasn't the Balanchine choreography."

"You're in for a treat! Mr. Balanchine choreographed the ballet for the opening night of this theatre. It's *my* favorite," Murphy said.

Knox turned to Tori, "Is it your favorite, too?"

She shook her head. "No, but it's definitely in my top three. My favorite is *The Sleeping Beauty*, our last ballet this season before *The Nutcracker*."

"But this choreography of *A Midsummer Night's Dream* is like seeing two ballets that complement each other," Murphy told him. "The first act is the entire plot of Shakespeare's play, complete with love triangles and feuding fairy kingdoms. It's probably the ballet you saw years ago. A warning—there will be an ovation after Act I because Act II is danced by different members of the company. Because Mr. Balanchine didn't like ending the story on love's misadventures, he created Act II—a poem about ideal love, told in the language of dance."

The orchestra conductor entered the auditorium and bowed to the audience. The house lights dimmed, the curtain rose, and they were transported to the city of Athens and the magical, mystical, and sometimes chaotic forest just outside its walls.

After a standing ovation and several curtain calls, the auditorium filled with light. Knox leaned down and whispered to Tori, "Balcony?". She nodded and followed him up the steps. The promenade filled with patrons looking to purchase souvenirs and refreshments during intermission. Together they navigated across the reception hall to the doors leading to the balcony. Outside, the full moon, the color of champagne bubbles, hung low in the sky—its reflection twinkling in the waters of the fountain below them.

They stood side-by-side on the balcony, not saying a word, for several minutes. Then they both began to speak at once.

"You go first," Tori said.

"I wanted to say how much I'm enjoying this evening. The last time I had such a great time was Thursday on the Union Clipper, before that Monday night's dinner at Leopard, and before that, the cruise on the Liberty II. Not to mention the match at the U.S. Open. You are the common denominator, Tori. I always have the best time when I'm with you."

"Thank you, Knox."

"What did you want to say?"

"I wanted to invite you to the next ballet. It's *Jewels*, and it's in three weeks. Please, say you'll think about it."

"I don't have to think about it. I'd love to come. May I ask you a personal question?"

She nodded.

"At dinner Tuesday, when you mentioned your divorce, you said it would be final soon."

Before he could say more or ask his question, Gemma's voice interrupted their conversation. "Knox, Tori, what did you think? Wasn't the first act beautiful?"

Tori and Knox turned to include Gemma and Graham in their conversation. They all agreed they had seen an extraordinary performance. "I think the best part of this ballet is yet to come," Tori said. "The wedding pas de deux is exquisite. Each move is a lover's gentle caress, and Mendelsohn's String Symphony No. 9 is the perfect accompaniment." She looked at Knox. "And I always bring tissues because I always cry."

Gemma nodded. "Me, too."

When chimes signaled the end of intermission, the balcony began to clear. Tori hung back, letting Graham and Gemma lead the way. She reached for Knox's hand to get his attention.

"October 3rd," she said. "My divorce will be final October 3rd."

Chapter 25
Grand Pas de Deux – Adagio

Sunday, September 10th

As Tori walked up the sidewalk from the parking lot to the Cloisters' entrance, she saw Knox getting out of a yellow cab. He saw her, waved, and walked down the hill to join her.

"Hi," she said. "Perfect timing."

He smiled and said, "I think our timing's been perfect since we met."

His blue-gray eyes held her gaze. She felt as if she'd been hypnotized. She couldn't look away. Imagining the feel of his arms around her, drawing her toward him, leaning down to kiss her, gently at first and then, with all the passion building inside her, caused her cheeks to burn.

"I'd give a lot more than a penny for your thoughts right now, Tori," he said, his voice husky, "Your cheeks have turned a lovely shade of pink," the knuckle of his right hand skimmed the skin of her left cheek, as he added, "and your eyes are…."

The conversation and laughter of four teenage boys walking up the hill from the bus stop broke the spell. Knox put his hand on her upper arm, and together they took a step sideways to the edge of the pavement so the group could walk around them. As the boys passed them, their complaints, "Mr. Corcoran teaches history, so why are we at an art museum?" and "This assignment is so lame!" made Tori snicker and Knox grin.

"So, what do you remember from your high school field trip here?" she asked.

"Not much. When I talked to my mom this morning, she told me the unicorn tapestries are here, but I don't remember them. I do have a weird memory of my friends and me lying on the museum floor. But that can't be right."

She laughed. "It might be. I had to my first time here, a field trip for world literature. We had to lie on the ground next to one of the knights' tombs to compare our height to that of a man from the Middle Ages. Anything else?"

"Nope, that's it."

Tori took a step forward, but Knox stopped her. "Before we go in. I want to say last night was incredible, but I'm happy today is just you and me."

He held out his hand, and she placed hers in his. They walked through the museum's Postern Gate and traveled six hundred years back in time. Tori led Knox to the Gothic chapel and the knights' tombs. The teenagers who had passed them on the sidewalk were there. Two of the boys were lying on the floor. Knox squeezed Tori's hand. "Should we?" he asked. She shook her head. "Not today."

They walked back and forth between the chapel and the Early Gothic Hall, comparing the colors and designs of the stained-glass windows. As they admired the glass-encased Belles Heures, a small prayer book of miniature paintings, Tori said, "The museum turns the pages every day to protect the vibrant colors of the paint. Each time I'm here, I can't wait to see the new page. I like to think the museum's curator changed it just for me." Knox read the wall-mounted sign next to the display case. "Jean, Duc de Berry commissioned the work in 1409. He and the three Dutch brothers who painted the book died of the plague before they were thirty," Knox said.

She nodded. "Yes, a sad reminder to make each day count."

Tori suggested they visit the Treasury Room next. "There's something in here that will make you smile," she told him as she led him to the display case with the Monkey Cup. "We begin here," she said, "and walk around." The story of a sleeping peddler robbed of his wares and clothes by dozens of mischievous apes was painted in enamel on the silver beaker. "According to this wall plaque," Knox said, "the cup celebrates man's folly."

The light in the rooms with the tapestries of the Nine Heroes and the Unicorn was soft and dim to prevent the cloth from deteriorating and the colors fading. From the pamphlet she picked up when they entered, Tori read the story of the *Hunt of the Unicorn* aloud. "'Together, the tapestries tell a tale of noblemen who, with their huntsmen and hounds, pursue a unicorn through a beautiful forest. They track down the unicorn, capture it, take it to a castle, and kill it. In the final tapestry, the unicorn is resurrected and is shown resting in a garden enclosed by a circular fence.'"

"Why were the noblemen hunting the unicorn?" Knox asked. "Does it say?"

"Yes," she said and continued reading. "'The unicorn's true magic lies in its horn's ability to detect the presence of poison and purify water.'"

The first tapestry showed the hunters entering the woods. "The weavers were master artisans and storytellers," Tori said. "Look, the hunters are in formal clothes, so we know what they're hunting is important." As they moved in front of the next tapestry, Knox said, "I see what you mean. Even in this one, the scout's signaling he's spotted something, but we still have no idea it's a unicorn."

When they were in front of the last tapestry, The Unicorn in Captivity, Tori suggested he give her his phone so she could take a picture of him to send his mother. Instead, he put his arm around her waist, tucked her close to his side, and took a selfie.

I need to suggest taking pictures more often.

When they entered the Cuxa Cloister, they had the courtyard and gardens to themselves. Knox led her to a stone bench under the covered portico where they could sit and rest for a while.

"So, October 3rd," he said, "it's only a couple of weeks away. How are you feeling about your divorce?"

"This minute?"

He smiled and nodded.

"This minute, I feel impatient. But give me a minute, and I'm sure that'll change. I'm all over the place—impatient this minute, frustrated the next, sometimes even worried."

"What are you worried about?"

"Oh," she shrugged. "Lots of things. For example, I have nothing legal that identifies me as Victoria Harrigan. I don't think of myself as Victoria Morgano anymore. Inside I feel like Victoria Harrigan. And yet, everything—from my passport to my voter registration card—says I'm not. I can go for days without thinking about it. Then I'll do something ordinary, like charge something in a store, and the clerk says, 'Thank you, Mrs. Morgano.' I want to shout, 'that's not me!' Why don't men have to deal with this mess? See, I change my mind every minute —now I'm annoyed."

"'In a minute there is time,'" Knox began.

Tori chimed in, and together they finished, "'For decisions and revisions which a minute will reverse.'"

"T.S. Eliot sure had my number," she said.

"How did you and Nico meet?" Knox asked.

"Murphy and Dylan's engagement party. Nico was best man. I was Murph's maid of honor. Neither of us was seeing anyone at the time, and there was an undeniable attraction. One thing led to another. I was living in DC at the time and flying to New York often—to shop for bridesmaids' dresses, have fittings. When I wasn't coming to New York, he'd fly to Washington. By the time Murphy and Dylan were married, our relationship was pretty serious, for one that was long-distance. So, I started to look for jobs in New York." She shrugged. "Sometimes I wonder...."

He waited to see if she would continue, and when she didn't, he prompted, "What do you wonder?"

She shrugged again. "Nico and I didn't just grow apart, Knox. He did some outrageous things—things that.... I wonder, 'should I have known?' Did I overlook a clue, something he said or did? I wonder what all that says about my judgment."

After a few minutes of silence, Knox said, "Thank you for telling me."

She nodded. "Sorry. I didn't mean to be such a downer. What do you want to see now?"

"Looks like a garden tour is about to begin. How about if we join in?"

She nodded and smiled. "Yes, let's. I like learning about how plants were used in medicine or art. Some are even said to have magical powers."

After the garden tour was over, Tori and Knox returned to their bench under the portico. The sun was beginning to set, and in the early moments of twilight, the rich colors of the garden's fall flowers, herbs and shrubs faded into a tableau of grays. "I've always thought of this museum as an infinite number of wonderful experiences," Tori said. "The exhibit rooms, the gardens, and courtyards change as the light of the day or the seasons change. It's always different. But I've never been in the courtyard at closing time. Never seen it by the light of a full moon. It's gorgeous!" He squeezed her hand. "But a little spooky, too."

They watched the moon until the guards told them the museum was closing.

Chapter 26
Grand Pas de Deux – First Variation

As they walked from the Cloisters to the parking lot, Knox said, "I don't want the day to end. Have dinner with me?"

"Okay, where should we go?"

"I don't know anything about this part of the City. Any suggestions?"

"In the past four days, we've sailed on a tall ship and traveled back to the Middle Ages. How about if we go to the '76 House? Keep up our history theme."

"I don't know where that is, but you always have the best ideas," he said.

"If you've never been, we have to go."

In the car, Tori made reservations and requested they be seated in the dining room with the King's beams and the portrait.

When she hung up, Knox said, "Sounds like you're a regular. Where are we going?"

"America's oldest restaurant and one of my favorites. It's right up the Palisades Parkway in Tappan." She explained the dining room where they'd be eating was over four hundred years old, and the ceiling beams had been cut from trees owned by the King of England at the time the room was built – King James II.

"Wow! And they're the originals?"

She nodded. "Yep. The bar rail is original to the tavern too."

"Now I can't wait to get there. What about the portrait you mentioned on the phone?"

George Washington had been at the tavern when he'd received irrefutable evidence his friend, Benedict Arnold, was a traitor, Tori explained. "Washington marched over to the fireplace, where a portrait of Arnold hung, took it down and rehung it upside down. That portrait is still there, and it's still upside down."

"Why have I never heard of this place?"

"Do you remember on the Liberty II I told you my family and I moved to northern New Jersey when I started middle school?" she asked.

"Yeah, when I asked you how you'd picked northern New Jersey over other areas to buy your townhouse. You said you and your mother had moved back to Pennsylvania to be closer to family after your father died, but you'd missed New Jersey and thought your memories had called you back."

She nodded, impressed he had remembered so much of her family's history she'd shared with him that day. "Yup, and because my parents and I went to '76 House often, it plays a role in lots of those memories. It's well known in northern New Jersey and this part of New York." The food was excellent, she told him. Her two favorite entrees were the blackened scallops and the brandy apple pork chops. "You can even order Washington's favorite ale," she said before admitting she didn't like it. "But I'm not a fan of dark ales."

As they drove along the Palisades Parkway, Tori opened the car's moon roof so they could see the moon and stars. Knox said, "This is nice. I miss having a car. Not relying on subways or Ubers to get around. With a car, you can just get up and go."

"I know what you mean. I lived on the Upper East Side when I first moved from DC to New York. Not having my car was a huge adjustment. And being able to have one again was a big factor in deciding where I wanted to live and buy a home. While I lived in the City, I kept my car at my mom's in Williamsport. I knew, deep down, I wouldn't be without a car for long."

Knox shared how his lease on the furnished apartment near Lincoln Center would be up in mid-February, and he was looking at places in and around Manhattan. "Since I left for college, I've only lived in dorm rooms or apartments. Even when Tierney and I were married, we lived in family-subsidized housing. A furnished one-bedroom over her parents' garage, and then my aunt and uncle's basement apartment in Boston. Now, I want a house, maybe a car." He told her he had appointments to look at Manhattan brownstones Tuesday and Thursday evenings with his agent and invited her to come along. As she was going to Philadelphia on business Thursday, she agreed to go with him Tuesday evening.

"We could have dinner afterward, discuss the houses. I'd appreciate a second opinion," Knox said.

Minutes later, Tori parked the car in front of a simple brick and stone building. Two American flags with thirteen stars and thirteen stripes hung on either side of the door. "There's not even a sign," Knox said. "If you didn't know about this place, you could drive right past it."

Inside, the host led them to their table. Knox chose Washington's favorite ale and Tori, a diet Coke. They decided on the pork chops and blackened scallops and asked the waiter to have the chef split the dishes in half. "This way, I can try both your favorites," Knox said.

Tori smiled. "I enjoyed today so much. Thank you. An afternoon at the Cloisters was just what I needed. I am, officially, refreshed and recharged."

As they waited for their entrees, he asked her about living in Washington, DC. "I was there three years," she said, "The first two I was in business school, and then I worked for the Treasury Department for a year."

"Did you like living in DC?"

"Yes, very much," she said. "Now, I go for meetings or conferences about four times a year. Sometimes more, so I get my Capitol fix."

"I'm working on several cases with the Securities and Exchange Commission," Knox said. "Maybe we could coordinate our trips—have an evening in DC together?"

"That could be fun. What about you? Did you like living in Boston?" she asked as the waiter served their entrees.

"Yeah, I did. Tierney was working on her MBA, and I was a law student. Our only funds came from the money we'd made working the year between college and grad school and student loans, and we pinched every penny. But we had fun those first two years."

"Two years? What happened your third year of law school, if you don't mind me asking?"

When Tierney finished her MBA, she found a permanent job with a hedge fund in New York, and Knox stayed in Boston to finish law school. "By that time, we both knew our marriage was over. Our high school infatuation had run its course. While it wasn't a foundation for a 'til death do us part' relationship, it was for a friendship." After law school, he'd moved back home to study for the bar. Eighteen months later, when their divorce was final, Tierney moved to Los Angeles.

"Thank you for sharing the story of your divorce with me. That must have been a tough year—the pressures of law school, your marriage ending. I'm so sorry," Tori said.

He nodded. "It was. I threw myself into law review and my studies. It was lonely at first. But, as the year went on, I found I enjoyed exploring Boston on my own. I attribute much of my career success to all my extra studying. All in all, it wasn't such a bad year."

"When did you start working for Sullivan & Casey?"

"The summer I graduated from NYU. Ben and I worked part-time at our parents' law firm during high school and summer breaks. That's where we both discovered our love of the law. Just not the trust, tax, and estate law our parents practice. By the time I graduated from high school, I'd become a pretty good legal researcher. The tax partner at S&C worked closely with my mom, and he offered me a job during my gap year between NYU and Harvard Law. When I returned to S&C the following summer, I started working in securities law. After a few weeks on the job, I was hooked. Two years later, I passed the bar and joined the firm full-time. The opportunity to go to London came up a couple of years later, and I jumped at it."

"An overseas assignment so early in your career—that's impressive," Tori said.

Knox nodded. "Thanks. But I credit my luck at scoring the London position to the legal training I got working for my parents and the 'nose to the grindstone' study strategy my last year in law school."

He raved about both the scallops and pork chops. "Yesterday, I couldn't have told you the last time I'd had scallops," he said, "and now I've eaten them two days in a row. But the dishes are so different. The Grand Marnier drizzle takes it to a new level."

"And don't you love the brandied apples with the pork?" Tori asked. "By the way, I want to compliment you on handling the interrogation you got over dinner last night. You managed very well and were a good sport. I know Dylan thought he was being subtle because he didn't strap you to the booth and shine a light in your face."

Knox laughed. "He's quite protective of you. Have you heard how I did? Did I pass muster?"

"You held your own," she assured him.

"It's good to know I got the 'friends' stamp of approval!" He paused before continuing, "May I ask—and you don't have to tell me, but you have terrific friends who look out for you. Above and beyond, I mean. Does it have to do with your divorce?"

She nodded. "Yes. This afternoon, I told you Nico had done some outrageous things." She paused before continuing, "For starters, he had an affair. He betrayed his brother and lied to his best friend—even tried to jeopardize Dylan's career for his own selfish reasons." She took a sip of water and focused her attention on the spoon beside her plate as the thumb and index finger of her right hand traced the spoon's handle. "For weeks, the gut punch I'd felt when I first learned of the affair would hit me again, when I least expected it, and the pain would take my breath. The day Dylan learned he couldn't trust the man who had been his best friend for two decades? Well, I had a ringside seat. Although he and I have only talked about it once, I know we both ask ourselves, 'what didn't we see?', 'what changed and why?' And Nico's brother…."

"Wow! Sounds like you've all been dealing with a lot. I'm so sorry, Tori. Thank you for telling me," Knox said.

"Could we change the subject? Maybe something a little less serious?" Tori asked.

"Good idea," Knox said. "Let's talk about next weekend. What shall we do?"

"Don't you have to go house-hunting? I feel guilty monopolizing so much of your time."

"I'm going Tuesday and Thursday, remember? Now, about the weekend," he said.

"You decide," she said.

"What?"

Tori looked down and straightened the napkin in her lap while she gathered her thoughts. "Knox, I like you a lot. But since we met, I've been the one to plan, organize, and suggest things we could do." She sighed. "What I'm trying to say, if you're interested in seeing where this goes, that's fantastic. I'm all in, but not as the camp counselor organizing events. And if you're not, that's okay, too. I know I'm dragging around some baggage for the next few weeks. No worries."

He reached over and took her hand. "Tori, I felt the attraction the minute I saw you. I'm all in, too."

She smiled and squeezed his hand. She fought the tears that threatened to fill her eyes. "Thank you, Knox."

He brought her hand to his lips and kissed it. "So, take out your calendar. Let's start planning."

He brought up the *New York Times* app on his phone and scrolled to the Arts & Leisure section. "I haven't been to a Broadway show for a while. Tell me what you'd like to see, and I'll try to get tickets for Saturday night or Sunday afternoon."

Together they selected two shows, a musical and a drama, they both wanted to see.

"What about the following weekend?" he asked. "Since Ben's going to New Haven to attend a law school buddy's wedding, I'm the designated son in a Father-Son golf tournament Saturday at my parents' club. But I'm free Sunday if you are, Tori."

"I'm going to the Yankee—Mariners' game," she said. "But I was given two tickets if you'd be interested in joining me. The seats are incredible, and we can have dinner at the stadium. There won't be blackened scallops with a drizzle of Grand Marnier, but I can promise delicious hot dogs with lots of yellow mustard, pickle relish, and chopped onions."

"Sounds perfect! We go to the best places! Today was incredible. Thank you, Tori." He pulled his phone from the back pocket of his jeans, and she watched him pull up the Uber app.

"I had a great time, too, Knox," she said. "Before I drive you home…." He began to object, but she said, "No, it's no trouble. I'm going to stop home first. Pick up Baron. The boys next door walked and fed him a few hours ago. Other than that, he's been alone all afternoon, and I'd feel better if he were with us."

Chapter 27
Grand Pas de Deux – Second Variation

As Tori pulled away from the '76 House, Bette Midler began to sing *From a Distance*, Lulu's ringtone, and her friend's name appeared on the navigation screen. She pushed the talk button and said, "Hi, Lulu. I have…"

"Where are you? You sound like you're in the car," Lulu said. "Murph's worried. She called you twice in the last thirty minutes, and you didn't answer. Why didn't you answer?"

"I didn't hear my phone ring," Tori said. "What's up?"

"My ringtone you heard, but you missed the *Star Wars* theme not once but twice? What were you doing?" Lulu asked. "Murph said you were supposed to spend the afternoon with Knox, but she expected you home hours ago. When she didn't hear from you, when you didn't answer your phone…She wanted to have Dylan drive to your house to check. But I told her I'd try. I'm texting her now, and I'll call her when we hang up," Lulu continued. "Verdict on Knox is he's terrific, and Murph said a real stud muffin. How was your afternoon at the Cloisters?"

"Hi Lulu, this is Knox. We had a fantastic time at the Cloisters and just finished a delicious dinner at '76 House. Thanks for asking. And for sharing the 'stud muffin' review. I hope to meet you and Tom in person soon."

Lulu laughed. "We're looking forward to meeting you, too, Knox. Sorry, Tor."

"No worries, Lu. I'm driving Knox home after we make a quick stop at the townhouse and pick up Baron. Please call Murph and tell her not to worry. It may be too late to call when I get home—it's a school night."

"Got it," Lulu said. "I'm glad Baron's going with you. I'll call Murphy, have her stand down. Have fun, you two. We'll talk tomorrow, girl."

"So, my reviews from last night seem to be pretty good. I'm a stud muffin!" He chuckled, then waited a few moments before continuing, "But what am I missing? Your friends are protective—I get that—but there's something more. You said earlier you were worried. At dinner, you told me Nico deceived you and destroyed his relationship with his brother and Dylan. Are you afraid of him?."

She nodded. "A little." She told Knox about the prowler on the porch when she'd been at the beach and running into Nico outside Fraunces Tavern.

"'Of all the gin joints,'" Knox said.

She nodded. "The creepiest part? He lurked outside the restaurant for nearly forty minutes to confront me. Nico was drunk and looking for a fight. I was so grateful your brother and Graham were with me." The phone calls to the office began two days later. "The caller ID just displayed a number, no name," she said. When she heard his voice, she wrote down the phone number and hung up. The security department investigated what she reported as a harassing phone call. The number belonged to a burner phone, and security blocked it. But a week later, she received another call—from a different number she also had blocked. "He called twice when I wasn't at my desk and left voicemails."

"What did he want? Do you know?"

She admitted she'd listened to the voicemails, hoping he would say something her attorney, Ivy, might be able to use against him. "But he didn't say anything that would sound threatening, although he knows just calling would upset me."

Nico hadn't stopped with phone calls, she told him. He'd sent a large bouquet of flowers to her office addressed to Victoria Morgano. "The receptionist called me when they arrived to check they were for me. I'm the only Victoria on the floor."

"Did you throw them out?"

"No. I pretended I had an allergy to stargazer lilies and asked her to keep them in reception. Although I know she had to be curious about my name, how the card was addressed."

A week later, a box of Fairy Tale brownies, addressed to Victoria Morgano, was waiting at her front door when she arrived home from work. "Each time he sends me something, calls me, he knows I'll get aggravated, which is exactly what he wants. But to a judge, to the average person—a glass of wine, a bouquet of flowers, or a box of brownies doesn't sound like harassment."

As she pulled into her driveway, Knox said, "He's devious. You're right. On the surface, all those things sound benign. Do you think he's capable of violence?"

"As late as three months ago, I would have said, 'No,' but now?" she shrugged. "Nico's world has imploded, and he's cast me in the role of the villain—his own personal Cruella de Vil. When he's angry, he lashes out. Which is why we're stopping to get my bodyguard."

Knox turned to look at her house, which was ablaze with light. "Your house is very nice and *very* well lit."

She laughed. "I feel safer knowing my home is visible from the International Space Station. Seriously, though, if the lights discourage anyone from walking around, I'm good with that. Come on. There's someone very important you need to meet."

When they entered the townhouse, Tori heard Baron's nails hitting the hardwood floors in the kitchen as he leapt and danced in anticipation of seeing her. After calming him down and introducing him to Knox, she said, "Baron's a ladies' man, and he doesn't take to men right away." Knox crouched down after she made the introductions, and to her surprise, Baron sniffed his hand and gave Knox a sloppy kiss on the chin after receiving a few pets and neck scratches.

Baron retrieved his leash from its hook by the side of the door and brought it to Tori. The trio exited the back door and headed for the boardwalk along the Hudson River. After a brief walk, they went to the car, and Baron curled up on his bed in the back seat.

They finalized plans for Tuesday evening during the drive to Knox's apartment. Then, he asked her how Nico's world had collapsed. "Since last December, Nico has been denied a promotion he wanted, been fired from his job, and had his CPA license revoked. Members of his family and his best friend want nothing to do with him. He can't accept responsibility for any of those things. So, he blames me for all of it."

After she put the car in park in front of Knox's apartment building, she turned to the back seat and said, "Okay, Baron, you're on duty." The dog opened his eyes, wagged his tail, and sat straight in his seat.

When she turned back to say good night to Knox, he cupped her cheeks with his hands and leaned forward so his forehead touched hers. "I'm so sorry he's doing this to you. And, just so you know, I'm impatient for October 3rd, too," he said.

Chapter 28
Grand Pas de Deux – Coda

Two Weeks Later

On Sunday afternoon, Tori decided to walk the twenty blocks from Port Authority to Columbus Circle, where she was to meet Knox to catch the subway to Yankee Stadium. The weather was perfect for a walk and a baseball game—mostly sunny skies, and cooler autumn temperatures. She hoped the exercise would exorcise the grumpy mood she'd been in all week and help calm her jittery nerves. Last Monday morning, she'd gotten up on the wrong side of the bed, and for the remainder of the week, she'd felt uneasy, unsettled, as if another shoe were about to drop.

And then it did.

Damn balloons, she thought. The confidence she'd gained after her first self-defense class had evaporated the minute she saw them and read the card. Why won't he leave me alone?

As she waited for the light on Central Park West to change, she saw Knox standing by the subway entrance, scanning the crowd of pedestrians looking for her. By the time the light changed, and she navigated her way across the wide street, he was at the curb. He put his arm around her waist and led her to one side of the subway entrance.

"Are you still shook up about the balloons?" he asked. "You look tired. I'm guessing you didn't sleep well."

She nodded and took a deep breath before pressing the index finger of each hand under her eyes to hold back tears.

Yesterday, she and Murphy had gone to the Short Hills Mall for a morning of shopping and lunch. Murphy was looking for a dress to wear to the managing partner's dinner at Dylan's law firm, and Tori was hoping to find something new to wear to Graham and Gemma's wedding. She also wanted to kick her lingerie up several notches. She was ready to feel desirable and sexy again.

The success of the shopping trip and spending the day with her friend buoyed her spirits. On the way home, she and Murph opened the car's moonroof, turned on her playlist of oldies, and sang along at the top of their lungs.

Until the security alert on Tori's phone signaled someone was on her front porch. Murphy grabbed Tori's cell phone, silenced the music, and opened the security app. "It's a woman," Murphy reported. Then, she flipped to the driveway camera and confirmed a white van from Creative Balloons, Custom Bouquets for Every Occasion, was parked there.

"I'll flip back to your front door, get a look at what she dropped off," Murph said. "Who do you think sent them?"

"Nico's the only person I can think of who'd send me balloons. You can look, but don't tell me. Their presence is upsetting enough—I don't need to know more until I'm home."

Sure enough, an arrangement of ten mylar balloons of the elongated face, hollow eye sockets, and open mouth of the Scream movie monster tethered to a weight with black ribbons was at her front door. The gentle afternoon breeze caused the ghoulish faces to bob and weave in a macabre dance on Tori's porch.

"Is there a card?" Murphy asked. Tori nodded and handed it to her. "The only word on the card is TEN. What the hell does that mean? I get there are ten balloons, but…."

"October 3rd is ten days away," Tori said.

Then she took a picture of the gruesome bouquet to send to her attorney, while Murphy went inside to retrieve two pairs of sharp scissors and a garbage bag. Together, they poked holes in, cut up, and threw away the ten gruesome faces. As Murphy stooped to pick up the weight that had kept the balloons from floating away, she said, "Geez! This is heavy. If someone clunked you on the head with this thing, you'd be a goner!"

It might have been the power of Murphy's suggestion or maybe just her own fears, but several hours before dawn, Tori's nightmare that Nico had thrown that balloon weight through her living room window woke her. She'd been unable to shake the image or go back to sleep.

Now, she took a deep, shuddering breath before looking up at Knox.

"Yes," she said, "The hideous balloons, the card with its one-word message? It has me wondering—what's next?"

"You think there's more coming?"

She shrugged. "Maybe. The good news is Nico's not creative enough to come up with something for every day. He knew this would upset me, and I'm reacting exactly like he wants me to."

"Divorce, even one as amicable as mine was, is never easy. But this guy," Knox shook his head, "this guy is crazy."

Tori nodded. "Let's not talk about estranged husbands or creepy balloons. I'm excited we're going to the game. It should be a real good match-up. And seeing you has brightened the grumpy mood I've been in all week."

Knox smiled. "Deal. I'm looking forward to the game, too". He took her hand, and they walked down the steps to the subway platform.

"By the way, before I forget, Knox. Dylan wanted me to be sure to tell you he was thrilled you missed him and thought about him all day yesterday. He can't wait to see you again either," she said.

When Knox had called her last night, Tori's phone had been downstairs charging. She and Murphy were upstairs on Murphy's iPad, talking to Lulu. Dylan had answered Tori's phone.

Knox rolled his eyes. "Yeah, I learned my lesson. I'll wait until I hear your voice, Tori, before saying anything. I did miss you yesterday. I kept wishing I was spending the afternoon with you and not in the rough looking for my ball. My game was so off—Dad and I had a terrible round. Ranked third—from the bottom."

"Knox, I promise the next time Murph and I plan an afternoon of shopping, I'll be sure to include you. She'll be delighted. Just mentioning Neiman's or Nordstrom's makes Dylan twitch."

When the doors of the D train opened, several passengers got off, and Tori and Knox found two seats. As they settled in for the ride to the Bronx, Knox said, "I have some big news."

"You made an offer on a house?"

He shook his head. "Better."

"You made an offer on a house, and it was accepted?"

"Better," he said again.

"Did you hire a new real estate agent?" She hadn't been impressed with the one who had shown them houses Tuesday evening.

"Yes, but that's not the news. Ben called me last night after the wedding. All he could talk about was a woman he sat next to at the reception. Kelly Barnett. She's a close friend of the bride's—they went to Pritzker Law School together. She clerked for a federal judge in Chicago for a year after graduation and joined one of the top firms there. Now, she's working on a big case with several partners from the New York office, and she'll be moving here before the end of the year. He seems quite intrigued. And he's flying to Chicago to visit her next Friday for the weekend."

"Ooh la la," Tori said. "I wonder if he'll mention meeting her tomorrow when Graham and I ask about the wedding."

"All he could tell me about the wedding was the food was pretty good, and the bride wore a white dress. But he described in detail what Kelly wore—an emerald-green dress that matched her eyes and showcased what he described as her 'sensational legs.'"

"Ooh! He's got it bad."

"I know, right?" he grinned. "Payback for all the ribbing I've taken lately."

Ribbing? About you and me? That thought made Tori smile.

Soon they were exiting the train and walking toward Yankee Stadium. As they lined up to go through the Stadium's security checkpoint and turnstiles, Knox said, "I've been thinking about something you said the other night. You called The Cloisters a place to reflect and recharge. And yet you didn't go there for nearly a year. Why not? I would have thought just the opposite."

As Tori placed her purse on the white folding table and opened it for the guard to inspect, she said, "No, too peaceful. My mood was more in line with Rodin's Gates of Hell."

"'Abandon all hope, ye who enter here?'"

"Yup. I think of Dante as one of my tour guides through the stages of grief. I sped through denial, got stuck in anger, and when I finally transitioned to bargaining, I wasn't interested in negotiating with the universe to get Nico back. I was more into revenge plots like if the judge tripled Eena's prison sentence, I'd give up wine and ice cream for a year."

"Eena. What an odd name! Was that Nico's mistress?" he asked.

"Yup. And his brother's wife. Correction. Ex-wife. As of a couple of months ago. Ben knew. Nico mentioned Eena that day outside Fraunces Tavern. Didn't your brother tell you any of this?"

"What? Nico had an affair with your sister-in-law?"

She nodded. "Yup. Double-header. Eena and I disliked each other from the start. But Sal, Nico's brother—I introduced you to him in the food court at the Open—has always had a girlfriend on the side. Once upon a time, I felt sorry for her." Tori shook her head.

As they started to walk around the stadium to their gate, Knox asked, "How did you find out about the affair? Did he tell you?"

"No. I learned about the affair while Nico and Eena were enjoying a romantic tryst in Paris. He told me he was going to London for a workshop, then business meetings. When he didn't call me or return my calls, I did a little digging, and with a colleague's help, I learned he'd escorted Mrs. V. Morgano to Paris. Just not this Mrs. V. Morgano. When he came home, I confronted him and filed for divorce."

"What a lowlife! Tori, I'm so sorry. No one, especially you, deserves to be treated like that, lied to."

"Thank you, Knox."

"By the way, Ben and I made a pact. I don't tell him what we talk about or do. What you share with him is between the two of you. But you were joking, right? Eena isn't really going to prison."

"Yes, she is. She pled guilty to fraud charges this summer, but I don't know when she'll be sentenced."

"Fraud?"

Tori nodded. "There's so much more to this story, and someday soon, I'll tell you the whole sordid tale. But not today. Let's have fun. Enjoy the game. We're almost at our gate."

"One more question?"

She sighed but smiled so he knew she wasn't annoyed. "Okay, one more."

"I'm guessing your bargain with the universe didn't work?"

"I had a glass of wine and pistachio ice cream at Shun Lee the night we went to the ballet. Believe me, if the universe had upheld its end, I would have, cheerfully, honored mine."

As they walked down the steps to the Field Level MVP seats, Tori heard Knox whisper, "Oh. My. God." Their seats were right behind home plate and the Yankee dugout.

"Tori, these seats are some of the best in the stadium. They go for hundreds of dollars each. How did you score such amazing tickets?" he asked as they sat down.

Just then, the opening bars of Take Me Out to the Ballgame filled the stadium. Tori stood. Laughing and jumping in place, she began to wave and then threw a sweeping kiss toward the scoreboard. As she sat down again, she said, "He saw us. He knows we're here."

"Who saw us? Who knows we're here?"

"My friend, Eddie. He's the organist and a New York legend. We're sitting in his seats. He played Take Me Out to the Ballgame, so I'd know he saw us."

Her phone buzzed, and she pulled it out of her jacket pocket to read the text.

Eddie: What's your friend's name?

Tori: Knox Cooper

She started to tell Knox how she'd met Eddie years earlier. "He lives in the same apartment building as Nico's mother. She wasn't particularly fond of me, so I often hung out at Eddie's."

"No way! Look!" Knox pointed to the jumbotron.

"The New York Yankees Welcome Tori Harrigan and Knox Cooper," followed by a giant red heart, filled the screen and was instantly replaced with a live picture of the two of them – with the words 'Kiss Cam' printed across the bottom.

"I'm not too embarrassed," Tori said through gritted teeth.

Knox cupped her chin with his hand and turned her face toward him. His lips touched hers, and his kiss was gentle.

Wow! Tori felt her cheeks flush. That one gentle kiss had been electrifying.

When they were no longer on camera, he said, "I'm following your lead, Tori. I'm waiting until October 3rd. When I kiss you the next time, I won't stop at one, and it won't be in front of a capacity crowd."

Chapter 29
Roses, Snakes & Signs

Tuesday, September 26th

Tuesday, Tori watched Knox's smile disappear as she entered Hale & Hearty for their lunch date. She knew he'd spotted her bandaged left hand.

"What happened to your hand?" he asked.

"Hi. How are you? How was your morning?"

"Sorry, I'll start again. Hi, Tori. I'm fine. What happened to your hand?"

"Let's find a table, order, and get our drinks first."

He led her to a table in the corner before going to the counter to place their order for two bowls of cream of mushroom soup. Then he stood in line to access the ice and soft drink dispensers.

"Okay. We have drinks. I ordered lunch. Now, tell me about the bandages on your left hand."

Before she had a chance to say anything, his name was called. Their order was ready.

When he was seated again, Tori took out her phone and clicked on a picture of eight black and gray snakeskin tubes lined up on her front porch.

"What am I looking at?" Knox asked.

"You know those fake snakes with springs inside that fly out of cans when you open them?"

"Yeah?"

"These eight serpents were stuffed in my mailbox. After work, I took Baron for a walk, and before we went inside, I stopped to get the mail. Like I do every night. I opened the mailbox, and all eight snakes sprang out at me. I was startled, stepped back, tripped over Baron, and fell on my butt—half in the driveway, half on the lawn. My left hand and wrist got cut up on the gravel."

"Tori, you could have been seriously hurt. How bad is your hand? What did you do?"

"Washed it, wrapped a clean towel around it to stop the bleeding, and fed Baron. Then, I gathered the snakes and put them on the porch before I drove to the doc-in-the-box down the street. They cleaned my hand again and wrapped it in the ace bandage. I had to have a tetanus shot because, when they asked me, I couldn't remember the last time I'd had one. When I got home, I lined these guys up and took the picture before throwing them in the garbage for today's pickup. And then, I iced my wrist. It feels much better this morning."

"You drove yourself? To an urgent care? With a sprained wrist?"

"Yeah, it wasn't a big deal. My hand doesn't hurt. My wrist is a little tender, but I'm just wearing the ace bandage because the doctor said to, and I want the attention. I'm fine."

He reached for her left hand, and she winced when he held it.

He shook his head. "Doesn't hurt, huh? Do you still have the picture of the flowers?"

"Yeah. Swipe right."

Sunday afternoon, just as the Yankees had retired the side in the fourth inning, Tori had received an alert on her phone. Her driveway and front porch cameras had confirmed the signature gray Amazon van in her driveway and a delivery person dropping off a box at her door. "Probably just one of my subscription orders," she told Knox, "like printer paper or ink cartridges."

That evening when she opened the package, she discovered nine black fabric roses in three neat rows. Nine plastic eyeballs, each with bloody red streaks, stared up at her from the center of each rose. When she called Knox to tell him she was home safe and sound, she told him about the flowers.

Now Knox said, "Nico needs to be stopped. I can't imagine what today's contribution will be."

"Oh, I already know—it was on the front lawn when I got up this morning. Swipe left."

He did. Next to the black mailbox was a yard sign—#1 Bitch.

Knox frowned, then said, "Okay, I get it. Day seven. Five letters, plus one number, and a character." He rolled his eyes.

"I texted a few neighbors, but none of them saw anything, and all my security cameras are positioned to catch someone prowling around the house and porch."

"I can't believe what a sick…." Knox shook his head.

"What bothers me the most is the planning. This creepy countdown calendar wasn't hatched last Saturday. Coming up with immature pranks for every day might be Nico, but figuring out Sunday's delivery would have to be from a place that delivers on Sunday, like Amazon, ordering a custom yard sign. It takes days to get those things printed. No, the planning has Eena's fingerprints all over it."

He handed her back her phone. "Eena must be a nasty piece of work."

"She is." Tori sighed.

"Talking about Nico and Eena is enough to give us indigestion. Pull out your calendar. Let's make plans for the rest of this week. Are you free for dinner tomorrow evening?" Knox asked.

She shook her head. "No, I'm giving a presentation at a workshop in mid-town tomorrow morning, and I'm part of a panel discussion after lunch. Since I was going to be in the area, I signed up to do the five o'clock docent tour at Lincoln Center. I'll just want to head home afterward."

"How about Thursday?"

"Book club at my house. Have to set up snacks and drinks for the ladies."

"Friday?"

She shook her head again. "Nope. Grocery shopping with Murphy. About once a month in the fall and winter, we get together and cook things—like chili, beef stew, and Bolognese. You know, dishes that are impractical for a single person or even a couple to make. But three or more? We each get enough to enjoy a couple of meals, but we're not eating the same thing once a week for months. We're shopping Friday, cooking Sunday."

"Wow! You are busy! So, when am I going to see you?"

"You're buying me dinner Saturday night, and then we're going to the ballet, remember?"

"And then I go to DC for meetings Monday and Tuesday. I won't be back until Tuesday evening. I won't be here October 2nd or 3rd."

"No big deal. Baron and I are planning quiet evenings before and after the hearing. But I will be accepting phone calls."

He chuckled. "Got it. What about the weekend after October 3rd?"

"Murph and I are meeting Lulu at a spa in the Berkshires for two days of pampering. Picturing mindfulness meditation sessions and Tai Chi walks, imagining I'm floating weightless in the cocoon envelopment bed while being massaged with warm vanilla cream is helping me get out of bed in the morning."

He smiled. "That sounds like the perfect way to relax after all the strain you've been under. The next weekend is my birthday. I want to spend it with you. Put it in your calendar now."

"Two things before I commit to anything—first, what about your family? Won't they want to celebrate your birthday with you? And second, your brother went whitewater rafting for his birthday. You aren't planning to have us jump out of a plane or repel down a cliff, are you?"

"No, no skydiving, maybe a little dinner and dancing. I'll talk to everyone, but I'm not spending the weekend with them. By the way, while you have your phone out, please text me George's information. I'd like to arrange for him to take me to the airport on Monday."

Chapter 30
The Beheading of Ursula

Wednesday, September 27th

"Ladies and Gentlemen, this concludes our tour of the David H. Koch Theatre. Are there any questions?" Tori asked, looking out at the nearly thirty faces staring back at her from the center orchestra seats. Then she turned her attention to the left section, where a handful of tourists had chosen to sit. A hand was in the air. Since the auditorium lighting was dim and the person was seated behind a tall, heavyset man, she could only see the raised hand.

"Yes," she said. "Could you please stand so I can see and hear you more clearly?"

Knox stood. His grin went from ear to ear. "Ms. Harrigan, can you hear me?"

She looked down at her feet, trying to compose herself. She didn't want to laugh. How? When had Knox joined the group? He hadn't been with them earlier when they toured the David Geffen Hall or even fifteen minutes ago when they'd been upstairs in the Promenade. Of that, she was certain.

"Yes, sir, you have a question?"

"You mentioned a couple of times this stage holds several surprises that contribute to the magic of certain ballets. Could you elaborate? Tell us some of the tricks?"

Tori smiled. "No."

She paused for several seconds before continuing. "But in late November, the company will begin performances of The Nutcracker, and the magic of Mr. Balanchine's staging uses many of those special surprises."

"I'd love to see that ballet. Do you think I might be able to get a ticket?"

"Yes, I believe if you wanted a ticket, one would be available."

"One more question?"

She nodded.

"A person whose opinion I value very much told me her favorite ballet is The Sleeping Beauty. I understand the Company is performing that ballet later this year. Could you tell us about it?

"Your friend has exceptional taste. Sleeping Beauty is one of the most elaborate productions performed by the Company. The costumes and stage settings are beautiful, and more than one hundred dancers, including students from the School of American Ballet, dance at each performance. The first performance of Sleeping Beauty is on October 18th."

"And how difficult will it be to get a ticket for that ballet?"

"If you wanted to attend, getting a ticket shouldn't be a problem."

She looked at the audience. "If there are no other questions," she paused. No one raised their hand. "Please exit the auditorium to your left. We'll pass the restrooms on our way to the lobby if anyone needs to stop. We'll meet at the fountain before we tour the Metropolitan Opera House, the largest of the three theatres we're visiting today."

Knox walked up beside her.

"What are you doing here?" she whispered.

"I missed you. Since you told me about the Chagal murals, I've been meaning to take this tour. So, I thought today would be perfect because the docent's a friend of mine." He smiled. "I hated not being able to call you today. How was the workshop?"

"Good. How was your day?"

"All right. I spent most of it in meetings. I never feel I've accomplished much on days like this." He lifted her left hand. "A few scabs but not too bad. Don't like to see you still wearing the ace bandage, though. Any updates on the countdown calendar?"

"It was a good day all around. Today's entry was pretty cute." She showed him a picture of six cookies, each a Disney villainess. "They came during lunch from Edible Art Bakery. Their stuff is delicious, and they can create almost any design you want. See? The Evil Queen from Snow White, Cruella de Vil, Maleficent, Cinderella's wicked stepmother, the Queen of Hearts, and Ursula."

"What happened to poor Ursula?"

"Sadly, Graham had already beheaded her before Coop took the picture."

"Before we continue the tour, I need to know. Did you just invite me to see Sleeping Beauty and The Nutcracker?"

She nodded. "I'm hesitant to extend this invitation, but if you'd like to see a rehearsal of The Nutcracker, we can do that. It's fun, but I must warn you. All the stage's secrets hidden with sets and lighting during the performance, things that make the ballet magical, are on full display in a rehearsal."

"I'd love to see all the behind-the-scenes stuff. Are you sure I can't take you to dinner after we finish here?"

"I'm sure. I just want to go home and put my feet up. But after we tour the Opera House, you can walk me to Port Authority."

Chapter 31

Day Five – Five Photos

Thursday, September 28th

"Thanks for coming so quickly, Chuck," Tori said.

"Of course," He took the seat opposite her. "Sounds like we've had a serious security breach."

"A convicted felon, awaiting sentencing, able to enter the building, access this floor, and leave an envelope for me at reception? Yes, I'd say so."

Chuck Flynn was the chief of security for One New York Plaza. Tori asked him to come to her office after opening the FedEx envelope she found on her desk after lunch. Instead of the new client forms she was expecting, she found five photographs, four of Eena alone and one of Eena and Nico together. All five pictures had been taken on their infamous tryst to Paris last April. Two provocative photos of Eena, one in a red lace bustier, thong, and garter belt and another of her in a black see-through negligee, Nico had taken in their room at the Hotel Splendid Etoile. The Arc de Triomphe framed by the room's open French doors. The other three pictures had been taken at some of Tori's favorite spots in and around Paris. Places she'd introduced Nico to on their trips.

When she first looked at the pictures, her stomach churned, and the back of her neck felt damp and clammy. Her mouth felt dry, so she grabbed the half-empty water bottle she'd opened before lunch and drank until it was empty. *Why am I so upset? I knew they'd gone to Paris.* The longer she stared at the photos, her shock morphed into anger. Her grip on the pictures tightened until one side of the photos was scrunched and crumpled in her fist. *Those places, those memories were mine! How dare he take her to my hotel, my favorite places?*

After several deep breaths, Tori lay the pictures on the desk and smoothed out, as best she could, the creases she had just made in them before placing them in a file folder and carrying them to the copy room. Then, when she was alone, she copied them. Finally, back in her office, she slid the originals into the envelope, tucked the copies in her messenger bag, and called Chuck.

Now, Tori handed him the envelope. "After I opened it and saw the contents, I looked at the shipping label. It's an obvious fake. The account number isn't even the nine-digit FedEx standard. Our receptionist told me a woman claiming the envelope had been delivered to her office by mistake dropped it off shortly after I left for lunch."

Chuck examined the label before pulling out the pictures. Eena—at Café de la Comedie, in Montmartre, at the Hotel Splendid Etôile, and at Malmaison with Nico.

"After you called, I checked this morning's visitors log," Chuck said. "No one named 'Morgano' was listed, but as you suspected, there was a 'Barsotti.' According to the log, a woman using that surname signed in at eleven fifteen, and the guard verified her identity with her driver's license. She signed out at twelve-thirty."

Tori nodded. "I thought she might have gone back to her maiden name."

"Do you know who the man is?" Chuck held up the picture taken at Malmaison.

"Yes. Nicolino Morgano. In five days, he'll be my ex-husband. He and the woman are," she paused, "involved."

"Tell me why you suspected this woman as the person who made the delivery," Chuck said, holding up the picture of Eena at the café.

"The photos. And the receptionist's description. A woman about my age, height, and build, with dark brown hair, pulled back in a chignon. She was wearing a Chanel suit, Louboutin's, and an unusual pendant on a platinum chain—three different-sized squares, one on top of the other, with a different shaped diamond in each square. That woman," Tori pointed to the picture, "my former sister-in-law, only wears designer suits, loves Louboutin's, and the necklace is one-of-a-kind. Her parents had it made for her. She never takes it off."

"Your photos will help us identify her on the CC-TV footage. She's looking directly at the camera and looks more like the description the receptionist gave me and less like the woman who entered the building." He handed Tori two screenshots. The first was a picture of Eena at the guard station signing in. Her shoulder-length hair was loose, parted on the side, and styled, so it partially covered the right side of her face. In the second—the photo taken for her visitor's badge—Eena was wearing glasses with large tortoiseshell frames.

"Whoa! She does look different in these pictures. Chuck, yesterday, I received a delivery from Edible Art Bakery at about the same time as today's FedEx drop-off. Unfortunate coincidence or dress rehearsal for today?"

"I'll have my team pull the film from the lobby, elevators, and this floor for yesterday and today," he said. "We'll account for Ms. Barsotti's movements while she was in the building. Why do you think she would go to this much trouble to harass you?"

"Do you recognize Ms. Barsotti from the news? She was arrested as part of that medical insurance scandal involving doctors and other medical personnel on Long Island. She tried to recruit me, and I told the authorities. She and my soon-to-be ex blame me for, among other things, her arrest. In the past several months, I've received harassing phone calls and deliveries, both here and at home. I'm sure they're behind them. But I can't prove it. Any evidence your team can put together will be the only proof I have she and my estranged husband are behind the stalking."

"We'll get right on it, and I'll keep you posted. Call me if anything else happens."

After Chuck left her office, Tori briefed Esta, Cooper, and Graham on the security breach and her meeting with Chuck. Then, Esta gathered the entire staff for an emergency meeting. She explained Tori had received suspicious packages on two consecutive days. "These deliveries may have been reconnaissance for something bigger. Because we have a responsibility to protect ourselves and each other and because we deal with confidential client information and sensitive proprietary data, we need to be careful about who's on our floor," she reminded them. "Meet every visitor at the elevators. Make sure you're always wearing your ID badge, and check that everyone you see has either an employee or a visitor ID. If not, call security immediately."

When the meeting was over, Tori looked at her watch—she was emotionally drained. It was not even four o'clock, and the walls of her office felt as if they were closing in on her. She took out her phone and dialed Knox. He answered on the first ring.

"This afternoon's been one for the record books. I need a drink, a shoulder to cry on, and a responsible adult to walk me to the ferry. In that order. Know anyone who might be available?"

"I'm your man. Meet up at Beckett's in fifteen minutes?"

At Beckett's Bar, they found a booth in the back and ordered. When the waiter had brought them their drinks, Tori told him about finding the envelope and her meeting with Chuck. "The good news is I may finally have evidence for a restraining order."

"Tori, I hope you know you can trust me. Last Sunday at Yankee Stadium, you said you'd tell me the whole story. How about now?"

"I do trust you. And now seems as good a time as any."

She took a sip of her Jack Rose before beginning. "Nico and I had a minor fender-bender New Years' Day. The passenger side took the brunt of the impact, and I had some pretty bad bruising. A week later, we had dinner with Eena before meeting Sal for the theatre. That's when Eena encouraged us to make some money from the accident."

For the next few minutes, Tori described the scam Eena had proposed that evening, how intrigued Nico had been by it, and how he and Eena had filed claim after claim for the next three months. "I learned about their affair on Thursday, and the following Monday, First Dominion investigators were questioning me about fraudulent medical bills, bank accounts I knew nothing about," Tori said. "It was a terrifying experience. Not to mention infuriating—they financed their affair with that stolen money."

Knox said, "That's some story. I can't believe they set you up like that."

Tori nodded. "I still shudder, get a sick feeling in the pit of my stomach when I think about those hours in the 'interrogation room.' So many things had to line up just right—so many 'if's.' What if Eena had waited to talk to Nico about the scam when I wasn't around? Or if she hadn't texted me the doctors' contact information, even after I told her not to? Or if I hadn't made the connection between the name of the acupuncturists' practice and a favorite short story?" She shook her head, and they sat silently for a few minutes.

Then, Tori looked at her watch. "As scary as that whole experience was, I was quite lucky in the long run. I hate to drop my story, drink, and run, but I'll need to head out soon if I'm going to catch the last ferry. When you get home, google Valentina Morgano and Fraudster Pharmacist. You were still in London when the scandal hit the papers."

"Tori, you are so brave, strong, smart," he said. "How you put that whole thing together, even while you were being questioned, accused? I am in awe of you. All that he's put you through…."

"I have my moments," she said. "Family and good friends have gotten me through this."

"I hope I'm among the good friends," he said.

"Yes, you are."

"Tonight's a beautiful night for a boat ride. May I ride with you so we can enjoy the sunset together?"

Chapter 32

A Visit from Arachne

Friday, September 29th

"Eewww!" Tori screamed. She'd reached for her mail, and instead, she'd grabbed something hairy. That moved! She felt it crawling over her right hand, up her arm, pricking her, pinching her. She banged her hand against the metal sides and rounded top of the mailbox as she pulled her arm out—trying to shake off or squish whatever was wiggling up her arm.

Something with glowing eyes fell to the ground and began to move. Several pairs of glowing eyes stared back at her from inside the mailbox. She slammed the door shut.

"Tori, everything okay?" Murphy called from the car.

She shook her head. "No. Bring your phone."

When Murphy was beside her, Tori pointed to the ground. "And there are more in there," she said, indicating the mailbox.

"What the hell are they?"

"Dunno. But it crept over my hand and up my arm and has orange eyes." She gently rubbed the back of her hand. "I banged my hand, trying to shake it off me."

Murphy aimed her phone's flashlight at the ground. A hairy, eight-legged spider crept laboriously across the grass.

"Eewwww! What is that thing?" Murphy asked.

Tori bent over and grabbed it. "The boys next door had some of these at their Halloween party last year. They're fake. Creepy but harmless." She carefully opened the door of the mailbox and threw the spider she was holding in with the others.

"Let's bring in the groceries and refrigerate the perishables," she said, "then deal with the critters."

"Dylan should already be on his way to pick me up. I'll call him, and he can deal with the creepy, crawling things in the mailbox while we handle the prep for our Sunday culinary extravaganza. I can't believe Nico put creepy stuff in your mailbox twice in less than a week."

"The cameras are focused on the house, not the mailbox," Tori said. "He can drive by, drop off, and make a quick exit with little chance of being seen."

Tori and Murphy had just finished unpacking and putting away the groceries when Dylan rang the doorbell. He was holding four large, black, hairy spiders—by the legs. Their orange eyes glowed, and they squirmed and twitched in a desperate effort to escape.

When Tori answered the door, he said, "You certainly do receive some unusual mail, my friend. I'll sit on the porch and remove the batteries. Do you have something I can put these guys in until I get to each of them? And then, what do you want me to do with them?"

Murphy came to the door with a garbage bag. "Just put them in the trash."

"No," Tori protested. "I need a picture." She pulled her phone from the back pocket of her jeans and handed it to Dylan.

"Got it. I'll take a video of the critters moving, beady eyes glowing. So what do you think—four spiders, four days to go?

"Yes, I think that's the message. You're a good guy, Dylan. Thanks," Tori said.

He returned minutes later, holding the garbage bag with the spiders in one hand and Tori's phone to his ear with the other.

"I couldn't agree more," he said into the phone, "Ivy knows her stuff. She's right. We have no proof Nico and Eena are behind these things. I'm hoping the investigation at Tori's work turns up something. See you tomorrow." He handed the phone to Tori. "It's Knox. I filled him in"

"Let's give them some privacy," Murph said. "You can help me prepare the dining room table for Sunday."

"Hi," Tori said. "Distract me. Tell me how your day was. Something, anything."

"Okay. My day was boring. I filed a motion to quash a subpoena, started on a brief, and had a conference call with the SEC," Knox said.

"I approve of boring. I will never complain about boring again."

"Anything new from Security on the pictures?" Knox asked.

"Yes, and it's good. Let me get to the dining room and put you on speaker. Dylan hasn't heard the news yet either."

Tori walked to the dining room, placed her phone on the table, put it on speaker, and the trio pulled out chairs and sat down.

"Everybody ready for the update?" Tori asked.

"All good," Knox said while Dylan and Murphy nodded.

"Chuck Flynn's team is brilliant! Tori began.

"Spoiler alert: Eena had inside help!" Murphy said.

"Yes," Tori confirmed, "Eena and Nico conned a Baruch College freshman working part-time into helping them. He works one floor below my office." After Eena had signed into the building yesterday, she'd taken the elevator to the cafeteria. The young man was waiting for her. While he went through the cafeteria line to get them lunch, Eena walked in the direction of the ladies' room. "The next time we see her on camera, her hair was in the chignon, and the glasses were gone," Tori said.

After lunch, the young man left, but Eena remained behind. "The cameras show him on my floor, speaking briefly with the receptionist," Tori said. "When Chuck showed her the video, she remembered the man in the video. He'd asked if I was in, and she told him I was at lunch."

Minutes later, the student was captured on video making a phone call, just as the cafeteria camera showed Eena receiving one. "She left the cafeteria, got on an elevator, and exited on my floor—carrying the envelope," Tori said.

"You got her!" Murph said.

"But proof against Eena isn't proof against Nico," Knox said. "He could argue this was all Eena. Her revenge against you for telling the police about the fraud scam."

"But wait—there's more," Tori said. Chuck questioned the young man who confessed he'd met Nico at an employment agency. "Seems Nico befriended several college students working with that agency, even invited several of them over for his girlfriend's famous lasagna." At dinner, Nico told them he wanted to play a joke on a friend who worked at One New York Plaza and offered the first one to land a job there $200 for helping him pull it off. "The day this kid got the offer, he called Nico," Tori said. "And today, that call cost him his job." The student was allowed to resign and provide a written statement about the incident in exchange for a reference.

"Chuck sent Ivy and the Nassau County Assistant District Attorney in charge of Eena's case digital copies of the footage his team spliced together and the student's statement. Ivy notified Judge Foti's clerk we'd be filing for a temporary restraining order on Tuesday as part of the divorce hearing. Fingers-crossed, the prosecutor petitions the court to rescind Eena's bail."

"Your suspicions might have been enough for a judge to issue a temporary order of protection, but if you didn't have the proof to get a final order...." Dylan shook his head. "You only get one chance to kill the king."

"The proof seems to be solid, and if Nico violates the restraining order, temporary or final, the penalties are stiff," Knox said.

"Tori, this sounds good. Maybe you're rid of him – forever," Murphy said. "Wait! I just thought of something. You said Nico met those students through an employment agency. Was he working with the agency? Could he have shown up at One New York Plaza for an interview?"

"No," Tori said. "The employment agency rep told Chuck they 'were not working with Mr. Morgano.'"

"That's what happens when your CPA license gets yanked," Dylan said. "State agencies are quick to report these things to any company doing a background check. And no bank wants a thief handling other people's money."

"What about the CC-TV footage from Wednesday?" Knox asked. "I know Ivy found out the bakery hadn't made the delivery. Do we know who delivered them?"

"No," Tori said. "The person who brought the cookies wore all gray —pants, jacket, baseball cap, and shoes. It isn't clear in the CC-TV footage if it's a man or a woman, and the guard on duty doesn't remember. But in the video footage, the person kept looking around, glancing up at the lobby ceiling, maybe trying to spot cameras? When the guard took the picture for the temporary ID, the person moved just enough to make it a little blurry. Chuck thinks someone was testing the system."

"But this is good, Tori," Murph said. "Really good."

"Yup. Just three more days," Tori said.

Chapter 33
Not My Favorite Ballet

Saturday, September 30th

"Achoo! Achoo!" Tori grabbed a tissue from the mosaic box in the middle of the ladies' room vanity. "Achoo!"

She blew her nose and reached for more tissues. I need to get this smell out of my nose. Just as the ushers had opened the auditorium doors and she, Knox, Murphy, and Dylan entered the theatre, Tori had smelled a mixture of bergamot, jasmine, and patchouli. That perfume, a scent she associated with Eena, triggered a bout of sneezing, just as it always did. She excused herself and went to the ladies' room to wash her hands and get tissues before taking her seat.

Now, the odor lingered in her nostrils. A spritz of her Sublime usually helped neutralize the more cloying fragrance. Tori sneezed twice more. Was the smell getting stronger? I can't sneeze through the entire first act of the ballet, she thought as she reached into her red leather clutch for the small bottle of perfume she'd started carrying when she and Nico began dating years ago.

"Salute, Veek Toria."

That voice made Tori wince. The reflection in the Murano glass mirror over the double sinks sneered back at her. A sudden wave of nausea burned the back of Tori's throat, and she felt perspiration form on her upper lip and the back of her neck. She wanted to take a deep breath, but the thought of inhaling another whiff of that perfume nearly made her gag. Suddenly, she felt lightheaded and gripped the edge of the white marble counter to steady herself. She stared back at Eena's reflection.

As the initial shock of seeing her nemesis subsided, Tori reached for more tissues, spritzed them with a drop of Sublime, and held them just beneath her nose. She started toward the restroom door, only to have Eena block her path. Tori held her perfume bottle as if it were a room deodorizer and depressed the nozzle. As the smell of floral vanilla and amber filled the room, Tori lowered the tissues.

"I'm leaving, Eena."

"No. Not yet. I've been watching you and your friends. I didn't think I'd have the opportunity to speak with you so early in the evening," Eena said. "First, what did you think of today's little presents?"

"Sex toys from my estranged husband and his mistress three days before our divorce is final? An unusual choice. But your threat was loud and clear. I'm guessing the ball gag was to remind me I should have kept my mouth shut. Should keep my mouth shut even now. And the hand-cuffs and flogger? A reminder I need to be punished for refusing to go along with your scam."

"Very good. You're smarter than Nico gave you credit for."

"Yes, I am. And Nico's not as smart as he thinks he is."

Eena nodded. "Touché! He can be," she paused, "juvenile. Now about your latest transgression. Getting a friend of mine fired."

"On behalf of my employer, I should thank you. Thursday's escapade uncovered a flaw in our security system and identified an employee with questionable integrity."

Tori again started toward the doors. Eena, again, stepped in front of her.

"I'm not finished with you yet," Eena said through gritted teeth.

"But I'm finished with you and Nico," Tori said. "Don't you know living well is the best revenge? Oh, but then living well isn't going to be an option in prison, is it?"

A sharp crack echoed off every hard surface in the room! Tori heard the sound of Eena's right hand connecting with her left cheek before she felt the sting of the slap. She was stunned. Her cheek was on fire. Tears filled her eyes, and she raised her left hand to soothe her now-stinging cheek.

The restroom door swung open, and Murphy's voice called, "Tori, are you still in here? I decided to make a quick trip before...."

As Eena turned toward the sound of Murphy's voice, Tori gripped her clutch with both hands and, holding it like a shield in front of her, pushed past Eena.

"Murph, go, run!" Tori shouted.

Her friend spun around, and they ran from the restroom.

"Help me keep her in there," Tori said as she leaned against the heavy wooden door, gripping the brass handle for leverage

Together the two women fought Eena's attempts to escape. On the other side of the Promenade, Tori saw three docents setting up the display of merchandise to be sold during intermission. She screamed. "Help! Help me! Get security. Someone assaulted me."

Seconds later, she saw a docent point in her direction. A guard was running across the reception hall toward her and speaking into a microphone connected to his earpiece. She said a silent prayer he was calling for backup.

Everything seemed to move at a faster-than-normal speed—as if someone had pushed the fast-forward button. One guard held the door closed, and another, who had appeared out of nowhere, pointed to a tufted leather bench across from the auditorium's entrance. When Tori and Murphy were safely seated on the bench, the guard holding the door stepped aside. Eena stumbled into the Promenade, almost falling from the sudden lack of resistance. She tried to push past one guard, but the other grabbed her and held her until her hands could be bound with a zip tie. Dylan and Knox exited the theatre and walked toward the bench. Dylan pulled Murphy to her feet and wrapped his arms around her while Knox sat beside Tori and held her hand.

One of the docents handed Tori an icy cold bottle of water. She held it against her still-stinging cheek and closed her eyes, allowing the cold condensation beading on the bottle to numb the pain. Static and the squawk of voices from a police radio startled her. When she opened her eyes, she saw a New York City uniformed officer standing beside her.

"I'm Officer Ryan," the young woman in uniform said, "May I sit down?" Tori nodded. The officer removed a small notebook and a pen from the back pocket of her uniform. "Can you tell me your name and what happened this evening?" she asked.

Tori lowered the bottle and brushed the moisture from her cheek. When she tried to answer, her voice was raspy. Knox took the bottle, loosened the cap, and handed it back to her. Tori took a long swallow of water. Then, she said, "I'm Tori, Victoria Harrigan Morgano." Suddenly, the shock of her confrontation with Eena and the slap hit her, and she began to shiver. Knox stood, took off his jacket, and draped it over her shoulders. When he sat down again, he pulled her toward him, supported her back, and wrapped his arms around her. The jacket was warm from the heat of his body, and the citrusy smell of his after-shave calmed her.

"We were walking to the theatre. I started sneezing. I went to the ladies' room. I just wanted to wash my hands, just wanted tissues, then, then...." Tori began to shake again, and Knox whispered, "You're okay. You've got this."

"Do you know who that woman is?" Murphy asked the officer. "Her name was, until about two months ago, Valentina Morgano." Officer Ryan looked up from her notebook. "Yes," Murph said. "That Valentina Morgano. She was part of that ring of Long Island doctors and therapists who stole millions until they were caught."

Tori sat up straight. She pulled Knox's jacket more tightly around her as she scanned the Promenade. "Where is she? I don't see her. Where is she?"

"Downstairs with my partner and one of the guards."

"I'll go. See what's happening," Dylan said.

"Why do you think she assaulted you this evening?" the police officer asked Tori.

"She tried to involve me in the fraud scam she's going to prison for."

"The Assistant DA in charge of her case needs to be notified about tonight," Knox said. "Tori, do you have the prosecutor's name?"

"Yes. In my phone. I have her office number, too."

Knox said to Officer Ryan, "She's scheduled to be sentenced in a few weeks. The judge allowed her to remain free on bail until then, but the prosecutor may want to petition the court to rescind that decision."

The officer gave Tori the case number for the assault and wrote down the contact information for the Nassau County prosecutor before she left.

Dylan passed her on the stairs as he returned to the reception area.

"What's going to happen now? To Eena, I mean?" Tori asked him when he'd rejoined the group.

"Officer Ryan's partner was going to charge her with a misdemeanor, issue a summons and let her go. Until I told him about her felony conviction. She's in the back of a police car waiting to be driven to the 20th Precinct."

Just then, the auditorium doors opened. The first act was over.

"I've lost all sense of time," Murph said. "It seems like hours ago I decided to stop in the ladies' room before the performance."

"Do you want to leave? Not stay for the second and third acts?" Dylan asked.

Tori shook her head. "Jewels isn't my favorite ballet. We've missed Emeralds, but we should stay to watch Rubies and Diamonds.

Knox squeezed her hand. "If you'd be more comfortable going home, putting your feet up…."

"No. I will not allow Eena or Nico to take away one more thing from me."

Chapter 34
Tomorrow

Monday, October 2nd

Tomorrow. Tori's mind drifted from the email she was finishing, and she turned her office chair so she could watch the orange and black ferries cross the Hudson River. The day that had once seemed so far in the future was almost here. *Tomorrow I will no longer be Mrs. Nicolino Morgano.*

Over the past five months, she'd often replayed the April afternoon she'd confronted Nico about the affair and told him she wanted a divorce. He'd begged her to give their marriage another chance. After First Dominion fired him, demanded he repay the money he and Eena had stolen, and the authorities began investigating Eena's role in the insurance scam, Nico no longer wanted a reconciliation. He wanted revenge.

In those early days, every time he'd thrown a punch, she'd counter-punched twice as hard. When, after a month, he still hadn't hired an attorney, Tori'd instructed Ivy to have a process server serve him with papers. When Nico made outlandish demands in their settlement conferences, she threatened to change the grounds for divorce from no fault to adultery, naming Eena as co-respondent. She'd even threatened to leak the salacious details of their affair to the Nassau Gazette. That Long Island tabloid would, Tori was confident, be happy to weave the titillating details of the affair into coverage of the insurance scam. Her gamble had paid off. Nico had backed down.

Initially, she'd been caught off-guard when the harassment began in mid-June, but she'd regrouped. Upgrading her security system had made her feel safer. Until that early August afternoon when an inebriated Nico had confronted her outside Fraunces Tavern. She'd felt physically afraid of him, and she'd enrolled in a self-defense training class. The past two weeks, however, were different. Every day's delivery had been a lunge she couldn't parry. The anticipation of what was to come, an advance she couldn't block. Every day she felt her spirit erode just a little more. Nico and Eena's determination to terrorize her, the time and money they were willing to invest to enact their revenge, frightened her. How far were they willing to go?

Last week she'd gone to a demonstration of Krav Maga, considered the best self-defense training in the world. She'd been impressed. The pamphlet she'd picked up was now crumpled at the bottom of her purse. She'd read it, cover-to-cover, countless times. Knew it by heart. I'm going to do it! Tori decided. I may not have what it takes, but I have to try.

Tomorrow would be the funeral for her marriage. The service would be held in a dingy courtroom on the second floor of the Bergen County Justice Center. Judge Margaret Foti was scheduled to hear her petition for divorce at nine-thirty. Since every one of Nico's issues, requests, demands, and delaying tactics had been addressed, the proceedings wouldn't take long, be only a formality. Tori didn't need to come, her attorney had said. But since she'd been present when she'd spoken her vows over four years ago, she wanted to be present when those vows were dissolved.

She tried to shake thoughts of harassment, self-defense training, and her pending divorce from her mind. Get back to work and get out of here, she scolded herself. Looking out at empty cubicles and offices, she realized many of her colleagues had left for the evening, including Cooper and Graham. A glance at her watch told her she'd just missed the six o'clock ferry and would have to take the subway to Port Authority and the express bus to Fort Lee. Wish I'd left earlier, she thought, but I can't have someone escort me to the ferry or subway for the rest of my life.

She forced herself to read the email she'd been working on one last time before hitting the send button. Surveying her desk, Tori reasoned she wouldn't do a lick of work tonight or tomorrow. So she pushed her messenger bag back in the nook between her credenza and desk, changed into flats, and grabbed her purse. As Tori locked her office door, she called 'good night' to the few remaining staffers. Within minutes she was walking across the plaza and heading toward the subway.

It will be dark soon, Tori thought. Rather than linger to watch the early October sun color the sky a bright yellow, orange, and peach as it sank into the Hudson River, she hurried across the plaza to the subway. As she approached the subway's escalator, she shivered from a sudden chill—not from the air but inside her. Pulling her pocketbook closer to her side, carefully looking both right and left before stepping onto the escalator, she thought, What's that old expression? Like someone walked over my grave.

Tori pushed through the turnstile and noticed there weren't many passengers in the station. Instead of taking the stairs down to an empty platform, she sat on a wooden bench beneath the sign that would signal an empty train was in the station, ready to begin its journey from the tip of Manhattan to the Bronx. She didn't have to wait long before the sign began to flash on and off.

As she started down the steps, she heard footsteps behind her and breathed a sigh of relief. Good. Another passenger. She always hated being the only person getting on a subway at the first stop of the run. It was creepy.

She was halfway down the stairs before a hand grabbed the strap of her shoulder bag. Her first instinct was to yank the purse away. Then she felt another hand on her right shoulder. Pushing hard. The power of the shove propelled her forward. She tried to hold onto the handrail, but her forward momentum made that impossible. For a second, she felt as if she were weightless. Then, her body slammed into the concrete. She raised her hands to protect her face. She tried to tuck herself into a ball, but each step smacked her legs and arms as she fell. The concrete's rough surface ripped her stockings and tore her skin as she somersaulted over and over again. Finally, she hit bottom.

When she opened her eyes, Tori saw her assailant's face, his triumphant smirk as he witnessed her ignominious splat on the platform. She watched him turn and saunter up the steps to the turnstile and exit. Her face and head throbbed. Warm blood trickled down the right side of her face and both legs. Her stockings were shredded. Strands of torn silk stretched painfully across her bleeding, swelling knees. The tender palms of her hands were scraped, filthy from the dirt, grit, and grime of the subway and her blood.

As she lay on the pavement, she closed her eyes and took gulps of air to settle her roiling stomach. She was shaking and hurt everywhere. When she tried to sit up, the effort made her lightheaded, and the black, white, and red subway signs went in and out of focus. Static feedback from a radio too close to her ear made her wince. Then a voice said, "Copy."

When she opened her eyes, a policeman was crouching beside her. "I'm Officer Hanson. I've called the paramedics," he said. "You took a nasty fall. Can you tell me your name? Where you are?" She tried, again, to sit up. "Don't try to get up," the officer said. "The EMTs will be here any minute."

"My name is Victoria Morgano. I'm in the South Ferry subway station. I did not fall," Tori said. "I was pushed. By Nicolino Morgano. He assaulted me. I want to press charges."

Chapter 35
Who's Anthony?

An ambulance brought Tori to Lower Manhattan Hospital's busy emergency room. Her head injury pushed her to the front of the line. After the EMTs wheeled her gurney to an empty cubicle, the nurse helped her change into a hospital gown and checked her vital signs. As she waited for the doctor to examine her, Tori called Murphy.

"That son of a bitch did what?" her friend had shouted from the phone when Tori told her what had happened and where she was. "Don't worry. Dylan and I'll take care of Baron. Do you need us to come get you?

"Maybe. I don't know. The doctor just walked in. Talk later?"

X-rays and a CT scan confirmed Tori had a severe concussion and several bruised but not broken ribs. Her right eye was bloodshot. The surrounding skin was swollen and already turning black and blue. After a plastic-surgery resident closed the one-inch gap on her forehead with ten stitches, a nurse cleaned and bandaged the cuts on her arms, legs, and knees. Then, the ER doctor returned to check on her.

"On a scale of one to ten, how would you describe the pain in your head?"

Tori winced. "Ten," she whispered.

"I see you've had a tetanus shot recently. Good," the doctor said as she reviewed Tori's chart. "I'm ordering an antibiotic and pain medication."

Although Tori was no longer dizzy and her blood pressure and pulse rate, both high when she'd been brought in, were back in normal ranges, the doctor would not commit to releasing her that night. "We'll re-evaluate after the antibiotic and pain medication have been administered," she said.

"I have to go home."

The doctor smiled. "We'll see," she said as she pulled back the cubicle curtain. That's when Tori saw Murphy, Dylan, and Officer Hanson, the policeman who had found her on the platform, waiting in the hallway.

"You came! You're both really here! I've never been so happy to see anyone in my whole life," Tori said, tears filling her eyes and spilling on her cheeks.

"Oh honey, of course, we came. My God, Tori, does it hurt? Of course, it hurts! What am I saying?" Murph said. Without taking her eyes off her friend, she dug in her purse, pulled out a package of tissues, and pressed one into Tori's hand. "Here. Don't cry! Please don't cry. You always get a headache when you cry."

"I already have a headache," Tori sniffled.

Dylan walked into the cubicle and placed Tori's overnight bag on the floor beside the bed. "What did the doctor say?"

"I've got a concussion, cuts, bruises. She won't tell me if I can go home tonight. I told her I had to. What time is it?"

"After nine," Dylan said. "You called us almost an hour and a half ago."

"Oh. That late. What's in there?" She pointed to the overnight bag.

"Your favorite yoga jacket and softest sweatpants. For when you leave. I thought they'd be easy to get on and off," Murphy said. "If we can't take you home, I'm spending the night. Dylan'll come for us in the morning."

"Thanks." Tori's voice was barely above a whisper, and she began to cry again.

Murphy replaced the wet tissue in her hand with a dry one and squeezed her friend's hand.

Officer Hanson cleared his throat. "I hate to interrupt."

"Tori, Officer Hanson has more questions for you. Do you need me to stay?" Dylan asked.

"I'm, I'm not sure. I don't think so."

"How about if I call Ivy? Tell her what happened. Let her know there's a possibility you won't be at the hearing tomorrow. And Murphy stays with you."

"That would be great. Thanks, Dylan."

"And call Lulu and Tom," Murphy said. "Give them an update. Tell Lu I'll text her later."

"Will do. I know they're pretty worried up in Boston. Do you need me to call your mother, Tori?"

"No. There was only time to make one phone call, so Mom doesn't know yet. I'll call her later. I'd rather she hear my voice, hear I'm okay when I tell her about—you know."

The nurse entered with an intravenous bag, a syringe, and a camera.

"What's the camera for?" Tori asked.

"Pictures," the nurse said. "The DA will need them for court. It's standard in assault cases. Could you give us a minute, Officer? Your friend can stay if you'd like."

The nurse took close-ups of Tori's black eye, the gash on her forehead, and the mottled bluish-purple bruises forming on her rib cage and thighs. She looked away and winced as the vein catheter for the antibiotic and pain medication was inserted in her left hand while Murphy, who had pulled a chair up to the side of the bed, held her right hand. "The antibiotic is slow and should take about twenty minutes," the nurse said, "but the pain relief should be almost immediate. I'll be back with an ice pack for your eye. Ten minutes on, ten minutes off."

On her way out, the nurse told Officer Hanson he could go back in.

"I was able to pull Mr. Morgano's DMV photo, and a couple of officers went to the West Seventy-First Street address listed on his license. No one was home."

"Maybe he's not there anymore," Tori said.

"His mother, Jenny Morgano, lives in the Kennedy House on Queens Boulevard in Forest Hills," Murphy said. "His brother, Sal, is a doctor at Mount Sinai. Someone in the Morgano family knows where Nico is. He shouldn't be that hard to track down."

Tori's phone rang. Knox's name and her favorite picture of them on the Union Clipper appeared on screen. That's when she saw he had already called several times and left several voicemails. He must be so worried I hadn't answered or called him back. She gripped her phone. She ached to hear his voice.

Murphy took the phone from Tori's hand. "How about if I step out and talk to Knox while you finish here? Does he know yet?"

Tori shook her head. "No. Make sure you tell him I'm all right," she called after Murphy.

Officer Hanson waited until Tori turned her attention back to him. "We'll send someone to question Mr. Morgano's mother and check his brother's schedule at the hospital. Do you remember what he was wearing tonight?"

"His clothes were dark—dark pants. Jeans, I think. Dark sweater."

Officer Hanson nodded. "A colleague is pulling up surveillance footage from the Water Street, subway entrance, and platform cameras."

"Ya gotta love those ubiquitous post-9/11 cameras," Murphy said as she returned to Tori's side. Turning to her friend, she said in a low voice, "Knox said he needs to hear your voice. Won't hang up until he does— even if you're just answering Officer Hanson's questions."

Tori smiled. Then she held up her index finger, signaling she needed a minute, and put the phone to her ear. "Hi, Knox."

"Oh, Tori. My God! How do you feel? Murphy told me you have a severe concussion and a black eye. Have they given you anything for the pain?"

"Yes. The nurse added it to the IV, and I feel it starting to work."

"Good. Murphy wasn't sure if you were going home tonight."

"I want to go home. I want to go home so badly."

"I know, Honey. But if you have to stay, she'll be with you. I wish I were there, holding your hand."

"Me too."

The nurse re-entered the cubicle with the ice pack and stood beside the bed.

"Knox, I have to lay the phone on the bed and put you on speaker. The nurse is here with an ice pack for my eye. And Officer Hanson has more questions."

She nodded to Officer Hanson. "Go on."

"Is there anything else you remember about waiting for the train or starting down the stairs?"

She closed her eyes for a moment. "Yes! I saw the train. In the station. It wasn't pulling in. It had already stopped. I was about halfway down the steps."

"Tori," Knox called from the phone. "When did you see Nico? While you were on the stairs or after you fell?"

"After. Nico just stood there, waiting until he knew I saw him. Then, he smiled and walked away."

Tori heard Knox's sharp intake of breath, his muttered curse, "Son of a bitch," coming from the phone's speaker.

"I think we have all we need for now," Officer Hanson said to Tori before he left. "If you think of anything else, please call me. My number's on the card I gave your friend."

Just then, the ER nurse came to check her IV. "Almost finished," she said. "How's the pain?"

"Better."

"The doctor will be in shortly. If you have someone to stay with you, wake you every few hours, she'll probably let you go home tonight."

"My husband and I will stay with her," Murphy said. She turned to Tori, "We dropped off our stuff at your house when we packed your suitcase and walked Baron."

"Knox," Tori said into the phone. "Did you hear that? I may be going home!"

"That's fantastic news! I'll say good night so you can get dressed," Knox said.

Tori said, "Good night, Knox," before she reluctantly ended the call.

After the doctor had checked Tori one last time and confirmed Murphy and Dylan would be staying with her, she told Tori she could go home. Murphy helped her get dressed. Then the nurse came in with her discharge orders, including instructions to stay home the remainder of the week, and told Murphy Tori's prescription for pain medication was ready to be picked up at the hospital pharmacy.

"I'll call for a wheelchair," the nurse said. "Transporation's backed up, so it may be twenty minutes or so. Plenty of time for your friend to pick up your meds."

"I'll text Dylan," Murphy said. "He can come back and sit with you."

When Dylan walked into Tori's cubicle, he wasn't alone. Officer Hanson was with him.

"The police matched Nico's DMV photo and your description with the surveillance footage from the street and subway cameras. I've watched the videos and positively identified Nico. The evidence is clear—he pushed you," Dylan said.

"Two officers from the Forest Hills precinct went to your mother-in-law's apartment. She wouldn't let them in. Stood in the doorway to talk to them. Said she hadn't seen her son. But one of the officers saw folded sheets, a blanket, and a pillow on the living room sofa. Like the couch was going to be made up into a bed. When he asked about it, Mrs. Morgano said she likes to lie down on that couch to read," Officer Hanson said.

"That sofa's a pull-out. And Jenny Morgano is no reader," Tori said.

"Officer Hanson's partner checked with Mount Sinai. Sal wasn't on duty, but the hospital gave us the number for his answering service. I called and told the operator it was an emergency. His sister-in-law was hurt," Dylan said.

Just then, Murphy joined them. "No wheelchair?" she asked.

"Not yet," Dylan said.

Tori's phone rang. She stared at the phone before showing the caller ID to Dylan and Murphy. It was Sal.

Dylan took the phone from Tori, tapped the phone icon, and put the call on speaker.

"Sal, it's Dylan Malone."

"Dylan. I got your message. What's going on? Is Tori all right?"

"An ambulance brought her to Lower Manhattan Hospital over three hours ago. Nico assaulted her."

"What? He assaulted her? How badly is she hurt?"

"Nico pushed her down the steel-tipped concrete steps of the South Ferry subway station. So yeah, she's seriously hurt. Severe concussion, black eye, bruised ribs. Thank God her injuries aren't life-threatening, but they easily could have been."

"Did she say it was Nico? With a concussion, she might be confused and only thought it was my brother."

"Stop it, Sal! The police have surveillance footage. I've seen it. Her assailant was Nico. He stalked her. He pushed her. If you know anything about where Nico is, you have to tell the police. If you don't, that's obstruction of justice—a serious crime with serious jail time."

Sal hesitated. "He's still my brother, and it would kill Mom if he went to jail."

"You don't have a choice. I must warn you the police are here with me now and can hear every word you say. If you know something…."

"Eena's Aunt Mehta told Nico Sunday morning he had until today to vacate the townhouse. Painters are coming tomorrow, and then the place goes on the market. Nico was planning to stay on Mom's sofa, but he called her a little while ago and said he was going to Anthony's."

"Thanks, Sal."

"Dylan, My mother said Tori had Eena arrested Saturday night," Sal said. "Is that true?"

"No, it isn't, Sal. The police arrested Eena because she assaulted Tori in the ladies' room at Lincoln Center." Dylan heard Sal's sharp intake of breath, his muttered, "Oh my God," before he continued. "It's a crime to go around New York City slapping people."

With that, Dylan hit the red phone icon to end the call.

"Who's Anthony?" Officer Hanson asked.

"Anthony Antonuccio," Dylan said. "He, Nico, and I grew up together. He and his wife have an apartment in the Park Slope section of Brooklyn."

Chapter 36
The Next Morning

Murphy came to check on Tori just before seven the following morning, but Tori was already awake. With the help of more pain medication and restorative sleep, her headache was manageable, and she was no longer dizzy. The muscles in her arms and legs were less stiff and sore. Murphy had sent her to bed with a plastic bag of crushed ice and replaced it when she woke Tori just before four a.m. The make-shift ice packs had reduced some swelling because she could now open her bloodshot eye.

When Tori came home in the early morning hours, Baron had been thrilled to see her—wagging his stubby tail, twirling in circles—but soon, he'd seemed to sense she was hurt. Instead of bounding up the stairs to the bedroom, he'd walked slowly behind her. Rather than taking his usual spot at the foot of the bed, he'd curled up right by her side. Now, he sat at attention as she sat on the edge of the bed before standing.

"Thanks for watching over me last night," Tori said as she gave him some early morning attention before heading to the bathroom to shower.

Warm water cascading from the showerhead caressed her muscles and joints. The soothing waterfall eroded the dam inside her, and the shower walls absorbed the sobs she had tamped down since the assault. When, finally, her tears had washed away the remains of her shock, she carefully began to rinse away the last of the soot, grit, and dried blood.

After her shower, Tori surveyed the damage in the large mirror over the bathroom vanity. Last night, she'd been so exhausted when she'd gotten home, it had been easy to avoid looking in the mirror. Now, her reflection shocked her. Among the pink, red, and mauve splotches on her face, arms, and legs were tender patches of black and blue. Her lips and face were still puffy, and her right eye was bloodshot—the skin around it bruised and discolored. Maroon blemishes dotted her ribcage and midriff. She winced as she patted dry the painful eggplant-colored marks that covered her thighs. Tears rose in her throat, and she stifled a sob. She took a deep, shuddering breath and closed her eyes.

A soft knock at her bedroom door and Dylan's voice calling, "Tori, could you let Baron out so he and I can go for a walk?" interrupted her thoughts and helped her regroup.

She tightened the belt on her bathrobe before opening the door. When Dylan called to him, Baron looked up at her. "Go ahead," she said, giving him a reassuring pat on the head. "I'll be fine. I'll see you both downstairs. Thanks, Dylan."

Returning to the bathroom, she averted her eyes and took another deep, shuddering breath before facing her reflection again. Then, she grabbed the vial of vitamin E gel the plastic surgeon had given her and slathered a generous layer on the black, blue and purple bruises around her right eye, on her left cheek, and below the stitches on her forehead. The discolored skin glistened. She wanted each bruise to stand out.

As she prepared to leave the bedroom, she thought of the stairs. She opened the door but held onto the doorframe until her heart stopped racing, and her legs felt steady again. Her breath quickened, and the palms of her hands felt damp. A flashback of feeling she was tumbling almost smothered her, and she gulped for air. She gripped the banister with both hands before putting first her left foot and then her right on each step until she was at the bottom.

In the kitchen, Dylan was standing at the stove making scrambled eggs and bacon. He was wearing her lavender apron with the imprint of a bunch of grapes and the saying, "Squeeze me. Make me wine" on the front, to protect his white dress shirt and tie. The sight made her smile.

"How are you feeling this morning?"

"Better, thanks. Not as foggy."

"Good. Murphy will be down in a minute. She's emailing lesson plans to her sub. You didn't eat anything last night, so you need to eat a little something now," he said. "Scrambled eggs with scallion cream cheese and bacon?"

Tori nodded. "Yes, please, sounds good. Dylan, before Murphy comes down, I want to say how grateful I am for everything. You and Nico were best buds for decades, and now you don't speak. I know how hard this has been for you."

He pulled out a chair and sat beside her. "You're right. It has been tough. Sometimes I think of the good times we shared, but then I remember he's a liar, a cheat, and a fraud. I don't trust him, and I don't see that changing. I like Knox, by the way. He seems like a good guy. I think you two are good together."

"Thanks, Dylan."

He squeezed her hand before he stood and walked to the stove.

Tori retrieved her phone from the counter, where it had been charging all night. There was a text from her mother, sent an hour ago. Tori had called Anna on the drive home from the hospital. She knew hearing her voice, knowing she was on her way home, had helped her mother handle the news of Nico's assault. In this morning's text, her mother wrote she hoped Tori was feeling rested and stronger this morning, wished her "good luck" at the hearing, and asked her to call as soon as it was over. Tori responded with the thumb's up emoji and three red hearts. She had hoped for a similar text from Knox—he had been so concerned, so sweet and kind last evening. She tried not to let her disappointment overshadow her relief that her divorce would be final in just a few hours.

Murphy entered the kitchen just as Dylan put a plate in front of Tori. She gave her husband a peck on the cheek before sitting down.

"That's what I'll have too, Honey. And Lulu's joining us for breakfast." She propped her tablet on the table.

When Lulu first saw Tori's face on screen, her throat and jaw clenched, telltale signs she was upset and fighting back tears. "Geez, Tori," Lulu said, her voice thick with the tears she was swallowing. "That looks so painful, and you can't even say, 'you should see the other guy,' 'cause that creep doesn't have a scratch on him. How do you feel?"

"Hi, Lulu. I'm feeling better than I did last night. A little nervous about today."

"Any news from the police? Did they arrest that scumbag yet?" Lulu asked.

"Haven't heard anything more this morning," Dylan said.

"I like today's addition of the vitamin E gel," Murphy said. "The judge and Nico's lawyer won't be able to miss your bruises."

Dylan placed his breakfast and Muphy's on the table and sat down. "Tori, Ivy called this morning. She'll ask you to describe what happened last night when you're on the stand. Since she hasn't received copies of the CC-TV footage yet, If Nico's lawyer objects and says it's only your word Nico pushed you, I told her I'd testify.

"I won't be able to hold it together if there's a problem, Dylan. Can you tell me what's going to happen?" Tori asked.

"This isn't my area of the law, but it should be simple. The divorce is no-fault, you've already split everything, and the temporary restraining order should be a no-brainer. But you never know."

"Will Nico be there?" Lulu asked.

"Oh God, I hope not! His lawyer told Ivy he wasn't coming. What if he changes his mind?" Tori asked.

"Remember there's a warrant out for his arrest," Dylan said.

"But that's New York, and this is New Jersey," Murph said.

"Ivy will tell the bailiff who will cuff him and the court clerk who will tell the judge. I'll call Officer Hanson, and that supercilious son-of-a-bitch will find himself on the way to jail," Dylan said. "But I don't think even Nico's that stupid. Don't worry, Tori. He's probably been arrested by now.

"And before I forget, I got an email from Knox late last night. He talked with the Nassau County ADA yesterday. Eena's still behind bars, and the hearing to revoke her bail is set for next week," Dylan said.

"Some good news to start the morning," Lulu said. "Auspicious beginning."

"Thank you," Tori said. "Did he say anything else? He didn't answer my text last night. I just texted him again. He usually answers me immediately unless he's in a meeting or court."

"There's your answer," Lulu said. "He's probably already in his meeting with that SEC lawyer. But he took the time out of his meeting schedule yesterday to follow up with the Nassau County prosecutor. That was so thoughtful."

Tori tried not to sound disappointed. "That's probably it. I'll try again after breakfast."

Murphy looked at the clock on the microwave. "We better get ready to leave for the courthouse. Lulu, we'll call when Tori is Ms. Victoria Harrigan again."

Chapter 37
The Divorce Hearing

At the courthouse, Tori, Dylan, and Murphy met Ivy Simon in the hall outside Judge Foti's courtroom. Together they went inside. Tori looked around the small, square room. Behind the judge's bench, peeling institutional green paint accented the ceiling tiles, stained rusty brown. The room had no windows, and the only light came from rectangular ceiling fixtures with harsh fluorescent bulbs, several of which emitted a persistent, annoying hum. She shivered. Could this be happening in a drearier place?

Nico's lawyer, Mitchell Margolis, arrived a few minutes later. Dylan and Murphy took seats in the gallery behind the table where Ivy and Tori were seated. Then, the court clerk entered the room, told them to stand, and announced the judge's arrival and the proceeding – Victoria Helene Morgano v. Nicolino Anthony Morgano, Petition for Divorce, and Request for Temporary Restraining Order. When Judge Foti sat down, she asked both lawyers if they were ready to proceed. Ivy said, "Yes, Your Honor." Mr. Margolis stood. Tori gripped the arms of her chair.

"Your Honor," Mr. Margolis said. "While I am ready to proceed with the divorce petition, I was only served with the plaintiff's request for a Restraining Order last Friday. Although I have made several attempts to contact Mr. Morgano, he and I have not yet had the opportunity to discuss this matter. Therefore, I request a continuance with respect to the restraining order."

Tori heard Murphy say to Dylan in a loud stage whisper, "Of course, he can't reach his client. He's on the lam."

Ivy rose from her seat. "Your Honor, my client was assaulted last evening and suffered a severe concussion, among other serious injuries. As you can see, she is badly bruised and spent last evening in the hospital. Her assailant was Mr. Morgano."

Tori took a deep breath and turned to face the judge.

"How are you feeling, Mrs. Morgano?" Judge Foti asked. "Are you in pain? Do you think you can proceed with this hearing?"

"I'm well enough to proceed, Your Honor."

"Mr. Morgano attacked my client in the South Ferry subway station at approximately six forty-five in the evening, according to this preliminary police report." Ivy pulled multiple copies of the report Officer Hanson had emailed her from her briefcase. She handed one to Mr. Margolis as she approached the bench to give the judge a copy. "I submit this as plaintiff's exhibit four. Mrs. Morgano needs and seeks the protections this court and law enforcement can provide. While last night's injuries are not life-threatening, they could have been. That is why we petition the court today to issue a temporary protection order."

"I object. Your Honor", Mr. Margolis shot back, "this is the first time I'm hearing about an alleged assault, and like the court, I was just handed this preliminary report. Furthermore, this alleged assault occurred in New York, not New Jersey. And finally, I don't understand how a petition to request a temporary restraining order can be filed with the court on Friday when the precipitating incident hadn't happened and wouldn't happen for three more days."

"I apologize for any confusion, Your Honor. Mr. Morgano's assault of Mrs. Morgano last evening makes this request for a restraining order all the more important. But the assault was not the precipitating incident. For the past two weeks, my client has been besieged by a daily barrage of items designed to inflict mental and emotional abuse. All arranged by Mr. Morgano. Photographs and descriptions of the items sent each day are attached to the petition sent to Mr. Margolis's office Friday morning. A sworn statement from the head of security at Mrs. Morgano's workplace citing evidence linking Mr. Morgano to at least one instance of harassment was also sent to Mr. Margolis. We submit these photos, descriptions, and sworn statements with the motion for the restraining order, as plaintiff's exhibits one, two, and three."

"She has to grant the restraining order. She just has to," Tori heard Murphy whisper behind her.

Judge Foti heard her too. When the judge's gavel banged on the square sound block, Tori flinched.

"Ma'am, this is your second interruption this morning. A third and I will have the bailiff remove you from the gallery," Judge Foti said. "You may continue, Ms. Simon."

"Concerning the alleged assault," Ivy said, "it is not just my client's word her assailant was Mr. Morgano. The New York City Police Department has surveillance footage of him stalking Mrs. Morgano, waiting for her to leave her office building on Water Street, and following her to the subway. Video from a camera at the South Ferry subway station shows Mr. Morgano committing this heinous assault. Efforts are currently underway to apprehend him."

In her mind, Tori relived the previous night's events, from the eerie feeling she'd had when she'd approached the escalator to feeling Nico's hand on her shoulder—pushing her. Her throat burned. She reached for a glass and the pitcher of water, but her hands were shaking, and water sloshed on the table. Ivy took the pitcher from her and poured the water before continuing her argument. Tori gripped the glass with both hands and took a drink.

"While I do not have access to the CC-TV footage this morning, I will present it at the final Personal Conduct Order hearing. An officer of the court, Mr. Dylan Malone, is seated in the gallery. He has seen the video, identified the assailant as Nicolino Morgano to the NYPD, and is prepared to testify this morning."

"I'd like to hear from Mr. Malone before I make my ruling."

Dylan rose and walked to the chair beside the judge's bench. After he was sworn in, the clerk asked him for his full name, address, and occupation for the record. Then Ivy asked him to describe the events of the prior evening, beginning with Tori's phone call from the hospital and ending with Dylan viewing the three surveillance videos.

"I have known Mr. Morgano since we were eleven. He was the best man at my wedding. Without any doubt or hesitation, I can say the man in the videos, the man I watched waiting for Victoria Morgano, following her and then deliberately pushing her down the subway steps, was Nicolino Morgano."

Since Nico's attorney had no questions for Dylan, he was excused and returned to his seat in the gallery beside Murphy. As he passed the plaintiff's table, he reached over to give Tori's shoulder a gentle pat. She looked up at him and whispered, "Thanks."

"Mr. Margolis, your request for a continuance is denied," Judge Foti said. "Please proceed, Ms. Simon."

Tori's body tensed. I don't know how much more of this I can take.

She heard Ivy call her to the stand. I can do this, she assured herself. But her head ached, and her bruised ribs made each breath painful. With her left hand on the Bible and her right hand raised, she swore to tell the whole truth. Ivy asked when she and Nico had separated and confirmed Tori still wished to proceed with the divorce and return to her maiden name. After Ivy had directed the judge's attention to the settlement agreement signed by both Tori and Nico, she advised the court she was not just seeking the temporary restraining order. She was also petitioning the court to assign a date for the final Personal Conduct Order hearing.

Tori turned to look at Judge Foti, but the judge's face gave nothing away. Please, she silently begged the judge, I need that final order of protection.

Finally, Ivy asked Tori to describe the extent of her injuries and how and when she'd sustained them.

She remembered her reflection in the mirror, her shock at seeing herself for the first time. Tears welled in her eyes, and her mouth went dry. Ivy handed her a box of tissues.

"Are you able to proceed?" Judge Foti asked.

"Yes, Your Honor. May I have a drink of water?"

Ivy poured her more water. Tori took a long swallow before describing her concussion, the stitches she had needed to close the gash on her forehead, and the bruises that now covered her face and body.

Then, Ivy said she had no further questions for Tori. Mr. Margolis rose and said he had no questions for the witness.

Judge Foti turned to Tori. "Mrs. Morgano, according to the settlement agreement, the joint assets have been split. There are no children. Can you think of any reason you and Mr. Morgano would need to see each other, talk, text, or email each other in the future?"

Tori shook her head. "No, Your Honor."

"Then, I see no undue burden or hardship on Mr. Morgano in granting the plaintiff's request for a temporary restraining order. A hearing on issuing a final order will be held on November 22nd at nine o'clock. Mr. Margolis, your client may not contact, call, email, message, threaten, stalk or follow Mrs. Morgano. Please advise him New Jersey is merciless about protective order violations, and failure to comply, even sending one angry drunken text, could result in fines in excess of one thousand dollars and jail time."

Judge Foti turned to the back page of the Judgment of Divorce. "Please confirm for the record that you signed this Judgment of Divorce of your own free will."

"I have."

"Mr. Margolis, I see your client has signed, and you have notarized the Judgment of Divorce," the judge said.

"Yes, your Honor."

"You may step down now, Ms. Harrigan."

"Thank you, Your Honor." Tori returned to the seat beside Ivy.

Then, Judge Foti announced the divorce was final, the temporary restraining order was granted, and she would see the attorneys in her courtroom for the final Protection Order hearing on November 22nd.

Court was adjourned.

Tori's marriage was over.

Chapter 38
What A Difference A Day Makes!

When Tori saw Knox sitting on the black wicker rocker on her porch, his head bent over his phone, relief spread through her. He was the one person she'd wanted to talk to and the only one she hadn't been able to reach.

"Knox, how? How are you here?" she asked when he opened the door to help her out of the car. He folded her in his arms and kissed the top of her head.

Dylan lowered the front passenger window and bent forward. "Glad you made it."

"Me too," Murphy said.

"You two knew and didn't tell me?" Tori looked from one to the other.

"In his email, the one I told you about this morning, Knox said he would get the first available seat on the first available flight. I didn't know when he'd get here, and I didn't want you to be disappointed. He texted me when he landed," Dylan said.

"The text came while we were in court," Murphy said. "That's when Dylan showed me the email."

"We're leaving you in capable hands," Dylan called out the car window. Knox released Tori from the hug but kept his arm around her shoulders. They watched the Malone's car turn onto the street before walking to the house.

"Tori, how do you feel? How did everything go this morning?"

"My spirits are great, but my body's a mess. The divorce is final, and the judge granted the temporary protection order. Knox, I'm so glad you're here and not in DC. But what about your meetings?"

"I wanted to come last night. But there were no flights," Knox said. "I was able to get a seat on the first shuttle this morning, and George brought me here. Jeremiah Sullivan, Sully, the SEC lawyer I'm working with, and I got through everything major we needed to get done. The rest we can finish up remotely. Staying wasn't an option. Coming back was too important. Tori, did you tell the police about Nico's history of harassing behavior—going back to last summer?"

She shook her head. "No, too much was happening last night. I didn't think about it."

He nodded. "I get that. But the pattern of escalation is clear, and it could mean the difference between the ADA pleading this down to probation and community service or pushing for jail time."

As they settled on the sofa in the family room, she said, "Okay, I'll tell Officer Hanson. The depth of Nico's hatred frightens me. I know the order of protection is only a piece of paper, but if he violates it…."

Knox nodded. "Let's hope the threat of fines and months in jail keep him away from you." He pulled out his phone and opened the calendar app. "Did the judge set a date for the final protection order hearing?"

She nodded. "November 22nd."

"Time?"

"Nine. Ivy's sending over a messenger later to pick that up." Tori pointed to a brown box in the corner of the room.

"What is it?"

"The box that came Sunday with day two's little gift—two dozen department store samples of Eena's favorite perfume and lotion. She must have been collecting them for a while. How long have they been planning this?" Tori shuddered. "The envelope with the photos, the spiders, and the sex toys are in there, too. Ivy said she needs them for the hearing."

"Mind if I look? I've never seen a picture of Nico, and I only caught a glimpse of Eena at the ballet. It dawned on me last night that if I saw them on the street, I wouldn't recognize them."

"No, go ahead. While you do that, I'm going upstairs to change into my soft, fleecy sweatpants and top. I've been fantasizing about them all morning."

Several minutes later, as Tori approached the top of the stairs, she felt her heart race. She took several cleansing breaths and waited for her breathing to slow. Knox called up the steps, "Tori, do you need help?"

She clutched the railing with her right hand. "I'm okay." Her voice sounded brittle as if she were about to cry. She heard his footfall on the stairs as he came to meet her. "I'm okay. Just a little post-traumatic stair disorder," she said, placing one foot first and then the other on the first step.

"Do you want me to go down first?" Knox asked. "Or do you want me to go behind you?"

"No! Not behind me!"

"Sorry. That was thoughtless. Of course, I'll go down first."

At the bottom of the steps, Knox put his arm around her and led her to the love seat.

"More comfortable?"

"Much. Although I know I'm not a pretty sight. Between the face and the clothes."

"What happened to you was…." He closed his eyes, and when he opened them, they glistened with unshed tears. "Your neck, your back could have been broken. You could have been paralyzed. You could have died. You see bruises, scratches, and stitches. I see shields that protected you from far worse. I. Am. So. Grateful. To. And. For. Every. Last. One." He punctuated every word with a gentle kiss—on the bruises around her right eye and left cheek, the stitches on her forehead, the scratches on her arms and hands.

"What did the doctor say about going away this weekend?" he asked.

Tori shook her head. "I didn't even bring it up last night. I know we can't go. Lulu canceled our reservations, and the spa is refunding our money. Murphy and I tried to convince her to put all three deposits toward a ticket to fly down here, but Jackson's a bit under the weather, and she'll be happier at home. Murphy canceled the dog sitter for me."

"Good. Resting at home is the best thing for you. And on a more selfish note, how about if we go away for my birthday? I didn't bring it up before because I didn't think you'd want Baron at the sitter's two weekends in a row."

She smiled. "Okay. Where should we go?"

"I have a couple of ideas."

Tori stifled a yawn. "Remember, no skydiving or rappelling down a cliff. You promised."

He rolled his eyes. "I remember."

"What did you think?" she nodded toward the box on the coffee table.

He stood and picked it up. "I was about to put this by the door, so it's handy when the messenger comes." As he walked to the front of the townhouse, he called back, "In the photo at Malmaison, they look normal."

"They're a good-looking couple. Eena's a beautiful woman," Tori called back.

"Think so? She's too 'in your face,' hard," he said as he sat down again.

"But she is beautiful. She always turned heads when we went out."

Knox took both her hands in his. "Do me a favor. Close your eyes for a minute. That's it. Now, picture the ballet we saw on Saturday."

Tori's nose wrinkled. "What are you picturing?" he asked. "Tell me."

"The music is staccato. The dancers' movements are exaggerated, sharp."

"Okay. Now, think about the second act of A Midsummer Night's Dream."

She smiled.

"Why are you smiling?"

"Because everything about that grand pas de deux is elegant and graceful. Murphy calls it 'Balanchine's love poem written in the language of dance.'"

"Okay, open your eyes," he said. "Eena is Jewels. Technically beautiful, but cold, harsh, flashy. You are the elegance and grace of the love poem. You are the true beauty—inside and out."

"Thank you. You are a sweet man." Her cheeks blushed. As she leaned toward him, she ran her fingertip across a tiny scratch that had scabbed at the base of his right sideburn.

"What happened here?" she asked.

"Nicked it shaving this morning."

She kissed it. "Be careful. I like this face and don't want anything to happen to it."

"Ditto."

As Tori nodded, she stifled a yawn.

"Much as I'd enjoy kissing you right now, I'm guessing you haven't slept well the past couple of weeks," Knox said. "How about you lie down on the sofa, we'll have Alexa play some soft music, and maybe you can catch a nap?" While she had been changing clothes, he'd set up the sofa. Now he tucked her in with a cashmere throw. "Comfortable?"

She nodded.

"Do you want anything? Water? Something to eat?"

She shook her head. "I'm fine. But if you want something, help yourself. There's leftover Chinese, cold cuts. We made cookies Sunday, but you should 'nuke' 'em a few seconds to make them soft and warm and the chocolate gooey," Tori yawned. "And could you turn on the fireplace? I just think it makes everything cozier."

"Absolutely. Why don't you close your eyes?"

"But I don't want to sleep while you're here. I've missed you."

"I'm not going anywhere until you tell me to leave. I'll be here when you wake up."

She smiled. "Promise?"

"Promise."

When Tori woke, the soft orange light streaming through the family room windows told her it was late afternoon. She'd slept several hours. Knox had placed a glass of water on the coffee table next to her, and she took a refreshing swallow. Her headache was gone, and her muscles didn't feel as stiff as they had. Knox was sitting at the counter, his laptop open. His back was to her, and he was talking on the phone.

"No, I'll be working remotely the rest of the week," Knox said to the person on the other end. "My girlfriend was assaulted last night, and…."

She smiled at the word, girlfriend, and because Baron was sitting next to Knox, leaning into him, his head on Knox's thigh, his eyes closed, while Knox stroked the top of his head. Until now, she had been the only person Baron would snuggle up to like that.

"Yes. It was frightening and frustrating being out of town. Unable to get back until this morning. Tori should be better in a few days. Anyway, I'm available by phone and email if anyone needs me."

When he ended the call, Tori asked, "You're not going to work the rest of the week?"

He swiveled on the counter stool to face her. "You're awake. How do you feel?"

"Much better." She stood and began to fold the throw.

"I'll do that. You sit down," he said, taking the blanket from her.

"You were right. I needed that nap. If this law thing doesn't work out…."

Knox chuckled. "I'll keep that in mind. While you were sleeping, the messenger came from Ivy's office."

"Good. I don't want to think about or look at those things again until the hearing. Hey, what are those?" She pointed to a vase containing a dozen roses in a rainbow of colors sitting on the counter by the sink. "And you didn't answer me about taking the rest of the week. Oh no! Poor Baron. He needs to be walked and fed."

"I fed Baron. One of the boys next door came by about a half-hour ago and walked him. Said his mother sent him. Yes, I'm working remotely. And these," he retrieved the vase from the counter and placed them on the coffee table in front of her, "came a little while ago."

"I feel like Rip Van Winkle. Lots happened since I closed my eyes."

He winked. "You have no idea."

"What? Tell me."

"Not yet. It's a surprise. I've been doing my research and planning our getaway. Now about these roses…."

She pulled the florist's card from the plastic trident and smiled when she saw the envelope was addressed to Ms. Victoria Harrigan. Her smile grew as she read the card aloud, "Tori, 'It is madness to hate all roses because you got scratched with one thorn.' XO Knox."

"'To give up your dreams because one didn't come true. To not believe in love because someone was unfaithful,'" she continued. "I love that quote from Antoine de Saint-Exupéry."

"I thought you'd recognize it," Knox said. "I believe there will always be another opportunity, another dream, another love."

"For every end, a new beginning?" she asked.

When he nodded, she said, "I believe that, too."

He kissed her softly. "Do you have any idea how important you are to me? Last night, when Murphy told me what had happened, my heart stopped. That's why I had to hear your voice myself." He kissed her again. "So, I am at your beck and call. How about something to eat? You haven't eaten since breakfast. I'll order anything you want."

"What about you? You must be starved."

"I'm hungry but not starving. I finished the leftover Chinese food earlier and had two cookies. You're right. They are amazing heated."

"Good. I'm a lousy host. You come over, I fall asleep, and you have to fend for yourself."

"You're a wonderful host. But I'm ready for dinner, and I bet you are too. What sounds good to you?"

"Let's not order in. Murphy and I spent Sunday cooking. How does Mediterranean chicken with wild rice sound?"

"Delicious."

Later, as they sat in the family room, Knox put his arm around her. "Last week, when I went to place the order for the flowers, I'd planned on ordering a dozen long-stemmed red roses. The very wise florist told me that if I was sending them to someone special, I needed to write a love letter instead. The color of each rose has a meaning, a hidden message, and I've written you a love letter."

"Read it to me."

"Pink roses symbolize admiration. These deep pink roses tell you how grateful I am that we met. How much I admire you. Yellow roses mean friendship and happiness. Our friendship makes me very happy. The two peach roses signify passion—your passion for life. I learn so much every time we're together. Which leads us to the silvery mauve roses."

"What do they mean?"

"Enchantment. You bewitched me that night at the US Open, and I fall further under your spell each time we're together. The white roses symbolize our new beginning. And I think the meaning of the two red roses is clear." He gently brushed the tears from her cheeks.

"Thank you. The roses are beautiful. I've relied on you these past weeks more than you could ever know."

Knox leaned in and kissed her softly on the lips. She breathed in the citrusy smell of his aftershave and ran the tips of her fingers along his jawline as they each deepened the kiss. He pulled away. "You okay? I didn't hurt you, did I?"

She shook her head. "You shaved?"

"Yeah. I was getting a bit scruffy."

She nodded. "Thank you."

Knox held her in his arms and looked into her eyes. "I have dreamed of holding you, kissing you for so long. And now I don't want to hurt you."

"I trust you. You won't hurt me. Do you remember several weeks ago, at Yankee Stadium, when Eddie put us on the Kiss Cam, and you told me the next time you kissed me, you wouldn't stop at one, and it wouldn't be in front of a capacity crowd?"

He nodded. "I remember." His voice was husky.

"Well, we're alone now. And an offer was extended, a promise made."

He pulled her to him. Her heart raced as she pressed herself against him and melted into him. His lips possessed hers, and his kiss tasted of the crisp grapes and tart apples from the glass of wine he'd had at dinner. His arms tightened around her.

She winced, and he pulled away.

"What's wrong?" Tori asked.

"Your ribs are bruised, and I hurt you. I'm sorry."

"Knox, if we put our heads together, we can figure this out." She stood, took his hand, and led him to the stairs.

Chapter 39

Just Your Ordinary, Everyday Con Man

Friday morning, Knox suggested they order dinner in that evening and invite the Malones. "This was supposed to be your spa weekend in the Berkshires with Murphy and Lulu," he said. "Just because your trip had to be canceled, doesn't mean we can't make this weekend special." He'd ordered her favorite dish, Chicken Caprese, from one of her favorite restaurants, Café Scalinatella, and even arranged a Zoom call after dinner with Lulu and Tom. She told him his plans for the evening were even better than the warm vanilla cream massage she'd scheduled and had to cancel at the spa.

Murphy and Dylan arrived just before seven o'clock. As soon as she opened the door, Tori could tell something was wrong.

"You both look so serious. What's up? she asked, looking first at Murphy, then Dylan.

The distinctive "pop" of a cork being pulled from a wine bottle filled the silence. "Wine. This needs to be discussed over a glass of wine," Murphy said. She led them to the kitchen, picking up two glasses of the Pinot Grigio Knox had just poured and handing one to Tori. "Go on," she said to Dylan. "Tell her."

"I got a voicemail from Sal this afternoon," Dylan said. "Nico was arrested. The arraignment was this morning. He's already out on bail."

Knox put his arm around Tori's shoulder. "You okay?" he asked in a soft voice.

She leaned into him and nodded. "It wasn't unexpected. But I hate he's out and angrier than ever, I bet." She took a swallow of wine.

"But you know we have your back, right?" Murphy said. "And now you've got protection orders in New York and New Jersey."

"I know. Thanks." Tori sighed. "I've felt so safe here in my little cocoon. And what about you, Dylan? You identified him to the police, and if he doesn't take a plea deal, this goes to court, you'll have to testify."

"Yes, but I doubt he knows I was the person who ID'ed him. And besides, it's you he seems to blame for everything."

"I've already promised my mom I'll leave work on time, won't stay late—especially now that it's getting dark earlier."

"Good," Murph said, and Dylan nodded.

"How much was the bail, Dylan? Did Sal say?" Knox asked.

"$15,000."

"Enough about Nico," Tori said. "Our delicious dinner should be here any minute, and then we've got a Zoom call with Lulu and Tom."

After dinner, Murphy and Dylan logged into the call on Tori's laptop while Tori and Knox logged in on his. The Roberts were waiting for them.

Tom, who hadn't seen or talked with Tori since the assault, asked how she felt. "It still looks painful. Wish we lived closer so we could help."

"Me, too. But I see a major improvement since Tuesday morning," Lulu said.

"It's all the TLC I've been getting for the past few days." Tori smiled at Knox.

"Are there any updates on Nico?" Tom asked.

Tori groaned and turned to Dylan. "Go ahead. Fill them in. I need more wine for this. Anyone else?" she said, reaching for the wine bottle. Murphy lifted her glass which Tori topped off before filling her own.

"Nico was arrested at Anthony's last night, and the arraignment was this morning. He pled not guilty," Dylan said.

"That's rich!" Lulu said. "The 'who are you going to believe? Me or your lying eyes?' defense. How are you feeling about that, Tori?"

"I'm a little nervous, but I can't stop living my life. If he comes any-where near me, I'll have him arrested for violating the protection order."

"Tori," Tom said, "was Anthony that obnoxious guy at your wedding? Very loud, was a bit overserved?"

Tori nodded. "Yup."

"He tried to impress us with the places he'd been, things he'd done," Lulu said. "Told us about an amazing ski trip he'd taken, how impressed the instructors had been at how easily he'd mastered cross-country skiing. It turns out he was talking about Chateau Grand Pente. Where my family went every year when I was growing up. Where Tom and I still go skiing. Where the Maine Alpine Skiing team practices. Where there is no cross-country skiing."

"He was so full of himself. Never made the connection Lulu's accent might mean she's from Maine and might have been to or known about the Chateau," Tom said.

"You didn't tell him you were from 'Bah Hahbah,' Lu? Shame on you," Tori said.

"No. She just called him on his BS," Tom said, "and he couldn't get away from us fast enough.

"Sounds like a prince," Knox said. "How do Anthony and Nico know each other?"

"Nico, Anthony, and I went to middle and high school together, lived down the street from each other. Anthony was the kid who always had a scheme, looked for the easy way out," Dylan said. "Why study when you can cheat? Why write a paper when you can buy one that's already earned a good grade? My mom didn't like me hanging out with him. Said he was nothing but trouble.

"He works for one of the smaller Wall Street firms, doesn't he?" Tori asked.

"Not anymore. Last I heard—from Nico, as a matter of fact—he'd been fired, lost his stockbroker's license, and was now promoting stocks," Dylan said.

"What does that mean?" Murphy asked. "What does he do?"

"It means he gets paid to hype stocks," Tori said.

"Some stock promoters are honest, but many more aren't," Knox said.

"The dishonest ones pump up the price of a stock they own by deliberately telling potential buyers information about the company that isn't true. Then, because the investors believe the hype, they buy the stock. The price shoots up, and the shysters sell," Dylan said.

"Hinting at an imminent takeover is one of their popular sales pitches," Knox said. "But there never is a takeover. It's all a scam. Some promoters even make-up dummy press releases about celebrity endorsements or lucrative contracts to lure people in."

"That analyst on one of the financial stations you watch? You know, the cute one who got fired several months ago?" Murphy asked her husband.

Dylan rolled his eyes and smiled at his wife. "Yeah."

"When I asked why he wasn't on the morning show anymore, you said he'd been fired. He was always recommending stocks. Was he a stock promoter?"

"Yeah, he had a great job at a top Wall Street firm and was an oil and gas industry expert. But he was recommending a lot of stocks he or members of his family owned to drive up the prices. Once he'd sold his positions, took his profits off the table, he walked back his recommendations, and the stock prices fell," Dylan said.

"I know the analyst you're talking about," Knox said. "Some of those stocks made big price corrections, and investors lost a lot of money. He wasn't just fired—from the brokerage firm and the television network. He was arrested."

"Tell me Anthony's not on television," Lulu said. "Please. I'm about to hurl at the thought."

Dylan laughed. "No, I suspect Anthony's just your ordinary, everyday con man—lying to investors, getting them to buy penny stocks he owns to drive up the price. Then he sells, the stock tanks, and the people he conned are left holding the bag."

"That's disgusting," Lulu said. "I only met him once, but I could see him doing that."

"Me too," Dylan said. "Anthony was never one to color inside the lines."

"Nico knew the medical insurance fraud scam was illegal and did it anyway. I don't think it would take much arm-twisting on Anthony's part to involve Nico in this scam, too," Tori said.

"Good point, although Eena did offer other incentives," Murphy said. "How much prison time could that analyst from TV get? If he's convicted."

"As much as five years, but since this is his first offense, probably less," Dylan said.

"The Department of Justice and Securities and Exchange Commission have beefed up their investigations into these types of scams because, with chat rooms, social media, crooks can cast a wider net, swindle more and more people," Knox said.

"Knox and his firm are working with the SEC helping swindled investors recoup some of their losses," Tori said. "He's one of the good guys."

"What do you do, Knox? To get the money back?" Lulu asked.

"Once the government's suit against a dishonest promoter is settled and the fines paid, the remaining assets are split among the investors. Many have lost everything. But getting back something when you have nothing left? That can mean a lot," he said. "That's why I was in DC on Monday. The SEC had just settled another case."

"If what you think is true, how are they doing it?" Tom asked. "Anthony's license was revoked, and Nico's not a broker."

"They could be working for or with someone licensed," Knox said.

"If they are part of a pump and dump scheme," Dylan said, "let's hope they get caught."

Chapter 40
A Day at the Beach

Saturday, October 7th

The early October Saturday morning was warm and sunny, and Knox suggested they drive to Sandy Hook. "It's only an hour away," he said, "and a walk on the beach is the perfect way to spend the day."

After breakfast, they packed two folding chairs, a small cooler, and Baron's tote bag into the trunk of Tori's car. Baron took his place on his bed in the back seat.

"He's so excited," Tori said. "He started twirling and dancing around the kitchen as soon as I took his new frisbee and the ball launcher out of the closet and put them in his bag. He doesn't know where he's going, but he knows it will be fun!"

On the drive, they talked about their plans for the next day. They were meeting Knox's parents, Ben, and Ben's girlfriend, Kelly, at '76 House for brunch. Although Tori had met both Margot and Dan Cooper before—once, Labor Day weekend when she'd run into Knox, Ben, and their parents at her favorite craft fair on the Lincoln Center Plaza, and again, when she and Knox had met them for dinner in the City, neither she nor Knox had met Kelly. After brunch, Dan and Margot would follow Tori and Knox back to her townhouse, where Knox would pick up his things and drive back to the City with his parents. Whenever Tori thought about him leaving, she wanted to ask him to stay. But he was returning to his office Monday morning, and she would be working from home.

"I'm going to try putting on make-up before the brunch," she said. "Try to tone down some of the bruises a little more." When she'd seen herself in the mirror the morning after the assault, she looked as if she'd had a fight with the box of sixty-four Crayola crayons and lost. But after several days of liberally applying vitamin E, her bruises were fading. Even the Purple Pizazz is more a Jazzberry Jam, she thought.

"You don't need to do that, you know."

"Yeah, but I'll feel better, more like myself. I've been thinking a lot about the women whose partners or husbands hit them, beat them regularly. Women I might see every day but never notice the bruising beneath the concealer and foundation," she said. "Thank you, by the way. When I was feeling sorry for myself the other day. What you said helped me put all this in perspective. Everything that's happened to me will heal. I'm very lucky and ashamed you had to point that out."

He reached over, took the hand resting on her leg, and brought it to his lips. "You have a right to feel a little sorry for yourself. And you're beautiful—bruised or not, make-up or not."

"Thank you." She smiled. "By the way, what time are you meeting the realtor Monday evening?" Before they left her townhouse, Knox had found a listing for a two-bedroom home in Hoboken near the river and scheduled an appointment to see it Monday evening.

"Six. I'll catch the five o'clock ferry, and the realtor will pick me up. I've enjoyed your boardwalk along the river this week. That's one of the things that drew me to this house."

"You'll call me after? Tell me what you think?" Tori asked.

He chuckled and reached over to squeeze her left hand. "You know I will. It's going to be hard to leave, not be here this week, but next weekend, we'll be on Amelia Island. We have that to look forward to, and it will just be the two of us."

"I can't wait," she said. "It's going to be a wonderful weekend. A perfect place to celebrate you and your birthday. Everything you've planned sounds amazing."

Next Friday evening, they were flying to Amelia Island to celebrate Knox's thirty-fourth birthday. The resort where they were staying had an infinity pool overlooking the ocean—a perfect place for a late-night swim. He arranged a private boat charter for Saturday afternoon. "I thought we could sail to Cumberland Island. Maybe we'll get lucky, and the wild horses will be on the beach," he said. A couple of weeks earlier, Tori had invited Knox to be her "plus one" at Graham and Gemma's wedding, and for his birthday, she'd found a beautiful tuxedo bow tie and matching pocket square—a paisley pattern in shades of grey with a thread of silver. She'd gift-wrapped them as soon as she'd brought them home, and they were ready to be packed for Florida.

They arrived at Sandy Hook just before eleven o'clock and set up their chairs near the water's edge. Then, they took off their shoes, rolled up their jeans, and walked, ankle-deep, into the frothy remains of a wave.

"It's not as cold as I thought it would be," Knox said.

"I like my ocean a bit warmer," Tori said. "It should be perfect on Amelia Island."

Baron chose that moment to run into the water after a seagull that swooped in to catch an early lunch, causing them both to laugh. When he'd chased the gull out of the water, he ran back to shore and shook himself dry. Together, they walked the nearly deserted beach. Periodically, Tori would stoop down to pick up a shell that caught her eye, or Knox would throw the frisbee he was carrying, and Baron would race down the sand, leap in the air, and catch it. He'd run back to join them, offering the frisbee to Knox. Then, he would wag his tail and spin around in a circle, clearly hoping Knox would throw the neon orange disc again.

"He's loving this," Tori said. "I just don't have the strength to throw it as far as you do, and he can't get this kind of a workout. Love to watch him leap up to catch it. He looks like a centerfielder out there."

When they returned to their area on the beach, Tori walked to the water's edge to rinse the sand off the shells she'd collected along the way. She laid them out to dry on the brown paper grocery bag she brought with her while Knox loosened the caps of three bottles of water, put two in the cup holders of the folding chairs, and poured the third into Baron's collapsible plastic water bowl. She and Knox enjoyed the salami, cheese, and fruit she packed for their lunch, and after Baron had gobbled down his snack, he sat, first next to her chair, then next to Knox's, waiting to see if either of them would be willing to share.

"What are you going to do with these?" Knox asked as he surveyed the drying shells beside him.

Tori shrugged and chuckled. "I know. I've got shells all over the house. But I can't seem to go to a beach without collecting more."

"I love your glass lamp, the one on the library table, with all the shells. Did you buy it like that, or are those shells you collected?"

"I collected every last one, washed and shellacked them," Tori said. "Try picking that lamp up when we get back to the house. It weighs a ton. Mom gave it to me as a housewarming gift. I picked out everything for that lamp—the size and shape of the ginger jar, the base. Even the finial is a shell I found on Sanibel Island. I love that lamp."

Later, Tori read the novel she'd started just before the assault, and Knox played catch with Baron. Using the ball launcher, he could send the yellow tennis ball far down the beach, and Baron had to run hard to catch and return it.

By mid-afternoon, they were ready to pack up the chairs, tote bag, and shells and head back to Fort Lee—by way of Beaches Burgers. They sat outside and enjoyed an early dinner of cheeseburgers and milkshakes. "Okay, the milkshake might not have been the best idea," Tori said as they got in the car again. "Brain freeze and I'm cold."

On the drive back, they were treated to a spectacular sunset, and just as the darkness was replacing the light, they were home. All in all, the day at the beach had been the perfect way to end the week.

Chapter 41
Her Altruistic Outreach

Friday, October 27th

Monday evening Knox had called her after he'd seen the townhouse. While he wasn't as enthusiastic as she had hoped he would be upon touring the property, he and his realtor were preparing an offer. Wednesday morning, the sellers rejected it. Knox decided not to submit another bid. "Something doesn't feel right," he said.

Their time on Amelia Island had been blissful. In the two weeks that followed their trip, Tori's bruises had faded, and with her doctor's approval, she'd resumed her self-defense training. She was feeling stronger, more confident. And she hadn't heard from or about Nico or even given him much thought.

She and Knox had fallen into a comfortable routine—they talked every day, texted often, and met for lunch at least once a week. Every Friday night, they boarded the ferry to Fort Lee, and Monday morning, they rode the ferry back to Lower Manhattan. That first weekend, Tori had been hesitant to resume her tradition of spending Friday evening with Murphy and Dylan—ordering a pizza or going out for dinner, playing cards at home, or going to a movie. How will Dylan feel about Knox joining us? The Friday get-togethers started with him and Nico. But when Murphy told her husband Knox would be staying with Tori for the weekend, it had been Dylan who'd initiated their first evening of pizza and bridge.

This Friday evening, they were going for burgers and then back to the Malones for cards. Tori pulled the car into the restaurant's parking lot next to Dylan's SUV and turned to Knox.

"I can't wait to introduce you to the Patrick Henry Tavern's Huzzah burger. The chef slathers cheddar pub cheese with a hint of horseradish on the bun, and when the bun connects with the hot burger—it is one yummy mess. If I order fries and you order onion rings, we could share."

"As long as you let me lean over and steal the fries from your plate —I love doing that," he said as he helped her out of the car.

Table manners be damned. Tori loved that too. For her, that simple gesture was a sign of the intimacy building in their relationship.

"This is my favorite way to end the week—having dinner with Murph and Dylan and then playing bridge or going to a movie," she said.

As they walked hand-in-hand across the parking lot, Tori's phone rang. It was her mother.

"You go on in, find Murph and Dylan. Order for me. I'm going to see what Mom wants. I'll be right behind you."

"Huzzah burger medium, fries, and a diet Pepsi?"

She smiled and gave him a thumb's up.

"I got it," Knox said before disappearing into the tavern. Tori stood near the restaurant's front door to take the call.

"Hi, Mom. What's up?"

"Oh, Tori, I have to tell you about two phone calls I received this week."

Tori was instantly on alert. Her mother's conversation hadn't begun with her usual "Hi honey. I'm not catching you at a bad time, am I?" Instead, Anna's voice was strained, and she spoke too quickly—hallmark signs her mother was anxious or upset.

"Okay. What's wrong? Start from the beginning."

Two days earlier, Anna had received a call at work from a guy named Ted Russo of Grand Piper Securities. He knew her mother recently participated in a fundraiser to help patients diagnosed with rheumatoid arthritis who couldn't afford treatments. Her "altruistic outreach" on behalf of those suffering from the debilitating disease was why he knew she'd be interested in a start-up pharmaceutical company developing a revolutionary drug. This once-a-year infusion could be individualized for each RA patient depending on the severity of the illness.

"Wait a minute, Mom." Tori dug in her purse for a pen and something to write on. She sat on the bench to the right of the restaurant's entrance and lay her pocketbook on her lap, so she had a surface to write on. Holding her phone in her left hand while anchoring the corner of a crumbled piece of paper with her left elbow, she began to jot down some of the things her mother had already told her. "Go on," she said.

"The company is called OPM Pharma," Anna said. "According to Mr. Russo, those are the initials of the doctor who first diagnosed RA."

The stock in this new company was selling for only $2.75 a share. The drug would be starting the second phase of clinical trials very soon, Mr. Russo said, because it had performed above expectations in the initial trial period. According to industry experts, he told Anna, FDA approval for this groundbreaking drug was almost a "sure-thing. " Finally, he delivered the coup de grâce—executives of OPM were in talks with professional athletes and famous actors who suffered from the disease to secure their endorsements.

"Tori, he told me both Lucille Ball and Edith Piaf had RA," Anna said. "Did you know that?"

"No, Mom, I didn't. And I doubt either one of them will be using the drug or giving their endorsements."

Her mother interrupted. "I had to get off the phone to go to a meeting. Thursday. I didn't get a chance to call Mr. Russo back. But today, just about three hours ago, I got a call at home from Mr. Gary Gunderson, who said he was the Chief Investment Officer of Grand Piper Securities."

Mr. Gunderson was following up to see if he could answer any additional questions Anna might have. "When I told him I was very interested but would need to speak with my daughter and investment advisor before going ahead, he told me I was making a huge mistake, taking an unnecessary gamble." The news about the trials and the endorsements could leak to the press at any time, and the stock price would soar, Mr. Gunderson said. Anna should invest right away.

Tori crossed her fingers and held her breath a moment before asking, "Mom, you didn't authorize him to buy shares for you or promise to send him money, did you?"

"No, Honey, not yet. I wanted to mention it to you first. I haven't talked to Larry either, but I don't think he'll be too keen on the idea. He's very conservative when it comes to overseeing the money your father left me."

Larry Membinger had been a long-time family friend and her father's investment advisor for years. Tori almost chuckled as she imagined Uncle Larry's appalled look as her mother relayed the story of the two phone calls.

"Good." Tori breathed a sigh of relief. "This whole thing doesn't sound kosher, but I promise I'll check it out. Don't tell Uncle Larry. It would only upset him. And Mom, promise me, swear you won't do anything—take their phone calls, send them money or commit to anything —until I check them out. Once some of these guys get you to commit to a few hundred or even a thousand dollars, they pressure you to invest more—tens of thousands. Remember what Grandfather used to say, 'If a man offers to sell you a diamond ring for a dime, he's offering you a piece of jewelry not worth ten cents.'"

Anna swore she would follow Tori's instructions to the letter. "Honor bright," she'd said. The solemn promise she and Tori's father had always made to Tori when she was growing up.

Promising to call back as soon as she'd researched OPM, Tori went to join Knox, Murphy, and Dylan inside. The tavern's owner greeted her —she and the Malones had been regulars for years—and showed her to their table. Knox stood, helped her off with her coat, and held her chair.

"Everything all right? he asked in a soft voice. She shook her head and put her notes on the table before sitting down.

"Uh oh, what's wrong?" Murphy said. "You've got your worry face on."

"My mom was cold-called this week," Tori said. "Twice. I'm sure it was a pump and dump pitch."

"Tell us what happened," Dylan said. "Looks like you took notes."

Tori nodded. "Yeah, I told her I'd research the company, and I will, but if it's what I think it is, I'm going to file an SEC complaint."

One server approached their table with a tray stand, and another carried a tray with their burgers. When they'd all been served, and the waitstaff had left, Tori continued.

"The first call came Wednesday morning—cold call prime-time." She turned the plastic ketchup bottle upside down and shook it before squeezing a large dollop on the side of her plate. Then she glanced at her notes before continuing. "A Mr. Russo called Mom at her office. The second call was this afternoon at the house."

"She didn't place an order, send him money, did she?" Knox asked. He leaned over to take a fry from her plate, dipped it in the ketchup, and popped it in his mouth.

"No, she told both men she'd check with her investment advisor and me and get back to them. But these guys were good. They'd done their research. The company they pitched her," Tori rechecked her notes, "OPM Pharma, has a drug that will, they claim, revolutionize the treatment of rheumatoid arthritis."

"Your mom posted pictures of her with your two aunts on her Facebook page at that RA fundraiser last weekend. The three sisters looked so cute in their jogging pants and sneakers, getting warmed up for the 5K. There was another picture, a fantastic one of them, high-fiving each other as they crossed the finish line," Murphy said.

"That's what I thought. The minute Mom told me Mr. Russo had complimented her 'altruistic outreach'," Tori said and rolled her eyes.

She reached over to take an onion ring from Knox's plate.

"Either of you ever heard of," she checked her notes a third time, "Grand Piper Securities?"

"What? What's goin' on?" Tori looked first at Knox, who stopped chewing as soon as the words left her mouth, and then Dylan, who was coughing and choking on his last swallow of beer.

Knox cupped her elbow in his hand and leaned closer. "Honey, let's not talk about this here, okay?" he said softly.

"We need to table this conversation until we're back at our place," Dylan said, his voice still husky from the coughing bout.

"What?" Tori asked, looking first at Knox, then Dylan, and then back at Knox. "Guys, you're scaring me. This is my mom."

"It'll be okay," Knox said, his voice low. "We'll ask for the check, finish our burgers, and head to the Malones." He removed his credit card from his wallet and signaled their waiter.

Chapter 42
Grand Piper Securities

On the way to the Malones, Tori repeated everything her mother had said on the phone and pleaded with Knox to tell her what he and Dylan knew about Grand Piper Securities. She was startled when he said, "I don't know what Dylan knows, but I'm positive it isn't what I know."

As soon as they entered the Malone's front door, they dropped their coats on one end of the sofa and walked past the card table, set up for the evening of bridge they'd planned, toward the back of the house.

"Let's sit at the kitchen table," Dylan said. Before he sat down, he pulled the magnetic notepad and pencil from the front of the refrigerator. Then, he drew a diamond shape on the top sheet of paper and wrote an X at each corner of the diamond. Finally, he placed a fifth X just to the left of the shape.

"When I was growing up, Gene Piper owned a popular pub and restaurant in our neighborhood. Piper's Tavern was the kind of place where families went on a fall Sunday afternoon to enjoy an early dinner and watch the Giants game or have a light supper on a summer Saturday after a day at the pool. Mr. Piper made the best pizza, and my mom still raves about his crabcake sandwiches. He sponsored our neighborhood baseball team. The Piper Pirates."

"The five of us who played the infield called ourselves the 'Grand Pipers.' The catcher was Gary Gunderson." He wrote a capital G beside the X at the bottom of the diamond.

"He's the one who called my mom this afternoon. He's the Chief Investment Officer of Grand Piper Securities," Tori said.

Dylan nodded. "Robert Masocci at second." He added an R beside the X at the top of the diamond. "Anthony Antonuccio on first." An A was added. "Nico Morgano, third base." An N was put next to the fourth X. "And yours truly at shortstop." He put a D by the final X next to the baseball diamond. "G. R. A. N. D. Our first initials and our nickname."

"No. No, No, No! Tori pounded her fists on the table, accenting each word. "Are you telling me this whole scam goes back to Nico? That now he's trying to swindle my mother? Hurt my mom?"

She pushed herself away from the table and paced up and down in the family room. Her hands still balled into fists. "Will I ever be rid of him? What do I have to do to be rid of him?" she shouted.

Knox wrapped his arms around her. She pounded her fists against his chest until finally burying her head in his shoulder and crying. He held her until the tears stopped. She looked up at him. "How do I share this news with Mom?"

"How about we do it together? In person. Tomorrow. Why don't you call her? Tell her we'll be there by lunchtime. And Tori, she told you she hadn't called either Russo or Gunderson back, so she has their numbers. Ask her not to throw them away."

Tori nodded. "I'll call her now." She took her phone from her purse and walked into the living room. When she returned to the kitchen, Knox asked, "All set?"

"Yeah, I told her you couldn't wait to meet her—my excuse for our impromptu visit. And I said I'd get Russo's and Gunderson's numbers so I could follow up with them on Monday. I didn't mention anything about, you know."

"Perfect because that's all true. I do want to meet your mom. Now come, sit down. Let me tell you what I know."

Knox took her hand in his before turning to Dylan. "Do you know anything about Robert Masocci? What he's doing now?"

"Yeah. He married Murph and me. We were his first marriage ceremony after his ordination. He's a Monsignor at a parish in Connecticut."

Knox nodded. "While you were calling your mother, Tori, I was doing a little research." He showed them his phone, open to the website of Grand Piper Securities. Gary Gunderson, Anthony Antonuccio, and Nico Morgano were standing, side-by-side smiling—the Chief Invesment Officer, the Chief Operating Officer, and the Chief Financial Officer. To the side and in the background were three men and two women, who appeared to be in their early to mid-twenties and who were identified on the website as "the sales team behind Grand Piper's success." Reading their names from left to right, Ted Russo was dead center.

Tori, Murphy, and Dylan reached for their phones.

"Look at their credentials," Dylan said, then turned his phone so that the others could see that section of the website. "Looks like Gary's the only licensed broker. Ted seems to be the only member of the so-called sales team who's taken the SIE, but there's no mention he took the licensing exams."

"What does that mean?" Murphy asked.

"No one at Grand Piper can sell anything but Gary Gunderson," Knox said.

"It would be unethical and illegal for anyone else to take an order. Although I doubt that technicality would slow them down," Dylan said.

"Ted Russo told Mom OPM Pharma, the pharmaceutical company he pitched her, was named for the doctor who first diagnosed RA. His initials were OPM. But when I search the doctor's name, I get Augustin Jacob Landré-Beauvais. Another lie."

Knox and Dylan exchanged looks. "What?" Tori asked.

"It's probably their inside joke. OPM—short for Other People's Money," Dylan said.

"It makes the scam more flexible," Knox said. "Your mother posted pictures at an RA fundraiser. Someone else's social media post might show them at an event for the American Cancer Society or the March of Dimes. Same company, same pitch, different disease."

"These guys are truly evil," Murphy said. "Really? Other people's money?"

Knox took a deep breath and turned to Tori. Tears of frustration welled in her eyes, and he squeezed her hand. "You okay?" he asked.

"I'm just so angry. I've never wanted to hurt anyone so much," she said.

"Just remember, we're partners in this. We've got this." He kissed her gently.

"Now, I'll tell you what I know, but it cannot leave this room." Knox looked at each of them, and they each pledged their silence with a nod.

"Jeremiah Sullivan, Sully, is the attorney at the SEC I've been working with. The last time I was in DC—the same day Nico attacked you—Sully and I were in his office when he received an urgent call. From a US attorney for the Eastern District of New York. I only heard Sully's side of the conversation, and he didn't say much at all—just agreed with what the person on the other end was saying.

"After the call though, he asked his PA to have two lawyers who work for him come to his office right away. When they got there, Sully told them he was putting the SEC's civil suit against Grand Piper Securities on temporary hold. He said they would add at least one more charge to the civil action before it was filed. Right after a New York federal grand jury issued criminal indictments against the three Grand Piper executives."

Chapter 43
On the Road to Williamsport

The following morning, as Tori was adjusting her scarf in the bedroom mirror, Knox walked up behind her, put his arms around her, and met her eyes in their reflection.

"You didn't sleep well last night," Knox said. "I reached for you several times, and you weren't there. I know you and Baron went downstairs at least once."

"A dream woke me. I don't remember it, but it left me," she paused, "unsettled, restless. I didn't want to disturb you."

"You could have."

"I wish your friend, Sully, would call back."

"Honey, it's not even seven o'clock on a Saturday morning. He might be sleeping in or maybe just waiting until later to call."

"I know. I'm just antsy. Could you drive this morning?"

"Of course. And maybe you can nap a little on the way," he said.

"Maybe. I'm going down to walk Baron. What if I start breakfast, and you set up his bed in the back of the car? I'll pull out his tote bag for the trip, and you can put it in the trunk with our stuff."

"Sounds good. I'll see you downstairs in a bit."

A little more than an hour later, Knox pulled the car out of the driveway. According to the navigational system, they would be at her mother's around eleven o'clock.

"Can you believe it's the last weekend in October? Graham and Gemma's wedding's next Saturday," Knox said. "I'm looking forward to our two-day staycation at the Hotel Pierre."

"I love that our big commute to and from the wedding is an elevator ride. Thank you again for arranging it," Tori said.

"And I'm looking forward to seeing that new play we have tickets for Friday night. It got a great review in the Times," Knox said. "Where do you think we should grab dinner? Joe Allen's? Jezebel's?"

"Either sounds good. Do you have a preference?"

"Crab and lobster rolls, I think," he said.

"Joe Allen's it is."

Knox was silent for a moment and then said, "When we get the phone numbers for Gunderson and Russo from your mother, I'm going to ask her permission to call Gunderson, as her lawyer, Monday morning. Tell him to stop harassing her, or I'll report Grand Piper to the SEC."

"Are you sure? I don't want any bit of this, whatever it is, to blow back on you. Jeopardize your career. I could call him."

"No, we talked about this last night. Both you and Dylan need to steer clear of this. Gunderson would recognize your name, probably wouldn't take your call. And Nico? No, it's too dangerous."

She nodded. "I could strangle Nico right now. He breaks the law, yet somehow I'm caught up in it." She shook her head. "I was afraid a blissful Nico-free month was too good to be true."

Just then, Knox's phone rang. The name, Sully, and a telephone number beginning with the Washington DC 202 area code appeared on the navigational screen.

Knox looked over at Tori. "Ready?" he asked. She nodded.

"Morning, Sully. Thanks for calling back," Knox said when he connected the call.

"Good morning, Knox. Sorry I couldn't get back to you last night. My eleven-year-old was hosting her first-ever slumber party. Six girls talked and giggled until almost three and wanted pancakes and waffles for breakfast. But their parents have picked them up, and my daughter's back in bed. Your message was intriguing. You have news about Grand Piper?"

"Sully, Tori Harrigan is with me. We're in the car on our way to her mother's in Williamsport."

"Tori, hi. It's a pleasure to meet you, by phone at least. Knox and I had just finished dinner last month when he found out you'd been assaulted. How are you feeling? No long-term aftereffects, I hope."

"I'm much better, thank you. Nice to meet you too. Do you mind if I call you Sully?"

"Everyone does. So, Knox, what news do you have about Grand Piper?"

"Tori's the one with the news, Sully."

She detailed her mother's conversations with Ted Russo and Gary Gunderson about OPM Pharma.

"OPM's a shell corporation set up for the sole purpose of running this scam," Sully said. "It has no employees, assets, products, or sales. And you know what the initials OPM stand for?"

"Knox told me last evening."

"There's more, Sully," and Knox repeated the back story of Grand Pipers' name that Dylan had told them the night before. "Gunderson was the catcher, Antonuccio, first baseman, and Tori's ex-husband, Nico, played third."

Sully's crisp, high-pitched whistle echoed through the car's sound system. "Nico Morgano's your ex-husband, Tori? The guy who assaulted you?"

"Yeah," Tori said.

"That's a twist I wasn't expecting! What's happening with that case?"

"He won't accept a plea. Trial's scheduled for the end of November," she said.

"We're on our way to Tori's mother's—to break the news her ex-son-in-law, as an executive of Grand Piper, was part of the group trying to cheat her," Knox said. "Should be there in a couple of hours. She told Russo and Gunderson she'd get back to them on Monday, but I plan to call them instead."

"Great," Sully said. "Text me their numbers when you get them. This group uses burner phones and other hard-to-detect devices to reach out to potential investors. The FBI is working that angle of the case, and I'll pass along the numbers when you send them."

"This may not be relevant," Tori said, "but Nico called me multiple times from multiple numbers last summer. The security team at my office discovered he'd used burner phones each time."

"You didn't happen to keep those numbers, did you?" Sully asked.

"Yes," Tori said. "I'll give them to Knox."

"That's great. Thanks," Sully said.

"Can you tell us anything about other shell companies these guys are peddling?" Knox asked.

"A little. One is called VMB Technology Management. They tell some potential investors it's advanced malware protection. Others investors are told it's the next big social media company. According to the incorporation documents, VMB has offices on West Seventy-First Street in Manhattan. My guys are in the office right now researching it. It's hard to keep up with these crooks—they start and shut down shell companies all the time."

"Oh my God! VMB could be Eena," Tori said.

"Who's Eena?" Sully asked.

"Nico's lover," Knox said.

"Valentina Marie Barsoti," Tori said. "Eena's her nickname. The initials work. And her godmother, Mehta Gagliardi, owns, or used to own, a townhouse at West Seventy-First and Amsterdam Avenue."

"You guys are a wealth of information this morning. You don't happen to know where I can find the mistress, do you?"

"Yes. Taconic Correctional Facility," Tori said.

"Whoa! You're kidding, right?"

"No, that's where she is. Serving an eighteen-month sentence."

"Any other companies you can tell us about?" Knox asked.

"You'll love this one—Resurrection Finance," Sully said. "A team claiming to be forensic accountants reaches out to Grand Piper's previous victims. People Gunderson and his sales team already scammed in a pump and dump scheme. Resurrection's so-called accountants claim they can recoup all or some of the money the victims lost in the stock swindle. For a substantial fee, of course. I can't wait to nail these guys."

"I can't wait for you to do that either," Tori said. "I know Nico hasn't been part of this group for long, but…."

"That's not true. He only became an executive of Grand Piper in late April," Sully said, "but he's been associated with them since the end of last year. Through a company, Broadwing Finance, he set up in December. Grand Piper hired Broadwing to do their books, and Nico signed the most recent tax returns for Grand Piper and all the shell companies."

"I didn't know anything about that."

"Tori, a piece of advice. Carefully review your last joint tax returns because the IRS is," Sully said. "The most recent returns filed for Grand Piper and all the shell corporations were signed by Nicolino Morgano and have all kinds of crazy shit—sorry, questionable entries."

"How far away from issuing a Wells are you?" Knox asked.

"Nice try, buddy," Sully said. "You know I can't confirm or deny there is or will be a Wells Notification. If either of you thinks of anything else or your mother tells you something, Tori, my team and I should know, call anytime. I'll be looking for your text with the burner numbers, Knox. Have fun, you two."

"Bye, Sully. Thanks," Knox said before disconnecting the call.

Tori groaned, then rolled her eyes. "'Be careful what you wish for. Sully finally calls, but I feel worse after our conversation. His comment about the tax returns sounded ominous. Nico always prepared them, and I reviewed them before I signed them. But I trusted him then too."

He reached over and squeezed her hand. "No worries. My mom is the best tax attorney I know. We'll ask her to give your returns a thorough review. And if something's wrong, she'll help you straighten it out."

"Thank you. If you're sure she won't mind. That makes me feel much better. Wonder what the FBI will do with the burner phone information. Do you know?"

"Every burner can be traced—whether it's a prepaid phone or a burner app you download on your cell. All mobile calls go through a cell carrier, and the FBI can compel those carriers to turn over data usage, call logs, and text messages that can be traced back to the user. Even a short call or a voicemail can provide a clear enough sample of someone's voice for the Bureau's sophisticated voice-matching software to identify the caller. And they can even track someone using a burner phone by tracing other phones that regularly move with the burner."

"Can the police do that too?" she asked.

He shook his head. "The feds have lots of toys local law enforcement would like to play with."

"How does it work?"

"Let's say I had a burner phone with me now. My identity could be traced through your cell because our phones are traveling together on Route 80, going through the same network of cell towers simultaneously."

"Okay, I get it. You asked Sully when, not if, he would be sending Grand Piper a Wells Notice. Do you honestly believe the SEC is getting ready to notify Nico, Anthony, and Gary it has evidence of securities fraud? Tori asked.

"Yes, I do."

Could this be happening? Could Nico be indicted on securities fraud charges? she wondered.

"I wish the SEC had the authority to bring criminal charges against them, throw all three of them in jail—not just bring a civil suit against them and the company," Tori said.

Knox smiled. "Remember the conversation I told you about last night between Sully and the two attorneys who work for him? He's brought in the Justice Department. And from what he just told us, probably the Criminal Investigation Unit of the IRS. Those agencies can and, it sounds like, plan to bring criminal charges."

Chapter 44
A Different Direction

When Tori woke early the following morning, she knew she wouldn't go back to sleep. She swung her legs over the side of the bed and stood as quietly as possible, then glanced back to see if she'd disturbed Knox. He hadn't moved and was still snoring softly. *Thank goodness Mom replaced that old mattress set,* she thought with a smile. The previous box spring and mattress had been purchased when she and her mother had moved into the house over twelve years ago, and for the past four years, that box spring had creaked in protest every time anyone sat down or got up from the bed.

She tiptoed to the chair where she'd set out her clothes for this morning. Baron, curled up at the foot of the bed, opened his eyes and watched her. When he was convinced she was really, truly getting up for the day, he stood and shook, causing his jowls to make a dull flapping sound as they moved back and forth, and his license and identification tags clinked together. Tori winced before putting her finger to her lips and whispering a barely audible, "Shh." Again, she looked over at Knox. He hadn't moved.

In the hall bathroom, she showered and dressed quickly before joining her mother and Baron in the kitchen. After giving her mother a quick peck on the cheek, Tori fastened Baron's leash to his collar and led him to the back door. "We're just going to take a stroll around the block," she said.

When they returned from their walk, Baron waited for her to unclip his leash, looked up at the kitchen counter, and then back at her. "I didn't forget to pack your favorite treats," she assured him. "I just didn't put them out before we left." She walked to the corner of the kitchen where she'd put the tote bag filled with his toys and treats, removed two of his favorite bacon and cheddar dog biscuits, unwrapped one, and gave it to him. After replacing the water in his dish, Tori poured herself a cup of freshly brewed coffee.

"Knox still sleeping?" Anna asked.

Tori nodded. "He's tired. We were up late Friday. Between the rain and the construction on 80, traffic was bumper to bumper near Harrisburg." She opened the refrigerator and removed a carton of half and half and the apple crisp her mother had made and just taken out of the oven when she, Knox, and Baron had arrived the prior afternoon.

Anna chuckled. "You haven't changed since you were a little girl. If there's leftover apple crisp, it's your breakfast of choice. Are you sure you don't want to scramble some eggs? I have both sausage and bacon."

"Nope," Tori said. "This is perfect! I swear I can still smell the cinnamon, nutmeg, and baking apples even this morning." She poured a little creamer in her coffee before continuing. "Apple crisp always reminds me of Grandmother. I can picture her in the kitchen of every house we ever lived in, peeling and coring apples." She dug her fork into the apple and buttery crumble mixture and let out a soft, appreciative groan. "This is so good. Thanks for making it, Mom."

"You're welcome."

"Speaking of Grandmother, I was really happy she was able to go out to dinner with us last night."

"Me too, Sweetie. By the way, I like Knox," her mother said. "So does your grandmother. And he seems to be crazy about you, Tori. We think you've found a good one this time."

Tori nodded. "I have. But since we met, I feel like it's been one thing after another. I keep expecting him to tell me he's going to look for a girlfriend who's not as high maintenance as I've been."

"I don't think that's going to happen," Anna said. "From what I can see, I'd say he's in love with you, Tori. And what's more, I think you're falling in love with him."

Tori rested her fork on her plate and took a swallow of coffee. "When we were on Amelia Island celebrating his birthday, he told me he was in love with me." She put her elbow on the table and rested her chin in her hand. "I kissed him, but I didn't tell him I loved him. I still haven't said the words, but I think you're right—I am in love with him. I'm just scared of being hurt again. Part of me thinks if I don't say the words out loud and he leaves, it won't hurt as much. And another part of me thinks if I don't tell him I love him, he might leave, find someone who will love him, won't be afraid to love him. But the thought of him leaving is so physically painful. It takes my breath."

"So, what are you going to do about it?"

"Mom, I want to be more than a hundred percent sure this time." Tori picked up her fork and cut another bite of apple crisp. "Picking the right man doesn't seem to be my superpower."

"Nico had a lot of people fooled, Tori."

"Not Baron," Tori said. "He barely tolerated Nico." At the sound of his name, Baron walked over and nuzzled her left arm.

"He seems to adore Knox—almost as much as he does you."

"Yeah," Tori said, taking Baron's face in both her hands and looking into his eyes. "But I don't know that I'm going to have you pick my next husband, Baron."

"Why not? As far as I can tell, he's the only one batting a thousand."

"Don't say that too loud. He already has a swelled head. He's even given me the 'I told you so' look from time to time, haven't you, Baby."

"Knox reminds me a lot of your father. Your grandmother saw it too. He's kind and generous."

Tori's eyes filled with tears. Her voice broke a little as she said, "Yeah, Mom, I think so too." She paused. "I see so many similarities. He's honest and straightforward like Dad was. Has a strong moral compass. Dad had an easy way with people, and Knox is like that, too. He protects me, looks out for me without being overprotective. He steps up. Suggests things, like taking Baron for the last walk while I get ready for bed. If he sees something that needs to be done, he just does it, like Dad did, and like Dad, doesn't talk about it."

"You've always known your own mind, Tori, tackled problems head-on. Yes, Nico was a mistake, but don't sit on the sidelines. Don't give him that power, Honey. If you're falling in love with Knox, well, life is too precious, time together too short. I say go for it."

Tori nodded and smiled. "I'm going to invite him to come back with Baron and me for the cousins' weekend. You'd like Knox to come back with us, wouldn't you, boy?" She unwrapped the other dog biscuit and held it up to show Baron, who was now dancing around her chair.

"Good morning, ladies," Knox said as he entered the kitchen and kissed Tori. "Did I hear I'm getting invited to something?"

"Yes, but it can wait until after breakfast," Tori said.

Anna cleared her throat.

"Okay, Mom. Point taken." Turning to Knox, she said, "My cousins and I try to meet up here at least once a year. This year, we're going to have an early Thanksgiving—the weekend before the holiday, so no one has to fight holiday traffic and crowded airports. We'll have a dinner, just the cousins and cousins-in-law, Friday night, and then Saturday, we'll get together at Aunt Claire's for a turkey dinner with all the trimmings. I'd like it if you came with me."

"I'd love to."

"Good," Anna said. "I'll let Lisa know to expect you both for the cousins' dinner and Claire to expect the three of us the next day. Now, Knox, I'm going to make myself some scrambled eggs and bacon. Can I make some for you? Or would you prefer Tori's breakfast of choice?"

"As delicious as the apple crisp is," Knox said, "the eggs and bacon sound even better."

A few hours later, Tori was directing Knox back to Route 80. With fewer cars on the road and no construction in the eastbound direction, the trip home seemed much faster. Soon, they were seeing signs for their exit.

"Would you stay with me this week?" Tori asked.

Knox smiled. "Of course, but I'll need to get some things from my apartment."

"Can Baron and I come up? We've never seen your place."

"Sure. But it's just a typical corporate apartment. Nothing special."

"I haven't given you much time to look for a place, have I? You haven't mentioned anything since your offer on that two-bedroom townhouse in Hoboken was rejected, and you decided not to submit another bid."

"The firm's paying for the apartment until mid-February, part of my relocation from the UK, and I always have the option to extend another month or two. As it turns out, the townhouse falling through wasn't such a bad thing. I've decided to go in a different direction."

"Oh? What direction's that?"

"Let's wait until we're back at your place. I want to show you something, and it'll make more sense when you see it."

Although Tori agreed to wait, she was hurt and a bit miffed. Knox hadn't mentioned anything about this "different direction" before. Afraid her voice would give her away if she continued the conversation, she turned on her oldies playlist. Those songs usually made her happy. Except Snow Patrol's Chasing Cars wasn't working its magic on her mood right now, and she was growing increasingly impatient to get to Knox's apartment.

He pulled into the semi-circular driveway in front of his apartment building and slipped the doorman a twenty-dollar bill so he could leave the car for the few minutes they'd be upstairs.

"Okay if I give Baron a drink?" she asked once they were in the apartment.

"Yeah, help yourself. The bowls are to the right of the sink. I'll pack a few things for the week and lay out my tux and clothes for the weekend. I was thinking, Friday at lunch, I'll take your clothes, stop by here, pick up my stuff and check us into the Pierre. I'll leave everything with the bellman to put in our room when it's ready."

"Sounds good," Tori said as she filled a bowl with water and set it on the floor. Then, she studied the living room and kitchen space.

"My parents and I lived in a corporate apartment for two months when we moved to Philadelphia," she said as she walked toward the bedroom. "I swear they all look alike."

Her eyes scanned the bedroom. Like the living room and kitchen, the walls were bare, and the room was sparsely furnished. But on the dresser were two framed photographs—the selfie Knox had taken of them in front of the Unicorn tapestries at the Cloisters and one of her in profile at Lincoln Center. He took that the night we saw Sleeping Beauty, she thought as she walked over to the dresser.

"I didn't know you'd taken this," she said, the tips of her index and middle fingers tracing the rounded edge of the frame that held her silhouette.

He smiled. "You were mesmerized by the fountain. You look so lovely, so at peace in that picture. It's hard to believe that was less than three weeks after Nico pushed you. All set?"

She nodded, her fingers lingering another moment on the frame, before turning to smile at him. "I'll pick up Baron's bowl and put it in the dishwasher."

Knox draped the garment bag over his left arm and picked up his canvas weekender. "On the counter in the kitchen, there's a manila envelope. I need to bring that too. Could you grab it on the way?" he asked.

Tori snapped on Baron's leash and picked up the envelope. "Is this for a case?"

He shook his head. "No. It's personal and one of the things I want to talk to you about. Part of the different direction."

"I'm intrigued." She examined the mailing label. "This is from a photographer?"

"All will be revealed soon, Ms. Harrigan."

Tori laughed. "Now I'm really intrigued."

Forty minutes later, they were seated at her dining room table, the envelope between them.

"Last week, my boss told me I was going to be made a partner next month," Knox said.

"Oh my God! That's wonderful! Congratulations!"

Knox put his hand up. "There's more. The only other people I've told are my parents. They're the best estate and tax attorneys I know, and I wanted their advice. Right after my mother gave me a lecture about how I needed to stop living in temporary housing, establish roots, build equity," he removed several eight by ten photographs from the envelope, "this became available."

Tori looked through the stack of staged pictures of the exterior and interior of a large two-story home. "It's beautiful," she said.

He nodded. "This house belonged to one of the senior partners. He and his wife moved to California last week, where he'll manage our San Francisco office. The firm bought his house. That's one of the relocation perks offered to partners. Tori, I'm scheduled to see the house tomorrow evening, and I'm considering buying it. I'd like you to come with me. Tell me what you think."

"Where is it?"

"Google Maps says eight and a half miles north, northwest of your townhouse."

"Of course, I'll go with you tomorrow evening, but are you sure this is what you want? Two months ago, you said four rooms with a bath were more than enough. This house has a lot more than four rooms. And it has a three-car garage. You don't even own one car."

"This is the first house that, I don't know, felt like home. When I saw the pictures, I knew I had to see it in person as soon as possible."

Tori grinned. "Okay. I should be able to catch the early ferry tomorrow if you can. I'll ask the boys next door to walk and feed Baron after school, so we can head out as soon as we get home. But now, we have about an hour before sunset. Let's drive those eight and a half miles and see the house that makes you this happy."

Chapter 45
At the Pierre

The First Weekend in November

"Should I try to hail a cab?" Knox asked as they left the theatre on West Forty-Seventh Street.

"Let's walk," Tori said. "The weather's lovely, and it's early. The other shows haven't let out yet, so there's no post-performance crush on the sidewalks."

She put her gloved hand in his, and they walked east to Broadway. As they approached Times Square, a young woman stood on the corner playing Tchaikovsky's Violin Concerto. The poignant, simple melody was in sharp contrast to the garish, flashing lights and provocative billboards just feet away. A scuffed leather violin case lay open on the sidewalk beside her, with several coins scattered on its nearly threadbare red velvet lining. They stopped to listen to the last bars of music and applauded when the young woman lowered her bow after the final lingering note. Remembering she had shoved the change from that morning's bagel purchase in her coat pocket, Tori removed two crumpled dollar bills and dropped them in among the coins. Knox did the same. Then, they turned the corner to join the sightseers, shoppers, and native New Yorkers on Broadway. The smokey, sweet smell of roasting chestnuts rose from each pushcart they passed and reminded Tori the streets and stores would soon be decorated for the upcoming holidays. She broke into a grin and looked up at Knox. She was looking forward to a Thanksgiving and Christmas holiday season without Morgano-family demands and drama.

"Thank you."

"You're welcome. But what am I being thanked for?" he asked.

"For being you. For being thoughtful. For tonight. In less than three weeks, it will be Thanksgiving. That means Christmas is just around the corner. I'm looking forward to the holidays this year."

He squeezed her hand. "You wanna give me credit for putting the magic in Christmas? I'll take it."

As they walked, they discussed the intense and brilliantly acted drama they'd just seen, the results of the inspection on the house Knox had successfully bid on earlier in the week, tomorrow's wedding, and their plans for Thanksgiving—first with Tori's mother in Williamsport the weekend after next, then with Knox's family on Thanksgiving Day. The walk to Fifth Avenue and the Hotel Pierre, where they were staying to attend Graham and Gemma's wedding the next afternoon, seemed to take no time at all.

When they walked through the hotel lobby and past the Two E Lounge, they heard the deep rich voice of a baritone singing *How to Handle a Woman*.

"Wonder what's going on there?" Knox asked.

"The Pierre's Broadway Cabaret," Tori said. "It's quite popular and attracts a lot of out-of-work actors and actresses waiting for their next gig."

"Let's have a drink and listen to the music," he suggested.

Most of the audience members in the lounge were seated at small tables close to the mirrored bar and the performers, but Tori and Knox preferred a loveseat by the lit fireplace. They placed their orders—a Bailey's Irish Cream for her and an Armagnac for him. He put his arm around her shoulders, and she snuggled in next to him. Soon the baritone was joined by a soprano, and the duo began to sing current Broadway duets.

When the set was complete and the singers and pianist took their break, the waiter came by to ask if they'd like another round. Knox looked at Tori, who shook her head.

"No, just the check," he said.

After he'd signed for the drinks and the waiter had left, Knox whispered in her ear, "Let's go upstairs. I want to tell you how much I love you."

"Oh, Mr. Cooper," Tori said. "Don't you know, showing is much better than telling."

The next morning, Tori woke in Knox's arms.

"Good morning. How did you sleep?" he asked.

"Wonderfully. You?"

"Same. I had an extraordinary dream. I dreamed the woman I'm in love with told me she loves me too."

"I do love you, Knox. Very much."

Then, he left her with no doubts about how loved and cherished she was.

After breakfast, they went their separate ways. Knox wanted to start his Christmas shopping, and Tori was having her hair and nails done before the wedding. He called as she was settling her salon bill and booking her next appointment.

"Hi," she said, "shopping trip successful?"

"Yep. Are you almost finished? I was thinking a light lunch at Amali's on Sixtieth," he said.

"Perfect. I'm just leaving the salon. I'll meet you there."

Over lunch, Tori asked Knox about his shopping trip and was surprised to learn his mother, Margot, had accompanied him.

"You should have invited her to join us for lunch," Tori said. "What did the two of you buy? Am I allowed to ask?"

"I did ask her, but she was meeting some friends for lunch. Then they were seeing that new David Auburn play that just opened off-Broadway. No, you can't ask me what I bought. And nothing is in our hotel room, so you won't find anything—even accidentally." He glanced at his watch, then signaled for the check. "Shall we head back there and start getting ready for the wedding?"

Later that afternoon, Tori checked her appearance in the full-length mirror on the back of the bathroom door before turning to the vanity and reaching for the small rectangular jewelry box sitting on the counter. Her fingertips caressed the bumps and ridges of its faded cognac-colored ostrich leather top. Tucked inside was a soft, burgundy velvet pouch which she removed before placing the leather box back on the counter. With great care, she inserted the tips of both index fingers into the bag's small opening and gently wiggled her fingers back and forth to loosen the fraying satin drawstring. Then, she carefully removed the antique hair comb nestled inside. The comb, a cluster of enamel pansies, had belonged to her grandmother, Victoria, after whom Tori had been named and who had died just before Tori was born. Each delicate flower was a shade of purple, ranging from lilac to amethyst. Sprinkled over each blossom's black center were small diamond chips that had always reminded her of fairy dust. She brushed back a strand of hair and secured it with the comb. The diamonds twinkled back at her first from the vanity mirror, then the full-length mirror, and seemed to promise tonight would be magical. Her grandmother's comb and her diamond stud earrings, the only jewelry she wore, were the perfect complement to her off-the-shoulder gown, the color of the silvery mauve roses Knox had told her weeks earlier meant enchantment.

As she started to walk into their bedroom at the hotel, she stopped to watch him. With his back to her, Knox removed his tuxedo jacket from the hanger and slid his arms through the sleeves. Tori shifted her position so she could see his face reflected in the mirror over the dresser as he straightened the cuffs of his dress shirt and buttoned his jacket. A wave of love and desire swept over her, leaving her breathless.

"Audacious, Mr. Cooper. Outshining the groom on his wedding day."

He turned to face her. She watched his blue-gray eyes darken in appreciation, his smile broadening as he walked toward her and took both her hands in his. She took a deep breath and closed her eyes, enjoying the familiar scent of his aftershave.

"Tori. Wow! You look heartstoppingly beautiful."

She pulled both his hands to her back and stepped into his embrace. "I didn't put on lipstick yet," she said, inviting a kiss.

He kissed her gently but pulled away when she tried to deepen it.

"I can kiss you, or we can go to the wedding," he said, his voice husky. "But we can't do both."

Tori kissed him and took a step back. "As much as I'd like to stay here, just the two of us, we need to go to the wedding." Then, she reached for the room key on top of the dresser next to them, slid the card key into his jacket pocket, and ran the back of her fingers provocatively up and down the wool before giving it a gentle pat. "Keep that right here, just in case," she said, opening her evening bag and removing her lipstick.

"In case what?" he asked.

She turned to the mirror he had just left to apply her lipstick, met his eyes in their reflection, and winked. "In case I suddenly need to be alone with you."

Once they exited the elevator on the second floor, they followed the signs to the Garden Foyer, where the wedding ceremony was to take place. As they turned the corner, they saw the guests leaving that venue and heading for the Rotunda, where the cocktail reception was to be held.

"Wonder what's going on," Tori said. "The wedding can't be over. It doesn't start for another fifteen minutes."

"I see my brother and Kelly. Maybe they know something," Knox said.

A waiter carrying a silver tray with champagne flutes passed them, and Knox removed two glasses before steering Tori over to where Coop and Kelly were standing.

"What's going on, do you know?" Tori asked.

"Not really. A woman, I think was the wedding planner, came out and said there was an unexpected delay, and we should come in here, enjoy a glass of champagne," Coop said, lifting his glass.

Kelly nodded. "Stuff happens. And we may never know. I hope whatever the snafu is hasn't upset Gemma or Graham."

Tori raised her hand and waved, "There's Esta and her husband. We're all sitting together at dinner."

After Tori and Coop's boss and her husband joined them, Coop said, "We were just talking about the delay. Wondering what happened."

"According to the ladies' room gossip," Esta said, "one of the groomsmen from out of town didn't try on his rented tux until just a little while ago. The pants were too short and the waist too big. The hotel concierge is checking maître d' uniforms for a pair of suitable pants. A year from now, it will be one of the most, if not the most repeated, story of the wedding."

Her husband chuckled. "She speaks from experience. Our rings didn't make it to the ceremony, and we each had to borrow a wedding band—Esta from her father, me from my mother."

Tori rolled her eyes. "The universe tried to warn me, but I didn't listen. The limo missed every green light on the way to the church, and then we got caught in the traffic from a high school football game. I was more than twenty minutes late. When I arrived, my former mother-in-law already had everyone on the groom's side of the church on the beads, praying I was a runaway bride."

Esta raised her champagne glass, "A toast to brides and grooms. May they all survive any wedding mishaps."

"To eloping," Tori said.

The six raised their glasses just as a woman announced, "Ladies and gentlemen. Thank you for your patience. The cause of our delay has been resolved. Please return to the Garden Foyer."

The guests filed out of the Rotunda, and soon the ushers had everyone seated again. As Gemma and Graham exchanged the vows they had written, Tori was surprised when an emotion she couldn't quite name—envy? longing?—swept over her. She turned to Knox. He met her eyes and mouthed, "I love you." She squeezed his hand and mouthed, "I love you, too."

Later that evening, after the traditional dances were finished and the band invited the guests to join the wedding party on the dance floor, Knox took her in his arms. He whispered in her ear, "So, we're eloping?"

"Not this year, Mr. Cooper. And tonight, we're dancing."

The next morning over breakfast, Knox said, "So, help me out here. What did you mean last night when I asked if we were eloping and you answered, 'not this year?'"

"I don't want to be married to one man on the first day of the year and another on the last. And let me remind you before we elope, a question must be asked, and an answer given."

"So, hang on. Wait a minute. Today's the twelfth of November. That means. You're saying fifty-six days from now, you'd marry me?"

"I doubt we could find someone to perform the ceremony on New Year's Day. And let me be more specific—that wasn't the question or the answer I had in mind."

Chapter 46
After the Cousins' Dinner

Williamsport, Friday, November 17th

"This evening was awesome," Knox said as he backed the car out of Lisa's driveway. "And your cousins are great! I can see why you all try to get together at least once a year."

"Yeah, they are," Tori said. "We've always been close."

"Dinner was delicious, too. I can't remember the last time I had corned beef and cabbage. And that dessert was amazing. Can you make that?"

"Irish trifle? Yup, Grandmother taught us all."

"Do you ever make it?"

"Sure. Christmas and on St. Patrick's Day, or as it shall now be known, the only day people eat corned beef and cabbage," she said.

"I didn't mean to offend anybody, but seriously? I thought the only time corned beef got rolled out as a dinner option was on St. Patrick's Day. Other than a corned beef sandwich at a deli, I don't think I've ever seen it on a menu except on St. Patrick's Day. You never make it."

"It's not something I think of making when it's just me or the two of us. But, you took everyone's teasing like a man," she said, smiling at the memory of nine napkins, including her own, launched at Knox from all around the table when he'd voiced his shock and disbelief they were having corned beef and cabbage for dinner. "But it's not March," he'd repeated several times.

Earlier that day, Tori, Knox, and Baron had returned to Williamsport for the cousins' reunion weekend. On the drive, she told him about her mother's three sisters, their husbands, their children, and their children's spouses. Now Tori realized she had never told Knox what to expect this weekend. The traditions she and her cousins had grown up with that would play a major role in the weekend's activities. She had just known Knox would jump right in, enjoy the fun.

They drove the rest of the way to her mother's, listening to a playlist of Broadway duets Tori had downloaded after their evening at the Two E Lounge.

As Knox pulled the car into the driveway, Tori stifled a yawn and shook her head as if to shake away any sleepiness.

"I'll walk Baron," he said. "You're tired."

She shook her head. "No, you two had your guy time last night. I need a little alone time with my best four-legged man."

He turned off the ignition and turned toward her. "Is everything okay? You're very quiet. Did I say or do something to upset you at dinner?"

She shook her head. "Everything's fine. Baron and I just need to talk."

When he helped her out of the car, Tori smiled and said, "Really. I'd tell you if something were wrong."

Anna had just taken four pumpkin pies out of the oven for their dinner the next day at her sister, Claire's. The aroma of freshly baked dough, cinnamon, ginger, cloves, and nutmeg filled the front hallway, and Tori and Knox followed the smells, like children following the Pied Piper of Hamelin, to the kitchen. As Tori passed the paper towel dispenser on the counter, she tore off a sheet, folded it, and wiped the tendrils of saliva from Baron's jowls.

"He makes me feel like the best cook in the world," her mother said. "He all but swoons every time I just preheat the oven. How was dinner?"

"Fantastic," Knox said, just as Tori said, "Interesting."

Anna raised her eyebrows and tried to catch her daughter's eye, but Tori avoided her mother's gaze. Then, she slid a dog treat into her coat pocket and took Baron's leash off the back doorknob.

"C'mon, buddy," she said. "I know it's hard to tear yourself away from this divine smell, but you need to go out." She clipped on his leash, and they walked to the front door.

At the bottom of the driveway, Tori asked, "Which way tonight? Right or left?" Baron turned to the right. They walked past the Kramer's house next door and then the Dolans before she said, "Dinner tonight was revelatory. And strange. There were times I felt I was watching a movie. No, not one movie but two. Like a split screen. On one side, I watched Knox being Knox—a great conversationalist and terrific listener. I could tell my family liked him, and he was enjoying himself. On the other screen, I saw past cousins' dinners, dinners with Nico, who wasn't joining in. Not listening to the conversation, just nodding and offering an occasional 'un huh,' his laugh, not fake exactly, but not authentic either.

"And everyone teased him, Knox, I mean, about his reaction to learning the dinner was corned beef. He got it from all of us. And he just laughed it off good-naturedly. You know Nico. Just imagine how different that scene would have been."

Baron turned to look up at her, his brow furrowed.

She sighed. "I'm not telling you anything you haven't known since Knox came to take care of us when I was hurt. But tonight, Baron, the penny finally dropped for me. I think, when Knox closes on his new house, he's going to ask us to move there, too. What do you think about that?"

He looked up at her with his soulful chocolate brown eyes.

"I know you haven't been inside the house. It's truly magnificent—and you will once he closes. He wants to make some changes before he moves in—update the bathrooms, build some bookcases on either side of the fireplace, replace the deck and add a screened porch in the back. He's planning on fencing in the yard, which I think is for you. Remember when we drove over there a couple of weeks ago and looked around outside? He said the backyard would be great for you to run around."

Baron stopped for a minute as if he were deep in thought. Then, he looked up at her and wagged his tail.

"Yeah. Okay. We're not talking anything immediate. But I think, if and when he asks, maybe we should say yes."

When they returned home, Tori sat on her mother's front porch while Baron enjoyed his treat. As they walked through the front door, her mother called to her from the living room. "Everything okay, Honey?"

Tori unhooked Baron's leash and hung her coat in the hall closet. "Everything's great, Mom. Knox already go up?"

Her mother nodded.

"Good. Lisa, John, Knox, and I are part of the set-up crew tomorrow morning at Aunt Claire's, so I'm going to head up too. See you in the morning." She bent down to kiss Anna on the cheek.

"Good night, Honey. I think Knox needs a little reassuring everything's okay. When I asked about the evening, he said you were very quiet on the way home."

"Thanks, Mom."

Baron raced her up the stairs. When she opened the door of her old bedroom, Knox, barefoot and dressed in jeans and a white undershirt, was taking his Dopp kit out of the weekender. Baron, tail wagging, went to get a petting.

Tori tried to wait her turn, but she couldn't. Instead, she walked straight to Knox, wrapped her arms around his waist, and rested her cheek on the soft cotton of his tee shirt. She could hear and feel his heartbeat, and she tightened her grip around his waist. He tossed the toiletry bag on the bed before wrapping his arms around her. He kissed the top of her head, then pulled away.

"Tori, what's going on? What's wrong?"

"Nothing. Can we sit on the bed for a minute and talk?"

When they were sitting next to each other, she took his hand in hers and turned to face him.

"I love you. I'm sure of that. But I haven't been sure of me. Of my ability to—I don't know—commit one hundred percent to a relationship with you? To be the lover, partner, and best friend you deserve? My heart felt it, wanted it, but my head kept getting in the way, arguing it was too soon, asking how I would recover if you ever left."

"I'm not going anywhere. I've told you that. Don't you believe me? What can I do to make you believe me?" he asked.

She smiled. "Nothing. It had to be me who figured it out. And I did. Tonight, at dinner. I watched you with my cousins and realized there has been a Knox-sized space beside me all this time. I tried to force Nico into it, but he didn't fit. Like me squeezing my feet into a too-small pair of shoes. They might look great on my feet for a while but are so uncomfortable. And when I finally do take them off, the initial pain is excruciating. But underneath that pain is a relief so exquisite, it quiets the ache and eventually overtakes it. Tonight, those too-small shoes and all the residual feelings of insecurity and self-doubt that went with them got thrown in the trash—never to be thought of again. I feel about five pounds lighter. I'm almost giddy with relief."

He pulled her into his arms and kissed her. Then, he traced her lips with the pad of his thumb before reaching for the Dopp kit behind him on the bed.

"My beard chafed you," he said. "Don't go away. I'm going to get rid of this," he rubbed the stubble on his chin, "and I'll be right back."

Saturday morning, Anna joined Tori and Baron on their walk.

"Are you ever going to tell me what happened last night at dinner?" her mother asked. "Knox was right, you were quiet when you got home, but after you and Baron went for a walk, everything seemed better."

"Last night, I finally realized that while Nico may have been the biggest mistake of my life so far, I was standing on the edge, about to make an even greater mistake—not loving Knox with everything I am, not committing to him."

"And you needed a little time and a walk with Baron to process it all?" Anna asked.

Tori nodded. "But everything's good now. Baron and I even discussed what we'd do if Knox asks us to move into the new house with him. We decided we're going to say yes."

"And the townhouse?"

"I love my little house, but it's time to purge myself of everything Nico touched. I bought him out, painted over the colors he chose, and purchased new furniture, but his ghost may still linger there. At the end of the day, Knox and I deserve a fresh start, a clean slate."

"Tori, when you told me Knox was joining us for Christmas this year, I asked Chris to make him a Christmas stocking," her mother said. "And right after you and he left a few weeks ago, I ordered him a 'Tori ornament.' They're at the house, wrapped. How about we hide them in the trunk of your car when we get back?"

Tori's Aunt Chris, her father's youngest sister, and her family lived in Michigan. She was the family crafter and seamstress, and over the years, she'd made Christmas stockings for all of them—even Nico.

"Oh, Mom. You always know just the right thing. That's perfect! I can't wait to see them!"

"I took pictures before I wrapped them. When I told your Aunt Chris about Knox, well, I think she put a lot of thought and love into this one." Anna pulled out her phone and scrolled to photos of a Christmas green velvet and needlepoint stocking of Santa, dressed in a green plaid kilt, high knee socks and clogs, and an Irish sweater with a shamrock embroidered on the front. On his head was a green tam o'shanter and by his side a Radio Flyer filled with toys. Knox's name was embroidered at the top of the stocking.

Tori gasped and swallowed the tears she felt building in her throat as she looked at the picture. "Aunt Chris outdid herself. It's beautiful. And after the ribbing Knox took over his reaction to last night's Irish menu? This is perfect!"

She swiped left to look at the next picture, a bright red Christmas ornament with Knox's name written in silver glitter. It was just like the ornament, her favorite, that her parents had given her the Christmas she was seven. Her "Tori" ornament's luster had faded over the years, the letters of her name had a little less sparkle. But her treasured memories of Christmas's past, when she and her parents had been a family, swirled around that ornament and, in her eyes, made it shine like a precious ruby. It always had pride of place on her tree every year. The first Christmas after she and Nico married, Anna had had a similar ornament in green made for him.

"I never thought to ask before," Anna said, "but what happened to Nico's Christmas stocking and ornament? Are they still packed with your Christmas things?"

Tori shook her head. "No. Remember right after I found out about Nico and Eena's affair, Lulu and Murphy came for the weekend? We went up to the attic—I knew exactly which Christmas box the stocking was in, and his ornament was right next to mine at the top of the ornament box. I put the Nico ball inside the toe of the stocking and," she paused, "stomped on it. Smashed it. When it splintered, it made the most satisfying crunching sound. Then each of them took a turn. Lulu refers to that weekend as 'the time we pulverized Nico's ball.'"

"Now that," Anna said, "really is perfect!"

Chapter 47
Thanksgiving Day

The clubhouse of the Long Island Country Club, where Knox and Ben's parents belonged, was an imposing two-story stone building. Lush cornucopia filled with squash, small pumpkins, corn, apples, pears, and acorns hung on the entrance's double doors. A gingerbread village had been set up on a large round table in the lobby.

"I've never been to a restaurant on Thanksgiving," Tori said. "Everything is so festive."

"And until last weekend, I'd never been to a Thanksgiving dinner that wasn't in a restaurant," Knox said. "I've told you before, when Ben and I were growing up, our parents' priorities were the two of us and their growing law practice. I don't remember my parents ever missing a soccer, basketball, or baseball game, a track or swim meet, but I also don't remember my mother cooking a meal or my father mowing the lawn. We had a cleaning service that came in once a week to take care of the house, a personal chef who came every Tuesday to prepare meals for the week, and a gardening service that appeared regularly to take care of the outside."

Tori nodded. "And, from the stories you and Ben tell, for years, you got to go terrific places to celebrate Thanksgiving—the Homestead, the Hershey Hotel, the Greenbrier."

They both turned toward a voice behind them, calling, "Knox, Tori." Dan and Margot Cooper greeted them, and Margot said, "Just got a text from Kelly. They got caught in parade traffic but should be here in about fifteen minutes. Let's wait for them at our table."

The maître d'led them through the dining room to a table by a wall of windows overlooking the ninth hole. At the center of each table was a wreath of rust and yellow mums with a white candle in a hurricane globe. Every candle in the room was lit and, together with the roaring fire, created an ambiance reflecting the holiday spirit.

"This room is magnificent," Tori said. "Thank you for including me today."

"You're an important part of our son's life," Margot said, "and I'm looking forward to hearing all about last weekend. Knox didn't tell me much on the phone, but he had a wonderful time."

"It was a shock to his system," Tori chuckled. "Friday evening, we had dinner with my cousins. I'm the baby, but not by much. That, they all believe, gives them license to tease me unrelentingly. And when we're together—there are ten of us—we are loud and opinionated. We also do a lot of reminiscing, and he heard many embarrassing stories about me. All ten cousins and their children, my mom, grandmother, my mother's three sisters, and their husbands had dinner at my Aunt Claire and Uncle Charlie's Saturday."

"How many of you were there?" Margot asked.

"Twenty-four," Tori said. "Knox hung in there, though. Things at Aunt Claire's are always a little like organized chaos. But my aunt and uncle handle a big crowd well."

"They share so many traditions and memories," Knox said. "It was a lot of fun, and Tori's goddaughter, Reagan, peppered me with questions. She is enchanting."

"She's four," Tori said, "and she announced she was in love with Knox between dinner and dessert."

"She confided in me that she hoped, and I quote, 'we marry you,'" Knox said.

Margot and Tori laughed.

"That's my goddaughter. She should come with a warning label."

"There's Ben and Kelly," Knox said, and he and his father stood as the couple approached the table. When they were all seated again, a waiter brought the bottle of wine Dan had selected, opened it, and once Dan had determined it was "excellent," the waiter poured each of them a glass.

"Dinner is a buffet," Margot explained. "It's set up in the other room, and we can help ourselves whenever we're ready."

"I want to hear about your new apartment, Kelly," Knox said. "I understand you found a great two-bedroom condo on East Seventy-Second Street. What a great location!"

"It is, and it's only a twenty-block walk to my office. I won't have to take a bus or subway in good weather," Kelly said. "I close on Monday, and I've hired a painter to freshen up the place. My furniture gets delivered the week before Christmas."

"How did the audition go the other night?" Tori asked.

"Great, thanks," Kelly said. "As of January 1st, I'm officially part of the Four Strings quartet."

Kelly, who had played the violin most of her life, and three friends had formed a string quartet when they were in law school, and leaving her friends and fellow musicians had been very difficult for Kelly.

"Congratulations!" Knox said. "That's great."

Kelly nodded. "Thanks to Tori and her Lincoln Center connections. Without her help, I wouldn't have found this group. I'm looking forward to playing with them. Thank you, Tori."

Ben grinned. "I'm looking forward to not traveling back and forth every weekend. I like Chicago, but I won't miss weekends at O'Hare. Or LaGuardia, for that matter."

"Are you and Ben still planning to spend Christmas in Chicago?" Tori asked as she looked first at Kelly and then Ben.

"We are," Kelly said. "After the closing, I'll fly back to Chicago, finish up there, and then fly back here. I'm shipping my clothes, and I've sold most of my furniture to a grad student. What was left wasn't worth hiring a truck for, so I donated it to a charity. It's been such a luxury to buy furniture specifically for this apartment. After the furniture is delivered, Ben and I will fly to Chicago, spend the holidays with my folks and return just before New Year's."

Dan raised his wine glass. "Looks like we have a lot to be thankful for this year and a lot to celebrate. Tori, Kelly, thank you for joining us. And to Kelly and Knox, who will join the rest of us in the joys of home-ownership next week. As my father told Margot and me when we bought our first house, 'Welcome to The Money Pit.'"

"Here, here," Ben said as all six glasses met in the middle of the table.

"We're decorating the townhouse for Christmas tomorrow, and I can't wait," Knox said.

"He's not kidding!" Tori laughed. "Even though I've told him heavy lifting is involved. Was he like this when he was little?"

Margot laughed and nodded her head. "Worse," Dan said. "And if Margot and I had plans for an evening out in December, the next day we'd find telltale signs these two," he pointed to his two sons, "had been snooping around looking for Christmas gifts."

"But we never found them," Knox said. "You and Mom had some good hiding places."

"They were next door, at the Brennans," Dan said.

They all laughed at Knox's and Ben's surprised expressions.

Margot suggested they head to the buffet. As they walked to the other room, she said to Tori, "Thank you so much for inviting Dan and me to celebrate Christmas with you this year. We're looking forward to it and to meeting your mother."

"And we're thrilled you're joining us," Tori said.

She gasped when they entered the room with the buffet. There were tables of appetizers, salads, soups, and side dishes, chefs carving turkey and ham, a table for vegetarian and vegan options, a multi-layered tower of desserts, and a chocolate fondue fountain.

When they'd helped themselves and were seated again, Ben said, "Now, tell us about last weekend. What did you do?"

Knox began with the cousins' dinner. Everyone laughed when he described his surprise at the Irish menu and his comments that had elicited the nine flying napkins. Eventually, Ben and Dan admitted they, too, would have been surprised corned beef and cabbage was served.

"After dinner, we opened our cousins' gifts," Tori said. For as long as she could remember, her grandparents had given each of their grandchildren a cousin's gift at Christmas. When they'd been children, the gift had been matching Christmas pajamas, a gift now reserved for the great-grandchildren.

"When my oldest cousin, Tess, turned fifteen," Tori said, "Grandmother and Grandfather started giving us slipper socks—the crazier, the better. And it's tradition, after all the socks have been opened, to put them on, sit on the floor and snap a group photo of all of us in our socks."

Tori passed around her phone, open to a picture of her four cousins, their spouses, she, and Knox on the floor, holding up their feet for the camera. Her socks were red and white horizontal stripes with Rudolf's face, his nose shiny red, on the toes. Knox sported red socks with a moose wearing a gray beanie cap with earflaps and a tassel on top. "And the tassels bounce on his instep when he walks," she said.

"The next morning, Tori and I went over to her aunt and uncle's. Several of us carried tables and extra chairs up from the basement. There were three sets of tables—one for each generation," Knox said. "And I never saw so much food."

"Did we go through the same buffet just now?" Tori asked.

"I meant in someone's home," he said. "Her aunt made two turkeys. We ate one at dinner, and the other one was just for sandwiches."

"The set-up, tear-down, and cooking are everyone's responsibility," Tori said. "My cousin, Lisa, and I have been responsible for the mashed potatoes since we were thirteen and eleven, respectively. But this wasn't my first rodeo! I got us on the set-up crew, which is much better than tearing down and putting away, and I signed Knox up for plating the cranberry sauce and corn."

"Then, after the dishes from dinner were cleared away," Knox said, "we each put together these amazing jigsaw puzzles."

"You mean you each had your own?" Dan asked.

"Yup, and they were, what? Forty pieces each, Honey?" Knox asked. Tori nodded.

"The puzzles were made of wood, and each puzzle has special pieces." He turned to Tori. "What were they called?"

"Whimsies," she said. "The puzzles are all Christmas-themed, and the whimsies are shaped like wreaths, sleds, and ice skates. The puzzles are a tradition in my father's family. One he introduced to my mother's family the Christmas they were engaged. That year he gave each of my mother's sisters and their husbands a set of twelve puzzles as their Christmas gift. I have my parents' puzzles packed in with my Christmas things."

"Wow! I didn't know you had puzzles, too. Can we put them together on Christmas?" Knox asked.

"Of course. And I'll tell you which ones are easy and which are hard in the car going home," she said.

Chapter 48
Decorating for Christmas

The morning after Thanksgiving, Tori woke with a start and looked around the bedroom. Baron wasn't curled up beside her on the floor, and Knox's side of the bed was empty, the sheet no longer warm.

"Alexa, what time is it?" she asked, her voice still groggy from sleep.

"The time is five forty-seven a.m. The temperature in Fort Lee is thirty-four degrees with patchy fog and a seventy percent chance of rain. Have a good day, Victoria," was Alexa's answer.

"Brr," Tori said aloud to the empty room. Reluctantly she pushed back the covers and got out of bed. When she opened the bedroom door, the house was quiet, and she called, "Knox? Baron?" No answer. As she started down the stairs, she could see three green and red plastic Christmas bins, two red ornament boxes, and the blue and white storage box that held her Nativity scene in the middle of the family room floor. On top of one of the green and red bins was the Christmas wreath. On another, a box of battery-operated window candles. The six-foot garland for the mantle had been laid on the coffee table.

She chuckled. Except for the Christmas tree and the candles for the second-floor windows, all the Christmas decorations and ornaments they'd be putting up today were in the family room. Wonder what time Knox got up this morning? He must have made at least three or four trips to bring all these things from the attic, she thought.

Last night, when they'd gotten home from Thanksgiving dinner with Knox's family, Tori'd taken him up to the third floor to show him what they'd be moving downstairs the next morning. He'd spotted three more red and green bins stacked against one of the attic walls. "What about those?" he'd asked. Those boxes, she explained, held her father's HO gauge model trains and the buildings, houses—even the utility poles and wires—that created the mythical town by the railroad tracks. Two plywood sheets painted green, and four sanded and stained two-by-fours were stored behind the bins. When assembled, she told him, they became the train's elevated platform. She ran her hand gently across the lid of the top box. "I don't have the room now. But someday." Her hand lingered on the top of the box, not wanting to break that physical connection to her memories of Christmases past.

Her father, Tori told him, had built many of the pieces from kits she and her mother had given him over the years. "The town is very 1950s. There's a movie theatre called the Rialto, Miss Molly's Diner, even a pharmacy with a US Army 'Uncle Sam Needs You' recruiting poster on the side."

"I'd love to see it," Knox had said. "Ben and I had trains growing up, but nothing as terrific as this set sounds."

Now, she climbed the stairs to the second floor to shower and dress for the day. Soft black leggings, a red turtleneck fleece, and her new slipper socks would be the most comfortable choice, she concluded. For a moment, she thought about laying out Knox's socks but then decided against it. He'd joined in the fun after the cousins' dinner, but maybe that was a one-time thing. Not a big deal, she thought. After all, he'd participated more in her family's traditions in one weekend than Nico had in four years.

As she headed for the kitchen, Tori remembered she'd added a box of her favorite double chocolate brownie mix to her grocery order last week and decided she'd make them this morning. By the time I've put the brownies in the oven and set the timer, Knox and Baron should be back, she told herself.

But they weren't. Tori glanced over at the storage bins. She knew what was in each one, and she fought the urge to stage the boxes, moving each closer to where its contents would eventually be displayed. But she didn't. Knox was so excited about decorating. She didn't want to spoil anything for him.

Turning back to the kitchen, she put a fresh k-cup in the coffee maker before putting the slow cooker on the counter and pulling out a rack of ribs, a large onion, and two bottles of beer from the refrigerator. Christmas carols would be lovely, she thought, and she instructed Alexa to begin her Christmas playlist. As she was rubbing spices on the ribs, Knox and Baron returned from their long outing.

"Good morning," Knox greeted her as he and Baron walked through the back door. He was holding a white paper bag with a bright red apple on the front. "We took a walk and then drove to Big Apple Bagel. We got there just as they were taking the bagels out of the oven, didn't we, boy?" As he bent down to unclip the leash, Baron turned away from him.

As Knox leaned in to kiss her, the savory smell of freshly baked dough and spices enveloped her. She took a deep breath, and her stomach growled. "Thank you. The perfect breakfast, and I'm hungry."

"Rough morning?" he asked, holding up one of the two bottles of Corona. "Or did Baron somehow let you know I'm in the doghouse, and these are for me?"

She chuckled. "Neither. They're for the ribs. What did you do?"

"First, I woke him when I got up. But I still wasn't in serious trouble because he wagged his tail. But then, after I showered and dressed, I kept him in the bedroom while I moved the boxes from the attic. I worried he'd walk in front of me, and I'd trip over him, which I explained several times during our walk. I've apologized over and over. Did you see how he turned his head when I took off his leash? He won't even look at me. Any suggestions?"

"The good news is he doesn't hold grudges. Once he forgives you, it's over. I suggest not one but two bacon and cheddar dog biscuits this morning."

"Thanks," he said, and took two biscuits from the pantry, opened one, and offered it to Baron, who took it greedily.

"See? He's coming around," Tori said. "Food is a great motivator."

Together they unpacked the breakfast Knox had picked up, poured themselves coffee, and sat at the counter. They were interrupted by the timer for the brownies, and Tori went to the oven to take them out.

"So, where do we begin?" Knox asked as she set the hot brownies on the counter to cool.

Tori surveyed the scene in front of her. She preferred to decorate the tree first, but since Knox had brought down everything but the tree from the attic and stacked it all in the corner where the tree would eventually stand, that wasn't going to work.

"According to you know who," she said, pointing at the Alexa device on the end table by the loveseat, "it's going to rain. I'll change into shoes, and then let's start with the outside, move to the living and dining rooms, and finish up in the family room."

"Sounds good. Just tell me what to do."

"Why don't you take these two red and green bins and the wreath to the front hallway? I'll follow you with the blue and white storage box and the window candles."

They made a good team. Soon the outside of the house was decorated, and as they stood in the driveway admiring their handiwork, the first raindrops began to fall.

"Once again, our timing's perfect," Knox said. "I think it's a sign."

"Yup, a sign we need to go inside," Tori teased and raced him to the front door.

Next up was her Nativity scene. When Knox unpacked first one and then another camel, he asked, "You have two camels?"

"Of course not!" she said. "I have three. I never bought into the idea three wealthy men shared one camel going across the desert. So I made sure they each had their own ride."

He shook his head and chuckled, unpacked the third camel, and asked, "Now what?"

Next came her Santas and elves. While she placed elves in places around the living room and on the staircase befitting their mischievous expressions, he climbed the step stool and positioned one bean bag Santa on the top shelf of the living room bookcase and another on top of the china closet in the dining room. "Cross their legs, give 'em a little attitude," Tori instructed when he asked how they looked.

Her white Christmas tablecloth, still wrapped in the dry cleaner's plastic after last year's disastrous Christmas dinner, was hanging in the back of the hall closet. Knox helped her straighten the cloth on the table. While he put new white tapers in the candlesticks, she unpacked the table's centerpiece—a train engine pulling a hopper car with a snow globe on top. In the globe were three snowmen—a father, mother, and child. "These are like cars from one of my father's trains," she told him. Once she put the batteries in the engine and flipped the switch, the globe lit up, and iridescent snowflakes swirled around the three snow-people. "Every Christmas eve, we leave the light on all night for Santa," she told him.

Knox took her in his arms. "Everything is so special, so magical," he said. "Thank you for inviting my parents for Christmas dinner. Both of them are looking forward to it. My mother told me again after dinner yesterday how excited they were to be coming."

"Your parents are wonderful, and I enjoy being with them," she said. "We'll have a great dinner and a terrific time."

"Let's get the tree from the attic and then take a break," he said. "It's almost noon, and I could eat a little something. Maybe a sandwich?"

"Perfect."

When the ten-foot slim balsam fir was standing in the corner of the two-story family room, plugged in and turned on, the archangel securely on top and the Velcro strips on the burgundy velvet tree skirt fastened and positioned behind the tree, Tori made them cups of steaming hot chocolate and marshmallows. Knox grated the cheddar and gruyere cheeses for their sandwiches. After lunch, they sat on the sofa and admired their handiwork.

"Before I forget, a colleague recommended a contractor for the work at the house," Knox said. "He emailed me his portfolio. When we finish here, I'd like you to take a look."

"Next week is an important and busy week," she said. "Making partner on Wednesday, becoming a homeowner on Thursday, picking up your new car Friday, and the ballet gala Saturday."

He tightened his arm around her shoulders and kissed the top of her head. "And Tuesday," he said, his voice low. "How are you feeling about Tuesday?"

"Nervous, although less so since my last meeting with Mr. Leeder," she said. "I just want to get it over with."

The Wednesday afternoon before Thanksgiving, Tori had met for the final time with Oliver Leeder, the assistant district attorney who was prosecuting Nico for the assault. The trial was Tuesday. Four more days. I can do four more days, she assured herself.

"How can people be expert witnesses?" she asked. "Testify all the time?"

"It's not personal for them. This is. It affects you, your life, our life."

She nodded. "Yeah. I guess so. I don't want to talk about it anymore. Let's talk about your house. Like what colors are you thinking about? What style furniture do you like? Are you going to hire a decorator?"

"Before I think about decorating…. Tori, I want you to have a key to the house, and I want you—and Baron, too—to feel welcome there any time, all the time. What I'm trying to say, what I want to ask you is…."

"Are you asking if I'll move in with you?"

He nodded. "I know you're independent, and…."

She put the tip of her index finger to his lips. "Baron and I have already discussed it. We'd love to move to the house with you, live with you."

"You would?"

She nodded, then put her cup and his on the table in front of them and kissed him, a deep, lingering kiss. "If this is our last Christmas here, let's decorate this tree and celebrate!" she said.

"Just a minute. I need to run upstairs," he said. "I want to put on my Christmas socks, too."

Tori was still seated on the couch when Knox returned. He stood in front of her, lifted first his left leg, shook his foot to make the tassel on that sock bounce, and then his right.

"This is such a cool tradition," he said. "It was so nice of your grandmother to include me in the cousins' gift this year."

"Of course. First, you're my boyfriend, and she likes you. Second, you gave her flowers the night we took her out to dinner. Then, you wrote her an old-fashioned thank you note for the socks. You've charmed my grandmother, Mr. Cooper. Why are you frowning?"

"Boyfriend. Not a fan of that word. I'm not a boy, and you and I are not just friends."

"Well, when you think of another word, let me know. I hate partner, and significant other has been used to death. Now, let's get started."

She opened the first box of ornaments and removed the red "Tori" ball. Wednesday evening, when Knox was on the phone with his mother finalizing their Thanksgiving day plans, Tori had snuck up to the attic and inserted the shiny red ball her mother had given her the prior weekend into the ornament box.

"All the figurines and ornaments have a story behind them. I won't bore you with every one today, but this ornament's special. My parents gave it to me when I was seven. It's my favorite, and it always goes on first." She held it up for him to see, then hung it on the most prominent branch right in front.

"Now your turn," she said as she reached over to pull the "Knox" ornament from its compartment and held it up for him to see.

"Tori, I don't know what to say." His grin lit up his face. "This is terrific. Thank you."

"It was my mom. She knew we needed a 'Knox' to go with the 'Tori."

It took them a couple of hours to trim the tree. As they added more and more decorations, they would stand back and decide some ornaments needed to be moved to a more prominent place on the tree, while others were relegated to less important positions. But the Tori and Knox ornaments never moved.

Afternoon had transitioned to twilight. The only light in the room came from the window candles, the Christmas tree, and the fire. In the background, Alexa continued to play carols. Knox looked around the room. "Wow. Everything is so festive!"

"Okay, the library table and mantle are the last two things. And then, we take the rest of these boxes upstairs to the attic, and We. Are. Done," she announced.

Tori reached into the last bin and removed the small plate protector on top. Inside were two porcelain plates—one for Santa's cookies and the other for the carrots and apples for the reindeer. Then she unwrapped a corn cob pipe and set all three on the top of the library table. "When I was three, Santa accidentally left his pipe at our house. Every year since, I've put it out for him to enjoy while he's here."

"That's adorable," he said. "Your parents certainly put a lot of thought into making Christmas special. Just like you're doing for me now." He reached for the garland on the coffee table. "I guess this is next?"

She shook her head. "Nope. Remember when we went to the rehearsal for The Nutcracker? There were no stage sets. So we saw the large trap door upstage right where the tree comes from, the machinery that makes it grow during the performance, and the slide on the floor that makes it look like the Sugar Plum Fairy is floating across the stage. Next month when we go to the performance, all those secrets will be camouflaged for the audience. Now, we're going to set up the mantle, and the garland is our camo. How about if I pull things out and you set up?" she said as she knelt on the floor next to a green and red bin.

"First come the stocking holders." She handed him four long bronze hooks. "The ends touch the wall. Yup, that's it, but space them out a little more. Exactly. That's perfect.

"Next, we weigh down the hooks because we don't want Santa to worry the stockings will fall if he fills them with lots of goodies. These go about two inches from the edge of the mantle." One by one, she handed him a bronze train engine, an open hopper labeled "Merry" and loaded with toys, then its twin labeled "Christmas," and finally the caboose.

"Now, the stockings." She pulled a chocolate brown velvet and needlepoint stocking from the box. Baron's name in capital letters was stitched at the top, above a scene where a Boxer sat in front of Rudolph, a plate, just like the one she'd set out earlier, with carrots and apples on the snowy ground between them. "Baron likes to be the caboose."

"This stocking is amazing," Knox said. "Where did you find something so perfect?"

"My Aunt Chris made it," she said. "She's amazingly talented, so creative—there isn't anything she can't do. And she always comes up with the best ideas. She's made all our stockings."

She handed him another. This one had Anna's name stitched in script above a tapestry of a man, woman, and little girl pulling a freshly cut Christmas tree. "Mom gets to be the engine."

"Now mine." She held up her stocking—Santa placing a doll and a bicycle under a tree, a little girl sneaking a peek over the banister. "I think I'd like to be 'Merry' this year."

She stood. "And now yours." She handed him the stocking of the Irish Santa and watched as his confusion turned to surprise. He grinned, and his eyes glistened with tears as he took the stocking from her. Reverently he ran his fingers over the stitched letters of his name and the shamrock on Santa's Irish sweater.

"Your aunt made this for me?" he asked, his voice husky.

She nodded. "Mom told her my new boyfriend was pretty darn special, and we think Aunt Chris put lots of extra effort and love into this one. What do you think?"

"It's beautiful. I can't remember, I mean, I don't think I've ever had anything so special." He took her in his arms. "Thank you. What we need now is some mistletoe."

"Coming right up," she said and took the clear glass ball with an open oval on one side from the library table where she'd put it earlier and headed to the kitchen. "I bought some the other day and put it in the vegetable crisper." She slid the mistletoe into the ornament and handed it to Knox. "The hook is right above the entrance to the family room. Do the honors?"

He picked up the white stepstool and unfolded it. "I thought you said when the tree-topper was on and the top of the tree was decorated, we were finished with this," he said as he climbed the small ladder.

She shrugged her shoulders. "What can I say?"

He climbed down and admired his handiwork before taking her in his arms. "Thank you for one of the most special days of my life," he said before kissing her. "And I still hate the word 'boyfriend.' But, I've thought of a better one."

As he got down on one knee, he pulled a small dark blue velvet box from his back pocket and opened it. Inside was an oval canary diamond set high in a platinum setting.

"Tori, for quite a few years, my priorities were centered around my career. Until one afternoon in August, when I met you. My world and my priorities shifted. All I wanted was to get to know you, spend time with you. It doesn't matter what we're doing. I'm happy because we're together. I love you. You intrigue me, enchant me, and I want to spend the rest of my life with you. Please marry me, be my wife, lover, and best friend?"

"Yes," Tori whispered as if she were making a solemn vow.

Chapter 49
The Fight in the Dog

Tuesday, November 28th

Tori looked at her watch and frowned. Nine thirty. That cannot be right, she thought. It couldn't be only thirty minutes since the courtroom doors were closed, could it? Maybe my watch battery's dead.

She gripped the rounded edge of the mahogany wooden bench she was sitting on to steady herself, leaned forward as far as she could, and looked up and down the corridor. To her left was the elevator she, Murphy, and Knox had taken earlier that morning. To her right and seated about ten feet down the hall, in front of Courtroom 2315, was a man talking on his phone. I wish I had my phone. But her phone was in her purse, and Knox had taken her pocketbook and coat with him when he and Murphy had gone to find seats in the courtroom's small gallery.

Tori turned to look out the window behind her. The skies outside the Criminal Court of the City of New York were steely gray and bleak, just as the weatherman had predicted. Although neither the meteorologist on her favorite morning news show nor the weather app on her phone had forecast snow, the damp, frigid air felt like a storm was brewing.

Now, she sat straight and crossed her right leg over her left. Seconds later, she uncrossed her legs and looked at her watch again. Nine thirty-two. So, it's not the battery.

She tiptoed to the double doors that led to courtroom 2316 and tried to listen. Nothing. Since there was no gap between the two doors, she couldn't see what was happening in the courtroom either.

Tori looked down at the black and white tile corridor. The tiles on the floor were large—at least a foot square and had been laid in a diagonal pattern. I bet there are twenty tiles between this bench and the one that man's sitting on, Tori thought. Careful to step on only black tiles, she counted her steps to the edge of the bench in front of Courtroom 2315. Twenty-one. The man stared at her a minute, then swiveled so his back was to her as if he thought she might want to eavesdrop. She shrugged before spinning on the ball of her foot, so she was now facing the elevator. For a moment, she wished she had the nerve to pretend she was playing a game of hopscotch and hop on one foot back to her seat outside Courtroom 2316. Instead, she returned to her bench, stepping only on white tiles this time. An even twenty. She looked at her watch. Not even five more minutes had passed. How much longer can opening arguments take?

Her next distraction strategy—try to recall every conversation she'd had with Robert Leeder, the assistant district attorney prosecuting the case of The State of New York v. Nicolino Anthony Morgano. She hadn't been impressed the first time she'd been to his office across the street. He looked like a boy playing dress-up in his father's clothes. His suit jacket's shoulders were too broad, and his shoes made a flopping sound when he walked. Only after he'd offered her a seat and sat down himself, did she notice gaps at the heel and side of each black tasseled loafer. Last week, however, when she'd met with him to review her testimony one more time, he was prepared and confident as he filled her in on his game plan. She finally understood why Dylan had said Leeder had a reputation for being a pit bull in the courtroom. "Remember, it's not the dog in the fight," Dylan had said, "it's the fight in the dog."

I wish Dylan were here, she thought. But as the final prosecution witness, he wouldn't take the stand for almost two hours. She, however, would be called to testify right after opening arguments.

Two weeks ago, Mr. Leeder called her to report on the status of two pre-trial motions Mr. Bartlett, Nico's lawyer, had filed. One challenging

Dylan's identification of Nico on the different surveillance tapes, which the prosecution had won. The other contesting the introduction of evidence showing Nico's escalating threats. The judge had ruled only Nico's voicemail messages left on her office phone during the summer, and the photographs of him with Eena in Paris could be admitted into evidence. Nothing else.

"But all the other things—from the ten Scream balloons to the two dozen department store samples of Eena's perfume—show that the assault was deliberate, pre-meditated. Everything Nico sent had to be planned. Are we supposed to believe he just forgot to send me something on day one? No, he intended the assault to be the coup de grace," Tori said.

"Although it's reasonable to assume your ex-husband is behind the other things, we don't have proof," Mr. Leeder had said. "but, hopefully, the videos will convince the jury the attack was pre-meditated. And I've talked with Loftus & Hunt's head of security, Chuck Flynn. He's agreed to testify about the photographs and phone calls."

That same day Mr. Leeder gave Tori the order in which he would call each of the six prosecution witnesses to the stand. Her testimony would be first, followed by Officer Hanson and the ER doctor who had treated her the night of the assault. Then Chuck Flynn's testimony would establish Nico's pattern of harassment at her workplace—beginning with the voicemails he'd left and ending with the delivery of the five provocative photographs Eena had personally delivered to Tori's office. Chuck won't be here for at least an hour, she thought. His testimony would set the stage for the next witness, the intern Nico had recruited to help Eena deliver the package to Tori's office. He was the only witness who had required a subpoena to appear.

Finally, a court officer opened the door. For the first time, Tori could see inside the courtroom. The jury was seated directly in front of her, under the windows, the prosecution table just a few feet in front of the jury box. To her left were the judge's bench and the witness stand. To her right the gallery for spectators. Knox and Murphy were the only two people seated behind the prosecution table. Tori knew the defense table —where Nico and Mr. Bartlett sat—was just to her right inside the door. And she knew Jenny, Nonna Morgano, and several of Nico's aunts and uncles were seated in the gallery behind that table. Except for Nonna, every member of the Morgano family had given her the evil eye when they got off the elevator and spoke loud enough for her to overhear their insults and derisive comments—especially Jenny and Nico.

Mr. Leeder gave her a reassuring smile before saying, "The prosecution calls Victoria Harrigan."

Tori looked straight ahead and walked through the double doors – right past the defense table and Nico's family in the gallery. Don't look right, don't look right, she reminded herself. The court clerk was waiting for her by the witness box. Tori unclenched her fists, placed her left hand on the Bible, and raised her right. Once she was sworn in and seated, the clerk asked her to repeat her full name and home address for the record.

Mr. Leeder wished her good morning and then, through a series of questions, had Tori describe the events of the evening of October 2nd— beginning when she'd left One New York Plaza and ending with Nico pushing her down the South Ferry Street subway steps. His questions and her answers were designed to show the jury how cautious she'd been – checking her surroundings before stepping on the escalator, waiting upstairs in full view of the toll booth clerk until flashing lights signaled a train was in the station. Later, when the surveillance tape of the subway entrance was played, the jury would see Nico lurking out of sight, waiting for those same signals, the ones that would set his plan to assault her in motion.

"I was about halfway down the steps when I felt a tug on the strap of my purse. Then I felt a hand on my shoulder, pushing me. I gripped the railing, but the momentum—I had to let go," Tori said.

A photo of concrete subway steps, each one tipped with a metal plate, flashed on a large screen visible to everyone in the courtroom.

"Steps like these?" Mr. Leeder asked.

"Yes."

Nico's lawyer rose to object. "Your Honor, this could be a picture of any flight of stairs."

With the photographs, Mr. Leeder entered into evidence an affidavit from the NYPD photographer who had taken the pictures confirming this was where Officer Hanson had found Tori.

The objection was overruled.

"Please describe what happened next, Ms. Harrigan."

"When I reached the bottom of the stairs, I turned my head to see who pushed me. I saw Nicolino Morgano. He pushed me, watched me fall, and did nothing to help me. Then Officer Hanson was there. He called the EMTs, and I was taken by ambulance to Lower Manhattan Hospital's emergency room."

Mr. Leeder waited until there wasn't a sound in the courtroom. Then, he swiped the tablet in front of him. Audible gasps from the jury, low murmured conversations from the gallery, and a familiar voice moaning, "No, oh no"—was that Nonna Morgano? Tori wondered—broke the silence in the courtroom. The closeup of Tori's face taken in the emergency room was projected on the large screen. Her right eye was blood red, the skin around it maroon and black. Dark, thin streaks of blood had dried on her cheek and neck and stained patches of her blonde hair mahogany brown.

The judge's gavel hit the sound block twice as she called, "Order. Order."

Tori looked at Knox. He was leaning forward in his chair – his jaw clenched, and his fists balled in his lap. He was glaring at Nico. She willed him to look at her. Murphy reached over to rub his shoulder, whisper something to him. After what seemed like forever but was probably only seconds, he turned to look at Tori. *It's over. I'm fine* was the message she tried to send. She smiled and held his gaze until his jaw relaxed and he unclenched his fists.

Then she turned to look at the jury. Some were staring at Nico, whose eyes were downcast. A few were looking at her. An older woman brushed away tears. Tori wanted to redirect their focus to the magnified image on the screen. She wanted to shout, Look at the picture! See what he did to me!

For the first time since she'd walked through the courtroom's double doors, Tori turned to the spectators' gallery behind the defense table. Nonna was dabbing her eyes with a handkerchief. One of Nico's aunts stared at her hands firmly clasped on the pocketbook in her lap. But Jenny scowled at Tori, and Tori met her stare. Take a good, long look. The monster you raised did this.

Before Nico's attorney could object to the graphic nature of the photograph, Mr. Leeder changed it. Every inch of Tori's thighs visible in the picture was covered in bruises. The picture changed again and again and again—close-ups of her bruised midriff, shins, arms, and hands.

"Ms. Harrigan, you received ten stitches on your forehead that night at the hospital?" Mr. Leeder asked.

"Yes."

"Objection, Your Honor. Ms. Harrigan is not a qualified medical professional," Mr. Bartlett said.

"Objection sustained," the judge ruled.

"Ms. Harrigan, do you have any lingering effects as a result of this incident," Mr. Leeder asked.

Her mind flashed to last Friday when she and Knox had brought the assembled ten-foot Christmas tree down from the attic. Even though it had been Knox behind her, her heart had pounded in her chest. She could hear it, feel it thumping in her ears. She nodded. "Yes. I don't like people, especially strangers, to walk behind me. I often step aside, let people pass me on the street or stairs."

Thank you, Ms. Harrigan. Your Honor, the prosecution has no more questions for this witness."

Mr. Bartlett began by challenging her identification of Nico. "Were you dizzy as a result of the fall?"

"Yes."

"Was your vision blurry at any time after you fell and before the EMTs arrived?"

"Yes."

"You are sure you didn't lose your balance, miss a step?

"Yes. I wasn't dizzy on the stairs. I didn't miss a step. I didn't fall. I was pushed."

"Despite your blurred vision, you are certain it was Mr. Morgano who pushed you?"

"Yes."

After several more attempts to shake her story, the defense counsel said he had no further questions. She was excused and took the seat between Knox and Murphy in the gallery. Murphy gave her a thumbs up, and Knox squeezed her hand and whispered, "You did great!"

Officer Hanson was the next witness. Mr. Leeder questioned him about the investigative process. Then the three surveillance tapes were played for the jury. On the large screen, Nico's face was visible in every frame. When the last video, the one that showed Nico behind Tori on the stairs, was played, Mr. Leeder froze the frame at the exact moment she began to fall. Murphy grabbed Tori's right hand, and Knox squeezed the other. The expression on Nico's face was almost demonic.

Next to testify was the emergency room doctor. She described the extent of Tori's injuries, and Mr. Leeder entered the medical report into evidence and again showed the photos taken at the hospital. The defense objected again, but the jury had seen them – twice.

Then Chuck Flynn was called to the stand. Mr. Leeder played the first of the two voicemail messages Nico had left Tori during the summer.

"Victoria, it's Nico. I know where you live, and now I know where you work. I'll be watching. Be careful. Downtown is deserted during the day."

The second message had been recorded a few days later.

"Victoria. Drove by the townhouse. Saw you painted the front door red. I was going to ring the bell, but it looked like no one was home. Found out you're going by Harrigan at work. Good to know."

Tori clasped her hand over her mouth to stifle any sound. The messages she'd thought months earlier as merely upsetting, now—after weeks of harassment and the assault—sounded menacing. He warned me. I heard his words, but I wasn't listening.

Then, Mr. Leeder had Chuck Flynn describe the events of September 30th, the day Tori had returned from lunch, to discover the five photos of Eena and Nico in Paris.

Mr. Bartlett stood. "Your Honor, I renew my objection to the CCTV footage from One New York Plaza being shown to the jury. Valentina Barsotti, the woman on the tapes, is not on trial."

"Mr. Bartlett, your objection is noted for the record, but my ruling stands," the judge said.

The young Baruch College student hired by Nico to help Eena deliver photographs to Tori's office entered the courtroom. Mr. Bartlett accused him of cooperating with the prosecution because he'd been fired and wanted to retaliate against Nico. But the young man's testimony was clear—he'd been recruited and hired by Mr. Morgano to help Ms. Barsoti deliver an envelope addressed to Victoria Harrigan on the forty-fifth floor of One New York Plaza.

Finally, it was Dylan's turn to testify. Mr. Leeder asked him to describe the events of October 3rd, beginning with Tori's phone call to the Malones.

"After we walked and fed her dog, we drove to the hospital. My wife, Patricia Malone, stayed with Ms. Harrigan while the medical team was treating her. I was in the waiting room."

"Is that where you first saw the surveillance videos of the Water Street, South Ferry subway entrance, and platform?" Mr. Leeder asked.

"Yes."

Mr. Leeder replayed the surveillance footage from each of the three cameras.

"Do you recognize the man in these videos, Mr. Malone? Do you see him in the courtroom today?"

"Yes." Dylan pointed to Nico seated at the defense table. "The man in the videos is Mr. Nicolino Morgano. He intended to cause bodily injury to Ms. Harrigan that night, and he did."

"Objection, Your Honor. Mr. Malone is not in a position to know what Mr. Morgano intended."

"Objection sustained."

"No further questions for this witness," Mr. Leeder said. As he turned toward the gallery, Tori saw he was smiling.

He looks pleased with the case he presented, she thought.

Since the defense counsel had no questions for Dylan, he was excused and joined Tori, Knox, and Murphy in the gallery.

"The prosecution rests, Your Honor," Mr. Leeder announced.

Mr. Bartlett stated the prosecution had failed to prove its case beyond a reasonable doubt and moved the charges against Mr. Morgano be dismissed. Tori thought he looked defeated. He'd even remained seated when he'd argued for dismissal.

"Motion overruled," the judge said. "You may call your first witness, Mr. Bartlett."

"The defense calls Dr. Margaret Parkinson, Your Honor."

After a woman in her mid-forties entered the courtroom and was sworn in, Mr. Bartlett had her detail her qualifications as an emergency room physician. She worked at Mt. Sinai Hospital. Dr. Parkinson testified it was common for patients with severe concussions to experience dizziness and blurred vision for some time after a severe fall.

On cross-examination, the doctor admitted she had never met or examined Tori.

Mr. Bartlett announced the defense rested.

Then, the Judge turned to the jury. "In a few minutes, the bailiff will escort you to the jury room for some last-minute instructions. Tomorrow, after both attorneys have presented their closing arguments, I will instruct you on the law. Then you will begin deliberations. You are not to discuss the case or the evidence presented today with anyone, nor should you try to research any aspect of this case, the defendant, victim, or witnesses. Court is adjourned."

Chapter 50
Going Viral

After the judge gaveled an end to the day's proceedings and the bailiff escorted the jurors to the Jury Room, Mr. Leeder thanked Tori and Dylan for their testimony and assured them he would call as soon as there was a verdict.

"Did I misunderstand you the other day?" Tori asked Mr. Leeder. "I thought Mr. Bartlett had several witnesses scheduled to testify on Nico's behalf."

"No, you didn't misunderstand. Mr. Antonuccio was scheduled to testify. I assume as a character witness. I don't know why he chose not to call him, but these things happen. I'm going across the street to prepare my closing statement for tomorrow," Mr. Leeder said. "I'll call you when the jury has reached a verdict. If Mr. Morgano tries to engage you in conversation, or intimidate you when you leave, call or text me immediately."

Suddenly, Tori, Knox, and the Malones were alone in the courtroom with Nico and his family.

"Blood sticks together," Murphy said, shaking her head. "That doctor from Mr. Sinai had to be someone Jenny pressured Sal to find. And what was Antonuccio going to say? Nico was with him in Brooklyn when you 'fell' down the stairs? And the guy in the videos was a doppelganger?"

Tori shrugged. "Who knows? I'm just glad it's over."

Out of the corner of her eye, she saw Jenny staring at her. The older woman's brow was furrowed. Her tight lips a bright red slash across her pale face. But Tori refused to acknowledge she'd seen Jenny staring or engage in a childish game of who blinks first.

"Jenny's getting ready to confront us, Dylan," she whispered.

"I'll go first," he said.

She shook her head. "No. Ladies first. We've got this, right, Murph?"

Her friend smiled, nodded, and patted the pocket of her coat. "Ready when you are."

Tori wrapped a rose cashmere scarf around her neck before turning to slide her arms in the coat Knox held for her. She snuck another glimpse of Jenny, whose body was rigid. You can't wait to say something to me, Tori thought. But I'm in no rush. You need to stew a bit longer.

Slowly, she buttoned her coat and put on her gloves. She took Knox's hand and walked toward the courtroom doors. Dylan and Murphy behind them.

"Veek Toria." Jenny stood as soon as Tori had taken her first step. Obviously, her ex-mother-in-law planned to block Tori's path to the courtroom's closed double doors.

"Jenny."

When the older woman didn't move, Tori said, "Excuse me. We're leaving."

Jenny stood her ground. Tori took a step to her left, intending to walk around the older woman, but Jenny countered with a step to her right and then stepped forward. Tori took one step back. "Back up, Jenny. Now."

"Not yet. I have a few things to say to you, Veek Toria."

Tori rolled her eyes. "Of course you do. You're nothing if not predictable, Jenny. And cruel. You're a predator. It's why you were so enamored of Eena. The two of you are kindred spirits."

"You are the worst thing that ever happened to my family, Veek Toria." Jenny grimaced as if just saying Victoria's name left a bitter, sour taste in her mouth. "I wish Nico had never met you. You destroyed his life. Splintered my family,"

"For once, we agree—I wish I'd never met Nico either. Now let us pass."

Jenny didn't move. "My son does not deserve this, Veek Toria."

"Again, I agree with you. But imposing a fine and sending him to prison is the worst the State of New York can do to him. If the jury finds Nico guilty and he's sentenced to prison, will you and the family join him for Christmas at Rikers? I'm sure the guards make the prison so cheery this time of year—festive wreaths on every cell door, white lights twinkling in the prison yard, garland and tinsel woven through the barbed wire fencing."

"Shut up! Just shut up!" Nico said as he came to stand beside his mother. "I'm not going to jail. If it weren't for you, Eena wouldn't be in prison, and I wouldn't be on trial. If you were a man, I'd…."

"If you were a man, I might be worried," Tori said. "But right now, Nico, you are violating restraining orders in two states. Mr. Leeder gave your attorney clear instructions. You cannot approach me or attempt to speak to me."

"Don't tell me what to do, Tori. I put up with your nagging, constantly thinking your way was better, acting superior far too long."

Nico turned and pointed his finger at Dylan. "And you were supposed to be my best friend. You were more like a brother to me than my flesh and blood. And yet you testify against me? All because your stupid cow of a wife is friends with my ex? Murphy cut off your balls years ago. And you," Nico next turned his venom on Knox, "be careful. Tori's just like her friend. If she hasn't already, she'll have your balls for breakfast before too long."

Then, in a voice just above a whisper, Murphy said, "We're in the New York Criminal Court. The older woman is Genevieve Morgano of Forest Hills. Her son, Nicolino Morgano, is on trial for assaulting Victoria Harrigan, the woman in the plum coat, who is his ex-wife. Both Victoria and Dylan Malone, once a close friend of Morgano's, testified against him today. Morgano has a history of harassing Ms. Harrigan. He is clearly in violation of two restraining orders against him."

Jenny and Nico had been so intent on confronting Tori and Dylan that neither had noticed Murphy videotaping their verbal assaults. Nico lunged at her, but Dylan stepped between them.

"I wouldn't do that if I were you," Dylan said.

"Jenny, Nico, you're already going viral. I'm emailing it to NY1 and the other local television stations. Oh, and I bet Page Six would like a copy too," Murph said.

"And don't forget Mr. Leeder," Tori said.

"Yes, don't forget me." Mr. Leeder stood in the doorway, a uniformed officer by his side.

"I was downstairs when I got your text," the prosecutor said to Knox.

As the court officer restrained Nico, cuffing his wrists behind his back, he shouted, "Go to hell, Tori."

"You. First."

Chapter 51
Krav Maga

Thursday, November 30th

Tori patted her coat pocket to assure herself her phone was there before rechecking her tote bag. The festive paper plates, napkins, and forks were at the bottom of the bag, her Loftus & Hunt ID in the inside zippered compartment. All set, she thought. She snuck another look at the cake from Edible Art Bakery. The one she'd had made to take to Knox's office this morning to celebrate the purchase of the new house—what would be their family home. As usual, Edible Art had done an outstanding job—the cake was a replica of the house, down to the welcome mat at the front door. Then, she closed the bakery's signature box—a pattern of white roses against a silver-gray cardboard background—and sealed the top with a piece of Scotch tape, just in case. She didn't want the top to open as she walked the one and a half blocks from her office building to Knox's, exposing her precious cargo to the elements. Finally, she slung the straps of her tote bag over her shoulder and carefully picked up the cake box.

She sighed, took a deep breath, and smiled. What a wonderful day! Today is a new beginning for Knox and me.

But yesterday had started as a terrific day, too. Knox had been made a partner in the Wall Street law firm of Sullivan & Casey. In the late afternoon, she and Coop had made the same walk she was preparing to make this morning to attend the reception celebrating the new partners. Margot and Dan were there, too. It was the first time Margot had seen

Tori wearing the engagement ring she helped her son design the morning before Graham and Gemma's wedding. Knox introduced her to everyone as his fiancée. Tori had walked back to her office floating on Cloud Nine.

And then the thunderstorm hit.

On her desk was a message to call Mr. Leeder, who delivered the news the verdict was in when Tori called him back. Guilty on one count of misdemeanor assault. Guilty of violating the restraining order. But since these were Mr. Morgano's first offenses, the judge sentenced him to a year's probation instead of jail time, and he was ordered to pay a fine of only $6,000. "I'd hoped, with the second violation of the restraining order yesterday," Mr. Leeder told her, "the sentence would be harsher."

Tori had leaned back in her chair and swallowed tears of frustration. "How can that be?" she asked Mr. Leeder. Then, when he had no response, she thanked him for his hard work. "Your case was strong, and you did an excellent job. That's why we have the guilty verdicts," she said.

Jessica Avery, the psychologist she'd gone to see when she and Nico were having marital trouble, and again after they separated, and again after Eena and Nico had assaulted her, was her next call. Talking about this latest injustice with Jessica helped. When they finished the telehealth visit, Tori was calmer, and her heart no longer felt like it would burst through her chest.

Nico is the past, like yesterday, Tori reminded herself. Today, Knox and I are taking another step toward our future together.

The elevator to the lobby turned out to be an express, and soon she was walking toward the intersection of Water and Broad Streets. Only one more block to Knox's office. While she waited for the light to change, her mind replayed their after-dinner conversation last Friday.

"Are you available to come to the closing Thursday?" he asked.

"I can probably get away. Why?" She smiled as she thought of the surprise she'd planned—the amazing French vanilla cake with raspberry filling, the paper plates and napkins with a two-story brick house that looked very much like the house he was buying, and the saying, "I'm Changing My Doorstep," printed on them. She planned on bringing everything to his office, leaving it with his PA while the closing was in progress for all the participants to enjoy after completing the paperwork.

"Because I'd like you to be there," he'd said, "especially since the house will be our family home. It will be in both our names, and I'd like to do this as a family—you and me."

The pedestrian light changing, signaling she could cross, brought her back to the present. As she was about to step into the street, she heard footsteps behind her on the pavement. It's nothing, she assured herself as she felt her pulse quicken, and she took what was now her usual one step sideways to let the person behind her pass.

But he didn't walk past her. He took a step right and grabbed her left elbow.

"Ouch!" she cried. Even through the layers of her winter coat, suit jacket, and blouse, she felt the painful grip of strong fingers pinching her elbow. She turned to look at her assailant, but she already knew who it was.

"Surprise!" Nico sneered. "What's wrong, Tori? You don't look pleased to see me."

How can I get away from him? started on an endless loop in her mind as he forced her to cross the street. She couldn't run in the heels and pencil skirt she was wearing. Downtown streets were deserted at ten in the morning—traders, brokers, and bankers were on the phones, in their offices and cubicles making money. Express buses only ran in the financial district during rush hour, and few cars were passing them by. No one would see what Nico might do to her. No one would hear her scream. Not for at least ninety minutes. Then there would be plenty of people on the streets—queueing up at food trucks, walking to cash machines and restaurants. But now, for ninety minutes, she and Nico were alone. He could do a lot in ninety minutes and get away.

"What have we got here?" he asked. "Edible Art Bakery, huh? Nice. But you won't need that where we're going."

With his other hand, Nico yanked the box she'd been holding like a delicate work of art from her hands. The box flew in the air. She tried to grab it, save it. The lid and sides popped open. Then, Tori watched in horror as the cake box fell with a splat on the asphalt. The cake house cracked down the middle from the impact, raspberry filling oozing between the cake's moist layers as if it were hurt and bleeding. Tori stared at the splintered cake in disbelief. Her surprise was ruined. She wanted to cry, scream, papercut Nico's eyes.

He took advantage of her temporary shock and was poking something hard and unyielding into her lower back with his right hand while his left hand maintained a vice-like grip on her left elbow. He walked half a step behind her, pushing her, forcing her down the street. He made her walk right past Knox's office building. Toward Pier 11. They were heading for the river.

"Do you know what this is?" he asked as he jabbed whatever it was against her lower back.

"I don't," Tori said, "but I'm sure you're gonna tell me."

"What does it feel like?" he asked, taunting her.

When she didn't answer him, he pushed whatever it was more firmly into her back. "What does it feel like?"

"A ballpoint pen," she said.

He jabbed it deeper into her back. "Don't you wish? Guess again."

"I don't know, Nico. Why don't you just tell me?"

I can't let him pull me behind the building, she thought as she stumbled down the street. *Or take me to the river.* She tried to picture the barrier that separated the land and the water. *Is he taking me to the Pier? How will he get us past the padlocked gate?* She was dressed warmly for the cold November morning. For a moment, she saw herself in the murky waters, the coat and scarf that now protected her from the near-freezing temperatures and gusting winds off the tip of Manhattan, weighing her down below the river's surface.

Tori knew they had to stay on the street, near a building. *It's my only hope.* She willed herself not to think about whatever it was he was holding to her back. *Someone might come out. A security guard might see us.* She forced her brain to go through the checklist she'd learned in self-defense classes. The ones she'd enrolled in last August after a drunken Nico had confronted her outside Fraunces Tavern.

It's all about timing and distance. She ticked off each item, one by one. *Leverage what you have.*

Nico's ever-tightening grip forced her to hold her left forearm and hand tightly across her chest. Once the cake had fallen, she'd lowered her right arm, so the straps of her tote bag could slide to the crook of her elbow. Now, she crossed her right arm in front of her. Until the fingers of both her hands could grab the straps. It's now or never.

She stopped. Nico slammed into her back. Tori kept her balance, taking advantage of him being pressed against her. She jammed the sharp point of her high heel into his instep. He stepped back, screaming in pain, hopping on one foot. She gripped the straps of the tote with both hands and swung it across his face.

Nico howled in pain and surprise. Tori heard the dull clunking sound of metal hitting concrete. His right hand was empty!

If that was a gun, she thought.

She could hear her instructor's voice, Incapacitate him. Find the weapon. Run.

She swung the tote bag back across his face and head. Ground her heel into his other foot. Nico moaned and bent over. She balled her hands together, making one tight fist, and slammed it down on his back. His knees buckled. He fell to the ground. She kicked off her shoes and began pounding the sharp heels into him—into any vulnerable place she could. She didn't stop. "Leave us alone," she shouted.

"Ma'am, Ma'am, stop," she heard a man shout behind her. It was a security guard. From the logo on his uniform, she knew he worked in Knox's building.

"Do you see a gun?" she asked, looking around her. "This man jammed it in my back. Made me walk down the street with him. He dropped it. Do you see it?"

Nico continued to writhe on the sidewalk. As the security guard looked for whatever it was Nico had been holding, she called 911.

"There," the guard said and pointed to a six-inch heavy-duty stun gun. She recognized it from her Krav Maga self-defense training. This model had ultra-sharp spike electrodes designed to penetrate heavy winter clothing. The security guard kicked the taser far away from Nico, who was still on the ground but seemed to be recovering.

The 911 dispatcher kept her on the line until a squad car and ambulance arrived. Then, she tried to call Knox's office, hoping his assistant would answer. The call went to voicemail. She was leaving a message when she saw him run out of his office building, his phone to his ear. He was running away from her toward Water Street. Tori shouted his name. He didn't hear her. She called his number. He answered immediately.

"Oh my God! I've been so worried. Where are you?" he asked.

"Turn around." Tori was dwarfed by the police officers and EMTs who surrounded her. She walked toward Knox and watched as his expression turned from confusion to fear and then fury. She knew he'd recognized Nico.

He was by her side in a flash.

"Tori, are you okay? Did he hurt you? What's going on?" he asked as he opened his arms, and she walked into them. "What did he do this time?" He nodded to Nico, who was being helped to the ambulance.

"And you are?" one of the officers, whose badge identified him as Officer Garcia, asked.

"Knox Cooper. Ms. Harrigan's fiancé. I work in 32 Old Slip." He nodded toward the skyscraper halfway up the street.

Tori pulled away from Knox and put the shoes she was holding on the ground. He steadied her as she stepped into them. "My feet are freezing," she said.

"Ms. Harrigan was just about to tell us what happened," Officer Garcia said.

Before she could begin her story, she saw Ben turn the corner. He was running, his unbuttoned overcoat billowing behind him. When he reached them, Ben bent over and put his hands on his knees, panting for air.

"You're okay. You're okay. Thank God," he gasped. "As I was leaving. Heard sirens. Saw police car, ambulance turn the corner. Then, the box in the street…."

"How did you know to look for me?" Tori asked.

"When you were late, I called your office. Ben told me you'd left in plenty of time. I asked him to start walking to my office while headed to yours," Knox said.

Tori reluctantly left Knox's embrace and went to hug her colleague. "Thank you."

"I'm just glad you're all right. Sorry your surprise was ruined," Ben said.

She nodded, but as she remembered the box, its sides forced open, and the cake split down the middle, tears filled her eyes and spilled down her cheeks.

"What surprise?" Knox asked. "What box?"

"It's not important," she said. "I'll explain later."

"Are you okay, Ms. Harrigan? Can you tell us what happened?" Officer Garcia asked.

Tori nodded, brushed the tears from her cheeks, and took a deep breath. "I was walking to my fiancé's office because we're closing on our new house." She turned to look up at Knox, standing behind her, his arms around her waist, and she leaned against him for support. "At the corner of Broad and Water Streets, I heard footsteps behind me. It sounded like the person was in a hurry, so I stepped aside to let them pass."

"She's taken a restraining order out against this man. He has a history of harassing and assaulting her," Knox said. "Last month, he pushed her down the steps in the subway. Ever since that attack, she tends to let someone pass rather than have them walk behind her."

When Tori explained how Nico forced her down the street with what she later learned was a stun gun at her back and how she had gotten free, she heard Knox's sharp intake of breath, and he tightened his arms around her.

Officer Garcia held up the stun gun. "This model is very effective, packs a hefty punch, and is easily concealed in a coat pocket because of its size. It's a good thing you disarmed him, Ms. Harrigan."

"We'll come by the station later so she can give her statement," Knox said. "But right now, I'd like to get her inside."

The officer nodded. Then, Knox shook his brother's hand. "Thanks," he said.

Ben gave Tori another hug. "Never a dull moment with you, Harrigan. Who knew you were such a lethal weapon?"

Knox led Tori into his office building. "What about the closing?" she asked as they rode the elevator to his office on the thirtieth floor.

"Everyone's taking a little break," he said. "When you didn't come, I imagined all sorts of horrible things. You learned all those moves in self-defense classes at the gym?"

"Yes and no," Tori said, "I learned a lot from those first eight classes. The night Eena slapped me, for example, I used my purse as a shield and took advantage of Murphy coming into the ladies' room. I learned those things in the training. They're common sense, but the repetition made them more natural. At our last class, we got a Krav Maga demo in case we wanted to go further. I signed up."

"The self-defense program used by the Israeli Defense Forces?"

Tori nodded. "It's intense. I wanted to feel safer, stronger, and more confident. Initially, the classes helped. But as the harassment continued, my confidence lessened. So after the demo, I decided to try it. I'm still at level one, and I may never be good enough to qualify for level two, but I've learned so much—about timing, looking for and taking that split-second when you can get away or defend yourself."

"The next time we're at the gym, will you introduce me to your instructors? I'm so grateful you signed up for that course, so grateful to them for training you as well as they did," Knox said. "I owe them so much. Now, how about we close on our house?"

Several hours later, Tori and Knox were the owners of a new dream home. After the paperwork had been signed and the impact of the morning's events hit her, when she realized all she could have lost and how lucky she was, Tori enjoyed a long cry in Knox's arms behind the closed doors of his office. Together they called Edible Art Bakery and ordered another cake, just like the one that had fallen in the street. Because, when all was said and done, today had turned out to be a wonderful day after all. And they needed to celebrate.

Chapter 52
The Indictment

January 9th

Tori snuggled further under the sheet and blanket, so the shell of her right ear was no longer exposed to the bedroom's chill. In the quiet minutes just before dawn, she concentrated on piecing together snippets of an unusual dream she'd had before the fragments were scattered, like a dandelion gone seed, by the rush of the morning routine.

In the dream, she and Knox were at a Pharrell Williams concert. The acoustics in the auditorium must have been terrible because the artist was singing Because I'm Happy, and she was cringing. Usually, Tori loved that song. It was Knox's ringtone for everyone but her and the one he downloaded the morning after she told him she loved him. Then, in the dream, Knox had made the too-loud noise stop with one word, "Cooper," and she'd felt the weight of his arm around her waist and the warmth of his body next to hers. He'd told someone standing next to him she'd be happy about something but couldn't remember what it was she'd be happy about.

Now, Knox's lips found the sensitive spot just behind her ear. His arms tightened around her. "You awake?" he whispered.

"Hmm," she responded as she turned to face him. "Good morning."

She was surprised when, instead of kissing her as he usually did, he asked, "What's your day like today?"

"I have nothing special on. Why?"

"I think we should call our offices. Tell them we'll work remotely today." His expression and tone were serious.

She frowned. "Knox, I've been trying to piece together a weird dream I had last night, but now I'm thinking it wasn't.... Did you get a phone call in the middle of the night? Is everyone all right? Your parents? Your brother?" She tried to tamp down the panic she was starting to feel—*Who calls in the middle of the night if it isn't an emergency?*

"Everyone's fine. Sully called. To give us a heads up. The grand jury issued indictments for Nico, Anthony, and Gunderson yesterday afternoon. They've been arrested, and the US Attorney for the Eastern District of New York has scheduled a press conference for seven this morning. In time to lead the network morning shows."

As the townhome's heating unit clicked on and warm air began to blow from the vent above her head, Tori felt her blood turn to ice water. She was suddenly cold and trembling and felt like a belt was tightening around her chest.

"Sully is certain Nico was arrested?" she asked.

"That's what he said. The FBI had all three under surveillance in anticipation of the grand jury's decision. According to Sully, although the operation had been kept quiet, the business reporter at NY1 had been doggedly following the grand jury proceedings, waiting for a decision. When he saw a flurry of activity yesterday, he followed his instincts, and TV crews were waiting. All the stations should have film of the perp walks by now."

"It's just, after everything," she began. "I just want this to be over. I don't get it. Nico's not this smart. How does he manage to slither off every time, like the venomous reptile he is, without serious consequences?"

"He's been quite lucky. I'll give him that," Knox said. "But I think his luck has finally run out."

"I hope DOJ, the IRS, the SEC—at least one government agency —can finally hold him accountable. Last spring, the bank's medical insurance company could have pressed charges, but they didn't. He just had to pay back the money he'd stolen. And last October's assault? Yeah, he was found guilty, but the judge sentenced him to a year's probation and fined him half of what he could have been made to pay. He assaults me with a taser, and his probation gets revoked. But he's only sentenced to a month in jail and then is let out after three weeks for good behavior—just in time for the holidays. And someone posted his $250,000 bail for the taser assault. I'm just so frustrated and angry."

"I want us to stay home today in case some enterprising reporter puts together last week's trial and yesterday's arrest. The last thing I want is for you to be harassed by a journalist trying to get a scoop. Ben can let us know if he spots a camera crew in front of your office building," Knox said.

He cradled her in his arms a while longer before they showered and dressed. Tori left a message for each of her direct reports that she'd be available by phone or email, and she spoke to Esta to explain why she'd be working remotely. "I'll let security know to be on the lookout for any reporters hanging around the lobby," her boss said.

Downstairs, Knox took Baron for a walk while Tori prepared their breakfast. After cleaning up the kitchen, Knox turned on the fireplace and the television, and they settled on the couch with another cup of coffee to watch the news.

Tori's favorite anchorman began his six-thirty broadcast with a story about the President's trip to South America. Then, minutes later, he announced, "Our next story is national and local news. Last night, a grand jury issued indictments against, and the FBI arrested three local businessmen. Our chief economics reporter, Kaitlin Miele, has that story. Kaitlin?"

"Thanks, John. Last night the three top executives of Grand Piper Securities, a New York brokerage firm, were arrested and charged with defrauding investors in a start-up company, OPM Pharma LLC. The three executives are Anthony Antonuccio, President and Chief Operating Officer, Gary Gunderson, Chief Investment Officer, and Nicolino

Morgano, Chief Financial Officer. An attorney with the Securities and Exchange Commission released a statement minutes ago, confirming the SEC is pursuing civil charges against Grand Piper and the three top officers."

Film clips of each of the men, hands cuffed behind their backs, were played. When Nico appeared on screen, his head turned away from the camera, Tori said, "That's Jenny's apartment building. I bet the neighborhood gossips can't believe their good fortune—the FBI, a high-profile case, on the morning news."

"The US Attorney for the Eastern District of New York, Pamela Goldsmith, has called a press conference for seven o'clock this morning," the reporter continued. "We will bring that to you live, and we should learn more at that time."

Tori stood and walked toward the kitchen, more to keep herself occupied than for any other reason.

"This coffee's tasting bitter. I'm going to switch to water. Can I get you anything?" she asked as she glanced at the microwave clock and did the mental math. *Nineteen more minutes until they learned more.*

She looked back at Knox, who shook his head. "I'm fine," he said.

"Okay if I wash the coffee pot?" she asked.

"Yeah."

She rinsed out her cup and put it in the dishwasher before emptying and washing the coffee pot. She left it on the counter to dry. Then, she fixed herself a glass of water.

Knox lowered the sound on the television. "How are you doing?"

"Okay, I think. I texted Murphy, Dylan, Lulu, and Tom while you were out with Baron. Murph's already left for school, but hopefully, the others will be watching the press conference. I sent my mom a text too."

He nodded. "This could be it."

At seven o'clock, Knox turned up the sound. After the two anchors introduced themselves and welcomed their viewers, they announced there was "breaking news." The scene switched from the television studio to a room with an empty podium, the United States Department of Justice seal on the front, an American flag, and the flag of the State of New York behind it. In a voiceover, Kaitlin Miele told the audience they were waiting for Pamela Goldsmith, the United States Attorney for the Eastern District of New York, to begin a press conference. She repeated the information Knox and Tori had heard earlier.

Suddenly there was a flurry of activity on screen as a woman in her mid-forties appeared, several men in suits walking behind her. Knox moved closer to the screen and pointed. "There," he said. "That's Sully."

Ms. Goldsmith took the podium. "Good morning. Late yesterday, a grand jury issued indictments against the three top executives of Grand Piper Securities, LLC. Last evening, the FBI arrested Anthony Peter Antonuccio, Gary John Gunderson, and Nicolino Anthony Morgano. Each has been charged with conspiracy, interstate transportation of fraudulently obtained stockholders' funds, creating false reports on a company, OPM Pharma, LLC, while having an undisclosed financial interest in that company, and income tax evasion. If convicted, each defendant could face as much as thirty years in prison," she said. "Now, before we open the floor for questions, Mr. Jeremiah Sullivan of the Securities and Exchange Commission will say a few words."

She stepped back, and Sully stepped forward. "Good morning. Thank you, Ms. Goldsmith. The Securities and Exchange Commission has filed a civil lawsuit against Grand Piper Securities, LLC and its three executives for manipulating the stock price of OPM Pharma, LLC and two other companies, Resurrection Finance and VMB Technology Management. All three companies were incorporated in Delaware but do business in the State of New York." He looked back at the US Attorney, who nodded. "We'll take a few questions," Sully said.

"Ms. Goldsmith, what details can you give us about the charges?" a reporter asked.

"In the indictment, we allege the three executives siphoned off funds from various so-called penny stock offerings where Grand Piper Securities was listed as underwriter and wiring those funds to accounts controlled by Messrs. Antonuccio, Gunderson, and Morgano for their personal use. We further allege that they deliberately and knowingly created and published false statements about OPM Pharma, LLC, in order to sell shares in that corporation. They also failed to disclose their proprietary interests in OPM to prospective buyers, as required by law."

Sully stepped to the podium. "For example, shares of OPM were initially offered at $.35 a share, rose to over $10 in October because of false and misleading statements made by the three executives. At no time did they disclose the extent of their ownership in OPM. When the stock hit an all-time high, the three began systematically selling off their positions. At yesterday's market close, the shares were worthless."

Another reporter asked if additional indictments against others at Grand Piper Securities would be forthcoming.

Ms. Goldsmith took the mic. "We do not currently anticipate additional indictments. Although Resurrection Finance and VMB Technology Management had their headquarters in the Forest Hills cooperative apartment owned by Mrs. Genevieve Morgano and a townhome on West Seventy-First Street, once owned by a relative of Mr. Morgano's former sister-in-law, neither Mrs. Genevieve Morgano nor the prior or current owners of the West Seventy-First Street townhouse are being investigated in connection with this matter."

"Eeew!" Tori said. "I'm no fan of Jenny's, that's for sure, but to have involved his mother in this fraud? And Eena's godmother? Not to mention a perfect stranger who just happened to buy a lovely townhouse once owned by Eena's Aunt Mehta. That's a new low, even for Nico."

"Sully told me the five members of their so-called sales team are cooperating with investigators. Even producing incriminating emails and texts."

Tori smiled. "This time, it feels different. Like it really and truly is finally over."

Our Spot on the Beach

February 14th

Tori pushed the curtains and blackout drapes aside and looked out at the day. Above the horizon, the faint outline of the moon and one feathery cloud were the only splashes of white in an azure sky. She opened the bedroom's French doors and stepped onto the balcony to watch the waves below crest and roll ashore, staining the white sand and leaving a lacey foam in their wake as they rolled back to the sea. The salt air mingled with the sweet smell of the scarlet and fuchsia blossoms on the carefully tended bougainvillea vines that crawled up the side of the hotel. *Today is magnificent,* she thought. *We couldn't ask for a day, a setting more perfect.*

The ringing of the phone beckoned her back inside. Before stepping into the bedroom and closing the door behind her, she took one more deep breath and watched one more wave crash ashore.

"Good morning, Ms. Harrigan. The time is eight o'clock. The current temperature in Charlotte Amalie is seventy-eight degrees. The high is expected to be eighty-four. The waiter is on his way up to your suite, ma'am. Have a wonderful day."

Seconds later, a knock at the door signaled room service was there. The waiter set a tray with a platter of mixed fruit, a basket of warm croissants, and coffee on the balcony's dining table, along with a single rose in a silver vase and a card. After she signed the check, he said,

"Leave everything on the table when you're finished, ma'am. I have in-structions to return just after eleven o'clock to clear everything away."

After the waiter left, Tori opened the envelope. A Valentine's card from Knox.

> Good morning.
>
> I missed you last night and can't wait to see
> you this morning. I'll be waiting for you at
> our spot on the beach at eleven. I love you. K.

"I love you, too," she said aloud. "So much." And she remembered that late August afternoon when she'd first met Knox. Even now, she felt her cheeks flush at the memory of the immediate and intense attrac-tion she'd felt. She remembered, too, how anxious she'd been her feel-ings might not be reciprocated. After their first dinner at the '76 House, she'd told him how she felt, and he'd assured her he felt the same about her. *I don't know what I would have done these past months without him,* she thought, *Murph, Dylan, Lulu, and Tom, too.* Tears filled her eyes. She missed her bests friends. *Maybe I should call them,* she thought, then decided against it.

She smiled as she remembered her FaceTime call with Murphy and Lulu the Sunday after Thanksgiving. She'd casually added Knox's pro-posal to the list of decorating chores they completed Friday, then held her left hand to the screen to show off her ring.

"I get to be the matron of honor, right? It's my turn," Murphy said. Years earlier, just before their graduation from Dickinson, they vowed they would be in each other's weddings. As they were sipping chianti and enjoying tuna grinders from George's Sub and Pizza Parlor, Lulu had handed each of them a turquoise post-it note. "Write your name on the post-it and fold it—like this," she demonstrated. Then they put the folded notes in a bowl, and each drew a name. "The name of our maids of honor," Lulu announced as she held up her paper to reveal Murphy's name. Murphy unfolded the post-it Tori had written. Years later, when Tori married Nico, Lulu had stood beside her.

So, when Tori announced she and Knox had decided to elope, Murphy was devastated. Until Tori told her she thought she'd found "the dress" in the window of a little boutique on Park Avenue. "I've made an appointment for us next Saturday," Tori said. As soon as she walked out of the dressing room in the simple ivory crepe sheath with cap sleeves that looked like perfect roses, the look on Murphy's face and the tears in her eyes told Tori she'd been right.

Although her mother and Knox's parents were disappointed they planned to elope, they understood. "We've both done the wedding thing," Tori said. "We want everything to be different. And this isn't about a wedding. It's about our marriage and our commitment to each other." But what neither of them had shared with their parents or friends was the date or the location. The afternoon Knox had proposed, they'd sat down with their calendars. Both had busy work schedules until June. "I don't want to wait that long," Knox said. So, they compromised. They would honeymoon in Tahiti in June but get married earlier. "On a beach," Knox said. "We both love the beach. It's one of our three Bs—ballet, baseball, and beaches."

They'd soon concluded with the work at the new house, meetings with the decorator, selling Tori's townhouse, and preparing to move, January was out of the question. But they'd both agreed they could each take a couple of days off in mid-February to make a long weekend. "It'll be too cold to get married on a beach," Tori said. But Knox countered by reminding her not every beach was cold in February.

He'd gone into planning overdrive. After he'd researched the laws governing marriage ceremonies in sunny southern climes, they'd decided on St. Thomas in the Virgin Islands. Two weeks ago, they'd flown to Charlotte Amalie to apply for their marriage license and see, in person, the secluded area on the resort's private beach reserved for wedding ceremonies. Last night after dinner on the suite's balcony, he kissed her good night before saying, "My suit and things for tomorrow are in another room." Then, he caressed her cheek, told her he loved her one more time, asked her to dream of him because he'd be dreaming of her, and began whistling, *I'm Getting Married in the Morning*, all the way to the elevator.

Tori smiled at her reflection as she applied the finishing touches to her make-up. *What a difference a year makes!* she thought. Last year, she and Murphy had been in Saint Martin, where she'd spent too much of the long Presidents' Day weekend get-away she'd given her husband for Valentine's Day stewing over Nico, who'd chosen to stay home and pout rather than share a romantic four days on a beach with her.

She shook her head free of thoughts of Nico and that awful time. He had moved to government housing in early January—a federal prison. Sully, whom she'd finally met in person when she and Knox had traveled to Washington, DC on business, called Knox regularly with updates on Nico, Anthony, and Gary. Each of them was trying to blame the other two, offering anything they could to bargain for leniency, but Sully said the case against them was rock-solid, and they had nothing the government wanted.

Mr. Leeder was again prosecuting Nico for assault and violating the protection order, with a charge for attempted kidnapping added for good measure. The thought of testifying against Nico, facing his family in court again, had been an irritant that was always there in the back of her mind. Until Mr. Leeder told her Nico's lawyer was looking to settle the state's case so he could concentrate on the upcoming federal trial—a trial she could follow in the news or not.

Just after ten, Tori took her new dress and strappy white and gold sandals from the closet. The blue topaz and diamond butterfly earrings Knox had given her for Christmas would be her "something blue," and the pearl bracelet that had been her Grandmother Helene's, her "something old." Around her neck, she wore the single pearl and diamond pendant her father had given her mother on their wedding day and which Anna had brought with her at Christmas. "Please wear this as your 'something borrowed,'" her mother had said.

Before she left the suite, Tori checked one more time her card and wedding gift for Knox—platinum cufflinks of a K and a T in script—were in the room's safety deposit box. Then, she closed the door and walked down the hallway to the elevator that would take her to the private beach and her new life.

Waiting for her when the elevator doors opened was Murphy, holding a box of tissues. "Do not cry, Harrigan. You'll ruin your make-up."

"Wha? What? How?" Tori stammered.

"Even when you elope, you need a witness," Murphy said. "I'd hug you, but I don't want to wrinkle you."

Murphy and Tori removed their sandals on the other side of the door just before they stepped on the sand. "They said someone would be here to take our shoes," Tori said.

"That would be me," Tom said, and he hooked his fingers into the sandals' straps.

Then, Murphy handed Tori one of two bouquets of Ginger Thomas and frangipani that had been placed on a small table. "Ready?"

Tori nodded, too afraid to speak, too afraid she'd cry. *I didn't realize how much I wanted Murphy and Lulu here until they weren't.*

As they turned toward the ocean, Tori gasped. Knox was grinning from ear to ear. The gold highlights in his hair glistened in the morning sun. In his eyes was the look every bride hoped, wanted to see from her groom on their wedding day. He was flanked on his right by Dylan and on his left by his brother, Ben. Sitting on white folding chairs were her mother, Margot, and Dan Cooper. Lulu was sitting behind them, Jackson in her lap, holding a bubble wand. Together, mother and son blew iridescent bubbles into the air. A violinist began to play *A Thousand Years*.

"Everyone's here," Tori managed to say.

"Dylan became an ordained minister of the American Marriage Ministries so he could perform the ceremony," Murphy said, "Take a closer look at the violinist."

"Oh my God," Tori said. "Is that Kelly?"

Murphy nodded. "Knox arranged everything. The only thing he couldn't figure out was how to get Baron here. All of us are booked on flights home tomorrow, so you have the next few days to yourselves."

When Tori was, at last, standing next to Knox, he whispered, "You take my breath away." And she whispered back, "I can't believe you did all this. Thank you."

In front of their parents and best friends, Knox promised her he would love, honor, and cherish her all the days of his life. Tori promised him she would love him with all her heart for all her life. Then Dylan pronounced them husband and wife. Knox took her in his arms and kissed her to a round of cheers.

"Well, Mrs. Cooper, are you ready to begin our journey together?" Knox asked.

"It's Harrigan-Cooper, remember? And I'm more than ready, Knox. I can't wait."

Acknowledgments

So many friends and colleagues helped me on my journey to tell Tori's story.

Thank you! First and foremost, Maureen Ryan Griffin has been a mentor, guide, and friend through this process. She not only has inspired me, encouraged me, and constantly challenged me, but she introduced me to an extraordinary writing community. Many years ago, I attended one of Maureen's Coastal Writing Retreats, where I first decided to try to write more than a short story or technical article. There, a supportive community took me under their collective wing: Savannah Stoner, Lori Oman, Patricia Borufsen, Jan Comfort, and our poet extraordinaire, Richard Thomas.

Maureen invited me to join one of her Under Construction classes at the start of the pandemic lockdown. Through the magic of Zoom, I met another group of exceptional and supportive writers, several of whom agreed to be my BETA readers. These talented writers and poets would offer suggestions to improve Tori's story each week.

My BETA readers are a patient and nurturing group. Their criticism was always constructive, helpful, and spot-on! Special thanks to Kelly Bennett, whose suggestions were invaluable, and Chris Daly, who always encouraged. Erika Lopez, whose probing questions made me relook (and change) my approach to several storylines, and Jonathan Heaslet, whose editing prowess shortened the text. He also reminded me my use of the Oxford comma was inconsistent and suggested I rewrite the ending (which I did, thanks, Jon!).

A special thanks to Lilianna Coriasco, who corrected my Italian, Janet Holman, who helped correct my spelling (especially those pesky errors that spell check doesn't catch because they're words, just not the right ones), and Susan Purves, who said the title needed to change! And she was right!

My friend, Suzanne Hetzel, a writer of children's books among so many accolades, painted the cover for me. What an honor, Suzi! Thank you!

Thank you, everyone!